pills, thrills, chills, and heartache

pills, thrills, chills, and heartache

adventures in the first person

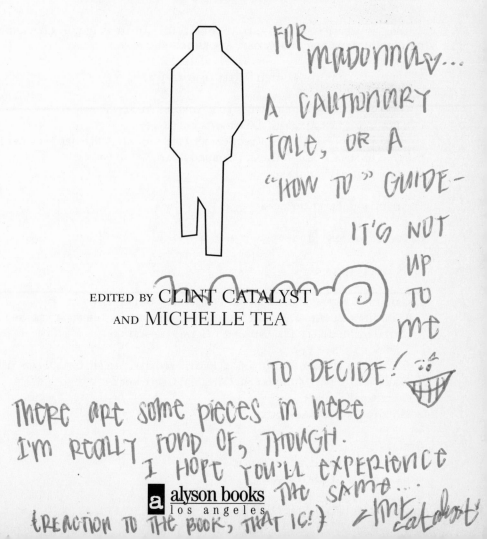

EDITED BY CLINT CATALYST
AND MICHELLE TEA

For Madonna...
A cautionary tale, or a "how to" guide—
it's not up to me to decide!

There are some pieces in here I'm really fond of, though. I hope you'll experience the same.... (reaction to the book, that is!)
—Clint Catalyst

alyson books
los angeles

MANUFACTURED IN THE UNITED STATES OF AMERICA.

THIS TRADE PAPERBACK ORIGINAL IS PUBLISHED BY ALYSON PUBLICATIONS,
P.O. BOX 4371, LOS ANGELES, CALIFORNIA 90078-4371.
DISTRIBUTION IN THE UNITED KINGDOM BY TURNAROUND PUBLISHER SERVICES LTD.,
UNIT 3, OLYMPIA TRADING ESTATE, COBURG ROAD, WOOD GREEN,
LONDON N22 6TZ ENGLAND.

FIRST EDITION: FEBRUARY 2004

04 05 06 07 08 a 10 9 8 7 6 5 4 3 2 1

ISBN 1-55583-753-0

LIBRARY OF CONGRESS CATALOGING-IN-PUBLICATION DATA
    PILLS, THRILLS, CHILLS, AND HEARTACHE : ADVENTURES IN THE FIRST PERSON /
    EDITED BY MICHELLE TEA AND CLINT CATALYST. — 1ST ED.
        ISBN 1-55583-753-0
        1. GAYS' WRITINGS, AMERICAN. 2. EROTIC STORIES, AMERICAN. 3. FIRST PERSON
    NARRATIVE. I. TEA, MICHELLE. II. CATALYST, CLINT, 1971–
    PS508.G39P55 2004
    813'.01083538'08664—DC22   2003058371

CREDITS
COVER PHOTOGRAPHY BY IDENTIKAL.
COVER DESIGN BY MATT SAMS.

Contents

CONTRIBUTORS...357

pills, thrills, chills, and heartache

Laurie Stone

STRUCK

I like fear. I like feeling where my skin ends when something strikes it, scratches it, tries to get underneath it. I like tension. I like the tension between what I want and what I need.

I fear I will touch too many people. My hand likes to go where it doesn't belong. I like the tension between being welcome and scaring people. It's such a thin line.

I like cruelty. Doesn't everybody? A man who has toyed with me gives a boring lecture, and I'm happy. I feel good. A woman who applauds my setbacks becomes fat as a hippo, and it's as if I've won the lottery.

I like shoplifting. Chocolate is good, but I don't steal chocolate cake. The pieces are too big. It has to be something I can palm. I like the tension of eating.

I like the way semen smells. I like being seized by a taste. I like being in a position to be corrected.

When people say they are going away, I say, "I will miss you," but I don't miss them. I miss people I want to fuck. Maybe it's only the fucking I miss, or not even the fucking but the idea of fucking. I like the tension of loving people one minute and forgetting them the next. I like

1

fucking people I don't like. I like being wrong about the people I want to fuck. The mistake is like healthy sleep.

I like mother's milk. I like not knowing whether I'm sucking cock or tit. I like having my mouth and cunt and ass penetrated at the same time.

I like being unattached. I like being tied up. I like making the wrong impression. I like penetrating a man's mouth.

I met a woman at a party. I thought her head would explode like something from a Cronenberg movie. Every word made her think about being misunderstood. She acted like her meaning was too precious to expose. I said, "It's annoying to be controlled, but it's funny. It's funny if you're not shocked."

Before my father took off his belt, he would say, "You're due for a licking." I would see a tongue on my skin. I like not knowing when I'll be struck.

When I'm with Oscar, I think I'm welcome when I'm scaring him. It makes me operate from inside a box. I like being loved for the wrong reasons. It makes me unsure whether I should protect myself.

I like a smell that is almost sickening. I like a feeling that is almost painful. I like having the same dream: A man is on all fours, over me like a dog finding a plaything in the woods. He sniffs at me gently and then licks, has friendly sex that makes me forget whether I'm in love or not, happy or not, gnawed at by doubts, losing money, giving away too much, failing at work, failing in friendship, symptomatic of diseases.

Fan is beautiful. She has clouds of hair. It's red, impossibly gleaming. Waves of it cascade over her forehead, dance around her cheekbones, fly down her shoulders. Her body is lean and statuesque. Her voice has a laugh. She holds her chin up. She likes being every man's desire, but it is not the most important thing. Being every man's desire shows her every man's desire, and she does not like what she sees. I like watching men fall in love with her. She acts as if she doesn't care. I think they like the whipped cream she places between herself and them. They think they can keep their footing in it. I imagine her cradled and sung to by men who can talk to cats.

A dominatrix told me she liked living out her fantasies. She said that not all women did. Some preferred to play with themselves, as if thinking about sex were not also a physical activity, as if the mind were not part of the body. She had made a living from her sexual activities. She was aroused by her work. It was her subject too. She had nothing else instructive to say. She thought she had devoted too much of her life to sex. She had missed out on other experiences. When she named them, they were dull, like going shopping for linens at Macy's.

I like being taken from behind. I like the tension of being trusted. I like prominent veins. I like knowing everyone can tell.

I like women with space between their teeth. Anything can happen. Everything they wear looks soft, smells good. They present their bodies as a gift. They can't be shocked. They bet on the future. They carry foreign money. They attract children. Their embrace is like a silk cord. They make an impression without leaving marks.

I like scars. I like cells that don't forget. I like fighting sleep. I like the intelligence of gorillas. I like being bent over a chair. I like healing on my own.

I was riding my bike up Sixth Avenue on a balmy night—late, so there were no cars—and I was sailing in that way that makes me forget what I'm made of. I was wearing a thin jacket I wanted to shed, but I didn't want to stop. The left sleeve slipped off, but the right cuff caught on my wrist, and the next thing I knew I was sprawled on the pavement, my left hand cut, my left knee showing a trickle of blood, my left hip bruised. Most of the damage was to my left hand. I groaned whenever I squeezed the brake. I groaned so loud, I laughed. The hand swelled. I applied ice. I thought I'd broken a bone. I couldn't decide whether to keep the hand still or flex it. I thought I should have X-rays, but I didn't go. Weeks passed, and it didn't heal, but in time the swelling went down, the bruises faded, the stiffness eased, the strength returned. The hand didn't forget the injury. A place I press below the knuckle sings.

Sammy's body is a machine. It is hard and has no fat. He likes women who behave like machines. He doesn't care if they mean it, as long as they do it. They park in front of him. They look like cars with shiny exteriors, women he can drive. He leans in close and leaves a space. Women swarm to the space. He likes women with leather seats and chrome handlebars—women who leave tread marks. He likes a machine that purrs when he turns it on and sleeps when he parks it. In a memory, he is 12 or so, in the woods, the fur on his body still downy, the pleasure of flowers already thorny. His father is wearing a red jacket, and vapor smokes from his nose and mouth. He looks like a ghost on an errand. Sammy wonders what his father is chasing or what is chasing his father, but every time he looks for his old man, he finds a map and a scribbled note.

Sammy's body is a getaway car. Pleasure slows him down. He looks at women through glass. They feel his breath against the window. He can cry if he doesn't smell them. He thinks they are filled with waiting. He doesn't like to swallow. He thinks there will always be something more tempting to taste. He sets tests he can't win. He remembers the strength in his dying father's hands. He remembers crying at the funeral and thinking about gunning cars on the flat roads of Kansas, blacktop sleek and hard as sinew ripping down the backbone of the land. When a woman touches new parts of him, he feels left out of the conversation.

I am looking at a man I barely know. His face is etched with old sorrow or his genes are. His wife is younger, or her genes are. The way he smiles looks like a wince because it tugs against the downward lines. She's wearing a white linen shirt that is crisp despite the fabric's tendency to crease. She casts sidelong glances at him. He worries about her if she's not nearby. Or maybe he needs to have her close. She appears to need the silk cord less than he does (or else she's better at concealing her needs).

I am looking at a man obsessed with himself in such a humorous way it seems he is talking about someone else. Stray need makes him sexy. He acts as if his life depends on his attractiveness, and he seems even to know that this need fuels his sexiness—a type that's touching in a girlish way. But he pretends he's shy. He pretends his hands are tied. He pretends he has to be seized or drunk. It's disastrous to play his way. He doesn't want to be right about his allure. He doesn't like the tension of that responsibility.

I like feeling where my desire ends when something is beyond it. It makes me unsure whether I should protect myself.

I met a man I both scared and excited (though many things had the same effect on him). Fear made him bold. Excitement made him shrink. He flattered and flirted. He didn't imagine my loneliness, though he knew I was alone. I didn't imagine his anxiety, though he detailed it for me. I didn't pursue him, but I met him when he asked. His interest made me hopeful in a way I couldn't control. Each time he appeared he reminded me he had nothing to give. I imagined he thought his flame was too tepid to hurt. He sent a gift, signed the note with love, and then he disappeared. When he resurfaced, my anger was equivalent to the self-reproach he'd tripped. I felt he'd left because I was unworthy, though I knew it wasn't true.

I like pornography intended for someone else. I like a mind I can penetrate, a mind that splits open for me like the halves of a papaya. A man once said he wanted to eat papaya from my cunt. He said he wanted to shave my pubic hair. He wanted me to wear a corset. He wanted to have sex that sounded uncomfortable but wasn't. His desire was touching in a girlish way. He liked the scars I had acquired through accidents. He liked giving me tests.

I like the footwork of boxing. I like encouragement that's confining like a corset. I like the discovery of irony by children.

A woman once told me she could *think* herself off. Her capacities seemed those of a mutant or a mythological beast. She could do it on the subway. She could probably do it anywhere, but I'm choosing the subway because of the vibrations. She would cross her legs and squeeze her pelvic muscles and somehow work up a cricket-like friction against her clit, or maybe friction wasn't necessary, the mind being sufficient. She would rock, or maybe not. She wasn't specific, or I don't remember. I liked the swagger in her smile.

I like women with passports that are heavily stamped. I like skin that's tattooed. I like the consequences of penetration. I like sex that's postponed. I like being on the receiving end. I like computers that talk. I like being slapped across the face. I like mixed origins.

My friend Andy fears that things can't change, but can only get worse at a faster rate. He fell in love with heroin, like a princess being awakened by a kiss. He was committed to oblivion. He bore the consequences of penetration. He liked sex that would put him to sleep. He thought of his dick as a needle. Women swarmed to his dead eyes. He liked women with nothing to lose. His curiosity was sweet. He was afraid of his ideas. He loved swallowing cunt. He didn't kill his intelligence. He treated his body cruelly. Women swarmed to his cruelty. He nursed his cruelty the way he did his drugs. Women with the power to think themselves off found him a good fuck. He didn't feign shyness.

He didn't need to be seized. He liked killing himself. He liked life. He could always express his beliefs. He found contact excruciating. His face grew skull-like. He kept the smell of cunt on his hands.

I like reversing my position. I like when honesty hurts. I like the thin line between masochism and courage. I told Sammy I believed in change, though when I gave examples it sounded like I was trying to cheer myself up. I find comfort in his size. He's too big to slam into a wall. I like separating because it hurts. I like being slowed down. I fear I will run out of patience and renewable cells. I like disliking Sammy. I like not having what I want, because it's what I need.

Ali Liebegott

EXCERPT FROM *THE IHOP PAPERS*

I'm 20 and I've never slept with anyone. I've been in AA for almost three years too. That's how I ended up in San Francisco. I'm trying to seduce Irene, my philosophy teacher from community college. Whenever I try to imagine having sex with a woman, I see myself drinking goblets of wine in dimly lit rooms, touching her clavicles as if they were the original pages of the Bible, so old and antique, thin and transparent. I just had a thought that the Bible was written on stone, not thin paper. Papyrus, stone—you know what I mean about the necessity of delicate touch, as if her clavicles were the thin, almost transparent pages of a very old Bible and I was the archaeologist who'd fallen into this glorious excavation.

You have to have some balls to title your book the Bible. That's not what I'm titling my book. I want my book to be accessible. I want to write a book that's really honest—*The IHOP Papers*—because it's about working at IHOP. I work at IHOP, the International House of Pancakes. You know, the chain of restaurants with the pointy blue-painted roofs. I wear what's most likely one of the most ugly dresses in existence. It is this blue shit thing with poofy sleeves and shoulders, and those god-awful white nurse shoes. I think I already told you what the

7

dress looks like. I got hired at 2 o'clock and Marguerito said, "Can you start today at 4?" So I had to walk home and get changed and put my hair up into the regulation IHOP bun—no wisps or braids or any hair hanging below the earlobe. I got dressed up in my new IHOP uniform, except for the white nurse shoes I still needed to buy. I wore a pair of black canvas hi-top sneakers instead. I hadn't moved into my own apartment yet, and I was still living with Irene, Gustavo, and Jenny. I was dying to show off my new uniform, but no one was home.

Wearing the IHOP uniform is like wearing a freak show costume, yet there was a part of wearing it those first days that felt like a badge of honor. I was a real worker, even though I'd had jobs since I was 15. Now I rode the bus in my waitress uniform. Before I went to work I had to go to Payless Shoes to buy the nurse shoes because that's where Marguerito said they sold them. There was an entire aisle of $16 white vinyl nurse shoes. For some reason I thought that ugly white nurse shoes were harder to come by, and I was shocked to see so many of them. I found a pair that fit me and wore them out of the store feeling, for a second, proud and grown up, like a waitress on a television show. I thought it made me look mature, like I had kids at home and an unemployed boyfriend who was chain-smoking at my kitchen table while I worked and waited for our extensive relationship problems to disappear. Somehow the stereotypical problems of waitresses on TV seemed more manageable than my own.

I waited for the bus in my new get-up. It finally came and I dropped my quarters in the slot. The bus driver looked me up and down and said, "Are you German?"

"Yeah," I said back. "I mean, I'm half German." He looked at me for a second, then pulled the bus away from the curb. I thought he thought he knew me from somewhere and then he realized he didn't—that's why he didn't say anything else.

Freaks are always attracted to me. I don't know why. Probably because I'm always sitting in bus stops on rainy nights with my arms all slit up. Normal people don't usually stop to chat in those situations.

The other thing is, I'm always lonely, so between attracting freaks and being too lonely to tell them to go away, I meet a lot of freaks. My brother used to call me a freak magnet.

When the bus came to my stop, I pulled the white cord and the bell went off. I walked up the aisle to the front of the bus and past the driver. "Edelweiss," he said as I stepped down to the curb. Then he laughed snorting once through his nose. As soon as the doors shut and the bus drove off down the street I realized he was making fun of my dress. I looked like I should be in *The Sound of Music* or painted on the box covers of Swiss or German hot chocolate packages. I told Irene the story when I got home, hoping for sympathy. Irene, Jenny, and Gustavo laughed and kept saying, "Edelweiss."

Being a waitress is universal, like love and death. It's good to stick with universal themes, but you also have to be careful not to be cliché. My community college teacher—Trudy, not Irene, the one I'm in love with—told me I was good at titles. Once I wrote a story called "A Girl Named Lightbulb." I told her sometimes the title comes to me first and the actual story later. Even though the book I'm writing now deals with universal themes, and hopefully is not cliché, some people still might not read it because it's about being gay. That's the way the cookie crumbles.

Lots of people hate gay people. They say, "It's not like I hate gay people," but you know they do. Once I gave a speech in my community college speech class on gay rights. I was supposed to convince everyone not to discriminate against gay people. I tried to be real low-profile when I went to the library because I didn't want anyone to see me near the gay books, so I grabbed one off the shelf and ran to the checkout desk. My speech ended up sucking, because the book I snatched was some speculative, gossipy almanac of gay people through history. "You should be careful who you make fun of because lots of people are gay—especially famous people like Michael Jackson, Anne Frank, Martina Navratilova, and Janis Joplin." That's how I ended my speech.

My teacher asked me for the source of my research material. I told her it was a book called *Top Secret Gay Stars*. She said I didn't know for sure whether these famous people in history were gay, especially Anne Frank. Then she gave me a C, since part of speech class was to do what she called "responsible research." I said, "The only reason you gave me a C is because you're a fucking dyke." I'm just kidding; I didn't say that. I'm sure she's a lezzy, though, now that I think about it. She probably had me pegged from a mile away too. I was upset about the C—but mostly I was glad Janis Joplin might be gay.

I used to drive around in a flower truck delivering flowers all day and pretending all sorts of things—things that are way too embarrassing to write here. For instance, I imagined that on my daily route of flower deliveries I'd meet famous people. My favorite fantasy was that I would ring a doorbell, holding a bouquet, and when the door opened it would be Hope from *Days of Our Lives*. She would let me in for a glass of water, stare into my sparkling eyes, and dab iodine on a mysterious cut across my throat. Then I'd bow my head into her chest and trace the tip of my nose across her collarbones. I'm real big on collarbones. They're so beautiful. I feel like there should be a collarbone museum, where the most beautiful collarbones in the world are displayed behind red velvet rope. If I ever went with Hope from *Days of Our Lives* to the collarbone museum, I'd point to all the beautiful ivory hued bones that looked like whittled willow branches and say, "That dog shit can't even compare to your collarbones."

Eventually Hope and I would live together in a one-bedroom apartment with Christmas tree lights strung up in the kitchen. After I made love to her, I'd drink milk right from the carton and shut the refrigerator door with a small click before walking back to our bed, my bare feet sticking slightly on the linoleum with each step.

I've always wanted Christmas lights strung up in my kitchen, but I've never done it. The kitchen I have now is small: There's a sink, a stove, a refrigerator, a wall, and the table where I'm typing this. It's an old apartment but I love it. The window in the kitchen opens onto a fire escape. Sometimes I sit out there.

Once I sat out there with my AA sponsor, Maria. We ate strawberries and I told her all my problems. Maria had gotten new combat boots that day and she'd put pink laces in them. I spent the whole time wanting to touch the toes of her boots—pet them like puppy heads. I wished Maria could stay forever, but she actually never stayed very long at all. You don't know about Maria yet. I'll warn you though: I love her too. In case you're keeping score, so far I love three people:

1. Irene, my community college Philosophy teacher
2. Hope from *Days of Our Lives*
3. Maria, my AA sponsor
(I'm not counting Janis Joplin as someone I love, because she's dead.)

I feel like the most awkward, ugly virgin of all time. I can't even think about how stupid I am, otherwise I'd want to slit the veins in the tops of my feet and watch all the blood run into the matted beige carpet like a spilled soda.

I used to ditch school every day so I could watch Hope on *Days of Our Lives*. When she and Bo got married, I was devastated. I kept trying to imagine instead of Bo it was Hope and I on a honeymoon in that big fucking mansion. Hope looked like a beautiful virgin in her white dress—I think on the show she was. The hardest part to watch was when he carried her to bed. He put her down so delicately, like she was his dog that accidentally ate a roach trap while he was at work. Her big, dying eyes looked into his, and his stupid eyes and cleft chin said, "I thought the roach trap was farther behind the refrigerator. Please don't die, please don't die." Oh, the whole thing makes me so mad.

Sometimes I want to beat people's faces with stones. And then I get scared because I can't tell whether I just thought, *I want to beat that person's face with a stone*, or whether it actually happened. I could see myself holding the bloody stone with tingling hands, feeling light-headed and lost. Anyway, Bo and Hope went to this estate for their honeymoon. There were tons of pretty flowers and moss everywhere and they spent the whole time walking around holding hands and barely talking. They gave each other meaningful looks. I guess because she was a scared virgin and she thought it would hurt.

I'm a virgin and I'm not a virgin. I got rid of the ol' hymen, if you know what I mean. I tied a little yellow ribbon 'round the ol' hymen tree. Actually, I lost my virginity to a giant black marking pen. *Eek, eek*—that's the sound of a marking pen writing on the page. I love that squeak—it's the sound of something getting done. Eek, eek—that's the sound I made when the marking pen went through my hymen.

I was hiding in my room because all these Marines were eating dinner at my house and I was sick of being a virgin, so I pushed the marking pen into my hymen, but it wouldn't go. I pushed harder, like I was trying to open a stuck door, and finally it gave. You know that ring that is supposed to hold the cap while you're using the marking pen? When I pulled the pen out of me after the skin broke, it was filled with hymen-skin. I'm not lyin'—the ring was filled with hymen. It sounds like a company jingle or bumper sticker: I'M NOT LYIN', IT WAS FILLED

WITH HYMEN. The more I write that, the stupider it sounds.

That's my problem: I don't know when to quit. "It's always overkill with you." That's what my brother says. Or he says, "Lighten up." When my family had to pick me up at the mental hospital, my brother said, "Why can't you just drink and not do drugs?" He's kind of moderate. I'm more loud, flamboyant, and desperate. For example, when we moved somewhere new, my mom asked me to take my brother with me and make new friends for the both of us.

I'd better slow down with my book. My community college teacher said sometimes when people get to the middle of their book, the book lags. I wonder whether Hope from *Days of Our Lives* is gay in real life. Oh, my God, that would be so rad. She doesn't look very gay. I wonder whether I look gay? Irene looks gay. I don't want to look gay. I mean, I don't want to look like the person that people think is the ugly dyke, with the short hair and flannel shirt and no bra on.

When I told my parents I was gay and was moving to San Francisco my dad said, "Good, now you can get a bunch of tattoos and look like a big dyke." I started laughing so hard when he said that. He started laughing too, and we both looked at each other laughing so hard, as if it was a contest to see who could stand laughing in the kitchen with their mouth open the longest.

Then my mom said, "Tom-m-m," and there was the long pause of astonishment as if my father had walked across hot coals.

The reason my dad knew what a lesbian looks like is because my brother's good friend Kerry McAdams had an older sister who ended up gay. My dad ran into her at my brother's soccer game her first year back from college. She sat in the bleachers with her girlfriend because Kerry McAdams was on my brother's soccer team too. The day after my dad saw her at the soccer game I went with him to buy a new shirt for work. We were parking the car before we went into the store when he said, "Kerry McAdams's sister Tracy is a lesbian."

"How do you know she's a lesbian?" I asked.

"Because I saw her at the soccer game with her lesbian friend. And the friend," he said, "was obviously a lesbian. She could just have easily been wearing a sandwich board that said LESBIAN." I asked my dad what a sandwich board was. He said, "Those big wooden signs that people wear over their shoulders when they walk through Times

Square trying to advertise something." I think I'm the only person who found out what a lesbian was before a sandwich board.

After that I could only imagine Tracy McAdams's girlfriend as a big butch dyke wearing a white sandwich board and sitting in the soccer field bleachers. And my dad said things like, "Good, go to San Francisco, you can look like Tracy McAdams's girlfriend."

My mom didn't want me to be gay either, but initially she was very calm because she thought all I needed was therapy. We did go as a family for one all-day emergency session to some therapist guy my mom had heard on the radio. My brother didn't have to go. "How come Aaron doesn't have to go?" I asked my mom. "Doesn't he care about the family?"

The radio therapist was late and my father was muttering about "paying all this money and the guy's late." When the radio therapist finally showed up, my dad sized him up like they'd met at a jukebox in a bar and my dad didn't want to hear another Johnny Cash song.

We all took our places on his leather couch that wrapped practically all the way around Los Angeles. The radio therapist asked us why we were there. My mom was convinced Irene was turning me gay: "Why does the teacher have a shaved head? Why does this older woman hang out with her students? Why are students moving to San Francisco to live with a teacher? Alexandra won't even let us meet her." These things were true, but my parents also lived two hours away, and I barely ever saw them.

We quibbled back and forth for a minute. I said, "How could they possibly ever have met her when they live two hours away?"

Then my mom said, "If she doesn't have anything to hide, why wouldn't she bring this important person to meet the family?"

Finally, the radio therapist, who was slouching across his couch with his expensive tennis shoe laces untied, asked, "Why can't you meet Irene now?"

That's when my mom said it. She said, "Meeting Irene at this point would be as comfortable as fucking a goat." I started to laugh so hard I was crying.

My father said, "Jesus, Marlene!"

And my mom said, "Well, that's exactly what it would be like."

Then the radio therapist said in his bored voice, "That's an interesting way of putting it." In a weird way I loved my mom so much for saying that. It just reminded me of how funny and smart she is, even if she hates Irene.

I wish I could've told Hope before her wedding night that it was going to hurt. "Hope," I would've said, "when you lose your virginity it's the same as when a dog runs really fast and smacks into a screen door. The dog feels shocked and some pain, a jolt maybe, but mostly it feels stupid and alone."

In AA sometimes people say, "I'm a piece of shit in the center of the universe." It means that you don't think you're worth anything, but at the same time, everything revolves around you. I have that problem.

Maybe it's different if Bo does it on your wedding night than if you do it to yourself with a marking pen with a dining room full of Marines in the house. Maybe if Bo does it you don't feel humiliated afterward.

I didn't exactly feel humiliated; in some ways I felt free, like I was happy and in charge. I was free, free, free—limping around the house by the time dessert came around. Free, free, free, with all the Marines eating bowls of whipped cream.

Did you know Marines like to eat only bowls full of whipped cream for dessert? There are a lot of Marines in my family. Some of them like cake or pie too. But whatever it is, Marines want extra—"Extra jalapeños, please. Make it so hot my tongue burns off." Then all the other Marines sit back and laugh, waiting for the other Marine to burn his tongue. They get the video camera out, and videotape the Marine burning his tongue off from too many jalapenos.

What I'm getting at is, people have to experience life for themselves. Hope might have a different hymen experience than I did. Who died and anointed me Queen of Hymen Information?

You probably think I am a megalomaniac. (That's a word I learned from Polly, this sexy waitress who wears leather suspenders.) Megalomania is a mental disorder characterized by delusions of grandeur, wealth, or power. Or a passion for doing big things—a tendency to exaggerate.

I love the dictionary. You can really learn a lot from it. For instance, when I was looking up megalomaniac, I read the definition for the word above it too. *Megalocardia—abnormal enlargement of the heart.* I have that too. That's why I love four women.

I really should lighten up. Maybe my brother is right about some things. I remember when we were growing up, his bathroom drawer was so neat. You could draw a line around everything inside: the razor, the brush, the toothpaste, etcetera. Aaron put everything back exactly in its place. I, on the other hand, couldn't get my drawer to open because it was so stuffed with shit.

Once my brother tried to come in my room, but it was so messy he couldn't push the door open. "You're going to be a loser in life. You're a loser because you smoke and your room's messy," he shouted through the tiny opening, where the door had jammed into a pile of clothes.

"You're going to be a rapist and a wife-beater," I shouted back. "Are you going to hit your wife like you hit me, huh, are you?" I'd say 50 times in a row.

"At least I don't smoke," he'd say back. "At least my room's not messy."

"No one's going to marry you, you're a wife-beater rapist," I'd shriek back at him, my words drifting out my open bedroom window for the entire neighborhood to hear.

When my brother and I hit junior high we stopped being friends and fought all the time. He was a year older and painfully shy. People were constantly coming up to him saying, "We saw your sister hanging out the car window, drunk and throwing up. We saw your sister being hauled off by the police. We saw your sister sing the National Anthem uninvited at the basketball game." We were growing apart as ungracefully as possible.

One time we were playing baseball in the backyard and I was at bat. My brother had made a baseball by taking silver duct tape and wrapping it as tightly as possible over and over. This made the ball lighter and harder to hit over the wall into the neighbor's yard.

My brother stood on the grass and delivered his pitch. I swung and missed. When I turned to pick up the ball, I saw a brightly colored king snake slithering near my feet. "Aah!" I screamed. My brother, who was a few feet away, saw why I screamed and ran into the house. He slid the glass door shut in front of me, locking me out with the snake.

"Watch out for the snake, ba-a-aby-y-y," he said. This was now my brother's favorite form of greeting. He spoke in the voice of this psy-

15

chopath we'd recently seen in a movie called *Tourist Trap*. This guy kidnaps women and holds them hostage in a basement, where one by one he turns them into mannequins. He covers them in plaster, leaving only their nostrils exposed. Then right before he slaps a handful of plaster over their nose holes he says, "Goodbye ba-a-aby-y-y!" The woman's chest heaves up and down a few times and she dies.

"Don't let the snake bite you, ba-a-aby-y-y!" he said, before locking the sliding glass door and retreating upstairs into his room.

My relationship with my brother began to revolve around slamming doors. He'd slam a door on me—I'd slam a door on him. Whoever had the most energy got to be the antagonist for the day. Another game we played involved one of us slipping into the other's room when they weren't there and hiding a piece of fruit. Depending on whether he or I was successful, weeks later, one of us would smell something rotten in his or her room. On one occasion, after hours of rummaging, I found a jet-black banana on the top shelf in my closet. I climbed up on a chair, slid a piece of paper under it, and tried to keep the putrefied pulp from oozing out of the swollen, black skin as I slipped it behind a box of baseball cards that were under his bed.

One afternoon while my parents were having drinks at the neighbors, my brother chased me around the house until he cornered me and whispered, "Hello-o-o, baby," in *Tourist Trap* voice.

"Stop it, you fucking asshole, get the fuck away from me, I fucking hate you," I said back. "Is this how you're going to treat your wife? Are you going to treat your wife like this? You're going to beat your wife, aren't you?"

I was taller than my brother even though I was a year younger, so when we fought I was able to hold my own. But this was the year he developed muscles and became stronger. "Open the door, ba-a-aby-y-y." He was outside my room, in the hall, trying to push the door open. I had a lock on it, but he'd slid a butter knife in between the door and the frame and unlocked it. He learned how to unlock all the doors with a butter knife the week before.

I leapt up and leaned against the door when I heard the first knife scrape against the lock. Now that it was unlocked, he was pushing as hard as he could, trying to open it, and I was trying to keep it shut by leaning my back against the door and bracing myself with bent legs.

My brother was stronger though, and I felt the door lurch forward.

"Get away from me, psycho," I said, huffing as I strained to keep the door from opening entirely. Then I threw all my weight into the door and heard my brother's long, terrible scream. I thought the scream was a trick to get me to open the door. *He's not going to fool me.* Only after he kept screaming and screaming did I become nervous and open the door. Blood was running down the doorjamb. The door had cut off the top of his finger and I could see the part of the wood that had been crushed where his finger had been caught in the door frame.

My parents, who were two houses down at the neighbor's having drinks, heard him scream and came running home to find him bleeding. When they wrapped a towel around his finger, the blood leaked through the six layers.

"How many times have I told you not to play grab-ass?" my father said. The top of Aaron's finger was barely hanging on by a piece of skin. My parents took him to the hospital and dropped me off at the neighbors where they'd been having drinks.

I hated the neighbors with my whole heart. All they did was drink scotch and look like they were about to beat you. The father neighbor, Mr. Broil, was the worst. He was an abnormally tall Air Force retiree. They had a lot of parties because even though they only had two daughters, their daughters were always about to get married or have kids or get engaged. The voyages to the Broil parties were always the same. My mother, father, brother, grandmother, and grandfather would walk the two doors down with a bottle of Seagram's V.O. as an offering and stand on the porch after ringing the doorbell. Mr. Broil would open the door.

"Hello," he'd say to my parents and grandparents, and then he would turn to me. "Hello, Alexandra."

"Hello, Mr. Broil," I'd say back in a tone that was somehow unsatisfactory to him—either too unenthusiastic or sarcastic.

Then Mr. Broil would say, "I said, hello," and grab my wrists and squeeze them so hard that when he was done there would be bruised stripes from where each of his fingers had been. My parents stood on either side of me, thinking it was some joke. After that we'd go inside and eat Mrs. Broil's famous ham spread.

Mrs. Broil was permanently lying under an afghan with a 15-year-old miniature dog with one tooth in its mouth on top of her. It was a race to see who would live longer, Mrs. Broil or the dog. They both had terrible arthritis and seemed generally unwell.

"How's it going, Lana? Feeling all right?" That's what everyone said whenever they walked by her.

My mother would whisper to my brother and me, "Go say hello to Mrs. Broil."

"Hi, Mrs. Broil. How are you?" we'd mumble obediently. Mrs. Broil was never really all right.

You spoke quietly and ultrarespectfully in the Broil house. There were pictures of Mr. Broil all the way up the staircase, in a progression of increasingly more important Air Force uniforms. Even when the curtains weren't drawn—they often were because somehow Mrs. Broil was adversely affected by light—the Broil house was dark. They had a pool, which was very exciting. But because it was such an emotional drain to be around them and their awful son, who was also abnormally tall, my brother and I rarely put in the begging work to go for a swim. Mr. Broil made you feel like you never really had done enough in life to be able to use their pool. If in fact they ever let you, you were too depressed to swim or to go on the beautiful light blue slide that curved around and dropped you into the water.

All the houses in our neighborhood were designed the same, and in every living room was a wet bar. Scotch was Mr. and Mrs. Broil's drink, so on their wet bar was the biggest bottle of scotch that you could buy at the liquor store. It sat in this strange sling that allowed Mr. Broil to tip the bottle with his fingertip until it filled his glass and then revert it to the upright position. Mr. Broil had only to recline in his recliner, which was strategically placed in front of the bar. When he wanted another drink, he'd reach over his shoulder and tilt the liquor seesaw.

Mr. Broil's son, Tony, was our age. Whenever he had a birthday, we'd be his guests to go wherever. One birthday he wanted to go to Knott's Berry Farm. We spent the night at Tony's house so we could get up extra early and arrive at Knott's Berry Farm exactly as it opened. Tony was a bastard like his father, and he'd spent the whole week doing that child thing where you threaten to uninvite your friends to the amusement park. "If you don't let me ride your bike, I'm going to tell my dad and then you won't be able to go to Knott's Berry Farm."

The morning of Tony's birthday came, and we all got into Mr. Broil's beat-up yellow station wagon with the broken speedometer. I rode in the front seat with Mr. Broil. The A.M. radio buzzed during the hour and a half drive to Knott's Berry Farm. I felt like I was going to a funeral as Mr. Broil crawled along at a responsible Air Force retiree rate and the stream of cars behind honked and swerved. Beyond nauseous, I looked over as the broken speedometer quietly turned circles like the hands on a clock, knowing when we got to Knott's Berry Farm I would be Mr. Broil's partner on all of the two seated roller coaster rides, since my brother was Tony's best friend.

I recalled that day at Knott's Berry Farm when my parents dropped me off at the Broil's before they took my brother to the hospital to try to get his finger sewn back on. Mrs. Broil was upstairs lying down and Mr. Broil was reclining in his recliner, his ice cubes clinking back and forth in his scotch glass.

I was in the sixth grade and went to a small Baptist school that stressed phonics and language skills. Each semester we were required to read 10 books. Instead of reading 10 books, I asked my teacher if I could read one big book. That is how I ended up sitting in the Broil's dark living room pretending to read the unabridged *David Copperfield*. Mr. Broil began his lecture from his recliner. "You know once I came home from work and Lizanne (one of his daughters) had a broken leg. Nobody knew how it happened. None of my children knew a thing. According to Lizanne she was walking across the floor and her leg broke all by itself."

I didn't know what he wanted from me; I never said I didn't slam the door on my brother's finger. It was like he was waiting for a confession. I couldn't tell whether he was saying one of his other children was responsible for Lizanne's leg breaking or whether he was going to break my leg. I guessed Lizanne was probably standing in front of his recliner when he tilted back to pour more scotch and she got clipped right below the knee.

I didn't feel guilty about what happened to my brother's finger. Instead I felt as if someone has taken all the blood from my veins and replaced it with dread. I dreaded the scorn of my brother for cutting his finger off, and the scorn of my father who would yell at me for an unnecessary hospital bill. Even more, I dreaded the next three hours because I knew my eyes would move over the same sentence in *David Copperfield* and I would have to participate in Mr. Broil's interrogation, Air Force style.

I should lighten up, like my brother says. You know who else should lighten up? Bo and Hope. All they did in the wedding episode was walk around the estate looking solemn, and the camera kept panning over Bo's slicked-back ponytail, in case we couldn't see for ourselves that he'd made an effort to look handsome for the day. "He's going to be boring, Hope," I shouted at the TV. Look at him: somber, solemn, walking, gazing—for Christ's sake, it's your wedding day! Have a drink. Who am I to talk? I don't know how to have a good time either. Honestly, I can't imagine their marriage lasting, because I think Hope feels pressured because Bo always tries to control her.

I want to be the best person I possibly can. I love Irene so much. She's the philosophy teacher I followed to San Francisco. She is the most beautiful, smart, caring person I've ever met. She lives here with two other students from our community college. They are all lovers— Irene, Gustavo, and Jenny—and they are living in this Gandhi-style household. They asked me to live there too, but I don't want to live with all of them. If it were just Irene, it would be different. We all met in this class called "The Philosophy of Nonviolence." Gustavo and Jenny weren't actually in that class, but they had been in Irene's other classes before I went to the community college. They knew Irene when she was married to a man.

Gustavo showed up in Irene's office one day and told her he was in love with her—he had a letter or something that he'd written to her. Irene told Gustavo that she never dates her students, so Gustavo dropped out of her class and Irene separated from her husband. That's how my headache started.

Irene loves Gustavo like I love Irene. You can ask anyone—they're mad about each other. Irene looks gay, but she likes dick. Dick is weird (like I've seen so many). Hi, nice to meet you, I'm the 20-year-old lesbian alcoholic pancake-waitress dick expert.

I loved "The Philosophy of Nonviolence" class. For my final project I created my own dance called "The Nonviolent Shuffle." I stood completely still, not dancing. Get it? Irene laughed so hard. She's so fucking beautiful when she laughs. Ever since she shaved her head she looks so fucking beautiful.

"Why does the teacher have a shaved head, Alexandra? Answer me that. Why does the teacher with the shaved head hang out with her students?" My poor mom. I think it's like Irene said: My mom's not well. Some groups of nonviolent people wear masks so they don't kill the little amoebas that float in the air. Jainism—that's what it's called. Other people don't step on the grass because they don't want to kill it. I want to be a really good person too, but stepping on the grass seems inevitable. There's a lot of grass, at least at the community college where Irene was my teacher. Everyone wanted to hang out with Irene, but only some of us got to. Even though she was nice to everyone, only some of us got to go to Denny's after class to talk about Jainism.

Before Irene moved to San Francisco with her two lovers, I loved her so fucking much. We did stuff every day together—only us. Everything is different now that she lives with her simplicity family. For the most part, I pretend I don't love her anymore. I'm playing it cool because I know she's never going to pick me over Gustavo. Even though Jenny is her lover too, I don't feel jealous of Jenny. I guess because I don't believe that Irene loves her with the intensity that she loves Gustavo.

When Irene taught at our community college, I'd circle her classroom, walking around and around the corridors, hoping her door would open and she'd look out and see me. Let me tell you what she used to dress like when she taught philosophy: She wore black jeans, a black T-shirt, and black clogs. Her keys hung off this key ring on her belt loop.

Irene has the most beautiful face: high cheekbones and big doe eyes. Oh, my God, and her hands! She has these big strong hands—they're so sexy. Sometimes she wears a few silver rings. Not too many, not like Liberace. After she shaved her head, she looked even more beautiful—as if that were possible. All her students loved her.

I loved her so much I'd drive by her house at night—even though it was 25 minutes from where I lived—just to see whether the light was on. I loved Divot. That's what we used to call Irene before we called her Chops or Choppy. She got that name one night when our whole group went miniature golfing. Irene put her ball down at the beginning of the hole and it rolled off the carved-out plastic mat where you are supposed to tee off. She said, "The ball rolled out of the divot."

"What did you call it?" I said.

And she said, "The divot. That's the name for that hole."

I thought, *Holy shit! She's the smartest, most intelligent woman in the whole world. She knows the name for that little thing at miniature golf.* That was the night my love metastasized.

A few holes later I said, "Can I call you Divot?" Then everyone started calling her Divot, which kind of pissed me off, because I was the one who thought of it. It took a long time for it to sound right, which I guess is only natural if you call someone Divot. It's not the most common name in the world. Divot. Divot. Divot.

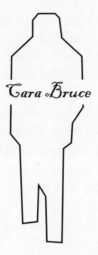

Tara Bruce

Love Boat and Lingerie

In 1988 I was 14 years old and in my freshman year of high school. Punk rock was still its own genre, Ronald Reagan was President, and postage stamps were 22 cents. I lived in a suburb of Washington, D.C. Like all suburbs it bred bored, troubled teens with no actual problems beyond the usual angst. Our boredom was solved in suburban teenage fashion: skipping school, hanging out at 7-11s, doing drugs, and going to the mall.

This was the year I really started experimenting with drugs. I smoked pot daily, took acid, drank until I puked, and snorted my first lines of cocaine. However, I was still waiting to lose my virginity. I had progressed to the point of blow jobs and getting fingered, but my proverbial cherry had yet to be popped. I wasn't waiting for anyone or anything in particular, just someone who wouldn't fuck and tell. I didn't want to be a girl whose secrets were revealed over Camels and Budweisers.

This particular day was hot but not too humid. I decided to ditch school early. While I was walking out I ran into my friends Elizabeth and Sara. They were going to the mall for a day of shoplifting. We grabbed some empty shopping bags and walked to the main intersection out of town. When the light turned red, we rapped on a car window. Hitchhiking was our main means of transportation and we were pretty good at it. We always hit up people who were alone. It was easier to manipulate people who didn't have someone to talk sense into him or her.

The driver we found was an aging frat boy. The kind of guy who, at 45, still thinks he's in Delta Omega Whatever. He rolled down his window, and we asked for a ride to the mall. This was the best way we had found to hitchhike. Nine times out of 10 people were so surprised to have a girl knocking on their window in the middle of the road that they simply said yes.

Elizabeth and I were sitting in the back seat. While the driver was attempting to impress Sara with stories of the wild things he did in his youth—like hitchhike—Elizabeth leaned over and placed something in my hand. It was a tiny square of tinfoil that stunk like sickly sweet death.

"What's this?" I whispered, wrinkling my nose as the distinctive aroma of formaldehyde filled the car.

"Love boat," Elizabeth whispered back, snatching the package out of my sweaty palms.

Love boat was a popular D.C. drug during the '80s. It was pot soaked in PCP, or "angel dust." I hadn't tried it yet, but I had seen all of the after-school specials featuring kids freaking out and breaking into convenience stores naked, or violently attacking police officers, or jumping out of windows thinking they could fly. But in spite of these *Reefer Madness*-esque exploitation programs, I wasn't afraid. I was conflicted. It was one of those really scary drugs, like heroin. The types that can make you go insane, or maybe even die. But I had plenty of friends who smoked boat, and they seemed to be OK. And there didn't seem to be a big addiction factor. You never heard of PCP junkies. Or about someone robbing a liquor store for his or her PCP fix. I took all of these things into consideration and decided to try it.

Elizabeth wanted to smoke the boat before we started our day of shoplifting. But it smelled really bad so we had to find a bathroom off the beaten path. Of course, employees were just as dangerous as customers when you decided to smoke PCP in a public rest room. We took an elevator down to the basement and wandered around underneath Macy's until we found a bathroom that had no toilet paper—only a few lingering cigarette butts. It felt safe. If anyone came in, our biggest problem would be that we would have to share our stash.

Sara and I leaned against the door as Elizabeth prepared the drugs. She smushed the tinfoil square between two coins to squeeze the PCP juice out of the pot seeds then carefully unfolded the package. It looked like moldy leaves and stunk like a bad science project. It was as if someone had done something really awful to pot, which I generally thought of as a very nice, pretty drug. The love boat seemed so fake. And even though I took acid, I didn't really think of that as being artificial. I guess it was my association with the whole hippie thing. Of course, this was when I still thought that hippies were really nice, loving people and not capitalistic smack addicts.

"Be careful," Elizabeth warned, after taking her hit. "Don't smoke too much. You don't want to become a patient."

She explained to us that love boat dealers were doctors and users were patients. That should have tipped me off to something.

But Sara and I ignored her and took huge hits. I worried about being cool and I didn't want to look like a lightweight. We passed the stinky bowl around a few times then lit cigarettes to mask the morgue-like scent. As soon as I took a drag of my cigarette, it hit me. I was fucked up. The kind of fucked up where you feel like you've been smashed against a glass wall. My arms felt like one hundred pound feathers, and my legs felt like rubber. I took a step forward, and it seemed as if I was gliding through quicksand. I thought about what a paradoxical feeling boat produced. And then my thoughts pretty much stopped. It was as if they were permanently stuck on the tip of my tongue. And my tongue felt as if it was swelling up to three times its normal size and sprouting hair. I stuck it out and looked in the grime-covered mirror. It looked fine, but I was suddenly convinced that it was going to puff up until it exploded.

"I feel weird," Sara said. She was talking OK but I felt weird too and was afraid that my words wouldn't come out with my tongue feeling like it was the size of my arm. I didn't want to look like an asshole, but I was sort of becoming frozen and that worried me. Of course PCP is an animal tranquilizer, and I was certain that I was becoming tranquilized to the point of coma. I consciously lifted my legs up high to break out of the funk. They were lead noodles.

I saw Elizabeth nod in response and wondered if she was having the tongue thing too. My entire body felt as if it was swelling. Walking was rubbery but felt really cool. After my moment of tranquilized panic had passed I began to really feel my body. It was like a super huge mass engulfed in fluid. I practiced walking again, pacing the bathroom floor.

I thought I liked the high, but I wasn't sure.

"I don't know," Sara said, as if reading my mind. "I feel weird."

"That's normal," Elizabeth said. And that made sense to me. You should feel weird when you take drugs. That's what they're for. I mean, isn't the point to feel as altered as possible? But, as the second wave of the drug washed over me, my stomach did that clench-heave thing that it does right before I'm going to vomit. I debated between good weird and bad weird.

"Are you OK?" Sara asked me.

"Yeah," I lied, trying to push the words off of my tongue rather than puke them out.

"Are you sure?" she asked. "You've been standing there for a few minutes with your mouth hanging open."

"No I haven't," I argued. "We've only been in here for a few minutes."

"Time gets fucked up on boat," said Elizabeth assuredly. "I forgot to tell you that."

We walked out of the bathroom. She was right. Everything was so much slower. The world was made of Jell-O. I started imagining myself completely made out of cubes of lime Jell-O. I lifted my right arm and imagined the globby Jell-O blooping down it. I quickly put my arm down. I didn't want to be the one to freak out on PCP. I prided myself on my ability to keep calm on drugs. Even if that meant holding on to the high with white knuckles and a bit lip. We made it to the elevator and went back up. As we entered the fluorescent world of mannequins and merchandise, I was overwhelmed. What if everyone knew we were fucked up? What if we were more fucked up than we thought we were? What if mall security arrested us, and my parents had to come get me, and they found out I was smoking PCP? They would be pretty pissed. It was too much for me to think about, and I started hyperventilating for a second until Elizabeth punched me in the arm. I didn't feel that until a few seconds later.

We slugged along through Macy's, heading to the lingerie department.

For some reason we always stole lingerie. I had the best collection of expensive bras, garters, and panties of any 14-year-old I knew. I had lingerie I never wore. In fact, I still have bras from back then that I never wear. I don't know why we stole lingerie—maybe it added an extra thrill.

We started picking through the racks of the most expensive shit we could find. Time was more than a little off, and we were going through every bra really carefully. We looked at each piece for at least 20 seconds before moving on to the next. I wasn't even completely sure what size bra I wore, other than small, so I usually ended up guessing and getting it wrong. It was at least half an hour before we had picked out around 15 pieces each to take into the dressing room. When we shoplifted normally we were good at it. We were in and out and didn't get greedy. But today was different. Today we were in the mall, shoplifting on love boat. Today we were taking our time.

"Cara," a familiar voice called. I thought I might be hallucinating. My mouth dropped as I saw Trish Barton's mother. Trish was in many of my advanced classes, and her mother knew mine. Mrs. Barton walked toward us. Elizabeth and Sara eyed me warily. This was *not* the time to be talking to parents. *Act normal*, I begged myself.

"How are you doing?" she asked. She was one of those parents who thought that her daughter could do no wrong. I nodded. The words *I'm fine* would not come out of my mouth. In fact, no words would come out of my mouth. She furrowed her brow. "Shouldn't you be in school?" she asked me.

"I, um…" I began. The connection between my brain and my mouth was frozen. The words were stuck in that short-circuited transit.

"We're doing a work-study thing," Elizabeth said calmly. "We're learning about real-life marketing."

Elizabeth was so fucking cool. I wanted to be that cool. She was like ice and her hard-ass attitude was very sexy. Besides the time I had spent the night at Laura Bigelow's house when I was 11, I hadn't really thought about girls this way. I couldn't decide whether it was the drugs, or whether I was suddenly a lesbian. Could PCP make me gay? Was there a gay switch in my brain that had just been turned on? I had heard about people crossing boundaries on drugs, and maybe this was one of them.

"Are you OK?" Mrs. Barton asked me.

Sara pinched the back of my thigh. "Yeah," I mumbled, trying to smile.

It was at that moment that Mrs. Barton noticed the bras in my hand. She reached over and touched part of the lace. She didn't say anything, but the look on her face was enough. If I was buying this many bras that must mean that I was having sex. Her face changed from friendly to snooty. I was sure that she was thinking how *her* daughter was not having sex, and that I was a slut. I was also sure I was going to hear about this from my mom sometime in the near future.

"Well," Mrs. Barton said tersely, "I ought to be going."

As soon as she left Elizabeth smacked the back of my head, "Act normal," she said.

I shrugged my shoulders and blushed. I was still thinking about what she would look like in her new bras.

We took our loot to the dressing room. A bored, gum-smacking attendant checked us in. This woman was a prime example of the hick quotient in Virginia. She had acne and wrinkles and was around 19. She also wore about a pound of makeup, making her face dark orange, like a bad fake tan. I sized her up. I loved to make up stories about people. I figured she had a kid or two and lived in a squat house with a Trans-Am on cinder blocks on the front lawn. Her boyfriend lived with her and worked construction. As I formulated this life for her, she counted our items. When she started counting them a second time, I giggled. She glared at me, like I was laughing at her, which I was. The love boat began to mix with a sudden fear of being pummeled by this chick that probably picked bar fights for fun. I started to shake. She looked at the bras, quivering in my hand, and then looked me in the eye. I smiled as sweetly as I could on PCP, but it came off really fake. She snarled and handed me the square plastic card that bore the unlucky number 13.

Elizabeth shook her head in disapproval. I was embarrassed but couldn't stop giggling. Soon Sara started too, and both of us were laughing like lunatics as we walked down the row, peering into open dressing rooms. The trick was to find one that had a lot of clothes left in it, so you could swap them out for whatever you wanted to steal. We found a large room that had a pile of unwanted clothing, and the three of us filed in.

"Shut up," spat Elizabeth. I put my hand over my mouth, but I couldn't stop laughing. I didn't even know what was so funny, but suddenly I felt good. I had forgotten that I was high and that you were supposed to enjoy being high. Sometimes I got too caught up in acting not high that I missed out on being high. I slid down against the wall of the dressing room and tried to compose myself. The room was in tunnel vision and all the edges were round. I got my laughing under control and watched Sara and Elizabeth as they picked out what they wanted.

I should admit that even though I love the rush of stealing, I'm not that good at it. In fact, I had been caught stealing cigarettes at Safeway and hair dye at Walgreen's. I had almost been caught the time we filled up a cart of groceries and walked out of the supermarket with it. But that time I ran. In general, shoplifting terrified me. And today I was totally out of my mind and my paranoia was growing by the minute. I sat back and watched. Sara and Elizabeth were pros. Elizabeth began shoving things into her bag, hiding bras in the sleeves of her jacket.

Sara pulled off her shirt and took off her bra. She put on one of the new bras and then started to put on a second. She had the clasp in front to hook it before she turned it around, but had only gotten through the first step. "I can't move," she said, frightened.

"What do you mean, you can't move?" I asked.

"I think I'm paralyzed," she whispered. I thought she was fucking with me and rolled my eyes.

"Help me," she urged. She was completely freaked out. I stood up, unsure of what to do. I didn't know what she wanted me to help her with. I lifted one of her arms and let it drop back down. She was like a catatonic schizophrenic who could be repositioned.

The only thing I could do was help her get the bra on so I started to spin it around. Her face clenched in concern. "What am I going to do? I'm stuck."

"It'll pass," Elizabeth said decidedly. God she was so calm. "It happens all the time."

I wasn't quite sure that spontaneous paralysis happened all the time, but I didn't want to say so. Instead I lifted Sara's arm and put it through one of the bra straps. I did the same for the other. I had to touch her breast to get the bra situated correctly. My lesbian fantasies resurfaced. I was now convinced that PCP made you gay. I could kiss her, and she couldn't do anything about it. My mind was circling around the possibilities. I was beginning to get lost in my thoughts when I noticed Elizabeth staring at me oddly. I realized I was standing there with my hands on Sara's tits staring off into space.

"Sorry," I said. "I was out of it for a minute."

"Thanks," Sara said. "I think one bra might be enough."

Elizabeth snorted, and I felt stupid. I stepped back, embarrassed. Now my friends thought I was queer and I wasn't sure that I wasn't. This was a head-trip I couldn't begin to deal with on PCP.

"God, you guys," I scoffed. "I just zoned out." Elizabeth was hanging clothes on hangers, and I was trying to coordinate getting Sara's shirt on for her.

"How are we going to leave if she's paralyzed?" I asked.

"It'll wear off any second," said Elizabeth. She seemed pretty confident, so I decided she must be right. I looked at my watch. We had already been at the mall for three hours, and all we had done was smoke drugs and look through bras at Macy's. Usually by this time we had a couple of outfits and were on our way home.

I slid back down the wall, and Elizabeth joined me on the floor. We sat there, staring up at Sara, who was still stuck.

"This is kind of creepy," I whispered to Elizabeth.

"Yeah," she agreed.

"I can hear you guys," Sara shrieked. "I'm paralyzed, not fucking deaf."

"God, calm down," Elizabeth snapped.

"Calm down?" Sara snarled. "You try being paralyzed. It fucking sucks."

I agreed that it did fucking suck but it also sucked that we were stuck in here waiting for her to become unglued. I wanted her to hurry up and be able to move. What if she was paralyzed for hours and we were stuck in this dressing room with the hick bitch out front and stolen bras on Sara's body? Just as my panic began to edge toward absolute frenzy, Sara fell over.

She shook out her sleeping limbs, and we left the dressing room. We began the long walk up the aisle toward the attendant. We handed her the things we didn't want with the corresponding plastic numbers.

"You girls sure were in there a long time," she drawled as she began to count.

"They were hard decisions," Elizabeth snapped. The lids of her eyes were half closed, and I wanted to tell her that she looked really high but I didn't think that this was the appropriate time. Instead I mumbled something stupid about needing to get home, and the mall worker looked at me like I was a nut case. I wondered if I was even speaking English. She grabbed my arm tightly, and I tried to pull away. I definitely was not experiencing any of those superhuman qualities that angel dust supposedly gives you. I wanted to ask Elizabeth if she was sure that this was PCP but when I looked up they were gone. I was totally confused. The woman yelled for security but Sara and Elizabeth had disappeared. After all of that slow motion and a brief stint with being paralyzed, the fear of cops had jump-started their inner clocks and told them to move it.

Before I knew what was happening, I was surrounded. Women poked their heads out of stalls to watch as I was led away by two security officers. I hoped Mrs. Barton wasn't in the room. I pleaded with myself to act normal. I made the usual bargain with God, that if he let me out of this one I would never do drugs again. The security officers were telling me how much trouble I was in, and I was sure they knew I was high. I tried to focus on what they were saying so I could come up with some sort of intelligent response, but their words were getting muddled with my own thoughts, and I feared that I was actually saying out loud all of the things that I was thinking. I lost track of how much trouble they were telling me I was going to be in as I concentrated solely on keeping my mouth shut.

The guards pulled me into a private office and dumped my shopping bag on the table. There was nothing in there. Suddenly I realized that they weren't busting me for doing drugs, but were busting me for shoplifting. I smiled, relieved. The guards looked confused—even I had been expecting something incriminating to be in the bag. The male guards left, and a woman guard asked me if I would please lift up my clothing so she could see what I was wearing underneath. With a new-found sense of righteousness I asked her if that was legal. She said that if I didn't do it, they would just take me to jail and have it done there. I was coherent enough to know that jail was one place I did not want to be. I lifted my shirt and pulled down my pants. Besides the fact that I was high on PCP, everything was fine.

The security people had no choice but to let me go. As I walked out of the mall a huge smile spread across my face. I was free.

The elation didn't last long—I realized that I was all alone and still high. When was this fucking trip ever going to end? I could be permanently fucked up on this shit. I shook my head; life would take forever at this pace, and I was way too impatient for that.

I didn't know what to do. I didn't want to hitchhike home alone on love boat, so I started to walk. It was only a few miles, but at the snail pace I was moving, it would be dark before I was even halfway. I walked down the street, trying to remember not to talk to myself out loud. After what felt like an hour, a car swerved onto the side of the road. There were no shoulders, only woods, and it almost hit me. I dived for the trees. The car door opened, and I screamed. It was probably some rapist who was going to abduct me and take me to an abandoned warehouse where he would tie me up and torture me with drops of water.

I turned around and told myself to run but my feet didn't want to move.

"Cara," yelled a voice. I turned around. It was Sara. I was so happy I began to cry. It was that emotional last stage of being high. Finally the drug was beginning to wear off. My vision became focused, and my mind started to process complete sentences. It was as if someone had turned me back on. I had survived my first cruise on love boat.

The guy dropped us off on a corner. We said goodbye, and I walked to my house. It was then that I realized I hadn't gotten anything. Sara and Elizabeth had new bras, and all I had was a bruise on my arm and the sneaking suspicion that I might not be totally straight. I entered the house, becoming more sober and more confused with each step. My mom was home, putting dinner on the table.

"What have you been doing all day?" She asked.

I quickly replayed the afternoon in my head. "Nothing too interesting," I answered. She smiled and we sat down to eat. Suddenly, I was starving.

Sara Seinberg

Twelve (Other) Easy Steps to God

i grew up all around, but suburbs are the same. ok, no, they're different, but the thing about suburbs is, no one *cares* that they're different from one other. even the differences are so boring you could sleep through a whole town like a geometry class, and still get a good grade just from guessing. or from lying.

now, lying is a big deal. when i was a kid traipsing from suburb to suburb, mall to mall, maybelline lip gloss to bonnie bell lip smacker, i could lie up a storm. nobody knew my story, so i could always make up new ones. life was never dramatic enough so...*poof*...i was dying of some rare and barely discernable disease or...*blam*...i was really a child in hiding because my parents were on the run in the witness protection program ducking out in walnut creek, california, from a mysterious posse of gangsters who might have trailed them there from new york or...*pow*...i had been the downy baby as an infant. always i pretended i had been so special in the distant past in order to have at least the tiniest bit of sparkle in the present.

i knew everything too. authority didn't count. i was a kid with a leo

33

complex. a madonna complex. the complex of the plain girl with the superstar trapped inside. a terrible thing. but everyone knows that apathy and bitterness are givens in suburban monotony. what is there to rebel against? what is oppressive? TV? what do you do?

smoke pot.

drink.

cut class.

fuck.

bo-ring.

i found a boy in tenth grade that did speed. his name was tommy. we started getting high together in the parking lot at fifth period. when it began, there was just the weed, back when a dime bag actually existed. when a dime bag could get you high for a whole week. but once he gave me some speed, i didn't even want to take the edge off. so i fucked him and he gave it to me. his dad was a dealer. he wanted to fuck me too. the dad's name was randy and he was this old crusty biker guy. huge antique jacked-up harley loud enough to wake the nodding. waking the dead was easy if you could get high enough. and we could. we did. randy had a single thick gray braid that fell down his spine and a matching beard in the same braid seven and three quarters inches down his neck. i'd come over and he'd say

yer lookin' pretty as a patent leather pump there, hester.

and even in tenth grade i knew randy knew something about me i didn't even know yet. his voice was real low. dirty. randy made me feel funny and i was too lily white to know whether that was good or bad.

so one day i headed over there and tommy wasn't home. i found randy on a cleaning jag. what was he cleaning? ledges on the windows between the bottom and the top sets of panes. a place that is supposed to be dusty. no one looked there ever. the tops of molding on the doorways, eight feet up in the air. inside the tank of the toilet where the guts push the water to sewers under the ground taking shit to who knows where while we walk the dog, while we fill yellow school buses with children, while we shop for overpriced bras and while we drink quietly alone in the dark because being a teenager leaves you very few options. randy was accomplishing the well-known speed side effect known as obscure cleaning.

hey randy
hester esther. my my my. don't you look lovely as a redheaded lobster with a big old pot of sticky drawn butter, he said, eyes all black like squid's ink. i never saw any color around them. all pupil. always.
don't i just? i said.

and then the weirdest thing. without tommy there, i felt calm. i felt smooth and calm like a lady. first time ever as a lady and i loved it. had him in my fist. that's what i thought. ha. i liked that he made me into a fifty-dollar main course. something to eat. something you eat with your fingers and a bib. rich and sloppy and wrong. with claws.

tommy went to get his bike fixed. told him he was a man now. time to fix his own bike. so he went down to ace's shop with my tools. old ace'll show him a thing or two.
yeah, i said. **kids like us sometimes need to be shown a thing or two i guess.**

he came down off the chair, dirty black jeans creasing at the knees, gray beard nodding at me like a knife blade. those marble-black eyes full of exactly nothing i could understand. insane. the speed, it made you insane. i would get there later.
hester, you need a little fun? a little crank?
sure, i said.

did i mention that i loved speed? it wasn't just a bad-girl thing. i actually loved it. i'd tried cocaine a bunch of times because it was around, but it never got me high enough. just made me want something more. crystal came through every time. no ducking into bathrooms for the crash. one line, two days. i loved it. if you could snort a winning superbowl touchdown as the clock ran calmly down to all those zeros and make that feeling last a whole day, that's it. that's speed.

randy was watching me like that again and i knew something bigger than me was happening. my neck started to tingle and then my shoulders started to ache and then i felt the sweat in my hands like water.

so you want to cut it?

you ever shot it?

shot it?

yeah.

uh…no.

well then, little lady, i guess it's your day for me to show you a thing or two.

too fast. too much. you want it. but you want it yourself, and it's too fast and it's not that you even want to stop it…it's that you can't. and he's so old and he's so handsome in the way that the wrong things always are and you love the smell of the sweat from his pores and it smells metallic like the spoon and what you taste in the metal on the back of your tongue is the fear of giving up the control you lost the minute you began to think you were a lady. that you had him in your fist. but you won't know this. you will do what you are told because you don't know how to do anything else in the face of this.

and because you want to.

spoon.
water.
cotton.
belt.
teeth.
needle.
skin.
pop.
blood.
push.
breathe.
breathe.

god.

and it feels like maybe your ears are bleeding or your skin is plastic or your lungs are in your throat or everything is finally loud enough. and fear is sitting in the belly of a spoon.

so there's one thing, randy. you said a thing…or two.

take your clothes off.

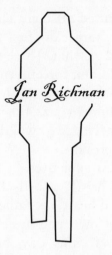

Jan Richman

YOUR MOUTH IS OPEN

I've wanted to fuck someone with Tourette's Syndrome ever since I can remember. At first the longing was simply a sexualized appetite for my father's proximity, wanting to feel the quakes and shivers of his regular Tourettic explosions from a box seat a few yards behind first base. I both craved and was repulsed by the compulsive flailing of his limbs, the tics and moans and perpetual knocking on wood, the heat that emanated from his seizures like sparks from machinery, smelling of oxidized metal.

As a kid, long before we knew that there was an exotic and French-sounding name for his condition, I'd imagine what it would be like to be continually wracked by uncontrollable shudders. I locked myself in my bedroom and created an elaborate ritual: I'd go about my regular routine—changing into my playclothes, listening to the radio, doing my homework—but every time the clock's little black rolodex flipped over to the next minute, I'd incorporate a carefully choreographed series of spastic jabs and expletives. First I'd shake my head no—no, no, no, no, no, no—delighting in the little twig-breaking sound my neck made with each oscillation. Still quivering, I'd vibrate my hands, palms out, hip-level, like I was performing some vaudevillian number, carrying out the

39

last note of a song as I strutted offstage. Then I'd punch myself in the crotch, the way I'd seen my father do, first with one fist, then with the other, in an alternating 3-2 rhythm. Three with the left, two with the right, not as hard as I could, but forceful enough to leave a little necklace of bruises along my pelvic bone. At the time, of course, I had no idea I was perfecting a modern jazz time signature with my flying fists—one, two, three, four-five; one, two, three, four-five—that would have made Dave Brubeck proud.

Finally, I'd gasp out a few expletives: "Goddamn it! Motherfucking cocksucking mommy of Christ!" Mostly I'd just ape the weird and nonsensical swear words I'd heard my father moan, but sometimes I'd get creative and splice my own pairings: "Jesus dick! Bitch sucker! Cunt-nosed pee-sprayer!" To this day, batty epithetical amalgams occur to me in episodes of road rage and end-of-my-rope domestic head-banging, but I know better now than to lapse into a wordy dance of neurological despair. Then, though, I must have cut quite a pose—a skilled mimic and miniapprentice to the master—in my corduroy clam-diggers and bobby socks.

But even highly adept masturbation gets old, and at some point I found myself wishing to be railed against instead of railing. I wanted to stay perfectly still and absorb the sparks and barks of someone with an intense boy-smell convulsing in my general direction. I craved the scent of fast motion, the frenetic fission of a body lost in time and space, puppeteered by a laughing, stuttering, ADD-addled god, a god without even rudimentary manners. The idea that I could be the recipient of all this uncontrolled flaying, the landing pad for unbridled wildness, was—and still is—the crucial detail of my erotic notion.

I am heat; barbed icicles melt against my skin. I am a smooth target; arrows grow kind as they pierce. My part in the sexual act has evolved, in fantasy, from my being just a kind of screen door to be flapped against to being an integral and emotional partner in crime, a trusted benefactress of escalated and furious longing. When I find him, I thought, he will be like a dream: I'll feel compelled to stay in any situation just to see what will happen next. There will be no explainable reason to get into the taxi, board the plane, follow the man into the Windex-colored river inhabited by flesh-eating neon tetras—I'll just do it. He will hold onto me as though I am a last raft in a biblical torrent;

he will know my sturdy, buoyant edges and my hard-won, handmade survival skills. He will know me underneath my skin. He'll know how I was formed, the tiny explosions of capillaries that dead-end at my blood-brain barrier. I already know him.

My friend Eli tells me he has a classmate with Tourette's who plays drums in a band called The Crying of Lot 49, which also happens to be one of my favorite novels by Thomas Pynchon. So we go to the Bottom of the Hill, a local San Francisco nightclub where antismoking laws are moot, and giant, obscenely cartoonish band posters line the walls like bright propaganda. In one, Lucy gives Charlie Brown a blow job; in another, Nancy and Sluggo go at it doggy style. It is a Friday night and the club is crowded. "I'm so fucking sick of fucking guitars," we over-hear a gaunt, pasty guy say to a gaunt, pasty girl. "I wanna see some-body get up there and play like a fucking fire extinguisher!"

Pattycake, the band onstage when we arrive, consists of three girls in miniskirts with varying shades of pink hair playing bubblegum TV theme-song music on tiny strap-on keyboards while posing and pout-ing. "Taste me, taste me, come on and taste me!" they sing in unison. We take our beers out to the patio. Sometimes it's hard to tell the dif-ference between experimental and insipid.

"There he is," says Eli conspiratorially as we step out the back door. He nods his chin up toward the staircase leading to the green room, a tiny redwood cupola built on top of the patio balcony—basically the only place where band members can go to smoke pot or shoot heroin or eat a burrito beyond the radar of rabid fans. I see a lanky man in brown suede pants slip into the room, his Beatleoid mop of hair dip-ping slightly to clear the diminutive door frame. His hair is the same color as his pants.

"Hey, Jamie!" Eli shouts. Jamie's chestnut head bobs back out of the portal just as swiftly as it had ducked in, and he quickly surveys the landscape of rock swine strewn across the patio. We are a motley assortment of sad sacks in sheep's clothing—mostly nerd-hip boys in horn-rimmed glasses and goatees sporting genuine bowling team jackets bought at Christmas time visits to thrift stores in their home-towns, a couple of neophytes in peg-legged black jeans and salon haircuts, a white guy with silver dreads and a chin piercing, and one chubby pigtailed chick in a cowgirl outfit smoking a clove cigarette.

Jamie spots Eli, turns, and salutes. His face, straight-on, is too wide and two-dimensional, the jaw spread out like a wingspan. His cheeks seem to go on forever, until they finally disappear into the shadowed borders of bone below his ears. The breadth and symmetry of his face is cartoonish and upsetting. On some level, I understand that he is simply handsome, but I feel a sudden and almost overwhelming urge to run quickly away from the bar and go get a cheeseburger.

It's probably reasonable that I expected Jamie to look like my father; after all, I already knew that he was much younger, and in a rock band, thus making him exponentially hipper style-wise than my sporty-casual, wash-'n'-wear, brought-to-you-by-Mervyn's dad, whose idea of dressing up is buttoning his sweater. But because I've never known anyone else who had Tourette's, and because I've been so long acquainted with my father's constant and consistent soap-operatic episodes, I unconsciously expected to notice an endemic, bellicose family resemblance. Sort of like expecting all Swedes to have blond hair, or all butchers to have meaty hands.

Just as I am puzzling over my disappointment and grappling with the urge toward flight, Jamie grabs the handrail at the top of the stairs. Slowly and deliberately he leans forward on it to pull his body up, like an acrobat in a circus. His shoulders thrust downward and his biceps bulge, his hips slowly begin to lift behind him—almost imperceptibly at first—and then his feet hover off the ground like disembodied souls. I wonder whether he is going to leapfrog the railing in slow motion, hurling himself into midair just to prove to me that he is worthy. That despite the disconcerting squareness of his jaw and his complete lack of genetic Richman-ness, he is indeed a kind of neurologically superfreaky superhero. I almost yell, "No!" but my voice seems to have melted into a slo-mo molasses dimension too.

I glance at Eli and he shrugs, still watching Jamie intently. Jamie has levitated now into a handstand position, and his legs wobble and kick delicately, like a swimmer trying not to make a splash. I think, *This is it: "Tourettic Indie Rocker Dies in Tragic Handstand Mishap."* But then his hips swivel and his feet descend to the ridge of wood that protrudes from the top of the door frame behind him. He rests them there, smiling, like he's done this a million times. Suddenly he lifts one hand

and slaps at his mouth five or six times in rapid succession, like a child approximating an Indian war cry. Somehow he manages to stay upside-down and vertical with just one arm supporting him, and then the hand comes back down to the railing just before he falls. He circles through this routine a couple of times, each time jabbing at his mouth in a furious, frenzied way while his other arm remains steady as a marble column. Finally, his hips gracefully descend back to the earthly plane, and he breaks into a drum roll, performed on the flat top of the railing, a little trill of fingered exuberance that punctuates his clown-alley act perfectly. He smiles and waves. I scrutinize his narrow back as he disappears into the doorway once more.

"Your mouth is open," says Eli.

I look around at the crowd on the patio and it seems that no one has even noticed the performance that just took place above their heads. The three goateed guys next to us continue their conversation about Krispy Kreme donuts. "They're not crispy, and they're not creamy, for God's sake," the one in the shiny gold Flagstaff Pie Alley jacket says. "I mean, somebody should sue them for false advertising." The other two nod their heads seriously like two yeshiva students contemplating the riddle of secular faith. Behind them, the cowgirl smokes and waits, and her deep dimples gouge her cheeks with every inhalation. The dimples make her seem perpetually cheerful, but when I look closely at her it's clear she is pissed off and afraid. She wears the precarious, defiant expression worn by most teenagers when adults are around—that combination of "I hate you" and "I fear you," the manifestation of which only hard-won pseudosophistication cures.

Ramona the bartender is one of those bartenders whose persona is so honed that you really don't have to do more than glance at her to know all the important facts. She spends most of her tips on clothes and make-up, she knows everything about everyone, and she used to be a man. She is vaguely Asian and vaguely Latin; with her smooth skin and dark, full lips, she is one of the most gorgeous women I've ever seen.

"Ramona the Pest!" Eli shouts. Ramona tosses her long black hair—a wig?—and marches right over to lean all the way across the wide bar to plant a kiss on Eli's mouth. I can hear the wet smack from three feet away as she makes a show of it.

43

"Eli's comin'! Hide your hearts, girls," she loudly warns the bored-looking short-banged girls at the bar. Her voice changes from a high-pitched feline squeak to a stage whisper just loud enough for everyone on this side of the club to catch. "Are you going to hang around after Lot 49?" she asks. "We're having a little private party. Only the crème de la crème."

"We're very crèmey," says Eli, handing me my beer. " No lumps at all."

"We regularly rise to the surface," I chime in.

Ramona doesn't seem amused, but she doesn't withdraw her invitation either. "Sweet!" she says dismissively as she turns to trot on her high heels toward a cock-rocker at the other end of the bar with a bleached-blond soul patch inside a black goatee. I don't know whether she's referring to the quality of the abstract crème or warning us about our spoilsport attitudes.

"Sweet!" I repeat to Eli, attempting to approximate Ramona's bitchy yet perky delivery.

He laughs and says, "As opposed to sour, I guess."

Pattycake's boyfriends are breaking down their gear when we approach the stage. The 'cakes linger offstage and receive compliments from male fans while three big punkabilly guys wind cord around their arms and tuck the sherbet-hued electric keyboards into tiny coffinlike cases. When one of the boyfriends picks up a pearly pink Casio with one hand and holds it above his head in order to disengage its cord, I picture King Kong holding a subway car in his giant mitt of paw like it's a piece of glittering jewelry. Jamie and his band mates are filtering in through the crowd with their equipment, hoisting big pieces of gear onto the stage and tripping up the beefy Pattycrew.

I always enjoy these transitional moments in live music clubs. Even in smoother, more high-class yuppie lounge venues, there is just no way to facilitate a totally smooth shift from one band to another unless you have multiple stages. And even then, somebody is always dropping some part of a drum kit and causing a brief expository head-turning clang. The Lot 49 band members—three guys and a woman—shuffle around the pussy-whipped Pattyserfs, mumbling "excuse me" and smiling short, polite smiles.

"Have you noticed that there seem to be an increasing number of band names out there that refer to certain snappish buckaroo literary wunderkind—Vonnegut, Pynchon, Henry Miller, Baudrillard?" I ask Eli. "I mean, leafing through the music section of the *Guardian* has become some kind of neo-postmodern lit trivia quiz."

Eli laughs and nods his head. "Kilgore Trout, Gran Faloonbus, Sexus, Gregor Samsa, Buddhakowski...er..."

"Obscene Goo!" I chime in.

"Even Steely Dan was cribbed right out of Naked Lunch. Remember the milk-spewing dildo that Burroughs wrote about?"

I think I knew this, but it is one of those facts that seems like a dream, one of those paisley psychotic dreams that always turns out to be real, one of those dreams where men rule the world. No one names their band after an Edna St. Vincent Millay poem, or a Flannery O'Connor short story. That's because rock and roll is like any other industry: It claims to be coeducational but is actually devoted to the stylish and thrilling and bullying antics of boys with tattoos on their triceps.

Jamie appears suddenly and gives Eli a one-armed hug while he clutches his cymbals with the other. I smile at his confidential face as it hovers toward me over Eli's shoulder. We each mumble "hi" as Eli introduces us. I want to say something about his earlier antigravity act on the railing, but before I can figure out how to word it, Ramona thrusts a pint of beer into Jamie's free hand. "On the house, lover boy," she says in a sultry whisper, her favorite flirtatious tone of voice. Then she pinches Eli's ass before she slithers back behind the bar.

The Crying of Lot 49 is a good name for this band, whose black-suited lead singer's delivery tends to lapse into the territory of an auctioneer at a county fair or a barker at a bankruptcy sale in an early American musical: "Twenty-five THIRty, thirty-five FORty, forty-five FIFty..." The songs are not so much melodic as incessant, like a sped-up church chime. The round syllables of vowely words repeat themselves in hurried, echoing rapture. I am almost moved to shout out a bid, but I become distracted by Jamie behind the drum set. It is difficult to frame him in unconstrained voyeuristic mode, to really gape at his full range of Tourettic motion—he's tucked away behind the bodies and big hairstyles and voluminous garments and various instruments and amps of the other musicians. You'd think drummers would have figured a way around this occupational hazard by now.

Of course, it's possible that they don't see it as a hazard. It's possible that drummers are drawn to drumming because the idea of pummeling objects while in obstructed-at-best view of others is appealing to them. Perhaps flailing tantrum-like behind a barricade of diverse figures provides some necessary closure on an obscure Freudian tableaux. Jamie, in any case, doesn't seem to mind, or notice, that his whole can only be seen in parts. He is watching the bass player intently, opening and closing the loop of his mouth like a fish. His playing is fiery and impetuous; he leaves open spaces unexpectedly, ducking out to create sudden scenarios where the singer presses forward into sharp relief, like an apprehended whisperer at a funeral. In between songs, Jamie slaps at his lips with the back of his hand, occasionally scrubbing at one side of his mouth as though it bears the traces of something that offends him—residual popcorn oiliness, or lipstick from the dry and powdery pucker of a skanky old lady.

"Life is short, but death is long. And that's the title of this song!" Jamie shouts in melancholic triumph. The ensuing number, their last, is a sweet and sad dirge about what will be missed most in the afterlife: coffee, White Castle cheeseburgers, the many nefarious smells of Chinatown, love, and even debt. Jamie sings it in a surprisingly pretty falsetto—not fake pretty but really pretty, an unadorned, attenuated cry that reminds me of a muezzin calling prayer. Only once do I notice him lapse into a carpish quaffing, sucking the air between verses. His gaze is fixed on a vague point on the back wall of the club. His wide jaw is mesmerizing now, his face a squared-off globe of moon peeking out from behind a curtain of clouds. I can't stop looking at it, even when a slow guitar solo careens in from stage left and everyone else's focus turns toward the red-velvet jacketed ax-master and his draggy manipulation of strings.

I hunch and sway to the right to avoid the fur collar of the woman in front of me. In this position, contorted slightly but not to Monty Python proportions, I can stare at Jamie with an unhindered sight line, framed softly by the prettying, wrenlike fur and hair of my compatriots. He is beautiful, chewing his cud like that, watching that spot on the back wall like it's sprouting Saturday morning cartoons. I vow to talk to him at the secret crème-de-la-crème after-party, to lure him into the smallest crook of my personal space, talk to him like this, just the two of us. To subtly let him know that I know that he knows that I know that he knows that I know.

At the after-party—the crème-de-la-crème turns out to be pretty much anybody who bothered to stick around until the end of the show—there is a raunchy 1950s B-movie showing on the back patio. Someone has hung a queen-sized bed sheet between two fig trees, and except for one small (menstrual?) stain, it makes a pretty good screen. The girl in the film has a tattoo on her back—some kind of segmented snake gnashing at its own tail, a fact that is accentuated by her alternating halter–midriff–crop-top costume choices. Or, the actress who plays the character of the girl in the film has a tattoo on her back, probably not even a real tattoo—no, definitely a fake tattoo. I wonder whether the makeup artist reapplied it every morning before the day's shoot, or whether it was done in some semi-indelible ink after the costume designer consulted with the art director who consulted with the publicist and the facile artifactual notion blossomed into a script change. I wonder whether she was told not to wash.

I don't like feeling manipulated by Hollywood leakheads. "I don't care more than you don't care," I say out loud. Someone mutes the sound and Jamie lifts an accordion from its ancient red leather case. There is something about the way his fingertips fit perfectly onto the mother-of-pearl buttons that is satisfyingly aggressive, and I feel like I want to scratch a hot itch, or punch the lock on the bathroom door right before someone on the other side starts jiggling the knob. During the sex scene he leans into the squeeze with a special cat-in-heat moan, milking the in-and-outs for all the polka laughs he can muster. Through the squeaky cacophony of sound, I can see the girl's hips moving up and down the screen, the arch in her back spelling out a snag, the curve of her ass orbited by that crafty, stop-action snake.

"Sometimes," Jamie tells me later when we're leaning up against the corrugated tin wall that separates the club's patio from the next-door neighbor's garden, a wall so flimsy that it does little more than provide the idea of a boundary, the illusion of tangible, civilized spaces between atoms, "the earth stops dead." I feel his breath on my neck as he speaks, and he's kind of rocking against the wall, which is emitting a rhythmic creaking noise. We have just smoked an enormous bowl of sticky weed. "It happens when I'm running around the polo field in Golden Gate Park. I can feel my legs pumping, but then suddenly there's nothing pushing against them, nothing keeping me in line. It feels like I'm falling...flying...straight downhill, my arms waving, but I know I'm on level ground." Looking around in the grainy night, the objects on the patio are transformed. The film, a different film now, this one featuring a girl motorcycle gang, casts shadows and throws silvery threads onto people's hair and clothes. The long, geometric patterns flicker around the patio in time to the tin wall's chirps and sensual moans—a familiar time signature that gathers momentum as it goes. Light fingers our bodies slowly at first, then races to a rumble as the metal vibrates and whines with Jamie's unbridled trills.

"All the usual landmarks appear," he says, staring into my left eyebrow intently, as though it is cueing him. He wipes his lips with the back of his hand, hard, and I can almost smell the satisfaction this gesture provides—an essence that emanates from his skin as a pall. "The black water tower sits on the sky like a hockey puck. The bleachers are peeling and gray, sitting snug in their coat of trees. My running becomes totally effortless." He lifts his torso to balance on one leg and holds one arm out straight, a weird modern dance accompaniment to his story. "I pass a Chinese lady and her dog, and a jogger in a Lakers T-shirt. It's like they're stuck in space, motionless, in some kind of blurred tableaux. I don't know how long the earth's rotation will pause, but I want to keep running, to catch up to all the lies that have had the edge on me since childhood."

There is a stretch of time that could be a minute, could be an hour. Inside it, I hear the muscly opening guitar chords from Liz Phair's "6'1" as clear as day, over and over in a circular abyss that calls me down into its whirlpool. Down, down. All I want to do is follow the alcohol- and pot-soaked egg of my brain, the spongy orb that has been doused with Jamie's odd and beautiful story, down into a cozy, mossy cove where Liz Phair plays her guitar relentlessly, strumming in giant extravagant loops, like she's churning butter. But in order to go down, I must first go left, follow the tilt that my body suddenly can't seem to resist, sea level's insistent pull, even though a voice in my head strongly urges me to catch myself and scamper back upright, no matter the vaudevillian indignity that would require. Or perhaps the voice, that long and cautionary creak, is not in my head after all, but the voice of the corrugated tin wall as it begins, with a metallic yowl, to give.

"Uh-oh," I hear Jamie intone, and as we succumb to gravity I start laughing out loud at the sight of his horizontalizing face, that square quickly becoming a diamond. "Mayday! Mayday!" he cries, alarm in his eyes. Our ship is going down. "The...pause...is...consummated," says the LED readout traveling across his forehead. I notice that we are both, for whatever misguided reason, clutching the sharp edge of the wobbly wall. It is only natural, I guess, to grab at whatever man-made object ought to hold firm in a moment of insufficient balance. But our grasp only serves to topple the entire fence faster and more forcefully than if we had clutched each other instead, or if we'd simply fallen like toy soldiers and lay down on the concrete, our heads pillowed by the wall-to-wall sea of standard-issue Doc Martens.

Evidently, the dozen others who have been leaning up and down the garden wall sensed this disaster coming, because there seems to be a collective effort at the last minute to stop the inevitable topple. An urgent, hand-held resistance greets our weight, but despite the attempt, our bodies gradually go over, and we fall in the way a building that has been expertly dynamited sinks gracefully into a breathtaking poof of dust. Slow-motion calamity. Thankfully, the neighbor's garden is plush, a cushion of dirt and vines that bolsters our fall almost comfortably in spite of the oafish clang and thump that ring out over the hushed patio.

Suddenly glossy black hair is everywhere I want to be, yards of stick-straight hair covering my face and Jamie's face and the carpet of tiny Cheeto-orange flowers I noticed as I hit the ground. My face is powdered with dirt, and I smell Chloe.

"Jamie, baby, are you all right?" a raspy, adolescent voice asks, the voice of the redolent girl belonging to the blinding black hair. "My silly man-boy! Did your little monsters make you fall over?"

Jamie glances at me through a skein of hair with what I assume is a thoroughly humiliated grin smeared across his face. His eyes are my father's eyes. They say what I already know is true: that we share the mystery, that we alone understand the tiny, perpetual pinhole poked in the laws of physics. We are traveling toward each other through the

tunnel that pinhole provides, clearly illuminated by the light of our riddle. The black hair lifts, and sways, and then there is a largish head
turned in my direction. The purple lips on the head are moving, and I
hear an eerily familiar, coquettish whisper. "My baby's OK," says
Ramona, holding onto Jamie's collar and kissing his mouth loudly, like
a car door shutting. "Let me help my baby up." As Jamie's head gets
tugged toward the sky, I notice that he is still beaming. I am sure I have
never seen a smile quite so unreserved. I follow his eyes to their object:
Ramona's sinewy biceps as she cradles the wingspan of his jaw. The
smile is the smile of a man in love, bathed in hair, in love with Ramona
the bartender. The two figures rise above me like Peter Pan and Tinker
Bell, floating up into the blinking atmosphere, and I am suddenly a lost
boy, weighed down by all the bad ideas in my dirty forever arsenal, destined to ride the pirate ship of sea-blue longing my whole life through.

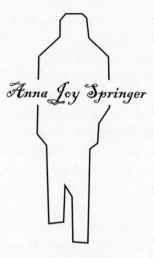

Anna Joy Springer

On My Planet

Last week my girlfriend's and my schedule kept interfering with our plans for fucking. Night after night she fell asleep early, and I'd lay there, blue-balled, looking at her fine, unconscious body, wanting to wake her, and stopping myself. On our fourth night together we set aside time for sex. I don't know how it happened, but she began channeling Colonel Sanders. (I think it came up after I reminded her of one of our in-jokes, where, after getting ass-fucked by a drumstick, a woman is later buggered by a penis. When the penis comes out of her ass, there is a piece of chicken on the end of it. Everyone is surprised, amused. Sometimes, when we are eating, one of us will flick a piece of wet food onto the floor to emulate the sound of the piece of chicken falling off the dick.)

So there she is during our special time, naked and ready for love, pretending to be Colonel Sanders. I get in role as Sanders's niece at once. She says, "No, no, no, sissy boy. You're no niece, you're my cross-dressing faggot nephew." We're laughing, and I try to fuck her. She offers her breast to me, saying, "Colonel-Colonel, are you thirsty? Do you want some milk?" I'm thoroughly confused, now that she has turned me into the Colonel, and this also makes me laugh.

"Well there, little lady, all this corporate expansion does make a man powerful thirsty," I respond. Is she now the ever-helpful Mrs. Colonel? I try to fuck my lactating wife.

"I have to go to the bathroom, Colonel," she tells me. "Unless you want some chocolate milk," she continues, flipping over to show me her bottom, giggling like a gross-out champ. Ugh! She knows that I absolutely cannot stand it when butt-sex is referred to in chocolate metaphors. We continue down this absurd path of mutual surprise and disgust for so long that we never get around to having sex. We laugh so hard it makes us tired and we fall asleep. Without having sex, we had sex-play.

I play easily and naturally with my lovers. During sex, parts of me that are usually dormant wake up and take over. In some ways this seems like a psychological or even therapeutic process, because during role-playing, my subconscious urges become conscious as my ego relinquishes control. In another way, sexual role-playing seems more spiritual; it's like my personality is somehow dismantled. All the people I might have been, under different circumstances, get a few moments to live in a body, to greet and touch those potential characters inhabiting my lover. Sex-play takes me to the boundary between some impossible world and my day-to-day reality. In different roles, I learn things about my every-day self that I can't learn by *being* my everyday self.

I began imagining I was someone else while having sex when I was still a teenager. I read stories in dirty magazines about people pretending to be meaner or weaker when they were fucking than they were in nonsexual encounters. But it wasn't anything I made a decision to try; it just happened. Maybe because I was nearly a child, it still seemed natural to become different characters and play-act different scenarios. But because I was also nearly an adult, getting more accustomed to the notion that I was a unified, monolithic self, what happened during sex-play carried over into my regular life too.

During these first experiences with sexual role-playing I began to understand that sexual intimacy was too complicated to try to hammer down. Through these complications, I began to realize that life was also much weirder than anyone had explained, and in this way fucking was a direct, if knotted, line into ethics. The first time role-playing led to one of these huge "whoa, life is very strange" revelations, I was about 16 and my boyfriend was 22.

I told him that I sometimes fantasized about being seduced by my pink-haired new-wave beautician, who was getting sober in Merced and staying with her parents. He was accommodating, telling me to close my eyes and imagine his hands were hers, as she groped around my lap for the scissors she had accidentally dropped, until she touched my panties. Another time, he suggested that I apply her punk-style eyeliner to his eyes, so that it would look more realistic when he ate my pussy while pretending to be her. A little while later, we went shopping for the lingerie she would wear. He picked out a light pink ensemble, including stockings and silk panties that he said felt nice against his cock. Oh.

I talked him through the penetration. I'd gotten him ready, and now he lay back on the couch while I pushed my way inside. It wasn't the first time I had been in his ass, but it was the first time I ever fucked a womanish creature. Somehow that made all the difference in my excited will to prod. There I was, in the act of becoming someone else— some*thing* else.

Aroused by his demure excitement as a prototypical girl, I suddenly thought, "He'd like to have a man doing this to him."

I didn't stop pumping when I asked, "You want a guy doing this to you?"

"No way, not no-how. Straight, straight, straight," he responded (while stroking his nipple beneath a sheer lace bra). After breaking him down for awhile, I got him to admit something. One night he had received a wordless blow job from a stranger on the beach. Maybe more than once, he finally added, but nothing more than a blow. I decided to press the issue, maybe wanting reassurance about my own queerness. I ran my hand over the front of his panties and said, "His big hand is so strong. It's touching the lace...you're getting so hard, so wet...you feel the calluses on those rough palms snag your pretty stockings...his bulge is pressing into your back, you don't know who it is...you want him to spread...to push..."

I discovered my boyfriend was bisexual—not just during this moment, but in real life, all the time. And that's when I realized role-playing was more than a fun way to pass the time. He never would have told me he was bisexual if his ego's defenses weren't already smashed to bits by his sexual excitement and less-inhibited role. Only as my lezzy beautician could he tell me this secret.

I've *almost* always loved it when, during sex-play, some curve-ball facet of the truth comes out and catches me off-guard. But it can get pretty fucked up and messy, like everything else people do. I used to have this regular customer who'd visit me at the peep show where I worked. It was a late-night shift, which meant that I had to act extra dirty. During the lunch rush, the guys wanted "girl-next-door" types. Never having been a girl next door, not even knowing any girls-next-door, I found this role a stretch—and boring. After midnight I'd spend the last hours of my shift trying to talk the come out of men so wasted they could barely get hard. We'd move from me being a farmer's daughter ready to do anything so that they didn't molest my father's prize sheep, to me, the transvestite, to them, the guy who loved to have their tiny penises laughed at by a booth full of girls. And so on.

One night a good-looking guy came in and I started in with my usual spiel. He told me to shut up. He was going to meet me after work in the parking lot out back. He was going to be behind a car. When I put the key in my door, he was going to come up behind me and push against me, put his hand over my mouth. My purse would spill dicks all over the ground and they'd bounce underneath the car. He was going to lift up my skirt and put his finger underneath the elastic riding up my pussy. He'd slide his knuckles along my cunt all lubed up from work. He would squeeze my nipples until they bruised, and nobody would see us. And then he would fuck me hard while I bit into the roof of my car. He knew where I was parked. He promised he'd be waiting.

Even though I didn't have a car, I started getting afraid. Normally I told violent customers to go find another girl, one who gave a shit about misogynist customers, if you get what I mean. Instead, I crawled closer to the glass while he was talking. His eyes were twinkling and sweet. He was smallish, with gentle-looking hands. He was a good talker, smart. Most guys just grunted inarticulate commands, but his details were convincing. Like a respectable enemy he showed no fear, so naturally, I became thrilled. I was still frightened, but like an idiot, I felt safe behind the bulletproof glass. His dick was pretty and stiff. It had been a long time since I'd felt a live nude cock. I played along. "I'll hit you, you sick fucker. I'll beat the shit out of you with the flashlight."

"No, you won't. You're too horny from jerking off all night. I bet you look at yourself in the glass. I bet watching yourself push that big black rod in and out of your box makes you hot. No one will know. I'll just fuck you and then I'll disappear."

Without willing it, I became possessed by some character, hearing myself respond, "You'll fuck me so hard..."

"You'll try to fight, but you won't be able to stop moving on me."

And on it went until I trusted that he was not actually planning to rape me. He got me off three times. Ah, love.

Whenever he came back I was happy to see him. I even told him my real name. He knew I was a dyke. Still, unlike my girlfriend, but like the best of whores, he was always able to gauge my mood within seconds and come up with the perfect accompanying fantasy. When I was sad, he'd talk about our vacation in Mexico, our slow lovemaking under the watery sky. When I was furious, I'd spit on his face pressed up to the glass and disembowel him for being a weak, stupid man. I'd feed his guts to my pet sharks, and stab his sandy corpse, *yippee*.

The week his girlfriend dumped him, I went to visit him in the real world. I was having drama with my girlfriend too. I was a little freaked out about meeting him in public: I was supposed to be a dyke, and he was a customer, not a real person—possibly a lunatic, probably a basket case. And, like all unknown drivers on the freeway, any girl who dated her customers for fun was clearly stupid, crazy, or high.

I marched like a zombie into the bar where he worked. He wasn't expecting me. I must have looked different with clothes on. I saw him standing behind the bar making Manhattans. I don't think he saw me. He was sexy, chatting up some clear-skinned straight girl. But there, outside his dark little peep show booth, with so much space and freedom between us, he looked like a smallish, manly poster boy. I left the bar quickly. He must have spotted me; I never saw him again. It was less confusing without him in my booth, but I missed the confusion.

So even though I usually think it's hot when reality and fantasy-play intersect, that complication can be disturbing. It depends on the balance of my so-called real personality and my roles, and on what's going on in my life at the time. A few years ago, after the breakup of a five-year relationship, I was convinced I would never get sex again and got that late 20s desperation that drives the sitcom plots. Being shy in public but a great hostess, I decided the best way to get sex was to throw a play-party. I called it an orgy. At an orgy, I reasoned, one of my guests would *have* to fuck me. As an added assurance, I held the event on my birthday.

A kind friend offered to arrange a preorgy abduction to get me in the mood. She would gather a group of masked girls who would gang rape me in a windowless van and take me home in time to smooth my hair for the party. I did not expect mundane, tedious despair to interrupt my plans. Who would? But it did.

The night before my party I got a phone call from my mother. She wished me a happy birthday, and parenthetically disclosed that she had finally cut ties with my childhood nemesis, her ex-husband.

When I thanked her, she seemed puzzled, but we left it at that. I wanted to believe that she had finally acknowledged what an asshole he was. In doing so, she became my witness and protector. My last few doubts about my history with him dissolved. She believed me, therefore the past was real. When the past became fully true, I was filled with an immense sadness I hadn't felt when the facts were still questionable.

So, under these circumstances, the idea of a gang rape didn't sound like so much fun anymore. Piss on my cornflakes, a natural disaster flying in the face of my party plans. I was already a mess, but became enraged when I couldn't overcome my dumb emotions and go through with the sex. I would have been crying through the whole fake, generous rape, remembering the real violations. My friend called and I had to apologize for my last-minute cancellation. I explained my situation to her. She assured me that it happens all the time.

Luckily, the need to protect my heart sometimes goes away as unexpectedly as it comes. Later that same evening, my living room was full of women who were ready to orgy. I didn't know whether I'd be in a state to join them. We all sat around having a few drinks and some synthetic heroin that was supposed to be ecstasy and writing exquisite corpses on each others' bodies.

As my sadness slipped away, I became a winking birthday slut. We started off with a rousing game of "Spin the Mango." I admit it was an immature beginning to an orgy, but it fit the aesthetic of our space. We played in the storage room of my house, which I had converted into a makeshift playhouse. I had positioned my roommate's futon and a box springs side by side on the floor, covered the windows with aluminum foil, and set votive candles along the walls. The rules: If you were the spinner you could elect to kiss the spinnee or to give them a task. Most often, my guests chose the task option. It all started out innocently enough: a spanking here, a diapering there. A butch I didn't know spun on me. She made me yank my own long hair up behind my head, and continue pulling it while she stroked my cheek.

I hadn't thought to invite her initially, but the friend I planned the party with pointed out that I'd only put femmes on my invitation list. As a second thought, I added the names of the few butches I knew who weren't dating my friends. The one who made me pull my own hair was a square little bottom, not taking the mysterious pill we all nervously swallowed. She'd been eyeing me shyly for weeks, and my friend was trying to fix us up. I thought I needed another butch in my life like I needed a second office job. I didn't like her; she was too careful, too controlled. I decided to ignore her, until she switched me and got me to pull my hair and crack my own neck.

For awhile, each girl played her sleepy, natural orgy role. But then, my best friend spun and the mango pointed toward me. We knew we shouldn't fool around with each other. But, as my best friend is a resourceful maker-of-games, sort of a femme Columbo, she quickly devised a solution. I was to be her interpreter, her singular Greek chorus, while she held court. The other girls had to perform dirty skits for Her Highness's pleasure.

We went into my bedroom and waited. The first girl was an experienced stripper, who bobbled around my bed while I narrated: "There's those big tits she wants any old body at all to suck, there's that apple ass, crunch crunch, Queen, crunch crunch."

The second act was a short massage for the queen's shoulders, which were already relaxed by the heroin. Third, a makeshift couple performed acrobatics while trying to fuck. The femme was obviously irritated by the butch's clumsiness when she dropped her on her head, then kept rutting without saying "oops." The finale came when two butches, a short one and a tall one, sucked each other off. The little one was the one who made me pull my hair—the drug-free loser. The other one had the largest, most masculine hands I'd ever seen and usually only fooled around with girls.

I announced that they were aliens from another planet, trying to get revenge on the goody-goody butch. Or maybe to see whether she had any sense of humor at all. "They seem to be attracted to one another. One of them is putting something long and bouncy inside its mouth." The irritating minibutch rose to the occasion by making up an alien language of bleeps and blips between her slurps as she sucked off the big one. She was good at sucking cock, and, in context, she really looked like your high-end fox-baby trade. The tall one shot her wad, shouting in gibberish ecstasy. I explained to the Queen that the ETs were performing a sacred coming-of-age ceremony, and that she needn't worry about the terrible morals of little green space teens.

That done, everyone fucked me and we ate some cake and got ready for bed. The little butch borrowed my pajama bottoms and slept on the bare box springs. The next day I found the pj's folded on a chair with a note on top. It said, "Call me if you need help cleaning up. PS: On my planet, we call it 'fellatio.'"

Ricky Lee

THESE STREETS
(A POEM FOR THE TRANSGENDERED WARRIOR)

mean cold black
sticky phlegm/come/gum
puke and shit
these streets
though i'd rather skip over piles of puke
and old condoms every morning
than wade through a starbucks fulla yuppies
these streets you know when they say
we're gonna clean up the trash
who they're talkin about

these streets
me, loose clothes
short hair, ball cap
typical mission dyke—i think
if that's a style yet
maybe in next month's vogue
can't wait for some validation
in the fashion industry for us

transgendered warriors
just kidding
anyway—clothes worn, patched and duct taped
let's see carhartts, black coat, big boots
big headphones, dj headphones
messenger bag

april 21st. 18th and capp st. 11:46 P.M.

hooker lady catches me walkin by
you gotta napkin she says
what? i say taking off my headphones
ya gotta napkin? i really gotta piss
naw sorry i say
it's slow tonight she says
slow and more cops than johns
that's a bad sign i say

when girls in short skirts gotta kneel behind parked cars
dodging the bright beam of the man
as they cruise by and their searchlights
cut through the night like some vietnam flashback
like soldiers bustin war criminals in sheer stalkings

a lot of the girls are workin in
jeans and sneakers though
you could say they have created
a more casual work environment
though more aptly it's called being broke
strung out and workin with what
ya got

the lady keeps talkin
bout business
then she goes—you workin?
huh? i say
you hookin—right?

naw i say i just live down the street
she ends the conversation abruptly
flips her hair and crosses the street

11:59 P.M. 20th and capp st.

guy pulls over in a busted-up red toyota
he catches my eye
how much he asks
how much for the sexo
naw man i'm off tonight i say sarcastically
and i wonder if he knows i'm a girl
or thinks i'm a young fag

12:01 A.M. 21st and capp st.

i round the corner toward mission and a
latin lady with almond skin
and a small silver dress
smiles wide
yuh need a date she says
no thanks i shrug
oh, you're a girl she says
and laughs
that's cool though
i give her a cigarette
like an apology
she smiles again
and i wonder if she would trick for another girl
though she probably knows at least in my case
it's not that economically feasible

these streets
where everybody's workin watchin
the johns lookin out for tits, hips, ass
the ladies are lookin for a swagger a fat wallet
and the cops are just lookin for everybody

april 22nd bush and grant 6:45 P.M.

me typical mission dyke
carhartts, dickies jacket, big boots, messenger bag
pull over on my mountain bike to take off my coat
an older man who is walkin by stops
you messenger guys really have a hard job
yeah i say
on the streets all day battling all that traffic
cars always tryin to run you down
you guys are real warriors you know
my coats off and he looks at me funny
oh, you're a chick he says
sorry—i meant no disrespect or anything
i just thought you were a guy
it's alright i say it happens all the time
by this point i don't have the heart to tell him
i'm not even a bike messenger
that i'm just peddling through downtown
unemployed lookin for a place to get drunk for free
well good job anyway
see ya he says

you never know when the coat comes off what's gonna happen
like you'll be adjusting your cap in the ladies room
and you hear the door open and you get all tense
cause you know you're gonna be met with a face of confusion
sometimes even pure terror
then recognition, then embarrassment
like you've watched someone go through some complete
gender catharsis in a matter of seconds
and the ladies room becomes this
cheezy self-help workshop
that you got stuck leading
and then there's the streets
these streets
like when your mama told you

when you were a kid you could be
whatever you wanna be—at least if you were lucky she did
these streets
where you're always somethin else in the minds of strangers
from block to block
hooker–faggot–bike messenger–john
cash in cash out–ride hard
these streets

Dodie Bellamy

PHONEZONE

In his first E-mail he called me a sex goddess, asked whether my real sex life was as incredible as in my writing. My sex life, I fired back, goes up and down like a seismograph. Our affair lasted 5.6 megabytes—that's four floppies worth of love letters, now entombed on a zip disk, a mere blip on the 100 mb zip. I wouldn't dare click open these ancient erotics, one glance at a SUBJECT: I WANT TO FUCK YOU my nostrils flare with smoke, my pupils whiz in psychedelic spirals, I growl, double over, upchuck my lunch *the toilet bowl is the fourth form*. The rest is much harder to measure. The phone bill cost a couple hundred a month, but he also called me constantly from work. Masturbating over the phone—is that tactile or merely aural? And then there were our real-time bodies colliding. We spent a weekend together in San Jose and six weeks in Chicago. What is the quantifiable difference between a hand held and a fuck? Or just lying there aching with arousal, alone, my body so charged with sex it glowed in the dark. After a few months his input became redundant, a formality. I was fucking him day and night—while eating a burrito, watching TV, every act I did was fucking Ed.

I was born Carla, but he called me Lala. Lala—when you say it your tongue drops down from the roof of your mouth, lah-lah, drops down twice as if you were licking my clit. I'm a stick figure with orgasms. Edward.C.Edwards writes to me from his computer at work, he can't come there so he holds it and by the time he jerks off at home he's so hot his come shoots over his head. "How do you jerk off?" I ask. With two fingers under the head, precisely.

Over the phone he sounded boyish with a tinge of New England. The first time we talked he burst out crying. For no other reason than the terror of loving Me. "That's OK," I purred, "I won't hurt you." In his next E-mail he wrote DON'T SCARE DON'T SCARE. *Sexspace is a dream that speaks back, endlessly erotic, undisciplined, tedious, pleasurable.* The highest circle of heaven is E-mail, the lower realm is the phone—earth is flesh hulking against flesh, leaking—hell is when all data transmission comes to a dead stop. I now believe that no living being ever walked on the moon *space suits and stage sets, a man named Ed* my nerves are jerked by electrodes like the legs of formaldehyded frogs. No one's at the other end of the prod. Here in the Sex Goddess graveyard my memories corrode with static UNLOVED UNLOVED and behind every door is a vivid turquoise light I'm never allowed to enter *gray sky bleeds into gray fields, no horizon* I watch the inexplicable actions of the humans around me, I grow fainter. This is the fourth form, when there's nothing left but you and the great mystery of What the Fuck Just Happened to Me?

He doesn't talk much—he just beats off and pants, and I babble, "I'd like to lick your big dick," etcetera. Invariably he comes before I do, and then he listens to me, silent as my foam mattress, silent as a black hole in space. I suggest that anything he'd say *you could recite the Pledge of Allegiance* would help me, but he doesn't answer, just waits. I know he likes to hear me heave and groan *Lala, lahdeedah* and I use that, his silent insistence. I have to come, his silence is a spotlight and I am so glaringly naked before it, my movements obscene and awkward, erect nipples pimples imperfect belly, everything exposed, my clit puffy as a pink orchid. With these thoughts I work myself into a frenzy.

From San Francisco to Chicago a fog of precipitous arousal jams the airwaves, obscures the stars, but that's OK, there's nothing to navigate, nowhere to go, we lie here WE suspended in romance WE breathing in unison *no more "I" death to the evil "I"* our souls float about us gentle as snow in a Christmas shaker *come-for-me, comfort-me* no world outside the curved plastic dome. "That was great!" he coos, and snowflakes flicker to the bottom.

Three green window shades, pine armoires facing one another, matching blond nightstands, battered, oil stains on the colorless carpet from feet slick with calendula lotion, pale green comforter, dull laundered bloodstains on cream sheets, diptych of Barbara Steele on wall above my head, lime Barbara, magenta Barbara, Caitlin's painting of a sad pensive Judy Garland in clown drag, leaning on cane, stubby cigarette, extravagant shadow flowing from her feet, a brocade puddle, gold webbed with copper, dotted with silver. Judy looks so exhausted, so burnt, as if all her glory were seeping out through her clunky booted feet *crossed at the ankles,* Jerome Caja ballerina with baseball bat, Fran Herndon's lithograph *Death of the Poet*, Ida Applebroog paint swatches, brownish black, golden yellow, bluish black, Harry Jacobus's explosion of pastels, floor-length mirror with a triangular top that points upward like a stake, shoe rack over the door full of dusty shoes that ache my ankles, shoes I do wear in a mangled heap beneath the left window, huge jade plant looming on top the right armoire, jade shadows, red-tinged cactus sitting on the dresser, three feet tall, many-pronged. A cat that looks as smug and tired as Judy Garland, long-haired black tuxedo, lamps with long black necks, white beaks, pink flannel bathrobe crumpled on floor, dirty terry-cloth slippers, a missing throw rug, clean rectangle of carpet where it used to lie, slab of double foam on a wooden platform, four pillows—two cream, two beige with red and green stripes—shelves in an open closet over-crammed with wrinkling clothes, wicker basket crammed with stinking clothes, crotch and feet. Teal blue phone receiver cradled between left ear and neck. "Touch yourself."

No more of this "who if I cried would hear me among the angelic order" shit. Daily I received visitations, sometimes hourly. He called me every morning, first thing. And then during his lunch break, and then at least once in the afternoon. We'd E-mail throughout the day, ten, twenty, sometimes thirty messages. A two-toned toot, happy rooster icon in the dialogue box: YOU HAVE NEW MAIL! On my screen materializes, "You're coming in loud and clear my fuck bunny, my cunt princess." I feel blessed, hot to merge, frantically type back, "Fuck me fuck me oh, fuck me!!!" If I didn't write to him by 11:00 A.M., he'd call to ask me what was the matter.

One day, between messages, I ran out to the corner store. When I unlocked the door the phone was ringing. His voice on the other end, urgent: "I called five times, Lala. Where were you?"

"I had to get some cat litter."

"You mean you left the house without telling me?" he joked.

Finally I'd found a universe I was the center of, I was Ed-obsessed, Ed-fused, a sex genie trapped within a technological bottle, bubbling over with devotion. I'd get him off over the phone a few nights a week. He was always horny and I love to talk dirty, heavy breathing and psychic communion, the sound of his fist slamming his cock. He'd climax quickly with a loud bellow, then, "Are you going to come for me?" Always the complete silence on his end as I finished myself off, his silence, his meticulous ear stripped me to the bone, my tits ballooned, the lips of my clit flapped like sails, his silence was a command a transcontinental tug of my leash as I humped myself against the toe of my black boot, faster and louder his silence demanded.

He was always wanting more from me *feed me love me fuck me* his need puddling my panties like snail snot. Top 40 love songs started to sound like documentaries of my life LOVE ME FOREVER YOU ARE THE YOU ARE NEVER LEAVE ALWAYS YOU ARE MY CAN'T LIVE WITHOUT YOU ARE TRUE SUNSHINE YOU ARE THE NOBODY ELSE suck me suck me suck the fucking marrow YOU ARE from my bones. In sexspace we were understood, our every whim, every mood cooed and coddled over, in sexspace there is no back, no forth. It wasn't always easy to maintain this high pitch—I had those dreaded unplug-the-phone days when I shuffled around utterly depleted. *I feel like I'm collapsing inward, like I've lost myself, the thought of having to write to him, of having to talk appalls me, I feel so unproductive, feel like a fraud.* But if 12 hours went by without him calling, I panicked because that meant he no longer loved me. The instant it's not there being pushed in my face, I cease to believe in love. Imagine closing the front door and the outside world ceasing to exist ALONE imagine that terror.

We we we we we we we we this little piggy had roast beef and now this little piggy has none.

Slime oozes through cracks and creeps up behind me, slime rears up like a giant slimy seahorse SPLAT and then there's a mysterious seven-minute black out. When I wake up I am the Sex Thing, my cunt won't stop, it's desperate, ravenous, aching for more and more and finally I meet Ed, my True Mate. I hurl myself through plate glass to get to him. To the naked eye we look like any two naked humans fucking but in Sex Vision you can see our gleaming striated kiwi-colored bodies, the dozens of snaky limbs that shoot out the tops of our heads, vine about our steaming torsos then poke through flesh with the ease of needles, snaky ropes leap out my nipples and stitch me to Ed's throbbing chest, we heave and grow enormous, two monstrous clouds pulsing above the horizon, glorious, crackling. Sperm rains down from the heavens seven days and seven nights.

I came for him over the phone this morning and again he listened in absolute silence—the kinkiness of this silence is astonishing. It took me ages, but he was patient, and when I finally gasped, he whispered, "Good girl." For months now my life has been ruled by this voice from beyond, these oozing endearments. I am Jesus' whore.

After I hung up I went to the bathroom and the toilet paper was soaked with lubricant, I was dripping with it, all slippery with streaks of blood—my cunt the stigmatic. I switched on the TV to a news report about a couple who tortured and murdered young women. There's a videotape of the woman going down on her unconscious 15-year-old sister, whom they also murdered. This is as real as it gets, the love swamp, monogamy squared, where you close your eyes, grow heavy and let go—sludge bubbles as you sink beneath the boggy horizon *her* blond *head bobbing between the doped sister's dewy thighs* I clicked the TV on mute and dialed Ed at work. "Hi. I love you."

It would take a physicist and a nuclear-powered camera to register the ultraviolet charge my clit carves through the universe—the computer monitor thrills my clit in seismic spikes, the thought of him arouses my body from neck to crotch, the thought of him unfurls my heart and groin like twin mandalas. Tumescences bloom across my 15-inch screen, a swollen garden of mouths, lips, labia, anuses, warts—Ed fucks them all. I dart to the store for some cat litter, and as the clerk makes change my phantom clit is ringing off the hook, the metallic taste of precome at the back of my throat.

His voice is digitalized then shot through two thousand of miles of wire, his voice arrives amplified. "Are you wet?" His voice sounds tinny and instantaneous.

"I don't know."

But there has to be a lapse, and that frightens me, to have him there yet not there at the same time. "Stick your finger in your pussy, check and see." His words congeal in my ear, viscous as the stuff that spurts from our bodies.

"Yes, I'm wet."

The receiver sucks up the ozone, the air turns thick and sticky, my self flows into it and is trapped, sex sap drops from my fingers in long drowsy columns, soft, yielding, clinging like a leech. The voice at the other end of the line weeps the voice pants acts impatient pleads, "Come for me." The physical world is reduced to props. Phone cord. Bed. Boot. Finger. Words are everywhere, inside my ears inside my cunt inside my nostrils hailing down from the ceiling, words like vermin always on the alert, words unite and seize the world order, words hold the world in its fist, squeezing tighter and tighter, words crush the world. Nothing dilutes their radiance. "Come for me," and I do come, a nova exploding in the afternoon, 2:30 P.M., Tuesday.

A bare lightbulb and a synchronized forlorn voice burst forth intermittently into the silent darkness of the bedroom. I am his convulsive possession, I am a telesomatic event.

I longed for his funky E-mails longed for his lips to ejaculate obscenities, my cunt on the other end of the phone line poised to catch them like a brass spittoon. Are you wet? YES Are you hard? YES What are you wearing? MY BRIGHT BLUE SWEATER AND A BIG PURPLE HAT I'd like to eat them off you with my mouth! Ed was a poet, he'd never stoop to linearity *do this do that and then and then* he waits in silence and two breath beings emerge bound by zillions of ethereal cords, line after faint white line, drooping in easy scallops, the thinnest white, soft focus, all these wavy lopsided positions. "Even though you're so far away, you feel like you're totally present." Our bodies turned porous, lighter than volcanic ash, our ectoplasm streamed through time and space and telephone lines *iridescent green kind of sticky like hair gel* we stepped a foot beneath the floorboards at first, before we learned to walk through walls, zoom across the night sky trailing glittering metallic streaks, turquoise, aqua, pale filmy yellow. We fucked like cumulus clouds, fat and fluffy, our circumferences bulging with each thrust, sunlight in sharp rays spilling through.

He said the head of his cock was rounder than most men's. I envisioned a long stalk crowned with a door knob *come on in* but eventually when I did get to see it, it was as pointed as any other *devil's tail* I lie on my stomach with Chinese needles forming a cross along my shoulders and down my spine, my head turned to the left, on the table beside me stands a dark wooden frame carved in an elaborate biomorphic design, vaguely floral with undulating lines, beneath its glass float three silk guppies, their bellies fat as Ed's but smashed flat as the screen he loved me through. I hate the third dimension, its fishy stench, I hate skin, Ed had acres of it, icy pink and delicate as a shaving of sashimi, delectable arc melting on a bed of sticky rice, flesh so pale that subtlety looms enormous, that white striation that bruised edge, fish egg garnish boomeranging with orange light. Ed's thick skin, so bulbous and taut, I imagined worlds birthing and dying and revolving beneath it, space stations soaring, shuttles zipping playfully to and fro—and there I was, stuck behind the anti-gravity screen. I was accustomed to the flash access of E-mail, those sexiest keys on the keyboard, "enter" and "return," thousands of times they launched me straight to his heart—in "real" life no matter how close I got to him I felt I was banging my tits up against the wrong dimension, that I was never ever going to get inside.

Lacan said the word kills the thing, but he was wrong. Life kills the word. Life is the death of the word.

I can't wait to fuck you—for months we said it, wrote it, daily, hourly—still I never quite expected my flesh self to come true. I hadn't prepared her for the ordinary, only for peak experiences. She was fluid, languid, libidinal, knew how to glide into rooms, how to fuck, to sparkle and attract attention but she didn't know how to wash clothes, cook dinner, maneuver Ed's ever-changing moods. Real life felt about as real as 3-D House of Wax, as if any moment my wraparound paper goggles were going to slip off my nose and Ed's apartment would go cross-eyed, everything doubled, shifting in blurry lurid colors. His flesh was so silent, like a TV switched on mute, especially the fat cells, which were totally soundproof. I missed the clamor of fantasy. His pale hazel eyes, eyes so pale they're practically translucent, his ass tight as balloons, squishy yet solid—I was drawn to his body, always clinging, rubbing myself against it, my cunt drooling. He seemed so tiny inside that mass of fresh pink, so trapped. I dreamed my cunt juices were acid that could burn through the silly illusion of skin—inside that palace of flesh there was room for two, I wanted to live there, the princess in his tower, the bat in his belfry, I wanted to whoosh with him through caverns of thigh and forearm.

My mouth a gaping cliché machine into which I empty myself.

I'm masturbating and you're not wearing any protection and neither am I. We're totally naked with one another both inside and out, and you're fucking me for the first time—that delicious moment of entry where I know I will never be the same again—I feel split open by your fucking me, my pussy belongs to you, I pinch my nipples to make sure I'm not dreaming. I want to stick my cunt inside your cock. I want to taste your tongue. I want to suck the words that are hiding at the base of your tongue. I want your words to grow inside my body so that you'll always be speaking to me, with each breath, each heartbeat. Each time my clit gets hard it will be you saying hello. The lover, dissolved to bytes, tries with great pains to return to the world of objects, banging pots, wailing in the night, a misty two-legged cloud drips from the ceiling and then the cold spot the war spot the eerie touch on the back of the neck, the flushed human shudders, its gushing heart banging against its rib cage, rattling the walls *are you wet, yes I'm leaking* the rationality necessary to maintain the solidity exhausts me. Who could keep it up? I know where I am but I do not feel as though I'm at the spot where I find myself. Space pursues me, encircles me, digests me. I'm afraid it will replace me. My body separates itself from thought, space devours my skin and spits me on the other side of my senses. I try to look at myself from any point whatsoever but my body dissolves like a warm snow cone, cherry-flavored. I am similar—not similar *to* something—just similar. I feel myself becoming space, dark space where things cannot be put. My cunt dwarfs the Grand Canyon. The one in Arizona.

Don Baird

PRIDE

When I made my first attempt to actually move into San Francisco I spent a brief amount of time temporarily residing with some friends in San Mateo. On the evening I moved all of my belongings into their garage, we had a U-Haul truck that needed to be returned to the rental place in Redwood City. There happened to be one little nondescript gay bar in Redwood City, so we decided to make the chore enjoyable and drop in for a drink after returning the truck. It was just about dark when we pulled up to the plain gray building with two doorways, one lit and one not. As an occasional man darted in the lit doorway with a speakeasy-like secrecy—collars up, hats forward—I noticed a figure standing in the dark doorway. Shame did not resonate from the form; in fact, this person leaned seductively, one hip protruding from the shadows, defiantly unrepressed. When my friends hopped out of the car and walked toward the door I stopped them and said, "Can I have the car keys? I'll be in in just a minute."

One of them looked at me curiously while the other smiled and knew exactly what was on my mind.

"Give him the keys," he said, "Let's go have some beers."

I wandered over to the dark doorway and gazed into the shadows tentatively, knowing that what was hidden by darkness might very well be something that should stay hidden. A young voice said "Hi," with a smile I heard before I saw—then it was all I could see—a perfect smile, small ultrawhite teeth in straight and flawless formation. Their brightness gave way to the whites of his eyes as my vision began to adjust to the darkness. I was taken aback by this young man's beauty. He was angelic yet cocky, possessing an attitude that even I hadn't the experience to pull off with such savvy. The urban edge and gay male nuances of a subculture I was only beginning to absorb and in some ways found frightening were already clearly present in him. I told him I was eventually moving into the city, just staying with friends in San Mateo at the moment. He said he planned to move to the city as well.

"I love it there. I've been to the Stud a bunch of times."

I was shocked by his boast about going to a place I was still afraid to enter, being a small-town boy and all. I suddenly had to know.

"How old are you?"

He smiled sheepishly and said, "15...no, 16. Today is my birthday."

"Really? How'd you get in the Stud?"

"I walked in. They didn't card me."

"Well, happy birthday," I said, my mind racing through facts regarding the age of consent in California.

"What's your name?" I asked.

"Pride," he said, with a hint of a southern accent, the first time I noticed it in our conversation.

"Did your mom name you that?"

"Yep."

"Cool name," I replied, approving only because his mother chose it. Had it been some modern name-change of his choice—some form of tribute to the annual gay and lesbian pride parade in San Francisco—I would have refused to call him that. The word pride was bandied about by a community with a false sense of well-being more appropriate to cocaine abuse than to the varied lifestyle choices of those who knew "the love that dare not speak its name." Even back then I was toying with the concept of Gay Shame Day as opposed to gay pride day.

"Do you hang around outside this bar often?" I asked.

"Just until I meet someone to go home with. I can't go inside; they know I'm underage here," he said, shifting coquettishly from one foot to the other, inside and outside of the shadows.

"Well, I don't have a home to invite you to tonight, seeing as how I just moved in with friends today—but I do have their car keys. Do you want to sit in the car with me until they finish their beers? They said we could."

"Sure," he said, smiling and giving the front of his sweatpants a tug, just like those guys in the movies, the ones I watched in closet-sized booths in a bookstore on Polk Street. How did this boy so young know so much about this big gay world that I only stood at the edge of, at long last poised and ready to jump into?

I unlocked the car, and he gingerly hopped into the driver seat. I suddenly had slight worries of him starting it up and taking off on a high-speed chase, a run from the law, criminal madness. I jammed the keys way down in my pocket and slid into the passenger seat.

We immediately started groping each other's crotches, somewhat nervous that a patrolling, persecuting Redwood City Cop would discover us. It wasn't unusual back then for gays to be unduly harassed when seen leaving the only gay bar in a smaller peninsula town and slapped with a nasty DUI violation or whatever else they could scrape up on a random homosexual. The cops lay in wait to catch the degenerates leaving their designated hangout or coming way too close to a schoolyard or a shopping mall to recruit innocent children into a life of depravity and sexually deviant behaviors. In fact, back then it wasn't too far-fetched a possibility that a pair of officers might even take the whole judicial process into their own hands and leave a gay man beaten and humiliated and too frightened to report the injustice to the same authorities who brutalized them. These thoughts in the back of my mind added a special sense of danger—an edge of exhilaration to our rushed sexual interaction.

As he shot his barely 16-year-old load in my mouth I was conjuring the cops flashlight beaming in, catching me like a vampire draining the boy's essence, sperm dripping from my chin. He quickly returned the gesture in a way that couldn't have possibly been construed as novice, pausing once to look up and smile sweetly and ask, "Am I doing it right?" This I'm certain he said for effect. I was able to confirm this suspicion, but not until several years later.

Relieved yet worried that my friends would be coming back to the car any minute, we made ourselves presentable and traded phone numbers. I promised to call him when I finally got settled into my own place in the city. We said goodbye and he wandered off into the darkness, flashing that perfect smile. The more prudish of my two friends gave me attitude when I stepped into the bar. As I handed his car keys back to him he looked repulsed as if I had soiled them, tossing them on the bar and wiping his hand on his jeans. The other one smiled wide with eyes that said, "Did you get any? Tell me all about it...later."

I said, "Thanks, you guys. Oh, yeah, could we find a car wash place somewhere—I'm really sorry but the car is going to need it." We all laughed and headed home.

Eventually I made the move to the big city. I found a place and a job and bought my first leather jacket, dyed my hair blond, found a boyfriend, moved in with him, moved away from him, discovered speed, made some fabulous friends, immersed myself in the punk rock music scene I had dreamed of. I even started writing a regular music column in one of the local gay papers. In all, I carved myself a neat little adventurous sort of life in San Francisco. Oddly enough, one of the main cornerstones of my social interaction turned out to be the Stud— the very place I was too afraid to go in to prior to a chance meeting with a 16-year-old who had been there several times and liked it. I decided not to be outdone by a mere teenager.

What I anticipated to be like a pit of gay vipers engaging in limitless sexual debauchery, severe drug abuse, danger, and dancing actually turned out to be a somewhat nurturing and friendly place, a place I would later describe as everyone's living room or the bar where I "grew up." I thought of Pride on occasion, usually when being carded to get in. I had tried the number he gave me a few months after we met but it had been disconnected. Many years later I learned that he was still around when I overheard a notorious chicken hawk who practically lived at the Stud talking about a beautiful boy named Pride. He saw my ears prick up and responded, "He said he knows you." I asked a few questions about him and wondered why we hadn't run into each other. But by that time I was probably pretty preoccupied with the third or fourth of my seven different boyfriends named Jeffery.

If I wasn't preoccupied with a Jeff then I was oftentimes fascinated with walking late at night around and around and around one block in the Castro. On the block were a school, a fenced-in playing field, an AIDS Hospice, a Cala Foods, and a street called Collingwood. This is where lots of people would go to cruise for dick, both on foot and in cars and only very late at night. It was an activity or ritual that not only addressed the reptilian manhunt urge of the gay night prowlers, but for me also really spoke to the drugs I was doing. It provided an activity to obsess on in a neat and contained way—marching around and around the block repeatedly with my eyes permanently opened wide like a shark taking in the potential prey that circled similarly around the block, seldom stopping, only slowing down for fear of drowning if stationary. Other nights I likened the heated stroll to tigers running around the tree so fast they turned into butter, then worried whether it was politically correct to even know that story. Or the one about the seven Chinese brothers: One of them swallowed the ocean while the others gathered gold and treasures from the ocean floor. But they got too greedy and went too far and the skinny one who swallowed the ocean couldn't hold it any longer and the greedy ones died, drowned in a wave of bulimic control issues; I wondered whether the skinny brother was really a sister.

Then I saw a very pretty boy sitting in a parked car, so pretty I risked certain shark death by stopping my constant motion. I stared into the car and the boy almost pointedly ignored my doting presence. I was persistent with my focus, yet trying to look somewhat casual about it. Finally he looked over to me and smiled and I said "Hi." He reluctantly acknowledged me in a slightly cocky and totally bored manner and I thought to myself, Oh, *great, he's going to be an arrogant snot.*

I approached the car, crouched down by the passenger window, and said, "So what are you up to?"

"Nothing...sitting here."

"What are you looking for?"

"I don't know. Maybe nothing," he said in a somewhat snotty and curt manner. "Dick, what do ya think I'm looking for? What is everyone here looking for?"

"I'm looking for a deep and meaningful love relationship with the man of my dreams," I said.

He smiled over my comment and it shook the chill away from the snide and arrogant attitude he had served thus far. He kind of looked familiar for some reason.

"It seems like I've maybe met you before."

He looked in my eyes and said, "No, I don't think so."

"What's your name?" I asked. "I'm Don."

"Pride," he said.

"Oh, my God, we have met before, then," I said. "It was a long, long time ago."

He looked at me more carefully and said, "I can't remember. God I hate it when this happens, when I can't remember someone I've been with but they remember me."

"Well think back, it was outside of a gay bar in Redwood City," I said, trying to jog his memory. He still couldn't remember, so I racked my brain trying to think of other associative details that would bring it back to him. "We just sat in a car and talked and blew each other," I said. Still nothing. He began to stammer out an apology when it hit me. "I know what will make you remember: It was the night of your sixteenth birthday that we met."

He paused for a moment and smiled and said, "Oh, yeah...now I remember." Then a look of shock came to his face and his eyes widened and he said, "That's really weird because tonight is my birthday."

"Really? No lie? Wow, so that would make it seven years to the day that we first met. That's incredible! Kind of eerie too, like it was supposed to happen."

Pride agreed.

Well, I guess this means we have an anniversary to celebrate. Want to go to my house and fuck?"

Pride agreed, and thus began our strange and wonderful friendship, but very slowly. After that night I probably didn't run into him again for at least six months—and I found him to be rather aloof and not very forthcoming with information about himself. I got the feeling right away that he hung with a crowd of people who were pretty hardcore and that he had embraced the darker end of a hedonistic drug culture even more fully and shamelessly than I had. Certain clues made this apparent, like the fact that he didn't ever seem to work at a normal job like everyone else yet he never seemed to want for cash or clothes or a place to live. I later learned that in his teens he actually was a model and made two commercials that probably paid very well—one was for Crest and the other was for Stridex medicated pads. But that's big money and I don't know exactly where it would have all gone. Who knew? Pride never really let anyone completely know all about him ever, at least not right away.

It had been many months since I saw him last, I was DJing at a new club in the Mission, and one night he walked in with my partner in this venture and was announced as the new go-go dancer, one of three we generally featured. He acted kind of standoffish toward me because he was involved with the club promoter, and I sensed there was a hint of jealousy over the fact that we knew each other previously, so he kept his distance.

The club didn't last as long as their relationship did, and during that period of time Pride actually seemed oddly tamed. I moved just a few blocks down the street from him and I would see him and his boyfriend on occasion—both dressed for work as waiters in crisp white shirts and black pants. This was highly uncharacteristic of Pride—holding a job and living the partnered domestic existence—but it went on for some time, two or three years. Yet during that time I found that as I met more people, did more drugs, enjoyed wild sex parties with people I had previously found too scary as bona fide residents of the darker side of life, invariably I would hear stories about Pride. They all seemed familiar with him, like everyone knew Pride.

Like the night my boyfriend and I were cruising together and got picked up by a short, kind of menacing Italian guy in a jaguar. The guy lived in the Castro, and his home was filled with a huge collection of taxidermed animals of all sorts: hawks, mountain lions, raccoons, bearskin rugs, a fox. The creatures stared at us from every direction as the guy led us to a back room with a sling and a wall of porn videos. We were expected to endlessly fuck the Italian guy, who turned out to be the kind of bottom who was so voracious it eventually began to render him unattractive. We came upon an impasse and he ordered breakfast for us from a nearby restaurant, making some comment about having to appear in court in the early morning.

When he left us alone to go pick up the food, I started putting details together and realized that this was the guy who had recently stabbed one of Pride's close drug-dealer friends and that he was just a very insane, hot-tempered ex-con. Of course there were many signs I should have recognized—like the gothic lettering across his abdomen that read CO CO COUNTY that I saw while fucking him. It didn't occur to me what it stood for; I just thought it was a reference to Chanel, and almost said that. On the contrary, it stood for Contra Costa County, it was definitely a prison tattoo, we were definitely playing with fire, and soon we would be sharing breakfast with the guy on his way to a sentencing for stabbing someone I vaguely knew. We ate quickly, and luckily another guy stopped by. He decided to get in one more fuck before his sentencing, allowing us the option to high-tail it out of there while he was distracted by the new guy's 10-inch cock. Total bottom.

I ran into Pride shortly after that one evening when I saw him wandering by my house. He told me he had been with friends who shot him up with heroin, which he'd never done before and hated. He was feeling wobbly and thirsty and out-of-sorts, so I took him in and sat him down and let him gather himself for a while. I believe this act of concern always touched Pride, like he found it unusual that someone would care enough about his well-being, and after that I felt much closer to him. He told me he had broken up with his boyfriend a while back and felt all the better in the long run being single.

Then he started telling me a bit about his childhood, which was fascinating. At 14 he was discovered having sex with another male, someone a great deal older than he was. At that point in time his family was going through a Jesus-freak stage, so they promptly whisked him off to church where they presented him in front of the entire congregation to be saved. They ordered him to redeem himself by asking the Lord for forgiveness and to solemnly promise to never commit this sin again, to never give in to the perverse temptation of pleasures of the flesh. He refused to say he would never do it again and the congregation began to pummel him with the usual sinner, damnation, hellfire for eternity stuff. So upon being handed an E-ticket straight to hell, Pride asked the sweaty speaking-in-tongues type Minister if the other members of the congregation that he had been enjoying those carnal pleasures with—*like that man there and that one over there sitting with his wife and yet another few looking nervous in the pews*—would be going to hell also. His family rushed him out of the church turned upside down by hypocrisy and lies and never once returned to the building or the faith. I was astonished and fascinated and loved him immediately. He gave me a warm hug and thanked me and was ready to head up the hill to his place.

After that I began visiting and hanging out with Pride far more frequently. I met lots of his friends, bought really good drugs, and felt like whenever I visited there I was stepping into a different world, a strange world that had little or nothing to do with what was normal and right and good. This was a world where people didn't hold regular jobs, where youth and beauty were used like currency and criminal activities were commonplace. It always seemed oddly heroic to me.

You never knew what would happen whenever the doorbell rang when you were at Pride's place. Who would it be? A really hot married guy scoring drugs, getting high, and wanting to get fucked in one quick efficient visit. One or two of the really tough dealer types you were always afraid of but found fascinating and sexy and longed to be liked by. A pair of concerned people bringing in their blue-lipped, overdosed friend for a clean, well-lighted place to recover. Or an occasional rough-trade-looking man who would walk in, notice Pride had company, say "Get rid of 'em," then go into the bedroom while Pride quickly ushered us out with a quick goodbye.

When you saw Pride next and asked him what that was all about, he wouldn't remember the incident or would say something like, "Oh, I got him high and he fucked me really hard." I'd look at him shocked, worry digging furrows in my brow, and he'd look back with that smile and his eyes sparkling and say, "What? I loved it!"

One morning, after I'd had a loud and physical altercation with my boyfriend at the time—a misguided actor who'd used me as a vehicle for that old, familiar downward spiral into the abyss of substance abuse—I found myself knocking on Pride's door. I needed refuge and a bit of peace and quiet. Pride's place was an illegal sister-in-law apartment, or red-headed stepchild apartment, as I liked to call it, located down a long, weird hall beside a garage and behind a relatively opulent house near Alamo Square. It had a hidden entrance, and I felt safe and protected there. When I arrived that morning and he saw that I had been in a scuffle with the boyfriend, he made a very heroic and touching promise that the boyfriend was never allowed there again and if he came there, he would kick his ass. Sweet.

Pride was obviously fresh from a bath and getting ready to go somewhere, so I offered to leave. He said, "No way, girl, you're coming with me on an adventure."

"OK," I said. I could use an adventure to take my minds off of things.

"Where are we going?" I asked.

"You'll see."

He was extra effervescent this morning, and I wondered why.

"Did you get fucked really hard by some mean guy last night or something?"

"Yeah, by an old ugly guy with a weird ugly dick," he said proudly. "And I loved it! Now do that big line on the coffee table because the cab is on the way." I rolled up a bill, eager for that familiar burning sensation. It was always followed by the sense that any form of fat clogging my veins and arteries was instantly melted away, allowing my blood to freely flow through at a new velocity, giving me a rush like that feeling you get when the roller coaster plummets from its highest point.

"Breakfast of idiots," I said aloud.

"No thanks, I'm not hungry." The doorbell sounded. "Let's go, girl," he said, swishing out the door in a most effeminate way. "Aren't I nelly?" he asked as he shook his hips down the hall. "But I can be butch too if I want."

We piled into the cab, which took us barely four blocks. "We're here," he said paying and tipping the driver extravagantly as we got out in front of a big apartment building.

"Who lives here?" I asked.

"Some spun-out, fucking bug-chasing fucking bitch," he said, smiling. "Not really, just a big drug dealer who needs me to shoot him up because he can't do it himself anymore. C'mon, he lives on the third floor," he said, starting to ascend the stairs.

"Well, aren't you just the little Florence Nightingale of the drug underworld," I said.

"Oh, yeah, butch it up, will ya? Like this," he said in a deep low macho voice as he applied his most manly gait to the first staircase. I was cracking up but followed his instructions. Upon hitting the next floor's landing he squealed, "OK, now nelly!" and exploded in a flurry of effeminate gesture in his ladylike ascent. He was slaying me. "OK, now butch," he said in a low voice. He was way ahead of me.

We entered the apartment, and the tone was much more somber in there than we were. I quickly stifled my giggly mood and let Pride do all the talking. There was not just the one dealer present but also another, even bigger and more notorious one in need of the same service. This puzzled me. How did people who were most definitely experienced in their drug use eventually reach a point where they weren't able to administer their own hits? I didn't ask any questions about it and actually averted my eyes while Nurse Pride did his duty; such things had made me actually faint in the past. When I heard cough number 1 and cough number 2, I knew it was safe to return my gaze in their direction. In the not-too-distant future one of those men would die suddenly from HIV/AIDS complications, and the other would be found bludgeoned to death and rolled up in a carpet at a place he had just acquired to open a small business. Since the two men didn't immediately rip off their clothes and initiate sex with us but rather prepared a package for Pride and handed it to him and called another cab, I knew this wasn't the only stop we'd be making.

We exited then entered a waiting cab and headed to our next destination, a long cab ride to a weird place in the shadow of the freeway and San Francisco General Hospital. It was a little red house with a fence and a very scary rottweiler guarding the place. A very handsome, stocky blond guy in leather pants and a wifebeater had to subdue the dog before we could enter the gate.

Pride had informed me that he was stopping here to do his service yet again to the boyfriend of another big drug dealer. Once safely inside I took in the surroundings in this oddly out-of-place little cottage under the freeway. Just off the front room, in a smaller room with no door, lay the sleeping drug dealer. He had a gun in his hand, which lay next to his head. He was snoring loudly. I was immediately frightened and glanced at Pride with widening eyes that said, "Let's get out of here." He just smiled.

The blond guy said, "Oh, don't worry about him—he's been up for five days and just fell out a bit ago. He's down for the count. Come on back here." He led us to a large back room. The cottage was situated on a slope, so the windows in this back room were high on the wall but right at ground level on the outside of the house. I kept seeing the gigantic paws of the rottweiler bounding by each window again and again as if he were on patrol.

Pride prepared the hit for the blond while I took in the room in all its sex-dungeon glory. There was a big X-shaped wooden structure with a variety of belts and cuffs attached to it for restraint purposes, a leather sling attached to the low ceiling, a weird sort of gynecological exam–bondage platform, and a video camera and monitor. A video sputtered on the screen—some indiscernible, fleshy homemade blur. From where I stood I could just see the gun in the sleeping lover's hand.

Nurse Nightingale apparently ran into a bit of trouble giving Mrs. Dealer her injection—they soon found it necessary to wrap his arm in saran wrap and say a prayer to the patron saint of abscess. His first attempt had "missed," and while I was curious about what that meant, whenever I looked over at them dealing with this complication I started feeling weak. I turned away and looked at the gun in the sleeping man's hand and thought about things like, *What if he decided to itch his nose in his sleep or something? What if he awoke groggily to the sounds of strangers talking in his house, like for instance me and Pride, or maybe just me?* I started feeling more uneasy about being there and turned to discover that the process of getting the blond high had encountered another even more unsightly complication.

I turned to the video screen and realized it was something the happy couple had filmed of themselves. Boy, the sleeping one certainly had a huge cock—probably 10 inches at least. Then it hit me: He was the same guy who had relieved us of top duties that morning with the Italian guy who had all the taxidermed animals and who faced charges of assault with a deadly weapon as soon as he hopped out of the sling. Small world.

Finally I heard the familiar cough that meant the hit worked and the toiling around with it had ended and I could confidently look toward them again without getting lightheaded or nauseous. Pride lit a cigarette and smiled like an emergency intern who had just saved a life. The handsome blond ripped off his clothes and approached me, dropped to his knees and started undoing my pants. Pride said, "I'll wait in the living room...don't take all day, OK?" He rolled his eyes.

I quickly found myself fucking the blond mercilessly hard against the wall, which I noticed had bullet holes in it—probably from the jealous drug-dealer boyfriend who was sleeping with a gun in his hand. The same guy who was slapping his 10-inch cock across the blond's face on the video screen, the one who snored from the adjacent bedroom with no door, just over my shoulder, where I glanced nervously.

"Don't worry about him; he won't wake up. Just keep fucking me...harder...fuck me hard, man," he panted and hissed far too loud for comfort, as if he wanted his mate to wake up and kill us both. "Fuck me like a bitch—make me your bitch, fucker."

I saw from the video that the blond seemed to like things a bit rougher than most. I reached up and grabbed his hair and pulled his head back next to mine and whispered harshly, "Make one more sound and I'm gone, you little bitch." I shoved my fingers in his mouth. At the window by our heads the rottweiler suddenly lunged at us, snarling and butting at the glass so hard I thought it would certainly break. I thrust my hips so hard I made bruises and shot my load into the condom, which I removed and threw down beside the blond. I said, "Yeah, real safe." I pulled my clothes back on quickly and headed out of the room, sneering at the sleeping guy.

Pride looked up at me from the couch and smiled. "You ready?"

"Yep," I said, sounding more like an ex-con or a cowboy than usual.

We both hit the front door at the same time and looked directly at each other, smiled, and simultaneously screamed, "OK, nelly!" We swished our way to a waiting cab.

Cheryl B.

Rope Burn

He was a part-time pot dealer who lived in my neighborhood. I met him at a party. We sat under the loft bed in the bedroom of our mutual friend and talked. He had a wooden pipe, carved with intricate, mesmerizing designs. When we went back to his posh East Village apartment, he showed me the large closet that overflowed with lamps, plants, and the weed. It was like a little jungle bursting with brightly hued leaves the color of green parrots.

He offered me some 'shrooms and we lounged about on his bedspread waiting for them to kick in. We exchanged stories. Tales of childhood pets: He had grown up with cats, I had two dogs. Levels of education: He had an MBA (his day job was on Wall Street, the pot dealing was a hobby); I was a junior at an arts college studying theater. Parents: Both mothers were neurotic, both fathers distant.

When the 'shrooms finally hit, his bedroom turned into a lollipop land of fascination. I had been admiring a Picasso print that hung on his wall when suddenly the blue dancer in the painting began to move—gyrating like a go-go girl. I spent some time studying the painting as he methodically stroked my dyed black hair. He told me he couldn't believe all the colors he saw in my hair. "It's like a rainbow," he said.

We kissed. We fucked. We held each other.

In the morning, I asked him to repeat his name and his answer was that his girlfriend was due back later that day. We exchanged numbers nonetheless.

"Jon" he wrote on the torn-off corner of a Chinese menu along with seven digits.

At our eighth meeting for casual sex, while the girlfriend visited her parents in Connecticut, he brought out a small bundle of thin rope, like twine, the kind you use to bind newspapers for recycling. He wanted me to braid the twine six rows deep, then tie it securely around the head of his penis, walk to the other side of the room, holding the other end of the string, and pull as hard as I could. I was concerned I would hurt him, cut him, maim him in some way.

But he pointed at the pile of twine on the floor with a look in his eyes that said, "Just do it." I took my time braiding the string in the hope that he would change his mind.

The last time we had been together, I took him to a friend's apartment where a group of us sat around and watched the movie *Carrie*. My real motivation for taking him to this friend's house was to get him up to the roof, which had an incredible view of lower Manhattan. I had already told the friend that this was going to happen. And as Sissy Spacek was pelted with feminine hygiene products and my group of friends chanted "creepy Carrie, creepy Carrie" at the TV screen, we made our exit.

When we got up to the roof, I leaned over the side of the building and looked out over the vast ocean of lights. He came up behind me, first holding me by my hips, then sliding his hands under my skirt. His warm hands felt good in the slightly chilly night.

He lifted my skirt up and undid his pants. I heard the distinct crinkle of a condom being opened and then I felt him against my ass, then between my thighs, then inside of me. He kissed me on the back of my neck and bit my ears as he fucked me. I held on to the edge of the roof and he held onto me and we stayed like this until we both came, our voices carrying through the air.

After we buttoned up and headed back down to the apartment, he grabbed me and kissed me, this kiss more passionate than any between us before. He looked at me: "I think Christie is suspicious," he said of his girlfriend, ruining whatever moment we were having.

As I braided the twine, I wondered whether he did this rope thing with Christie. It didn't really go along with the image of her I had concocted in my head: executive, pin-striped suit, gold watch, and thin lips. Maybe he needed an impoverished art student like me to do such things with. The last time he had me over, we frolicked on the couch until a sharp metal object stabbed me in the back.

"Ow," I yelped. Jon lifted me off the couch, where we discovered a large tortoiseshell barrette. I picked up the barrette and noticed the strands of blond hair that clung to it. It reminded me of my first night in Jon's apartment, how he had stroked my head, telling me he saw a rainbow in the dyed black mass of my hair.

"I'm sorry about that," Jon said, taking the barrette away from me.

From then on I felt Christie's presence in his apartment. She was staking her claim.

I reminded myself that I was only in it for the pot. And the ensuing sex, but mostly the pot. The last thing I wanted was a relationship with someone who wore a suit to work.

After about half an hour of braiding, during which Jon sat on his couch reading the *The Wall Street Journal*, and calluses began to form on both of my forefingers, the rope was ready.

To go through with this task, I needed at least one hit off of the gigantic bong that lived in the corner of Jon's apartment, between two adjacent windows. My eyes moved from one window to the next, taking in the thwarted, panoramic view of Avenue B. I took the hit, watching the smoke rise neatly through the long blue cylinder. I breathed in and held it. Jon was now fondling the rope I had just braided for him.

"It's nice," he said, caressing the itchy, dry surface of the rope. I looked away.

He called my name. I turned to face him and he held the rope out to me like an offering.

I took it in my hands, trembling slightly. He smiled and raised his arms in surrender.

Once I had the makeshift rope securely fastened about the head of his dick, I began to walk across the room, the lead of the rope uncoiled off the floor as the resistance tightened. I watched his eyes broaden and could see his anatomy rise. I continued backing up, inching toward the pot closet, then farther back to the front door, resting my back on the far wall.

The rope was now fully extended. For some reason, I was thinking about squirrels: their eerie resemblance to rats, the way their cheeks quivered when they were full of nuts. I thought about the all the weed we had shared—the kind of bud that smelled like a summer's eve would smell, if there really were such a thing. I thought about Christie and her blond hair kept neatly back in her sadistic barrette.

I pulled a bit harder, watching the tip of his penis grow crimson, then purple, then a color I don't know how to describe except maybe that it was meaty. I watched the sweat pour down his face, his chest. It was almost as if his ears, his nose, and his pores all drizzled sweat. The sight was both intriguing and monstrous.

He looked about to burst. He closed his eyes and motioned like he was about to make a dive and his come shot out in a steady stream, hitting the Picasso print whose figure had once danced for me. I watched the come drip down the blue woman's body and I was filled with a strange satisfaction.

I walked over to him, gathering up the rope as I went. The look of complete happiness on his face was creepy. He fell back on the couch and motioned for me to sit next to him.

"Thanks," he said, catching his breath. "That was good."

"No problem," I said. I knew that when I left his apartment shortly, I was not coming back.

I stood up and leaned over to kiss him for the last time and noticed the red welt that ran down the top of his penis like a nasty burn, and I wondered what Christie would think when she saw it.

Mark Ewert

Dancing for the Beats

In 1988, when I was 17, I went to the Naropa Institute with the express intention of sleeping with either Allen Ginsberg or William Burroughs, thereby joining my life to theirs, and speeding up my own ascent into greatness. William wasn't teaching that year, but Allen was, so it was he I made my play for, on the very first night of the Summer Session, with the immortal line, "Hello Mr. Ginsberg, my name is Mark Ewert, and I'd like to make you a breakfast, lunch, or dinner sometime." This gambit worked like a charm, and thereafter Allen and I were boyfriends. He wasn't the least bit weirded out by the fact that I was still interested in sleeping with Burroughs. Quite the contrary.

"It would be great to get William laid," Allen declared, "He *loves* getting fucked. And you really care about him and his work." Allen was 62 at the time, and Bill was 74.

At this time in my life, I wanted to be *anything* that I could be the best at: actor, writer, filmmaker, painter, whatever. It changed almost daily. Within a week of meeting Allen, he told me that my writing "sucked." (Context: I *was* at that moment walking away from him with another young poet whom I was about to go fuck, and when Allen had asked whether he could join in, or at least watch, we had both said no.) Though you may find it hard to believe, at 17 I was more than a little bit impressionable, and so to hear from the world's most famous living poet that my writing sucked had, shall we say, an impact on me. OK, so writing was out.

Instead I decided to focus my efforts on art forms that had no real criteria you could judge it by, such as butoh, the avant-garde Japanese dance that I had seen all of a minute's worth of footage of on CNN. From what I could see, butoh consisted of people writhing around on the ground meaningfully, as if in agony. Well, I could do *that*. Besides, as a teenager, I had such an aversion toward my body, and was so all-around worked-up and miserable—with bad posture and four layers of clothes, expecting the world to end at any minute—I thought I surely could channel some of that intensity into this wonderful, ungradable, new kind of dance. I would be great.

Strangely enough, of all the ways I sought to win Allen's approval, it was butoh that did the trick. Allen *loved* my butoh dancing, and, for a long time, it was like our little parlor game to spring on his unsuspecting famous artist friends. (It's now 1989, and I'm living in NYC, attending my one and only year of college, and staying with Allen on the Lower East Side on the weekends.) At some point at the gathering, perhaps when conversation was beginning to lag, Allen would announce, "And now, my friend Mark would like to show you this special kind of dance he does. It's really something." Our guests would politely settle themselves into attentive postures while I began to strip: shucking off shoes, peeling off sweater, shirts, pants, underwear, socks. I folded all my clothes neatly and placed them on an empty chair.

Allen would dim the lights. I'd stand no more than a few feet in front of our shanghaied audience, straighten my posture, and close my eyes. Then the dance would begin.

Typically, I'd start by letting my spine crumple under the weight of my head, which motion would eventually bring me to a prone position on the floor, with my blazingly white ass sticking up in the air. After that it was just a matter of moving as the spirit moved me—succumbing to the million minute pressures of gravity and anatomy until my body contorted and deformed in unique, uncontrived ways. Once Judith Malina (cofounder of the Living Theater) came over, and I was getting so into the infinitesimalities of my prone-on-the-floor movements, that I was, for all intents and purposes, not moving at all. Fearing that I was losing my audience, Allen called on me to "Rise! Rise!" so that my motions would at least return to the realm of the visible.

Another performance I especially remember was the time Allen and I went to visit Francesco Clemente, a very regal Italian of aristocratic background, who I was both crushed out on and scared of. His studio was a dark, wood-walled cavern, a full city-block long in the heart of New York. For my dance, he and Allen sat in block-shaped, throne-like chairs, and this time I had a space the size of a theater stage to fill with aesthetic presence. As I moved, I was very aware of my shriveled little peeny hanging down from my pubic thatch, and my ribs shuddering in my scrawny chest, but I tried to turn such patches of self-consciousness into badges of honor, projecting their energy outward with courage and acceptance. I also stayed on my feet more, and entered into, and held, a series of static, yoga-like poses—like that of an archer pulling back a taut bow. This "Indian" flavor was in honor of Francesco being a Hindu. I also recall pantomiming the picking of a beautiful, long-stemmed rose that was apparently growing out of my butt, and then bringing the imaginary blossom to my nostrils, to sniff. This was in honor of the earthy, shit-and-stink theme of many of Francesco's paintings.

It's Thanksgiving, 1989, and I'm staying alone with William Burroughs in his little wooden house in Lawrence, Kansas—a humble piece of Americana, like something out of my parents' childhood, or possibly their parents'. It's evening, and everyone else has gone home for the night. Bill is well into his fifth or sixth scotch, and is getting quite sloppy and jocular. He lists around the little front room and den, scaring his cats, and pulling things off cluttered shelves, ostensibly to show them to me: a scorpion englobed in a paperweight, a book about alien abduction, a wooden cane that conceals a sword. It's been a long, action-packed day, and we're running out of things to say to each other. It's late. We drift into the little bedroom, where we'll be sharing the bed tonight. Suddenly, Bill lights on an idea.

"And now, you *must* show me this dancing of yours," he drawls, campily emphatic. "Right this instant. If you don't, Allen will have...our...heads! Our *heads*, my dear."

"OK," I say, stalling. "I think maybe I could use some more of that pot..."

"Then pot you shall have, my dear." William scuffles out of the room, to look for pot, rolling papers, and matches—a procedure that even in the best of times (that is, when William is sober) takes several minutes. Slapstick sounds from the other room: things breaking, cats yowling, William bellowing.

I'm smoking the joint slowly and carefully. "I think," I say, "I think I need some music."

"Ah! Music! *Music!*" William cries, and once again he bustles around the length and breadth of his entire domicile, until he produces a black and yellow Walkman, and a tape of the Master Musicians of Joujouka.

"Yes, that should do," I say. "William, why don't you sit on the bed, and I'll just stand here, and sort of get ready, get into the music. Then I'll begin."

William agrees gamely, and climbs into bed. His eyes, which have been slits all night, are now all but fully closed with alcohol and sleepiness. The skin on his bald head hangs loosely, and he's tucked snuggly in bed in his pale blue pajamas.

I take off my shirts but keep my pants on, standing two feet from the bed. I hook the clip of the Walkman onto the right hip of my jeans, and carefully untangle the headphones' cords before placing the metal band over and around my skull. I press PLAY.

I close my eyes, and let the blaring horns of the tape shuttle my mind along snaky trails: through the ceiling, through the roof, out into infinite starry expanses. William is snoring lightly, but it no longer matters. *I must become one with the music,* I say to myself. *I must lose myself completely.* Slowly I begin to raise my arms over my head, and pivot faintly around the axis of my spine.

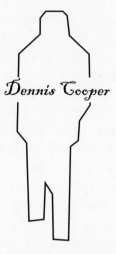

Dennis Cooper

ONE NIGHT IN 1979 I DID TOO MUCH COKE AND COULDN'T SLEEP AND
HAD WHAT I THOUGHT WAS A MILLION-DOLLAR IDEA TO WRITE THE
DEFINITIVE TELL-ALL BOOK ABOUT GLAM ROCK BASED ON MY OWN
PERSONAL EXPERIENCE BUT THIS IS AS FAR AS I GOT

It was 1972–73. There was this club, Rodney Bingenheimer's
English Disco, now a bad Turkish restaurant, where everyone who
was remotely involved in Glam—Bowie, Sparks, Roxy Music, T. Rex,
Slade, Suzi Quatro, Jobriath, The Sweet, et al.—hung out all the time.
I was just out of high school, and very pathetically "glam"—plat-
forms, shag haircut, shimmery clothes—so I gravitated to Rodney's,
like people did, and became a semiregular. We just hung out, like I
said, maybe danced, or did drugs—mostly quaaludes and downers—
talked to Rodney, who was sweet but a moron, and waited for Glam
celebs to drop by. Then we'd schmooze them and/or try to get in their
pants. It was very competitive. A few of us made up this graph with a
point system indicating which stars were the most trophylike—Bowie,
Bryan Ferry, Marc Bolan, Todd Rundgren, and I forget who else. We
had the scene charted all the way down to the "only when desperate"
types—say Lou Reed, or the drummer from Silverhead, or any local
band member, no matter how foxy and unknown, or famous but
unbelievably disgusting, like Flo and Eddie. Or OK, but too old and
insane, like Arthur Lee.

I wasn't that cute, obviously, but I was smarter than most of those overdressed airheads, so I was a top-notch schmoozer, if a loser as a groupie. Everyone glamorous dropped by Rodney's club at some point. All the names: Paul Lynde, Andy Warhol, Eric Estrada, Debbie fucking Reynolds, Raymond-fucking-Burr. Even enemies of music like Jackson Browne and the Eagles. And since Glam was all into a very loose, floaty sexuality, stars tended to treat the place like a brothel.

Like Bowie picked up this cute boy whose name I forget, took him home, tied him up, fucked him, then pissed all over him in a bathtub. Actually, his name was Karl, and he was the bass player of a really well known band, you can figure out the name of if you want. Fuck him.

Several regulars—boys and girls—did Iggy Pop, who was such a total junky back then that he wasn't as trophy-like as you'd think. After a while, Iggy would stagger in yet again, and we'd just go, "Puh-lease." Anyway, it was wild and stupid.

So one of the semiregulars was this very cute pimply boy a little younger than me. Everybody was into him. His energy was just adorable, I can't tell you, although when he got really, really famous a few years later, it became obvious that all that energy was just the foundation of one of the creepiest, most careering, back-stabbing personalities in the history of showbiz, if you ask me. Anyway, he's a joke dinner theater actor now, so ha ha.

Point is, the energetic boy had a rock band, a kind of tinker-toy Iggy and the Stooges meets something really horrible like when the Bay City Rollers went Heavy Metal, if you remember that phase, and one night they played at the club. They were so pathetic that it was almost sublime. Here's this little 16-year-old, perfect-looking rich kid screaming suicidal threats, and miming shooting up, and just acting all wasted and animalesque. We were all just like, "Yum."

After the show he joined us at our table, which was extremely unusual. I guess he was tired. For a while in its history, Rodney's had these big, round tables where we regular types sat around strategizing and saying, "Look...yawn...it's the guitarist from Zolar X...yawn."

Anyway, I was sitting at a table with Chuckie Starr—that's two r's—who was sort of famous at the time for wearing seven-foot platform shoes on *The Mike Douglas Show*. And with this girl named Michelle, who was fucking Rod Stewart—in fact he wrote this famous song about her—I forget its name—that goes, "Red lips, hair, and fingernails / I know you're a mean old Jezebel," and some other bullshit. She was there. And Sable Starr—again two r's—who ended up snagging Johnny Thunders, and even marrying him, which impressed us totally at the time, but really, it can't have been all that much fun. And there were all these other people—nice, creepy, cute, not cute. Anyway, I was pontificating, like I used to do, about how, like, the Raspberries' songs were so hermetic that they were holy, or something, and the energetic boy became very impressed. But then he wasn't, like, brilliant.

So our eyes started flashing back and forth. You know, that way. Sex. No one could believe it, because he seemed so unavailable. After a while he said, "You should, um, come home with me."

And I was, like, "Done. Say the word." So I drove him to his house—this big white mansion a block or two south of Sunset—and we snuck inside—it was like five in the morning—so as not to wake his parents. But his mom was awake for some reason, I don't know why. I think she was a diet pillhead. Her eyes were really weird. And she stopped us in the hallway. And that's when I thought, *Oh, my God.* Because she was the star of this hugely famous TV series, which meant she was also the mother of this hugely famous teen idol-actor-singer of the period, which meant that the energetic boy was, like, royalty. I was thinking, *I fucking scored.* Because he'd never exactly let on that he was you-know-who's little brother.

Anyway, his mother, who's a Republican scumbag in real life, was actually nice, and she didn't give a shit that we were completely 'luded out. She was just, like, "Have fun, you two." It must have been the diet pills talking.

Then he and I went to his room. We took some more quaaludes, and smoked some pot, and I forget what else, frankly—probably talked about his famous mother and brother—and I was beginning to see what a superficial little narcissist he was underneath all that cuteness. But at that point, who cared? And I think he eventually said, "Let's, you know, do it." Not an exact quote. And we took off our clothes, and then...it's all sort of hazy, I guess because of the drugs. But we did all the obvious stuff. I remember that, at one particular point, I had been rimming him for, like, an hour, as I tended to do, especially when I was on downers, and thinking, *Wow, he must really love to be rimmed,* and *We were made for each other,* etcetera. And I looked up, because I needed another hit of his face to stay interested, and that's when I realized that the look on his face, which I'd been reading as slack-faced delirium—as in, "Oh, I have found the sublime," or, "Oh, Dennis. How could I have lived so long without..." etcetera or what-ever—had nothing to do with me. He'd been asleep the whole time, the self-involved little piece of shit. Yeah, like that stopped me.

Eileen Myles

Liquid Sky

Somebody had a party in a loft. Steve Hamilton was there. I think it was after a reading at the Ear Inn. It was Saturday. Someone had a bright white loft. Lots of cheese on the table, brie. There was plenty of vodka. Big bottles of Welch's grape juice. Which made a pretty strange drink. You wouldn't mix vodka with wine. Here it was like the vodka had to keep its head under the water of the grape juice. Know what I mean. If it peeked out it would be vodka with this Kool Aid aftertaste. Which would be pointless. Insulting to both drinks. So I'm drinking these. Someone had a little bit more money and a bad idea. Then we left and walked home along the Bowery. You were really mad. I had no idea why. You'd just slip into these things, and I'd be really quiet like a child even though I was the adult. Seemed so.

I remember going inside. You were yelling ferociously by then. It's quite possible I had been saying something fucked-up at the party. I was capable of standing two feet away from you and telling someone we were breaking up. I wanted to be free. In little pieces. In other people's eyes. It was my first relationship. I always liked going out with you. I wanted it to be that way. Us. Yet there was always something better for you at the party than me. It seemed so clear. I brought you to places

99

and you found something good. You were very young and you got so excited. And I loved that. But why not me? I fell in love with the love in your eyes for Rose. It started there, and continued on. Once in a while I'd bob into view. You were pushing me. "Asshole," you yelled. I had to get out. You pushed me into the giant mirror—it was propped up on bricks like a shrine to our vanity. It crashed loudly. Huge shards on the floor that I kept for years. For drugs and later because it fit on the tiny shelf over the sink and I never forgot. I looked great that day and I was full of that. I didn't want to stay in with you and be dark. It was early summer, full of white. Walking out the door with my nice ass. Framed by the door. Suddenly you kicked. I went flying down the stairs. Head first, knee first. Before I hit the landing you smashed the door shut. Smeared down on the second floor landing. Sprawled. Dead. The door upstairs to my home was shut. I lay there.

Someone was inside of me. She picked herself up. My knee felt like a watermelon. I lifted it, crying. Probably about five o'clock. Richard. I needed a beer. Moving up First Avenue. My arms and my legs. Space between them so anyone could see the world between my limbs. Me moving and waving. Very slow. Sobbing. The bodegas were now owned by Koreans. I called her Mah-Jong because she reminded me of the woman in Steve Roper. Normally she was cautious but tonight she extended me credit for a six of tall Millers. I was being like you. Getting the most. I sat on Richard's stoop. I felt settled in a way. Smoking and crying. Like I was at work. In about an hour, when I gathered myself, I buzzed. I got up there real ragged. There was a ca-clump to my leg because someone could hear it. I had someone to show it to. My own door was closed. Dead home.

I sat on his chair. A swivel chair painted white from a play. I was always finding things and giving them to other people and then regretting it and going out and visiting my thing. Touching my chair or my desk, using it and feeling sad like it was some lost god. My life was always leaving me. No big deal. You want it?

That night I spread out my life on Richard's floor. I can stay here? Yes. I had a sleeping bag. It was summer and I was very warm. I do believe in the soul because I have seen it several times. This was the first. In the sleepy pale blue of the morning I saw a portion of milky white, my soul, leaving me. I thought I died. It was chilly being gone, watching the thing you knew slip away. I definitely died. That glowing snot I called myself no longer home. Is it safe to say it was cool for you? You woke up at dawn and wondered where I was. Then you remembered something and sat there and cried. My soul came by and comforted you. Like a glowing slipper. Boo-hoo, boo-hoo. Hello.

We came back to earth. We always do. You did not take me to the hospital. I was alone. Do you drink heavily? No, I said. He was a young doctor with curly hair who asked me that question. He wore glasses. He was younger than me. It began to be strange. The nurses called him Bambi. Dr. Bambi. Do you drink heavily? No.

I'm not really interested in the institution of alcoholism. I know its cathedrals and tiny pews and dirty glass. Its cigarettes and long yawning days that quiver as the light adjusts kindly. The cool perfume that fills the screen of the day with fantasy and cancellations and mad peaks of joy. I have never hurt anyone. Not really. But the hand of violence lifts the broken stick and everything stops for a moment. I am simply flesh. Born mortal. Lying there on my watery brief shelf. Brought down by you in a rage as I fled. From your scary church. Brought down. Dr. Bambi, oh, no.

Once I woke up in the morning and the TV was still on. It was color, a sporting event. The cheers of the crowd. I had come home and collapsed on the smooth velvet couch. Brown like a big old casket it seemed. I fooled around, stuck my hand under the pillows. Voila! A marigold flask full of vodka. I had gone into the bathroom at somebody's party and filled it from a fifth and tucked it in my pocket and slipped out.

Embarrassed if anyone saw me going into the bathroom with a fifth. I wanted to be a boisterous drinker, but I was not anymore. So somehow it wound up under the cushions. I had just seen *Liquid Sky*. You know that pumping orgasm music. Where the brain of someone would become illuminated by pleasure and then they'd die. Well I shot bolt upright, I stood there with my little flask and knocked it back. I was the movie. A derelict in a coat with the tails of it waving and one foot further back for balance and my head thrown back as I tipped the flask and I saw it. The glowing white pouring down, spirit, firewater, and I survived. It was such a vision. I knew I was a drunk. In movies. With special effects.

Once when you called me, but you were a different one—older, later, smaller, darker, just not the same—or I called you and it seemed possible we would see each other soon, and I was scared so I decided to go walk the dog. I'll call you back. *Slam.* The single strong thing I had done in my life was to leave you. I was so hurt. Then I became red, huge, demanding. Sometimes very small. I walked around New York and the countryside, changing sizes. In the country I became small, part of the scenery. Occasionally had a good sad cry. I had loved you. That New Year's Eve all alone in Pennsylvania, there was no right party. I even visited America Online, the sober room. It was full. And all of the other rooms were drunk. Margaritas all over America. I created my own room. Literary butch on small estate needs company. I was calling out. I elaborated. No one home. I posted again. And again. Alone on acres of land on New Year's Eve and alone in the Net, waving and flagging girls down, begging for company. I sat in my electronic room alone. I turned it off. Better to be alone in a house in Nature. At the moment when the circle turns and we slip into the next century of seasons I stepped to the door. It was sweet. Light rain on the pond and gently tippling on the flagstone. I prayed to the rain. *I love you*, I thought. "Happy New Year's," I said to the floods of gentleness.

So I'm walking my dog. There's a big school on Norfolk. I'm sure you know it. On Rivington too. With a giant playground behind it. Dark and surrounded by fences. I'd throw the ball. And watch her go. I'd go get it, pick it up, throw it again. A thing was going on. A white thing. I saw my power pouring out. In a tiny hole in my chest where Joe now has tubes where medicine pours through. An important spot. There are several important doors to the soul. There's one here, a tiny circle. Mine opened up. All my white poured out. The same soul? The same contaminated firewater. A white glowing substance was throbbing away pouring into the atmosphere and I was afraid I wasn't free anymore. My anima fleeing into the March air, becoming a cloud. Milky sock.

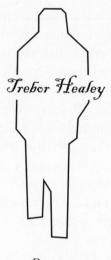

Trebor Healey

BLAME

We were five, or that night we were anyway. We were actually two relationships in ruins and the fifth was whom we blamed it on. But truthfully, we were just five flies circling the same pile of shit, which in this case was a little coffee and cake shop called Just Desserts on Church Street in San Francisco. The shop was one block far enough out not to have been swallowed whole by the bourgeois bovine mad cow disease—yes, it makes a sponge of your brain—of the Castro District.

The two sorry halves of the ruined relationships worked at Just Desserts and had been screwing each other among the cakes after hours for a good two months before Jake and I realized it. I ran into Jake one dusky fog-swollen afternoon. He always had overly arched eyebrows, and they looked particularly concerned or hurt or worried or something that night.

"Can you believe it? They should have told us." I didn't know what he was talking about, but he soon filled me in. A drag perhaps, but I wasn't devastated by the news and Jake shouldn't have been either. We were both in open relationships, after all. But what miffed us was that they'd kept it clandestine, even when we were all friends and had been hanging out a lot together all during the said affair-ette. I didn't mind being a cuckold, but being a chump kind of sucked. Then again, things hadn't been going well with Freddie and me for some time, and I actually felt a sudden sense of relief that maybe this would wrap it up and put the sorry thing to rest once and for all.

"So how into Lawrence are you, anyway?" I asked Jake.

"Oh, fuck, it's been like 10 years. We're family, man." The math didn't add up—they were both 24—but I got the point. "I don't expect him to be having sex with just me, but screwing Freddie is like screwing my sister or something." *Not quite*, I thought, but I understood his point. "It's just, I don't know, it's tacky."

"Tacky? Cool Whip is tacky, Jake. It's more like sloppy. I'd just like to know who he's fucking so there aren't any surprises."

"I think it's tacky."

"Well, how about lame, Jake, can we agree on lame? That's kind of like tacky and tasteless and sloppy and stupid and just kind of pathetic in general—a good compromise."

But Jake only smiled and looked at me one second too long. I'd never thought of it, actually. I'd mercy-fucked plenty—sad friends and lonely, socially inept types—but I'd never revenge-fucked. Jake was cute and all, but I didn't like how his brows moved, and imagining how they'd react when he came was mildly revolting to me. Mildly. So I held his gaze.

As we climbed the stairs to his flat on Guerrero Street (Freddie and Lawrence were both working tonight and probably fucking later), I was thinking that if I could just maneuver things so I could do him from behind, I wouldn't have to see it.

The most I could manage was a 69—which wasn't half bad—and I didn't have to witness it, though I heard it—a brow-arching gasp, if ever there was one.

Maybe it would have all ended there if Johnny hadn't entered from stage left. He was Freddie's ex and I'd never met him, but I knew him from pictures and I would've recognized him anywhere. He was a demonic-looking little satyr of a boy, and I was glad he was back in Manhattan because I would have been tempted to do him, and doing him would be a step past sloppy, tacky, or lame because of the agreement I'd made with Freddie. It was an open relationship, sure, but everyone has some limit, and Freddie's was history.

"Just don't fuck my ex-boyfriends, OK?" he'd pleaded.

I hear it like an echo now, as I gaze out the bus window at him. He's unmistakable, looks just like the photos: the black eyes, the tattered raincoat, the painters cap turned backward on his head, the pierced nose and stubble, the telltale tattoo on his neck of the molecular structure of LSD.

My neck swiveled—and not just from recognition. I watched him stop for a signal, watched him chug from a bottle he had wrapped in a paper bag. I'd later learn the bottle was a pint of morphine he'd lifted from the bedside of a dying friend.

He was damn good bad news, as all heroin addicts are. I don't know why I like junkies. I like potheads too, which is what Freddie was a year ago. What I loathe are speed freaks, and Freddie was now fast becoming one, no thanks to Lawrence, who in his epic sense of himself had decided speed was a part of the current zeitgeist and thus to be embraced.

Lawrence was what you'd call an art fag, which means he was always doing art and calling himself an artist and even attending the Art Institute, but his work was atrocious, derivative, and pretentious. And most importantly, totally unimportant. Of course, as an art fag, he was proud of his oeuvre's lack of quality and content, even its unimportance. It made him a rebel, misunderstood, a stylist. And style was everything to people like Lawrence, even though they had none. His painfully gauche apparel was a case in point. At Just Desserts he'd wear these billowy white shirts—sort of Errol Flynn knockoffs—with some kind of medallion pinned to his chest. He'd wear drawstring military pants, and his hair was all fucked up with gel into some kind of purposefully malformed pompadour. The effect of all this made him look like either a corny musketeer, a clean pirate, an overly well-scrubbed postgoth wanna-be with nary a clue, or exactly what he was: a clueless art fag.

Lawrence primarily used speed and ecstasy because those were the drugs of "his generation," he'd tell us. Freddie had no such parameters, even though he was falling victim to them. In fact, Freddie's chief characteristic was that he was hopelessly malleable, and like a sponge absorbed whatever crossed his path, which at this point was speed and Lawrence's semen. I'd wonder sometimes how Jake could put up with him. Of course, Jake was 24 and horny, and he tolerated him for the same reasons everyone else did: Lawrence was cute and had a big dick. Amazing and tacky and pathetic and lame, how far that could take you.

It was nobody's fault, what happened, but someone always has to take the blame and certain people seem to invite it or make things expedient by offering little resistance. Or they already possess such a depraved reputation that for everyone else it's simply irresistible to scapegoat them. But he was the hero and the villain both, Johnny was, and when he said good riddance he meant it, and that pretty much said it all.

But the whole fucking thing was my idea. And yet it was Lawrence's show, and Jake was the one who just stood there and let it all happen, like some will-to-tragedy. Freddie was the one who got all mopey and started crying. Johnny was just Johnny, which was enough. Which was plenty.

"Why didn't you just tell me, Freddie?" I asked him, annoyed. "It's not like I'd care." But that last was the wrong thing to say because I'd answered the question for him. Malleable Freddie couldn't imagine life without me. Some part of Freddie wasn't formed, I guess, and he became whoever he was with. It was getting creepier by the week; he'd taken to wearing my clothes and even thinking my fucking thoughts. He hadn't actually been to his own apartment in several weeks.

"Freddie, do this for me," I requested or demanded. I have to admit I was tempted to order him about since he liked it so much. "Just find someone who doesn't do speed or bad art. That little fuck will ruin you. You need to choose your friends wisely." I probably sounded like his daddy, all right. Exactly what I didn't want to be, but I couldn't help myself; I knew him by now. "Freddie, you just better pick the right fuckin' pond to swim in or you'll end some sad little maggot at the wrong end of the food chain."

"Well, he wants to have a threesome," Freddie sheepishly offered, combing his thick block-cut of black hair behind one ear. *Freddie would have been the cutest Beatle, I thought irrelevantly.*

"What about Jake?" I asked.

"Jake gets jealous."

"Come on, they've been together 10 years."

"What?"

"Never mind. But I'll pass on the threesome. I mean, in the interest of peace and all that shit, Freddie, shouldn't we be making this a foursome to sort of clear the slate and then everyone can live happily ever after?"

"You don't understand," Freddie said earnestly. I looked at him inquisitively. "Lawrence wants to have like a 3-way relationship. He wants to dump Jake."

I rolled my eyes. "Freddie, I could barely stand him for an hour, let alone a day. A relationship?" I looked at him like he was insane.

"I'm just telling you what he said, I didn't say I wanted to," he said defensively.

"First he gives you speed and dick, and now he gives you bad ideas."

"It's no biggie, Kip. I'll just tell him no."

"Do that."

"Can I still fuck him?"

"Go for it; I don't fuckin' care. But have him deal with Jake, would you?"

He nodded.

"Oh, guess what, Freddie," I then said, trying to be subtle. "I think I saw that guy Johnny today."

"Yeah, you did," he said dourly.

"Oh, you already talked to him?"

"Yeah, sort of. He came into Just Desserts."

"So is he, like, moving back here?" I asked, half dreading it, and yet my heart was racing with excitement all the same.

"Well, you know, he's staying with Lawrence. And…" he hesitated. "Well, I should have told you this." I rolled my eyes. "Well, it just happened—and I tried to stop him."

"What do you mean by that, Freddie? Did he force himself on you?" I said mockingly.

"Well, not exactly. I mean, I know Johnny. He's a fuckin' user. He came on to me and I knew what he was doing. He did it just to seduce Lawrence; I know it. 'Cause he needed somewhere to stay and to store some acid he's dealing."

I just looked at him. He rolled his shoulders.

"He fucked us both." Then he laughed. "It was kind of funny. He was lubing his cock with this disgusting jelly shit they put in cakes, you know between the layers? And then he shot one of those spray gun frosting things up Lawrence's butt, and fuckin' emptied it."

"And Lawrence liked it?" I asked.

"Actually, he looked sort of scared."

"Jake must be stoked about all this."

"He doesn't want Jake to know."

"Of course not."

"Anyway, Lawrence has a show at the Art Institute. I want you to come." I couldn't think of anything I'd rather not do, but I had an idea I couldn't shake.

"Yeah, sure," I answered nonchalantly. "Jake coming?"

"Yup."

Maybe I shouldn't have asked because I know he saw the light in my eyes. "How about this Johnny guy, is he coming?"

"Why?"

"I don't know," I said defensively. "He lives with Lawrence. I just thought..."

But before I could finish, Freddie answered me in a clipped tone, casting his eyes downward. "Yeah, he is." Silence. Then: "Do you want to fuck him?"

Of course would have been the honest answer. "Freddie, we made a deal. I won't fuck him if you don't want me to."

"If?" he erupted. "That's the deal! You can't fuck my history."

Your history. We're about to alter all that, Freddie. We're about to make some. Some damn ugly history. Necessary but ugly.

I suppose I shouldn't have smoked four bowls with Freddie on the bench up those steps on Russian Hill. Just as Lawrence shouldn't have done X and then later speed. Nor should he have done me—nor any of us, for that matter. Jake should have done something, anything.... Johnny did lots of things. Johnny was a user and a fuck-up, thoroughly charming.

The show was a blur. Lawrence, thinking himself sensitive and open-minded, had, as he called it, "integrated" his day job with his art. Large glossy penises cut from porn magazines graced the walls, framed in thrift-store frames and touched-up with acrylic paint to accentuate whatever uniqueness he'd discovered on the various genitals he'd lifted. You know the ploy: blue veins highlighted in navy and purple cock heads. And from the holy mouths of the plagiarized phalluses shot jelly and dried frosting from Just Desserts, some of which actually flaked off during the show, proving "the ephemeral nature of beauty" according to the 19-year-old critic's liner notes in the program.

When I met Johnny, it was far worse than I'd imagined. He had that magnetic presence that bound up your drawers and made you want to lick the salt off his neck and just fuck him right then and there. Like a dog, I wanted to get a whiff of his asshole and chase him around the gallery until we fucked each other to death in some corner.

"Nice to meet you, finally," I said to him as Freddie introduced us. "I recognize you from Freddie's pictures."

He looked at Freddie crossly. "Why do you show people that shit?" Freddie looked at me as if to say, "See what I mean?" before looking back at Johnny and sheepishly rolling his shoulders.

"So, which of these cocks looks the most like yours?" Johnny asked sardonically, sweeping his eyes around the room. But when they returned, he drilled them into my own and I think I must have blushed, four bowls or not. I looked at Freddie, whose self-esteem was in free fall, his eyebrows looking heartbreakingly Jake-like.

I stuttered, but Freddie cut me off. "That big one over there," he said.

I didn't agree, but I appreciated him delivering me from the awkward moment. I grinned a cursory smile.

"Anybody want a drink?" I offered, desperate to change the subject.

"Yeah," Johnny immediately answered, stepping right in front of Freddie as he headed to the bar without inviting him.

I looked at Freddie. "It's just a drink, Freddie." He stormed off.

"You're not as stupid as most of Freddie's boyfriends. Lawrence is more his type," Johnny informed me as he gulped a glass of wine.

"Gee, thanks, but you're not exactly stupid either."

"Oh, you don't know." And I didn't.

The show was bad. It went on and on. There were performances. People pierced each other's backs. One girl did a monologue about a guy shitting in her pussy, which she claimed was the new frontier of sex: asshole-pussy intercourse. Perhaps.

Then Lawrence offered to paint people's penises. It was nice to see all those guys whip them out, but only the few that got hard could really be painted. A limp cock is a limp canvas. I couldn't bear to watch Lawrence wallow in his self-perceived talent. And now that he'd dropped the X he'd brought along, he was a cheap, lovey-dovey poster-boy for PLUR. Though, still being Lawrence, he discredited any ideal he came into contact with and made it look cheap and insincere. *Stop him*, I thought, *before he destroys rave culture entirely.*

I went to the bar, where I drank some more with Johnny, who'd never left his perch. Freddie was avoiding me, and Jake had still not appeared.

When he did, he was all smiles. *Twice chumped*, I thought, and for Lawrence. What a crime; how pointless. I had an urge to save him then. But I couldn't, of course, and besides: The tearful thank-you would likely be accompanied by those arched brows, which would make me regret even the most necessary of good deeds. He invited us all back to his place for a party. He seemed so innocent. *He is a marked man for sure*, I thought.

When we got outside, Jake pulled out a huge bag of sensimilla. I had a precognition that this night would be a wise one to ride out sober. I ignored it and we headed for the bench and all got ludicrously stoned. Freddie even smiled at me now. It would be pointless to recount what we laughed about on the walk home, as anything would do: the color of MUNI buses was suddenly hilarious, as were the plethora of streets in San Francisco named after bad presidents. Pierce, Fillmore, Buchanan. "Where's Nixon Street? Where's Harding?" Freddie kept asking passersby.

Johnny was my problem. He nudged me, looked at me, whispered, "We need to fuck" in my ear. Later he kept asking, "When?" I liked him, he was interesting, intelligent, dangerous, a shit. He'd lived in Portland with all the rest of the Gus Van Sant junky boys; he'd read everything; he hated Lawrence's art and told him so to his face. He told me off-handedly that after two nights in Lawrence's house, he'd decided to destroy the little fuck. I'm a nice guy, generally, but that idea excited me.

"I'm fucking starving," I said to him then.

"Then let's go to Just Desserts," he said, with a sinister gleam in his eye.

It took no effort to get the others to agree, and before we knew it we were rounding the corner to our fated pile of shit, Just Desserts, which had just closed. We strong-armed the new kid who was closing into letting us in, in the only way you can strong-arm any little San Francisco fag boy: with drugs. My God, what a pharmacy Johnny had in his little backpack: blotter, X, 'ludes, 'shrooms, etcetera.

Lawrence assured the kid we'd finish up, and we packed him off to Dolores Park with mushrooms, where I hoped he wouldn't get jumped wandering around like an idiot, marveling at the pink and purple trees while he sang Pink Floyd tunes. Meanwhile, we plowed through the tollhouses and black bottoms as Lawrence started spreading out lines of speed on the glass counter. Yes, it was my idea; I accept the blame for that.

"What about that threesome, Freddie?" I said it loud enough for Lawrence and Johnny both. Yes, it was a kind of entrapment, but I figured if Freddie was there, then I wasn't really fucking with his history, was I? I was just participating in it. We could all have our cake and eat it too, which is what faggot sex is about, right? And in Just Desserts, no less. Boy, did we get ours.

"Sure," Freddie smiled, having missed my motive in his sensamillic bliss.

"If two heads are better than one...do the math," Lawrence shouted excitedly, snorting the fat line before him like a pig.

Johnny yanked me around by the shoulder and buried his tongue in my mouth. Lawrence was all over Freddie, and Jake—well, Jake was just standing there, his eyebrows rising like a flood, and I knew something had to be done. I reached over and grabbed him by the belt, pulling him into Johnny and me as I fumbled with his fly. I don't remember much else: moving into the back kitchen, Johnny's insane grin as he prepared the frosting pump-guns like hypodermics, then Johnny and me fucking really good while everyone stopped and watched us as we slid around in Crisco on the stainless steel food prep table.

Everyone knows a love fuck when they see one. And it stopped them dead, and it changed history, all right. When it ended, Johnny and I slid over the side of the table, nearly fracturing our collective bones. Freddie burst into tears and fell into Lawrence's arms. Jake just stood there. Even his brows were at a loss.

"Those two deserve each other," Johnny said coldly, as he rifled Lawrence's pants for his keys. I felt myself agreeing, but it seemed so cruel. Is this how flies treat each other around shit?

Then Johnny was out in the front of the shop, with a big malicious smile on his face. "Watch this," he said, picking up a chair and heaving it through the big front glass window. "So much for Lawrence, the espresso jerk," he laughed.

A loud alarm accompanied the shatter; then Lawrence yelling, and Freddie wailing.

"Come on!" Johnny said, as he pulled me through the now-empty window frame. I looked back to see Jake, just standing there, watching. I knew Freddie needed me then. But that was just the problem. Freddie was a black hole of need, and if I stepped in it now, I'd never climb out.

I yelled, "Sorry," in a pathetic attempt to retain some semblance of innocence, and followed Johnny out to save my own skin. Johnny ran down the street, laughing. He ran all the way to Lawrence's house, with me following him, though not totally sure why, and realizing that in doing so I was going to have to explain. If I stuck around, that is. I knew I'd done something irrevocable.

Johnny knew I had a car. Johnny was now busy burglarizing Lawrence's apartment and gathering whatever valuables he could find while explaining where we were now heading. But there was no way I was going to go with him. I realized in that moment, in that clarity that comes only from the depths of a drug-addled mind, that the only escape from this sick five-cornered vortex was to make a clean break, and alone.

And it never hurt to dump the blame on someone else. And Johnny was willing. I gave him my car keys. It was only a shit-beat Toyota anyway, and I had insurance and way too many tickets besides. I could shirk responsibility and dispense with a white elephant. I knew as he hopped in with all of Lawrence's valuables, his brows clenched as he insulted my lack of guts, that he was saving me some difficult explanations, which I was already rehearsing in my head.

"You're as pathetic as the rest of them. Good fucking riddance."

I couldn't agree more. In fact, I'd agreed with everything he'd said since the moment I met him. And yes, I hadn't known how stupid he was. And he was a fuck-up and a user. He was beautiful in it. Go, Johnny, go. He set me free. He took the blame, the night, and Freddie, even that awful car. Johnny set me free.

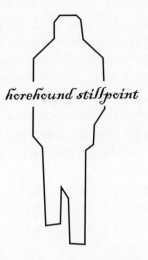

horehound stillpoint

PIGBONES IN A BATHTUB

The most beautiful boy in the world, and the man I loved most in the world, plus the 13 other guys milling around the yard, were all insisting I drop acid. It was *important*, they added; we'd be able to connect on a level you can't get to any other way. Tripping would make this Motorcycle Run more than just 16 fags in the forest.

These were butch queers with an agenda: get high, fuck around, lose our minds, and bond like mad. All in the name of getting so close to the Earth, we would remember where we came from.

I was scared.

Scared, shit, I was monumentally insecure, socially paralyzed, desperately in love, and my whole future—I had decided—rode on what happened up here in Mendocino. The pressure to join in fought with the need to keep my head from flying off my shoulders.

Oops, too late.

It felt like my emotions were already scattered from here to Neptune.

Wind hustled through the forest beyond our host's country home. I heard voices shivering in those treetops, whispers full of muffled threats and future regrets.

For one thing, the most beautiful boy in the world had the acid and he said it came straight from the laboratory: 100% pure. Clean, like in the old days. Skull-shattering powerful. Seeing as how it was still in liquid form, he had filled a syringe, you were supposed to stick out your tongue, and he would not let the needle touch you. No, I swear, he said, I'll just let a drop or two fall into your mouth. You swallow, that's it, no muss, no fuss. Just the most eyeball-popping mind-twisting soul-jerking trip in this pan-psychedelic universe we call home.

And hey, it was my turn.

Jokes about Morgan Fairchild, a dark tool shed, and Dumbfuck the dog sailed right over my head. All around me I saw lean, mean motorcycles, rough-'n'-ready tent gear, and authentic Mexican blankets. I saw men with gorgeous masculine smiles, muddy masculine boots, easy masculine muscles. I hadn't felt like such a lost little sissy since the seventh grade.

In the face of all this gay male camaraderie—the high-fives, for example, that these guys executed flawlessly—I could not find the balls to say no to the communal drug of choice. Unfortunately, I had sworn off drugs 10 days earlier. For the first time in 17 years I was clean. In the process, anyway.

The man I loved most in the world—he was not clean. Dedicated pothead. Just what I was trying to get away from. But damn, the man oozed everything I ever desired, inside and out. His clothes were post-Armageddon cool, his apartment was furnished in reconstructed hardware, his pet tarantula ate crickets while we fucked in a drawbridge bed *he had built* with his own two hands. The bed was a real piece of work. He had outfitted it with chains, cuffs, leather curtains, plus an overhead pole that held a hundred cock rings of every size and material, style and configuration known to man. And his eyes—his big brown eyes—reminded me of all those corny songs about letting your love light shine on down.

When he turned those eyes toward me, all moist and wrecked and sad, I wanted to lay myself right in the middle of traffic for him. (You know, to show him how *sincere* my love was.) I wanted to take him inside, no matter what the cost. I wanted something of him to become me. Those molecules that had been in his lungs, I inhaled them. Molecules that had been part of his tongue, his spit, the lining of his mouth, I needed them to be in me. I swallowed as much as I could. Pink cloud...blue Heaven...Shangri-la: A kiss from him made everything else seem dim and lifeless. The sweat on his balls I licked as single-mindedly as any boy with ice cream.

I loved him so much, I wanted to be straight—as in not, uh, stoned—in order to drink him in undiluted. His smell was the only drug I wanted. When he left a shirt over at my house, I went crazy for it. The armpits, my God. His B.O. was sizzling bacon, newly cut grass, horse sweat, and the Okeefenokee Swamp all rolled into one. I sniffed that thing in the morning, snorted it at noon, and dragged it around all night. Getting dizzy, I realized I had to space out my inhalations. The most righteous ganja in Jamaica could not do for me what that one stinky T-shirt did.

OK, he was a black man. Some powerful fucking African-American pheromones rose up out of his pores; no one else had ever sent me into hyperdrive like Marcus did. (There, I said it, I used his name. A little piece of my heart just splintered off and became dust in the wind. Big sigh. Ancient stab of pain. I hope you're happy. I hope he's happy.)

Hell, I hope he's still alive.

And he wanted me to drop acid.

He rode his motorcycle, with me on the back, for four ball-tingling hours of winding back roads, so we could stay up all night and watch the stars rotate. Not to mention roasting the pig and telling jokes around the campfire.

So, I stuck out my tongue. Beautiful boy said a tender benediction. Then, ever so gently, the merest whisper of a squeeze on the syringe, a drop, a single drop...oops, unexpected stream, ha ha. Beauty snapped my jaw shut for me, and his eyes told me to *swallow*.

He positively radiated laughter, mischief, and daring, this black-haired German 18-year-old. Creamy skin, sinfully cherry lips, huge noble nose, long gangly arms, and solid "carve me up for Thanksgiving" thighs. Looking at him for the first time, I thought, *Jesus Christ, there's a young man I would leave Marcus for.*

So much for my faithful undying love.

Anyway, I did what his eyes told me to do.

I swallowed.

(I swallowed everything that came from these two guys. Call me a sucker: At an age when I should have known better, I was still falling for beautiful, funny, smart, fearless guys with broad backs and big dicks. Go figure.)

At first it was all right. We chopped vegetables, gathered wood, made two fires, and cooked shish kebabs in a friendly chaotic commotion. Lots of flirtation and hustle-bustle. Dinner started out normally enough—then chewing became really weird, really fast. People's eyes got intense, questioning, unnerved. Laughter erupted for no reason. Phrases and half-sentences hovered around the edges of making sense. An unreasonable amount of face-touching ensued.

We were coming on like gangbusters.

They were dealing.

In lieu of digging a pit, our host had built the pig-roasting fire in an old-fashioned bathtub on cat-feet. The pig, wrapped in massive amounts of foil, was placed on a rack atop the tub. These guys could drink a quart of liquid LSD and still figure out an original and fabulous way to cook tomorrow's brunch.

My focus zeroed in on the question: What was inside and what was outside? The bite of bell pepper at the end of my fork: Was that outside me, until I ate it? But then if it became me, in my stomach, through digestion, if it became me, what about the fiber part that would come out of me again the next day? Food became me, but only for a while; that didn't make sense. Where was the boundary? The air that I was breathing. The dying sunlight. Ooh, the sunset. Was that inside me, or outside?

Trip-*ping*. On and on, the flow of thoughts, the attempt to figure out this infinitely tangled web of cause and effect. Then giving up and giving in to hysterical laughter at God knows what. I think one moment was when a squirrel watched one of the guys stick his hand into his jeans and scratch his nuts. (But that could have been before, hell, it could have been the next day, this is all from memory, so—you know—grains of salt, right, enough of them to fill the Dead Sea.) Anyway, liftoff accomplished.

People wandered off. Someone got into cleanup duty, and I mean, got *in* to it. Next thing you knew, we were sitting around the campfire, in the dark, like a real tribe. Peering into that fire as if it were the most vital and significant thing on Earth.

Fifteen of us bantered. I had devolved into a member of some speechless species. Marcus hugged me now and then, rubbed my back, tousled my hair. I knew he wanted me to join in, but it was beyond me. I needed to pee, and I didn't know...how to anymore...or where I should go...or what to do at all. Five hundred trees in every direction, but I didn't know where I should go.

After about ten thousand hours of being the odd man out, I finally spoke.

"I have to pee," I muttered to Marcus.

Of course they all heard. It got quiet as death.

What was I, 8?

"So, go." This was the love of my life being helpful.

"Where?"

Falling, falling, I knew I was falling into depths of idiocy, but I couldn't find anything to hold onto.

"So long as you don't piss on the fire or in the tent, you can go pretty much anywhere."

The fire twisted with his words. The logs contorted. The flames licked out and turned to evil in front of my eyes.

This was the Holocaust. Those were human skulls in the fire. Women. Babies. Burning, dead, but still screaming. Still in pain. Begging for release. Begging for the waters of life to cool their suffering. If only I were a man...if only I would piss on the fire for them, for their lives, for their deliverance from hell.

Marcus told me not to pee on the fire.

But it was within me, golden liquid, the answer to all their prayers.

My urine could finally do some *good*. It would be a symbol. It would soothe their burns and put out the cause of Evil and Affliction. It would change the meaning of Final Solution forever.

Marcus had firmly told me not to.

That might have been a challenge, though.

Maybe he was testing me, to see if I would do the Right Thing in spite of what he said.

I was so confused. I wasn't sure if I could remember how to stand up.

So I held it in.

The banter had come full circle, back to Dumbfuck the dog. He was just a stupid puppy, they smirked. 'Cause his balls were so puny. No balls whatsoever, they laughed and agreed. Dumbfuck was old enough to be a fully grown adult, but his puny little balls had never dropped. So he was destined to be Dumbfuck the puppy all his years.

Of course I knew they were talking about me.

I have always been sensitive about the size of my balls. Even Marcus, usually the ultimate gentleman, had remarked on them: "You got the smallest balls I've ever seen."

Thank God he had the grace to add: "I don't know how you manage to come so much."

They were talking about me in code. Marcus was the Big Daddy of the group, and his friends couldn't talk *out loud* about what a loser he had brought with him to this pig roast. So they talked about Dumbfuck, the ball-less moron. Dumbfuck had a one-inch dick, but that didn't matter, because he couldn't fuck anyway. Too skinny, too nervous, two balls short. An eating, napping, shedding, shitting waste of space.

"It's up to the new guy to do it."

Wait, did someone really say that? Was that inside my head or did it come from out there, from one of them?

"It's up to the new guy to do the right thing."

The Holocaust burned on. The tribe was castrating me in front of the man I loved most in the world (not to mention the most beautiful boy in the world). I had to do something. Anything.

"It's up to the new guy to start the orgy."

What the fuck? That couldn't be right. No way these guys would remove my balls with one breath and demand that I jump-start a group sex scene with the next.

Real words or imagined, inside or outside, it hardly mattered, with boundaries so thoroughly collapsed. I was a spectacular failure either way. Spectacular in a pathetic kind of way.

Marcus leaned into me.

"We're trying to send you a message."

Ha! Those were real words. A message, coded, from outside.

All of a sudden, I understood.

They were *aliens*. All these guys hailed from a superdistant planet. That's how they could all speak and be so cool and know what was going on. Of course! It all made sense. This was a test. To see if a human could break the code.

"I wish I were a robot."

Omigod, those words were real too, and they had come from my mouth. It spoke!

The aliens gawked as if the fire had turned into a waterfall, only they were staring at me now.

"So," my mouth continued, "I could have an adapter in my back...side."

Dumbfuck the ball-less wonder dog chose this moment to yip at the moon.

"Then I could get hooked up."

Apparently, no words on Earth could have been more embarrassing for the aliens to hear. They turned away. They gave each other significant looks. The silence that followed was this terrible tangible thing and it made my last remaining one inch shrivel up and die.

Dumbfuck slunk away, totally whipped.

The Experiment from Outer Space had concluded. Humans were hopeless. Useless.

Eat, sleep, and shit: That's all I was good for.

And dying.

I was dying to take a piss and—POW—the next heartbeat was suddenly too late. I jumped up and grabbed at my fly, but the piss was already spreading through my jeans. When I did get my dick out, the flow increased tenfold and shot through the air, hitting—yes—the fire, but also the *aliens*. A sizzling sound filled the air as part of my urine jet stream hit the burning wood and the red-hot embers. Shouts flew around as one guy after another got splashed in the face, all over the hair, on jackets and boots and blue jeans. My dick did its best imitation of a fire hose completely out of control. Shooting and spraying in 10 directions at once, while the rest of my body did this odd little dance, squirming, high-stepping, leaping, all limbs and parts with minds of their own.

What a show.

The grand finale for the worst trip of my life.

Wait!

It hadn't happened yet. Out there. In the real world.

That image had been inside my head. There was still time. I could still do something right, even if it was to just go piss in the woods.

I got up as awkwardly as any robot ever had. Stiffly, weirdly, containing, still containing, all focus on containing, not pissing yet, not pissing my pants, no, not yet, one step, one foot further, another step, continuing to contain, I made it to a tree, to the other side of the tree, and whipped my dick out as if I knew what I was doing.

And pissed.

Ah-h-h. Amazing! Success.

Whew. Just as I was shaking the last few drops off—with my eyes closed because both the world and my pecker were too strange to look at—Marcus plunged his tongue in my mouth. I coughed on his lips. Then hiccuped, while fumbling around to button up my jeans. At this point, I didn't know whether to shit or wind my watch.

He picked me up. Marcus took me in his arms and carried me to his tent.

That man always did know how to sweep me off my feet. His follow-through usually fell short, but this time he let me down softly, and safely, on our sleeping bag.

I fell in love all over again. Marcus could break promises left and right, never showing up when he said he would, always refraining from any real communication, but damn, he came through in the crunch.

It lasted for only a moment, though.

He went to town on my nipples before I knew my ass from my elbow. He went down on my dick and started sliding fingers up my butt.

Another time, I would have been thrilled.

He slapped my cock on his cheeks, he polished the head with his amazing tongue, he grabbed and stroked and pumped that thing like a professional football player turned hooker.

My cock had about as much chance of getting hard as a recently salted garden slug.

There was the acid, of course. There was also my psychic castration in front of all the guys. Plus, my failure to do anything about the Holocaust. All in all, I felt cosmically unsexy.

Furthermore, I had been wearing one of Marcus's cock rings for about 12 hours now—a sensation I was not used to and found not only uncomfortable but absolutely deadening to my senses.

My mouth had dried up to such an extent that I didn't have enough spit to speak, let alone suck dick. I tried to get into the moment, thought I could at least lick his beautiful black butt. Even Marcus couldn't lie still for that though; it must have felt like I was brushing his asshole with sandpaper.

He shrugged me off. I was secretly relieved.

We both gave up.

He sighed. I died a little.

Eventually, Marcus started snoring. I wanted to cry.

It was over.

We might eat the pig tomorrow morning—real queers' brunch in the wilderness—we might hold hands, get on his bike and travel together, we might be able to make love a few more times, but it was over.

Well. My goal for that weekend had been to find out whether Marcus and I could truly be lovers. I had my answer, just not the one I wanted.

While Marcus snoozed his way through the night, my mind raced with a million and one realizations, the one being that I would never sleep again.

In the morning, which came in spite of all my fears, the rebel queers had become a bunch of washed-up, wrung-out, raggedy-ass rejects, with croaking voices like Tallulah Bankhead's. A few of the guys tried to crack wise, others barked a mirthless laughter. No one could look in anyone else's eyes for more than two seconds.

Half the pig was incinerated, the other half cooked to perfection. We ate what we could, then filled up on sticky buns.

The guys, though—these tough motherfucking fags—did in fact turn out to be aliens, even in the light of day. Nothing else could have explained, to my mind, their decision to drop more acid and go climb a cliff.

Not me.

Not a chance in hell.

I was not going to do more acid. Not going to climb any goddamn cliff. Didn't care what the view of the ocean would be. Didn't care that this was actually the secret double-handshake bonding climax of the Gay Men's Motorcycle Run and Pig Roast weekend in the woods.

They did it all, though. They brought out the syringe, stuck out their tongues, laced up their boots and took off in a flurry of activity that left me feeling like a tree stump.

Except for one.

One other guy declined the acid and stayed behind.

The most beautiful boy in the world.

Ten minutes after the gang split, we were playing pigbones in a bathtub.

He took a vertebra. I got some other damn ham bone. We were like kids with toy jet fighters in our hot little fists.

"Red 5: I'm going in."

"Look at the size of that thing!"

"Cut the chatter, Gold 2."

"Luke, pull out!"

"I'm a little cooked, but I'm all right."

"I've got one on my tail."

"Cover me, Porkins."

"They came from behind!"

"A-a-i-i-e-e."

We reenacted the entire *Star Wars* dogfight. We had Zorrolike duels in the dust while the sun rose in the sky and the day became white with joy.

He knew the names of all the bones. Singing "the tibia's connected to the femur," this playful and gorgeous young man took me on a tour of a pig's skeletal structure. He showed me how all these bones fit together.

Zephyr. He wanted me to call him Zephyr. And he wanted my phone number in the city. He kept hugging me too.

When the cliff-climbers got back, they were horrified at our faces. Do you guys know, they asked, you have the ashes of a cremated pig all over you?

It seemed disgusting and unsanitary, now that they mentioned it. By the time we washed up, the afternoon had turned gray.

The only other thing I remember about that weekend was Marcus coming back from town after putting gas in his motorcycle. He told us that the young stud-mechanic had squatted down, checking out the customized 1100 Kawasaki and saying to Marcus that he would do anything for a ride.

Our own ride back to San Francisco was less of a sex fantasy. We were both quiet. The same miles and roads that had been so stimulating two days ago seemed just ball-busting this time.

Marcus dropped me off and that was about it. He stopped calling, stopped showing up at my door. The love light did not shine out of his eyes whenever I managed to find him at one of the South of Market bars. I spent whole days staring at the walls of my apartment, smoking one cigarette after another.

I kept thinking if things didn't get better, somehow, I would do it, tomorrow. I would take a razor blade with me into the shower. I would take a long walk out to the Golden Gate Bridge. I would start collecting pills and dry cleaner bags. Thus began my Summer of Suicidal Ideation.

Then out of the blue, Zephyr popped back into my life.

"Hi, Greg! Guess where I'm calling from. What? No, that's just my roommate's harpsichord. Butch, huh? Anyway, I want to go dancing. Come on, it'll be great. How about the End Up?"

So again we met under the stars, this time out on the patio at the End Up. We didn't do much dancing.

I asked him back to my apartment, but just for conversation. Till then I hadn't talked to anybody about what had happened up in Mendocino.

Much to my surprise, he hugged me, kissed me, and rolled us into bed almost the minute we got in the door.

"I don't know if I can do this," I started.

"What's up?"

"It's just...that pig roast where I met you...I feel like...it was such a horrible experience."

"Got that right," he agreed. "Those guys couldn't cook a breakfast steak, let alone a whole pig."

"No, I mean the campfire, and everybody else talking...."

"I know. All those stupid jokes about Morgan Fairchild; I couldn't get into it at all."

"But, it was worse than that for me. I had this hideous, awful trip."

"You did? Aw, come here."

He held me with equal parts of tender nurturing and lust.

"That was one fucked up weekend for both of us," he added.

"It was?"

"Yeah. The only fun part was playing pigbones in a bathtub with you. If you really want to talk about it, I guess that'd be OK. But the thing is, I'm going to start crying if I think about how those creeps treated me like a piece of meat after you and what's-his-name took off."

Mind bombs galore went off in my head.

"The only fun part...?"

"Those creeps...?"

"*What's-his-name...?!*"

We did cry that night, later. We confided our sexual histories, our STDs, and our psychic scars. We sobbed in each other's arms, but we laughed just as hard, and we took turns fucking each other till morning.

That night, it felt as if Zephyr handed me back my balls. Not on a platter, thank God, but on the tip of his tongue. With shared pain and salty tears and sweaty lust and cascades of laughter. We bonded like mad, all right. He came at me with so much love, all my bones seemed to reconnect. My soiled, wrecked, old heart flooded back to life, and the flow of blood carried with it the memory of where we came from.

Kathe Izzo

THE BLACK HAND

I promise everything. I promise every part of myself and I mean it.

I count over the years each time, from one thing to the next, sometimes the same things, sometimes new things, counting forward and backward, and sometimes there is a year missing. I count over my lovers too, with years overlapping, years overlapping with jobs, where I slept in the house, or whether I lived somewhere else. I can never remember, no matter how many times I have counted, how many years there are between things, how long I have lived in this town, how many years ago I left my husband. Sometimes I don't even trust the ages of my children; I think there must be an extra year in there, I have to count from season to season, from event to event, sometimes several times in one day. I know it was four years ago this May I met her, well, it was April 26 when I had my reading at the library, but we didn't even meet eyes that day, really. I saw her in her black raincoat and thought, *Finally there are some more interesting women in town*, but I left right after I read because I felt like the straight girl, which I guess I was. And then it was May, a few weeks later, when I celebrated my ninth wedding anniversary at Franco's and I wore these weird bell-bottoms and a lace shirt my husband had given me that day. I found out later that her friend—who had been the bartender that night—called her and told her I was there, and she came and sat at the bar, sat close enough to hear our conversation. I didn't even see her, I don't remember her there, but later she told me things that were said and how she saw me that night, not yet knowing me or my situation, except for what she had heard in town. Sometime after that I smiled at her in the post office and she came right over, asked me for a copy of my book. Could I bring it to the hair salon where she worked? After that I seemed to run into her every day. A couple of weeks later, two days after her birthday, I left my marriage, not for her although I know it doesn't seem that way, I know she doesn't believe that and neither does half the town. I walked away and never went back—not really—except for an occasional roof and for protection from myself.

I remember her and I count the ways: the bad way, the fucking way, the skin way. A few tender moments and then I see her, walking down the hallway at Orleans district court with T, her AA sponsor, after our restraining order hearing, just like in the movies, a silhouette against the dim light, her back, the swagger, T's hulking shape advising her, *consigliere*. I'm standing there with my therapist, whose name, no shit, is Blossom (it was a nickname her husband, the reverend, had given her), who is also, no shit, holding her knitting in a little bag. Don't ask me how we got hooked up, my shrink and I; this kind of famous dyke-poet-idol of mine recommended her. Blossom was like the post-trau-matic-stress-incest enforcer of the outer cape, we beat the pillows with a tennis racket and screamed, or at least I did, sometimes, if I could get her to leave. I hated it when she watched. She told me later she watched me stare down the hallway that morning, and could tell how much I loved Lita right then and would never forget it, but she couldn't have possibly known what was really going on. There is no way a Laura Ashley girl like her, no matter what tricks she had cooking up for the reverend, could have possibly known what was going down between a housewife-mother of three in a short skirt and a girl who looked like Al Pacino with a few pounds. Not when he was young and fresh but at the end of Godfather II when he was tired, after he gave the order to kill Fredo, his weaker brother—actually his older brother—you know after the big forgiveness scene at their mother's funeral? He doesn't have Fredo killed then, at the funeral, but a couple of days later, on a cloudy silent afternoon, while Fredo is fishing, in the middle of the lake, saying the Hail Mary.

I wouldn't talk to her there, in the court, when I had my chance. When they asked me whether I wanted to renew the order I said yes, indefinitely, even though I was sweating and had a hard time standing one inch away from her. I was not afraid; I kept my eyes on her hands, her fingers holding on to the edge of judge's desk. She had an order against me as well so I hadn't been able to call her either, couldn't change my mind if I wanted to, had no choice unless I gave up the whole thing. He had called us up to the front of the room, because we were two girls, I guess. All the other cases had read from the back, speaking into a microphone so everyone could hear. We stood up close and spoke in low tones. I looked at her only once but she was looking straight ahead. She had those doe eyes that wrapped all the way around her face, so I knew she could see me. I sent her a single rose in a bud vase the next day. Sent it to the hair salon where she worked. Sent it anonymously and made them swear they wouldn't tell my name. The next morning the police were at the door. The sergeant, to be exact. I lied, I said I was set up. Why would I do something like that, she's sick, she's dangerous, everybody in town knows, someone's just trying to start something, and the sergeant looks me in the eye and says this is serious, if you sent the flower you are breaking the law.

You know, the way she was—well, the skin way anyway—it's not what you might think, not for a rough girl like her. It's not like the bad way or the fucking way. I don't mean skin against skin, or broken skin. It's more about real skin, the kind that covers your bones, and our skins were not that different. She had buttery dark skin like my grandmother. We were both Italian. I can see it now, the skin around her eyes. I always thought how beautiful it would be when she grew older, softer over time: smooth, oily skin on the palms of her hands, soft for a butch girl, a welder. Her hands...I can't believe myself, even now creaming over those hands, those fucking hands. Bringing my hand to her lips in the car, on the street, fingers dialing the phone over and over in the middle of the night, getting a busy signal, getting through to the machine, pressing the phone to her lips. "You motherfucking white piece of shit, I know what you are doing right now..." The hands on the glass of the useless locked door, knocking, shaking, breaking, "You are so stupid, so very, very stupid." Those hands around my throat, around my dog's throat, around the tube of the vacuum cleaner, against my head. Her hands, loyal to my body and I want it now, even now and now.

The source of love is not shallow; it goes down deep in the heart, as deep as our suffering.

In Lita's bathroom there was a big photo collage under glass on the wall opposite the toilet. It covered the whole wall. She had made it herself. It was full of girls, hundreds of weird pretty girls, the ones you'd expect next to a lot of ones you wouldn't. It really turned me on, brought out the competitive streak in me, checking out the bodies, the pouts, the poses. I could describe every girl to you right now in detail—that's how much time I spent in there with the door shut. Different girls at different times, you know what I mean. The girl with the big lips pressed to a black shoe. The naked girl looking over her shoulder cupping her own breast. The scraggly girl with her butt in the air.

Everything was spotless, perfect, at least in the beginning. Lita herself was well-groomed and obsessive about her personal hygiene. She couldn't understand how I could go to work without taking a shower. She felt it improved her self-esteem and performance. She was always talking like that, like out of a book she knew too well, keeping on track. She told me once how she had taught herself to have things, how she had taught herself to live in an apartment, like she had taught herself to read and write and how to swim. Like all my butch girlfriends, she swam with her head above the waves and never in dark water.

She liked me to read to her, especially poetry, things I liked, even though she often told me she didn't understand them. She loved to be read to. She talked about her career as a jewelry designer. She would walk down Newbury Street in Boston and count the women on the street wearing her earrings. She told me about the day she crashed, bottomed out, and how the police had come and broken down the door, removing her from her too expensive house, where she was found shattered, curled up on top of her beaten girlfriend. She told me how there was no furniture, just the girlfriend, the Doberman, the gray Volvo, the coke, and the Harley in the living room. She told me about the clothes, the suits, the shoes, the money. She told me about meeting married women through the personals and what they would wear when they met her in a straight bar. She told me to hurt myself, and I did.

She had all the pretty girls. Straight girls all the time, coming up in restaurants, on the street, nervous, leaning in. I gave her my life. Thank God for the kids or I might have been too queer for her; sometimes I worried about that. She had all the candles burning the night I showed up for the first time. She knew everything about me. She knew what I wanted, what I liked to do. She knew I would not leave. Not until I couldn't. It started like that game, you know, you be this and I'll be that, we're so perfect for each other, isn't it funny, we like the same things, fantasies fitting together like immaculate puzzle pieces. I think about it now and my hips move. I started everything, I somehow assumed I was in charge. I would start a story; she would lie back and smile. In the end I was always gone, gone down, dissolved into a wet crumpled mess. No one had ever been able to quite pull it off before, do the things I asked them to do, in detail, not to such effect. I had a sweet girlfriend once, with a safe word, I think it was *fur* or *cur*, but this, now, was above negotiation.

I had to call the police. I just had to. I couldn't lie to myself anymore. I knew it would give me time to breathe. Time to think, which I wasn't doing too well on my own. I called the police because I just couldn't stay away. I've never said that to anyone before but I bet 9 times out of 10, in this peculiar brand of love, that's true across the board. It's like quitting smoking; it depends on whether, in the deepest regions of your heart, you really want to quit. If you don't tell anyone then you can start smoking again at any time and no one will know you failed. If you know you're going to go back and you will hate yourself for it, you have to let people in on it, get other people involved. The whole town knew. It was winter. Everyone was waiting for one of us to get arrested.

The five axioms of forgiveness:
1. Forgiveness starts in our own hearts.
2. Forgiveness is not conditional.
3. Forgiveness of others is always superficial.
4. There is no conflict that cannot be brought to peace by forgiving oneself.
5. Every gesture of forgiveness is sufficient in its own time.

I could try to tell you that the girls saw her by accident, but I would be lying. I drove them to the salon, parked my car in front of the library, and waited. I sat in the car and let them run in, two sisters, 6 and 9, hand in hand, shaking a bag of Girl Scout cookies between them, anxious to be in the middle of something they thought was love, anxious to be in the middle of their mother's tunnel vision, to be in her vision, period; the tunnel was so small, so specific, you could hardly be in the middle, only one thing could fit at a time, everything else running on automatic by some strict internal discipline, every base covered, even better than usual, all the homework done, all the housework done really fast so there was more time to lay on the couch and think about double suicide, watch Sally Jesse, and think about real tears, real life. The girls ran back to the car, breathless. They said she was crying and I drove home and called. I knew if I talked fast enough, I could beat the revenge call to the cops. I could catch her, even though I knew those tears had been working up for weeks, way before the hearing, before the rose, lying still and quiet behind her eyelids just waiting for me, worked up before my birth, waiting for me to show up. I called. I left my oldest girl in charge. I ran over and rang the bell and she looked around as she stepped out to see if it was a scam, as if the joint was cased. She stepped toward me, I touched her, I buried into her neck and broad shoulders and it only took a second. A second to go from a world where things happen one at a time to a world of multiple fracture and division. The inside of my head was banging:

You are my family. I am tired.

I want to lie down and have no place left to go but you.
I know the truth now and when I doubt it, I know you will tell me.

You will say, "Come to me before any whisper or sob,
after any instinct to move, I will be there.
After any instinct to reach out or touch,
I will be there.
I am at the end of every reach.
I will fill the palm at the middle of every grasp."

I was on my knees. With total gratitude, I said, "Forgive me."

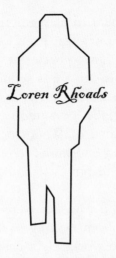

Loren Rhoads

ANARCHY IN CALAVERAS COUNTY

I'm fully aware that when the revolution comes down in the cities, the naive will be eaten for breakfast. No doubt I'm on the menu. Despite that, the process of societal change fascinates me. I was glued to the television on April 28, 1992, watching Los Angeles on fire like the opening scene of *Blade Runner*. The LA police, so quick to kick up the hornets' nest, crowded together in frightened knots. Anarchy in the streets: It was something to see.

Being naive, I expected the LA uprising would transform this country. If nothing else, history proves that social revolution comes slowly. The kind of change that's accomplished in one night of violence never lasts. There's always the assassination of the assassin, a coup to overthrow the coup. Even as technological advancement escalates in our world, people and the institutions they create evolve ever so slowly.

Barabbas appeared to be working toward something better. He'd founded Anarchy Village 13 in the Sierra foothills of Northern California. Long before the Simi Valley jurors issued their incitement to riot, Barabbas had been organizing a music festival for May Day, 1992.

My lover, Mason, had rehearsed with the duo Turbo Messiah, who planned to drive us up to the Sierras for the weekend. Either Mason could honor his commitment to play guitar with them or we could sit around and watch the country tear itself apart on TV. Too many people seemed dependent for him to back out.

Originally, I'd pushed to go. I was seduced by the idea of an anarchist music festival: "All musics welcome." I wanted to camp and explore the untamed foothills. I wanted to be exposed to new bands. Fact is, I was 5 at the time of Woodstock. I wanted to experience wilderness on acid with an enormous crowd of my peers, entertained by industrial musicians and punks. I had grand expectations for the weekend.

Friday afternoon, Turbo Messiah were late picking us up in San Francisco because they'd been waiting to see whether Glen (the bass player) would be called to work. He'd been up half the night filming the rioting as a freelance cameraman for channel 4. Someone snuck up on his blind side and punched his head into the camera. He wasn't so much angry with the coward who hit him as at the reporter supposedly watching his back. His head felt a little fuzzy, but he was glad to be getting away for the weekend.

Six of us formed a caravan. John of Turbo Messiah and his wife Sheila would drive up in a rental truck packed with tents, coolers, and drums. Glen, Mason, our friend Ron, and I would follow in our van. We brought water and beer and enough chemicals to pass the time. Necessities.

The festival flyer promised level campsites and a pit toilet. I have to admit I was pretty curious to see an actual anarchist commune. AV13 had 40 acres of wilderness, complete with trout stream and outdoor stage. I wondered what kind of people lived there. Who would abandon civilization, as screwed-up as it is, to live cut-off from everything? They didn't even have a telephone! I couldn't conceive of politics devoid of society. What did these anarchists hope to accomplish secluded in the mountains?

It was past 10 o'clock and fully dark when we finally reached the anarchist "ranch." After 20 minutes of dirt driveway twisting past sheer drop-offs, we were as close to the middle of nowhere as I'd ever been. Darkness engulfed the festival site. A mere handful of people huddled around a single campfire.

Turned out there was no commune. Barabbas lived alone in a house

134

trailer with his dog Boris Badenov. Grizzled and wild-eyed in the fire-light, Barabbas conversed like anyone living in exile. Dressed in black from Stetson and bandanna to jeans and combat boots, his age was difficult to guess. He hunched over on a black staff—walking like an old man, Sheila observed. I found out later that he suffered from lupus.

Barabbas spoke in the imperial "we": "We would like to build a recording studio up here, with a dormitory where bands could stay while they record." At the time, however, AV13 had no electricity. Barabbas hoped to recruit malcontents to live on the property in exchange for their help in improving the place. Living there meant abiding by his rules: "No sexism. No racism. No bigotry will be tolerated. No fighting. If you drug, you do *not* drive." (Having seen the roads, I guessed you wouldn't get far.)

Of course he had rules, John pointed out, like every anarchist. Given the codification, I'd expected a big gathering. Instead, the other three people represented, in varying combinations, the two other bands to play Saturday night. Barabbas expected two punk bands from Reno and an industrial band from Sacramento. One band might be bringing a P.A. The whole P.A. thing seemed ridiculous. Why did the music need to be loud? To scare the bears? The air was so clear that sound traveled perfectly.

Before we'd unpacked the rental truck, Barabbas bragged that when he was in jail down in LA, the Bloods believed he was Charlie Manson's little brother. The nickname pleased him. He said he used to wear a goatee and shave his head. With his eyes twinkling in the fire-light, I could see the resemblance.

When Ron returned from reconnoitering the camping area, I whispered to him about "Charlie Manson's little brother." He reported that earlier Barabbas had said, "This thing in the cities, this race riot, it's just like *Helter Skelter,* man."

I stared around into the night. Ron muttered, "I almost expect the Family to come out of the woods."

Yikes. Calaveras County, site of AV13, previously played home to Leonard Lake and Charles Ng, two antisocial boys who killed everyone that dropped by: neighbors, people lured by fake for-sale ads, buddies, and coworkers. No one knows for certain how many bodies they scattered across the Sierra foothills. They might have gotten away with it if they hadn't videotaped torturing their victims. Lake offed himself in jail by swallowing cyanide. Ng was brought to trial in a cage. Who knew how many serial killers kept hunting lodges in the mountains?

I worked myself into an anxiety attack. Mason calmly pointed out that Barabbas expected other bands. Flyers had been posted on Haight Street. People knew about the event. People knew where we'd gone. Barabbas would be really stupid to kill us. He'd have to dispose of our bodies, our camping gear, and the vehicles—all in complete darkness.

When Alisa of Big City Orchestra stood up to go to bed, Barabbas warned her not to go to the trailer where she was staying alone. He added quickly, "It's not that a woman can't protect herself; it's that no one should walk around here by themselves, unless they're armed."

I'd forgotten that the flyer warned against brown bears and cougars. As we'd driven down the dirt roads, I saw a suspicious shadow, a black bear shape, but didn't tell anyone. I could have imagined it.

OK, OK. Reality check. Maybe it was the pressure of all that *space* around us, but I felt really isolated. I'd expected a weekend community in the wilderness, not two tents alone on a hillside. I'd camped in bear country before, in a truck camper with my parents. Mason had gone camping exactly twice. Ron's idea of camping was a Dead show at Laguna Seca. Lucky for us, John, Glen, and especially Sheila could cope. They insisted on locking the food in the van.

Later, cocooned in my blankets, I felt my uterus contract. Are bears among the animals that attack menstruating women? I imagined one biting through the wall of the tent, crushing my skull like an eggshell. Waiting for death, I dozed off.

Before dawn, I had to pee desperately. The morning was absolutely silent. Even the birds were sleeping. My body wouldn't stop shivering. I knew that if I got up and dressed I'd be warmer.

I considered finding the stream—it had to be downhill—to see what animals would come to drink at dawn. When I zipped the tent closed behind me, my breath fogged the air. The sky was pearlescent gray.

The area *was* incredibly beautiful. Blue lupine spilled beneath an oak not far from our tent. The bluish purple flowers spiked up beneath a blue plastic hammock like a painting.

Glen had just climbed out of the Turbo Messiah tent and was headed down the slope to the vehicles. I followed. I could get a drink since he had keys to the truck.

When I caught up with him, he was rolling a joint.

"I wonder what's going on in the world," I said, missing my morning newspaper. "I feel like we're missing everything."

"Everything's probably settled back to normal."

"Doesn't that make you sad? This could have been the turning point of American civilization."

"When was anything changed by looting?" Glen asked. He sucked fire into the joint, then handed it to me.

Changing the subject, I asked, "Do you think anyone else will come today? Maybe they're all out marching and getting arrested."

Glen shrugged. He was a man of few, usually well chosen, words. To fill the silence, I said, "It surprises me that Barabbas would want to be up here away from all the action."

"I think he just wants a place where he can walk around armed."

"What do you mean?"

"Didn't you see the pistol on his hip last night?"

"I'm glad I didn't. I was paranoid enough."

We finished the joint in silence. I realized I didn't want to wander around stoned, on the off chance that I met a bear or took a wrong step. There were 40 acres, sure, but mostly vertical and covered with poison oak. After a friend developed the worst case of blistering poison oak the Haight Street Free Clinic had ever seen, I held a healthy respect for the stuff.

I decided to go back to bed and write in my journal. I'd been awake an hour when the sun finally climbed over the eastern mountain. Birds are better than alarm clocks. They zoomed from tree to tree, singing their heads off. Why is birdsong such a symphony when it's so random?

When Sheila came out of their tent about 8, she advised us to put on bug spray first thing. The bugs were out in force.

By 9:30, the thin mountain air had warmed past 80 degrees. Powder-fine dust clung to our sweat. AV13 had no running water, not even a well. Barabbas bathed in the creek. We were welcome to try it, though he suggested we avoid getting water in our mouths. Our "citified" digestive systems might not cope with unfiltered, unchlorinated water in its natural state.

Barabbas offered us a ride. The creek was half a mile down a steep trail. I would've walked, just to see what I could see along the way, but everyone else wanted to ride.

Barabbas jump-started the jeep. Glen recorded the proceedings with his video camera. When the motor sputtered to life, Barabbas called us all to climb aboard. Sheila rode shotgun. Mason, John, Ron, and I squatted atop toolboxes in the jeep bed. Glen knelt behind the jeep to get an art shot of the expedition's beginning.

Barabbas put the jeep in reverse. It lurched back toward Glen's head. From my overview, I expected to see Glen's head crushed like a melon under the military tire. I was too horrified to move.

"Stop!" Mason and John shouted. "Stop! Stop!"

Barabbas protested that the jeep had no turning radius. We had to back up to turn around.

Ultimately someone conveyed that Glen was about to be mashed. The video footage captures the moment very well.

Glen clambered into the jeep and off we went. From the "parking lot," the creek trail dropped at a 45-degree angle. There was nothing to hold on to but the rim of the jeep bed. We bounced around like a roller coaster with no restraints. As we reached the hairpin, Barabbas warned that the transmission slipped. We rounded the curve on two wheels. The jeep wavered above the abyss—the lush green hillside below was dotted with plenty of trees to snap bones as bodies careened down. My stomach plugged my throat. I imagined the seven of us killed when the jeep rolled over, miles from a hospital or even a phone.

At the cusp of destruction, Barabbas righted the jeep and cursed its slipping gears.

Beside me, John swung his legs over the tailgate. "I've been in a jeep that's rolled," he told me very earnestly. "I won't do it again."

I grabbed hold of the tailgate myself. "I'll jump when you do," I promised. "I'm trusting you with my life, John."

Our eyes met and my resolve strengthened.

Like the best of tour guides, Barabbas said, "This is where the 'dozer went off."

"What happened?" Ron asked.

"The brakes failed when I came down to pull the truck out."

"Stop the jeep!" everyone chorused. It took some repetition to convince Barabbas. Everyone scrambled out to peer over the edge to see the bulldozer, 30 feet down the slope, with its blade braced against the trunk of a cottonwood tree.

"When you guys are ready," Barabbas called. The jeep engine idled like a purring lion.

"I'm going to walk the rest of the way," John decided.

"Me too," I said quickly.

"I can't turn around here," Barabbas pointed out. "I have to drive all the way down before going back up."

Only Ron rode down to the creek.

Building the trail must have been a Herculean task. Trees had to be felled, then the brush pulled out before the surface could be graded relatively flat. The people from whom Barabbas purchased the property had done that work.

When we reached the bottom of the hill, the creekside was like Eden. Undomesticated, unscarred by a graffiti-covered bridge or green 30-gallon trash cans, the water chattered as it crawled between flat granite slabs. Barabbas explained that the round depressions were where Miwok Indians used to grind corn.

He pointed out flat stones stacked into rudimentary fences on either side of the creek. He claimed Chinese gold prospectors had built them over a century ago. Across the creek and up the trail were remnants of a Chinese village. Barabbas called it a ghost town on his property. Abandoned pails and other "gold-seeking equipment" lay all over. I wished I'd dressed for exploration—boots against snakes and jeans against the poison oak. Next time.

On the sandy bottom of the creek, a box turtle mimicked a rock. John reached in to pick him up. In another pool lurked a diamond-shaped beetle. Eggs like freshwater pearls covered its back. Legs outstretched, the beetle wasn't as big as my palm. Still, she was largest bug I'd seen outside the zoo. I couldn't bring myself to actually bathe with her.

After we hiked back up to the only level area, Ron and I voted not to trip. Too many elements were uncontrolled. We got very high instead. The pot hit me right between the eyes. I'd forgotten how pleasant it could be to sit around a campfire, high, with the breeze against my bare arms. We roasted corn in the coals and burned chicken on the grill.

Alan and Das of Nux Vomica and Big City Orchestra hung a variety of metal above the junk plywood stage. They banged around a little, joined by Mason, John, and Glen: five men with drumsticks flailing. Barabbas declared, "*That* is the music of the apocalypse. Those effete musicians in the cities will have to adapt their music when the world ends."

I suspected the music of the apocalypse would sound more like crickets and birdsong, but I held my tongue.

Barabbas declaimed about this "event." No one had shown up but the nine of us. Still, he saw this as an anarchic occasion, a challenge to his neighbors. I worried about the cops arresting us for the noise. The police had visited AV13 twice before, looking for a pot farm or a speed lab. Barabbas believed they were threatened by his anarchism. I suspected they were keeping an eye out for the next Leonard Lake. I threw the acid out. There wasn't much of it, but it was in separate wrappers. They could claim it had been divided for sale.

With an almost sinking feeling I watched a rental truck pull in, followed by a beat-up van. It was 5 in the afternoon, and another band had finally arrived. In less than 24 hours I'd adjusted from disappointment at the size of the crowd to enjoying a retreat among friends.

The new band came over to the campfire. Barabbas struggled to explain the permutations of Trance–Turbo Messiah and Nux Vomica–Big City Orchestra.

A woman with dyed black hair asked, "This is everyone who came?"

Barabbas pointed out he was still expecting two bands from Reno, a tattoo artist, and some fire walkers.

"We thought there'd be a crowd," the spokeswoman said.

I knew how they felt, but it had been a *really* nice day. More people would have ruined it. There weren't enough chairs around the fire as it was, and Barabbas warned us not to sit on the ground because of scorpions and fire ants.

The cumulative beers caught up with me, so I withdrew to our tent to nap, serenaded by the drone of insects. I could tell the difference between bees and flies just by the pitch of their humming. Something zipped by so fast its whine Dopplered.

Inadvertently, I eavesdropped on the other band. They'd withdrawn to the hammock to discuss their options. They wanted money to cover the rental of the U-Haul and the P.A. At least some of them wanted to leave. This isn't what they expected and they didn't want to waste their time. One guy said he really admired Barabbas for living what he believed, instead of just talking about it. I admired that too. I just wished Barabbas had accomplished more than a ramshackle stage and a pit toilet. And three or five disappointed bands, depending on how you counted them.

Eventually the new band decided to leave. If they returned the truck and the P.A., they'd only be charged one day's rental, rather than for the weekend. Barabbas gave them some cash to defray the cost.

Once it got good and dark, Turbo Messiah–Trance stepped gingerly onto the plywood stage. Mason would play noise guitar, John stood behind the drums, and Glen shifted between his bass guitar and an old reel-to-reel tape player.

They had rehearsed a set list grounded in rhythm with structured mayhem over top, but that quickly became unfeasible. The uneven power provided by Barabbas's generator played hob with Mason's effects. The set devolved into unfettered waves of sound and guitar lamentation, which Barabbas dubbed "scary music." It sounded great, but clearly the men were unhappy. It was one of those cases where Mason would have to listen to the tape afterward to be at all objective.

To end their portion of the music, John pulled out a hundred feet of white PVC hose. Glen collected "every knife! I need every knife," and hacked the hose into uneven lengths. We each took one and to twirl over our heads.

"Sounds like the whirlybird UFOs are landing on my property," Barabbas said, immensely proud.

By the time Nux Vomica reached the audience participation part of their set, I was tired and chilled in my T-shirt and wool coat. Despite Barabbas's warning, I went off alone to go to sleep.

I shone my flashlight around as I climbed up to the tent, but saw only trees. I stripped off my jeans and T-shirt, pulled on thermal tights and a long-sleeved top, and burrowed into my blankets. The heavy comforter was a smothering sort of comfy. I left the tent flap folded back so I could see out. The stars looked like grains of salt scattered across velvet.

Big City Orchestra began a beautiful Tibetan-sounding acoustic piece. Crickets chirped the perfect accompaniment. It was a shame I was so tired. I wanted the peaceful moment to last.

Sleep washed over me like the sea. I fought it, opening my eyes again and again, until I was submerged.

A crash on the hillside above woke me. It sounded like a rotted log tipping over. I guess a falling tree makes noise even when you're sleeping. So much for Zen conundrums.

The crashing didn't stop. The most rational explanation was a bear scavenging for grubs. I wasn't sure bears came out at night or could see in unbroken blackness, but I didn't want to think it was human.

It surprised me that whatever it was would come so close to my tent. Should I make noise to scare it away? Scream for help like a girl? Shine my light around and maybe antagonize it? The bravest, most sensible thing, I decided, would be to go back down where the people were. Nothing would attack us en masse. I pulled my jeans over my tights, my sweater and coat over my top.

As I came down the slope, Barabbas was glaring into the woods. "Was that you?" he demanded.

"I'm glad you heard it too. What was it?"

"Could be a bear."

"That's what I was afraid of."

"Could be somebody up there stealing wood off my land."

"In complete darkness? I didn't see any lights."

"It could just be deer walking over the brush. Sounded too big for that, though. Whatever it is, it's something big."

Before I came down, Barabbas had called for John and Glen to explore with him, gun drawn as a pointer. Sheila put an end to that. Thank goodness Barabbas hadn't shot me by mistake.

Barabbas announced, "I'm usually in bed by now, so I don't hear things moving around in the woods at night. I'm going back to my trailer. Anybody who wants can come with me."

"I'm ready to go to bed," Sheila announced. "Johnny, come with me."

"I'll come too," I said.

As I tracked Mason down to say good night, I wondered if I was kissing him good night for the last time. He didn't seem concerned, so I shrugged and went back toward the bonfire. Sheila and John had gone up to the campsite without me. It wasn't far, but it was scary to climb the hill alone now.

John and Sheila were down at the outhouse. I zipped my tent closed with the flap down over the door. If a bear strolled past the tent, I did not want to see it.

Barabbas hoped for a second show on Sunday morning, but the day was already growing hot as we ate breakfast. We were eager to go home to shower. I wore a layer of bug spray, a layer of sunscreen, a coating of orange dust, more bug repellent, powdered down with more dirt. It would be worth braving a revolution in order to wash. I was eager to get home and switch on CNN to find out what was happening in the world.

While we broke camp, a white RV pulled into the clearing. Parking that big old thing in the limited flat space was a major accomplishment. The tattoo artist had finally arrived.

Tara Jepsen

SWIMMING WITH THE DOLPHINS

Friday I picked up my friends Fern and Judy to head up to a yoga retreat held at a hot spring in Northern California. The retreat was being led by a yoga instructor–psychic healer woman I had gone to for massage and energy work. Energy work is the business of taking a broom to a person's aura and various other manners of spiritual damage control. This woman, Shakti, often tells me I'm having trouble digesting my food because I can't "digest" the world around me. The body-heart-mind connection: That's her specialty. The retreat, which was called the Inner Dolphin Retreat because of the emphasis on fluidity of thought and feeling, promised lots of yoga and relaxing in the healing waters of the hot springs. There were workshops planned— sketching your inner child, for example—that I hoped we would never get around to. The weekend would be fueled by vegan meals, which made me worry that I would spend the weekend never quite full and bedeviled by with digestive trouble. But I kept my hopes high, as I had attended a similar retreat the year before and hadn't felt particularly emotionally destroyed by it.

We drove into the quaint city of Middletown, oddly enough the town where my dad moved to find himself after my parents divorced.

We navigated our way into the country over rutted dirt roads and final-ly through the guarded gate of Heavenly Hot Springs. The hippie guy in the tiny brown wooden booth had to take our names and license plate number. We found our way to the designated lodge and parked among BMWs, Volkswagen buses, and a mixed salad of other vehicles.

We grabbed our sleeping bags and satchels and headed up a little green hill to the lodge. This was no Elks Lodge—it was more of a groovy Northern California job with high, angular ceilings and beige carpeting and lots of windows and sliding doors to an outdoor seating area that got plenty of sun. We dropped all our stuff in a corner on top of everyone else's and joined the opening circle that was just beginning. Everyone sat cross-legged on the thick carpeting, and pillows were available for those concerned with their posture. We were instructed to pass around a big femur-looking bone and introduce ourselves as we received the bone. Each person would hold the bone in his or her lap, pause thoughtfully, look everyone in the face with that "finally relaxed after my crazy life" gaze with wide eyes and closed-lip smiles, then say their name and why they came to the Dolphin workshop. Everyone had deep reasons for coming, punctuated by white-light buzzwords. "I want to learn to be more mindful of [insert something to revere here]. I just feel very out of touch with myself and I want to get more centered and grounded." Some people were working on their relationships, and most had escaped fast-paced, stressful daily lives to get more in touch with their spirituality. I introduced myself, having to hold back from explaining that I did not name myself Tara after the goddess and my parents never thought about Buddhism when they named me. I said I was trying to be "open" to my experience that weekend, secretly pat-ting myself on the back for making a comment both accessible to this group and true to my feelings.

Following the opening circle was an invocation ritual. I'm not sure who or what exactly we were invoking but it must have been spiritual-ly beneficial or otherwise crucial to an enlightening weekend. Incense and candles burned on a wooden altar in the middle of the circle while some guys hovering on the periphery played their didgeridoos to warm up the psychic air. The musicians all looked like nice guys who were dorks in high school. Shakti led everyone chanting in a language I did-n't understand but guessed to be Sanskrit because that's the language these new age people seem to use most often. Once our voices and the music got a little energy roiling in the room Shakti had four specially chosen people invoke each of the elements: earth, air, fire, and water. She told us these people had deep connections to their respective elements. So each person did a dance that basically involved a lot of spinning around.

I could identify Shakti's boyfriend right away. She always had a boyfriend around—she did at the last retreat I attended as well. That's proof enough, plus she told me attachment is her "jewel," meaning it is the personality trait that can hurt her or make her strong. Mine is anger.

Anyway, I knew her beau was the hippie named Onelove, dressed in a green shirt and green skirt—which, I found out later, helped him to focus on his heart chakra. His element was water. He swirled about, dipping his fingers in a little handmade wooden bowl of water and flicking droplets in the air in what appeared to be a low-rent mimicry of a dance Stevie Nicks does very well. Right away I could tell he was a Pisces. He had long yellow hair and a beard and that floaty look in his eyes of someone nonverbally telling you they are tuned into a different and more spiritually elevated frequency. That look makes me feel violent.

Fern, Judy, and I knew there would be few dykes there besides us, if any at all. These retreats can be appallingly homogeneous in the realms of race, sexuality, age, spiritual beliefs, and eating habits. But this time around it turned out there were two lesbians at the retreat. After an initial excited moment, I realized I didn't feel any connection with them; they seemed like everyone else, so acceptable and not weird or a step off any flag.

After the long and elaborate opening ceremony, it was dinnertime. I hadn't eaten for several hours so I was looking forward to the food, even if it was vegan. Turns out the macrobiotic cook only made miso soup because she said it was too late to eat much. I got the idea she just started too late to make anything decent. The soup was watery with the vague flavor of miso and some vegetables. How could she leave us this way? I did notice that the cook was a cute, natural-looking number who could really work the librarian-to-sexy-lady seduction angle if she wanted to, so I didn't completely give up on her. I finished eating with a disappointed feeling in my stomach, which I knew only felt full because it was sloshing with broth I would pee out soon enough.

A movement session was planned for after dinner. I dreaded the movement thing because I knew it would be hokey and require me to express my feelings in an embarrassing way. The crowd always seems to have a feeling of "I would *never* do this in my regular life but I'm here at a retreat with loving and supportive people so, what the hey! I'll shed my corporate America 'tude and let it all hang out here in the trees." It all seems so insincere. I stuffed down my feelings of being cheated by dinner and tried to roll with it. Maybe I was just too cynical and I should give in to this activity that seemed cheesy but was really another effective way to keep the body healthy. Ugh. The whole group congregated in the back of the main lodge room while Shakti stood up front. She bellowed, "Sometimes I'm walking around feeling on top of the world and then suddenly I feel angry! Walk *angry!*" She stomped around the room with reckless abandon, Iron John at Drama Club.

One by one the emotionally available masses crossed the floor shooting their pent-up anger out of their heavy feet. I tried to throw my hat in the ring. I made fists and poofed my socked feet against the ground. I couldn't bring myself to hunker my butt down in the gorilla-caveman style others were using so I just heaved across the floor, homo sapiens erect, trying to channel my deep-seated anger but finding only disenchantment with these bizarre people. I couldn't believe how stupid the whole thing felt, and I've done plenty of weird shit in therapy.

When everyone had gone one angry lap, Shakti was back at the front of the room. She yelled, "Sometimes I'm just so *busy!*" She bustled around the room like Melanie Griffith in *Working Girl,* and that one was easy for me. Busy, no problem. I can access that feeling.

At the announcement of each new emotion there would be a thrilled whoop from the crowd of comfortably clad retreatgoers. Permission was granted to feel those nasty, oppressive emotions everyone bottled up inside, and it was time to let 'er rip. I wondered whether we would all rent pornos later to let off a little steam. The crescendo of emotions felt like a soccer game. Shakti went on and on through several emotions and then I left. I snuck out to the kitchen and slumped down against the wall crying, like Molly Ringwald after the dance in *Sixteen Candles.* How annoying to be in a room of people who want to have a big pillow fight to deal with our troubles together. I didn't come to the woods to hunker down with a bunch of floaty hosers and reveal my innermost self. I just wanted water, yoga, and the woods. I had my own problems, traumas—whatever—and this gathering felt wrong. Shakti came in the kitchen and asked me what the deal was and all I could tell her was that the whole thing felt terrible and I didn't belong there and I needed to leave. I packed my stuff for the first time that weekend. It was late and she implored me to stay so I did; I figured I could always leave in the morning.

Shakti asked whether there was anyone I would allow to be with me in my broken-down state so I named my two pals. We got to leave the group activity because of my obvious trauma. We went for a walk up a hill in the clear, sharp dark. Fortunately my friends and I had the foresight to bring some chocolate bars so a little justice could occur after that useless meal. The night sky was incredible at Heavenly Hot Springs because there were no lights around. All the space above you is big and deep blue and tall; majestic trees surrounded you. The air is cool and clean and being alive feels like the most gracefully insane gift.

As we walked up over the rutted dirt road I thought about how the land we stood on was historical, sacred Native land, stolen from its original inhabitants, and how now the people running Heavenly used this fact to promote their facilities. *This is sacred Indian land,* they said to visitors, like any voyeur could just suck up the magic juices by standing there or while puttering around in the hot tubs. Most land in this country has been stolen or disgraced in some way, but it struck me that mission command at Heavenly purported to be doing the best, most empathetic work with the land. And really, if they meant that, I couldn't believe that charging admission to a hot springs where people could park their fancy cars and fuck in the tubs was the most enlightened scenario. And there I was, mucking through it all, wondering who ran the place and whether there was any justice where there appeared to be none.

After our walk we went to the hot springs to soak. I had to ignore the people fucking in the pool to avoid getting completely grossed out. Many men are brazenly lecherous, staring and inventing reasons to talk to ladies right there while you're hanging out naked. You enter the pool in the buff and there are all these shining faces watching you as though you were the star at a debutante ball. I didn't look at anyone. I floated

Fern around for a while—meaning she lay on her back and I supported her and moved her around the pool—which was a wonderful experience. You close your eyes and completely lose your sense of space and
distance while the perfectly warm water washes over your naked body.
The procedure is related in nature to a rebirthing ritual, though it is certainly not the whole enchilada.

The water was just warm enough to be comfortable for long peri-
ods of time. Like the sweetest liquid blanket. After soaking, we walked
back to the lodge in the dark and I discovered someone had taken my
sleeping bag. The second or third time I felt ripped off in one night. I
grabbed an old bag and went outside to share a one-person tent with
Fern and Judy. I slept between the girls with watery dreams and not
much sleep or actual rest. And a fear of contracting tuberculosis.

The next morning this girl named Crystal was supposed to ring a
bell so we all knew to wake up for yoga. We didn't hear Crystal's bell.
So we stumbled into the lodge an hour and 10 minutes late, looking
like the Jeff Spiccoli yoginis from the city.

After yoga we were allowed to feed again—a bowl of fruit with oatmeal this time. And the thing was, I felt full after this. I thanked the gay
goddess for allowing my stomach to shrink in less than 24 hours. We
then had to get ready for the rebirthing ritual Shakti had planned, pretty much the main event of the weekend. A rebirthing ritual involved a
lot of heavy breathing and then Shakti crawled over you like a mother
giving birth and you were reborn. The lodge was loaded with pillows,
so everyone started building a personal rebirth nest. I arrived late to the
rebirthing kick-off so I was left with a few small pillows and my sleeping bag, sort of the jalopy to everyone else's sports coupes.

Shakti started out with a demonstration, using this girl who was such
a teacher's pet as the model. She was a quick rebirther and we were suit-
ably prepped for the event to come. Shakti told us that one of the nerdy
musician guys would be walking around didgeridooing at our bodies as
he sensed was fit. He was intuitively gifted and would know where we
needed the pain boomed out, and if we didn't want to be didgeridooed
in our private parts we should make that known right now. No one
needed to shield their loins from the horn, so we carried on.

Shakti put on some dramatic music and we all started breathing. I
think I started too fast too soon because I didn't understand how the

rebirthing was supposed to progress. After a while people started wailing and crying out and my carpal tunnel got inflamed. The pain boomer guy walked around throttling his didgeridoo at us while the speakers blared with some intense music that I think I listened to in high school. We sounded like individually packaged hounds of hell. I heard Shakti coaching different people through their rebirthing and I became resentful that my rebirth would be one of the last because Shakti didn't think much of me. I didn't say the right things to belong to this club. And what about that time she said I was too masculine for a girl (anyone who knows this finds it nearly impossible to believe)?

Onelove was cochampioning the birthing with Shakti so that each new baby would have a daddy as well as a mommy to hold them. I had many giggles over the weekend at the sex play–rebirthing terminology. Finally my turn came to shoot the tube and there I was crying again. This made me look like a good student. Shakti crawled over me and when she got to my feet she said I was stuck; she said I had to really want it. So I screamed and hollered and cried, I was really in the zone, and as I finally pulled my feet through and was reborn she said I was beautiful and then she started yelling, "*This girl needs some male energy!*" And she kept emphasizing the male energy part, which I know was because of my gayness. Not only was I too male, but I needed more men in my life to supply real maleness. Onelove was petting my head saying something caring and then this other guy, Peter, came over and took over as Team Daddy when Shakti and Onelove had to move on to the next birth. He was cradling my head in his lap and I didn't know how to ask him to leave so I just sat there and kept crying for my own damn reasons. I felt like my tear ducts had opened to the size of dinner plates. All these new age people were owning my sadness as something they had helped me find, which pissed me off. I am the sole captain of my personal grief regimen.

After everyone had been reborn, we all lay around on the floor completely spent and looking like crazed aerobicizers who had reached our collective max in someone's living room. We then rounded up the wagons for another circle. This time we passed around an eagle feather as each person shared his or her experience. God. The first few people who shared threw the feather to the next person as they finished speaking, so Onelove stopped everything and explained that he had acquired the feather when he was living on a reservation, emphasizing "reservation" to imply his authenticity and authority with this symbolic object. He then launched into a broken English attempt at a Native American accent that I can only imagine he picked up off 1950s TV. He said, "Eagle feather not touch ground. Feather sacred."

I fucking packed my bags after this circle too. I can't believe the derelict lows this retreat reached in the name of higher ground. But we went on and everyone shared their cosmic moments with the rebirthing. Contact with ancient Egyptian relatives from past lives, standard stuff like that. I swallowed my insane frustration with Onelove and told everyone about my inflamed carpal tunnel. I knew I sounded so unevolved. Mr. Fancypants Onelove told us that he felt very accepted by everyone as a daddy and how happy that made him because as a male he has been saddled with a legacy of violence and power. He told us about the men's retreats he facilitates to help his brothers deal with their anger and pain. I wondered whether he and Robert Bly had compared notes.

Onelove then got an extraserious look on his face and slowly gazed around the room, revealing that he walks down the street (dramatic pause) and oftentimes women won't even look at him. We were to see how deeply this hurt him and understand that the women's movement had now officially taken things too far. Caught up in liberation fever, we had unthinkingly alienated our allies, the sensitive guys, by looking at what we want to rather than into their kind, goddess-worshipping faces. This incensed me so much that I ceased looking at Onelove for the rest of the weekend.

Dinner was swiftly approaching, and I had signed up with my lady friends to help with prep. Sandy the macro cook turned into über-Virgo in the kitchen. She set up little stations for us to work at and as she finished her own tasks she would turn to me and say, "Tara. Try this. I have created nectar." And she would say this to me in a voice quiet and husky, intoning that we were sharing something akin to a sunrise. She went on to tell me about various colon-cleansing retreats she had attended. "You wouldn't believe what came out of me," she hummed in her special voice. "Ghosts."

Tonight's dinner was the main meal of the weekend. Everyone dressed up, the girls in sexy floral-print dresses and the guys in all fash-

ions of hippie wear. We had all been asked to do a writing exercise earlier in which we chose one element and described what we liked about
it. I thought water was my obvious choice, being a Scorpio, so I chose
fire instead. Everyone handed their little manifestos in to Shakti except
for me because I lost mine, and she kept them next to her plate while
she ate. She also kept Onelove at her side, who was eating out of two
wooden bowls he carried around with him. He would only eat out of
those bowls and use his fingers for utensils. Some homage to minimal-
ism or stepping lightly on the earth. There was no dessert after dinner—not even vegan cookies like last year. Shakti started reading everyone's papers. When she read she would replace the name of the element
with the writer's name, so that each paragraph would start with "What
I like about Steve is..." (instead of "What I like about earth is...") and
everyone delighted in their hidden ability to praise themselves. I never
found my piece of paper though I dug through mountains of sleeping
bags and canvas satchels in my vain attempt.

After dinner, Fern and I headed for the hot springs. Judy decided to
go to bed early; she was pooped from her own teary onslaught during
the rebirthing ritual. When Fern and I arrived at the tubs we nudely
descended the staircase into the water and stood by the side and took
in the warmth. Some guy hovering by Fern told her that he was a student at the watsu (which is massage in the water) school and he had to
work off some hours and could he give her a massage. She said not
right now. I noticed this other guy in glasses scoping her out.
Fortunately, this stuff didn't happen to me, for whatever reason. Fern
went off on her own and I just leaned back and had what I think is my
closest achievement of an empty mind. No one hand clapping, no tree
falling in the woods. What a wonderful and mysterious feeling.

After a while I went to sit down on the in-pool bench and I looked
over at Fern, and the guy in the glasses was talking to her. I wondered
whether I should go rescue her but then I witnessed her being willing-
ly massaged by the guy. Not Watsu, but a regular shoulder job. I looked
away and then when I checked back, I noticed a pained look on her
face and I thought, *If I didn't know any better, I would think Fern was
getting fucked.*

She floated over to me a couple minutes later and said to me in an
exhale, "Well, I just got fucked." I couldn't believe it. She spoke mat-

ter-of-factly about how weird that was and half-laughed about it. She told me the guy had been massaging her shoulders and then her tits, which really turned her on, then he moved back down her butt and next thing she knew he slid some fingers inside her and was fucking her with his hand. I laughed because it all seemed so incredible and she laughed, probably for similar and different reasons.

I told Fern I would float her again if she wanted, and she did. I floated her for a long time until I noticed that she was crying. She started sobbing and I held her for a while and she told me she felt awful for getting fucked by that guy. She couldn't handle the fact that if anyone asked her whom she last fucked she would have to answer, "Some hoser in the tubs at Heavenly." We sat over in the corner and she waxed loathing while I murmured sympathy. I know that feeling so well. You hate the beast and you hate your pathetic judgment for throwing the door open wide to let it in.

After sitting together confused for a while we noticed this guy from our retreat taking his clothes off to climb into the pool. Fern said, "Oh, look—it's Peter," (who took the second shift of Team Daddy), and we watched him undress. He walked outside and got in the pool with his pal Moondoggie, and they came over to talk to us. Peter had a low, resonant voice that sounded a lot like a didgeridoo. We chatted for a while and I couldn't figure out how comfortable I felt standing so close to the guys with everyone's stuff hanging out all over the place. I wondered whether this meant I had weird sex issues I didn't know about.

Eventually it was time to go, so the three of us minus Moondoggie decided to walk back to the lodge together. We walked back in the pitch dark with Peter between Fern and me, and he had an arm around each of us. It felt like we were on a yucky team. Charlie's Angels with a twist.

When we arrived at the lodge he said in that rumbling voice, "We should all sleep together," so we said OK. *I was trying to be open.* Fern went to get her sleeping bag. I went to the bathroom to begin my tooth care regimen before bed. When I emerged in the large sleeping room, it was already filled with snoozing retreat people. Peter had set up a sprawling bed of blankets for the three of us, and he was nestled right in the center. Fern still wasn't back. I decided to bring my sleeping bag over so I could seal myself into my own world. I lay down a little ways from his side and fell asleep quickly. I knew Peter had probably planned on a little pillow talk, but no way. I started to suspect Fern would not return. Somewhere along the line, I woke up to Peter's didgeridoo noise in my ear, and then his arm flopped over my body. I couldn't believe it. I took the passive route. I turned away from him and curled up into an armadillo ball. He soon got the hint and went away. I fell back asleep and next thing I knew didgeridoo was in my ear again. Peter was steam-rolling into my ear and once again had his arm over me. I was pissed to have to ball up and move away, again but I accepted my burden like a good martyr. There was just no way I was going to confront this shit when I needed precious sleep.

The next morning, the yoga bell woke us. I leaped up to pee before the festivities began. Before I was even out of the room, Peter started crying—I mean *wailing*—all primal and desperate. I have no idea about what. I felt like I was supposed to comfort him, but I didn't want to. I felt too pissed about his big dumb arm swinging over me all night. So then I had to wonder, *Am I just not a loving person? Why do I hate this person who seems to be in a lot of pain?* Peter kept crying and a few women hurried over to help him. I hoped that meant I was off the hook. He bellowed for a good half hour; I couldn't believe how long he could maintain such a volume. We finally started yoga and still the bursts of animal agony came out of him. I feared that I somehow made him this sad because of not letting him put his arm around me. But this seemed so ridiculous and arrogant that I shrugged it off.

After yoga, we had a little free time before the next unsatisfying meal and the mandala demo. I went on a little walk up the hill in the sun and lay on a flat rock hoping to bake a little. The land and plants and trees were so peaceful, and the expanse was sprinkled with Heavenly people who lived on the land in tents. On my way back down the hill I heard a mewing noise, and a white cat with one blue eye and one green eye—just like David Bowie—came out to talk to me. She rubbed around my ankles and I kept walking down the hill.

Lunch was ready back at the lodge. Vegan sushi. Of course it tasted good. When I was mostly done eating, macrovirgocook approached me and said in that special voice, the voice just for me, "Tara. Come here." I thought something special was going to happen; I don't know where that little slice of optimism came from. I walked over to her and she said, "Come dance with me."

Shit, I thought as I went in with her.

We boogied around to some groovy '70s dance music that was unexplainably playing in the background. She said, "We have great lives. You know, if you want something, you just have to put it out there and you'll get it. The universe works that way."

"Yeah," I said, because there I was.

"Let's go out dancing. We should go out, just the girls," she said to me conspiratorially. After a couple of minutes I told her I had to pee, and dancing was over. I planned to wander off to read or soak but everyone was talking about the mandala demo like we had to be there, so I thought I could stay for the intro then leave if I wanted to. Terry Blair was leading the mandala workshop. She was a skinny lady. She somehow seemed very fragile—I guess because of the slow, soft, and inhibited way she talked. She told us she started drawing mandalas when she divorced her husband and had an odd physical response that left her without vision most of the time, and when her eyes would randomly open she would draw these round symmetrical pictures that were healing her.

Terry told us that mandalas are drawn in Tibet as well as some Oceanic countries and that there is a seven-year process to learning about mandalas for Tibetans. She reported that some woman from the United States went to Tibet to learn about mandalas and she had consolidated the learning process so Americans could learn in a few short hours. How perfectly McDonald's. I got up to leave as Fern was coming in, and she convinced me to stay. I did have a morbid curiosity about how this would all play out. We sat in the eating area, and Terry said, with a soft and unobtrusive voice, that all she assumed was that you could lift a pencil and get it to a piece of paper. They were there to pad the rest of the way.

I drew a big circle with umbrellas, anchors, a turtle, and some teardrops on it; I figured my mandala was about my relationship to water. After an undisclosed amount of time, we went into the living room and put them all on the floor in a circle. Everyone walked around and looked at each other's work. There were a lot of dolphins and a fair number of vaginas. We sat around and talked about our pictures, the highlight being when Fern explained how she ended up drawing a pussy and a clit (her words), which was because she started with a bird and it evolved.

Finally we were free to pack up. My body almost couldn't handle the excitement. I felt like seventh grade was finally over. My shit was packed in two minutes flat and I felt positively radiant. During my shlepping around I noticed that Fern and Peter were deep in conversation as they sat on the lodge floor. They proceeded to give each other rather intimate-looking hugs. Later I found out a little kissing had been going on. As he left, Peter said goodbye to me and said he felt we had shared a special experience that weekend.

The final event before we could leave was a closing circle. This took fucking forever. The men were asked to group in the middle of the room and the women surrounded them, holding hands. I can't count the number of times over the course of the weekend that the men were thanked for being sensitive and wonderful and great daddies. As the ladies surrounded the studs someone said, "Every man's dream! Surrounded by women." I made the gay retort, "Not every man's dream." The women then started rotating around the men and the point was to *stare into each other's eyes*, have a big meaningful moment and share closed-lip smiles. I thought I was going to explode with fury. I gave everyone the most vacuous look I have. The men then turned inward and hugged each other. Shakti instructed us to say ohms around them. We ohmed away and the guys stayed in their embrace for so long that we heightened the volume of the ohms to hopefully make them turn outward and pay attention to the rest of the group as well. But it didn't work so finally Shakti said, "Hey, you guys, face us and ohm."

There was exaltation in everyone's face. There was a little hugging and kissing and then we all danced to Earth, Wind, and Fire's "Shining Star." I wanted the hell out. I helped clean up a bit and this guy gave me a CD of his didgeridoo band. Finally Fern, Judy, and I loaded up the car and headed back to San Francisco, stopping only for French fries and Pepsi on the way home.

Charles Anders

I Am So Smart

The pigeon looked impassive as a saint. It smelled of nightclub bathrooms at three in the morning. All around it, the San Francisco Cat Fanciers groomed their pets One Last Time. I heard one woman in a power suit lecture her cat, in a whisper, on deportment. The cats wore little contestant numbers pinned to their fur. Barnstable and I each held a handle of the pigeon's wicker basket, near the bleachers in the open-air marquee.

We hadn't named the pigeon anything. In the drunken meetings of the San Francisco Local of the National Pranksters Union, we'd mostly drawn up fevered choreographies of a stunt that would finally make our sister chapters in Los Angeles and Portland pay respect.

"Are you sure we should be doing this?" I asked Barnstable.

"You're the one desperate to show off to your girlfriend." Barnstable's twice-broken nose dilated. He scratched his shaved head with his free hand. Barnstable and I have sex from time to time, after meetings and the like. But I didn't think he'd be jealous.

"She's not my girlfriend. She doesn't love me; she never will." I'd already spotted Andi in the stalls, talking on her cell phone, as usual. And sitting near her was the reporter from a local weekly we were hop-

159

ing would write up this stunt in her column. The damp grass sponged the soles of my shoes.

I brushed the pigeon feathers off my dress. I'd worn my most professional drag for this crowd, and kept my makeup and false eyelashes subtle. I looked around the crowd. I recognized a few friends among the cat-fanciers, and felt a touch of shame.

My eyes tripped over Andi's from a dozen yards away. She had the most gorgeous blue-green eyes I'd ever seen. Her eyelids curled into epicanthic sideways minarets. Exchanging gazes, we were each both top and bottom in an eye-fuck that my skin only wished it could join.

"If only I could tell her," I muttered.

"So, we going to do this or not, Roy?" asked Barnstable.

I started to shake my head. Surrounded by all these decent people and their perfect cats, I cringed. Why ruin everything just to be an attention slut? We could just take the wicker carrier back to the car and forget the whole thing.

Then I saw Roach—Andi's sometime ex-boyfriend. He lurched from the men's room in the direction of the bleachers. Judging from the smirk on his pasty face and the way he strutted to the bleachers, I guessed he and Andi were back together again. His curly brown hair flopped over his eyes. His booty-call beeper hung from his belt, primed to lure him to a new lover when the first lover's expiration hour arrived. From our hours of shared introspection, I understood Roach's need to find his "safe place," and that the "safe place" could be a moving target.

Roach caught my stare and winked.

"Let's do it," I said.

We hoisted the carrier, then undid the latch. I reached in and pulled out the pigeon, which gave me a glassy stare and offered no resistance. I reached into its grubby butt and twisted the dial within. The pigeon thrummed and shook. I picked it up and cocked it over my shoulder like a football.

Roach had almost reached the bleachers when I tossed the vibrating pigeon at him. For good measure, we'd stuffed it with organic catnip. (The good stuff. I know a pot grower in Humboldt who does catnip as a sideline.) The vibration made the wings twitch convincingly. Roach instinctively caught the pigeon with one hand. Good man.

I heard a growl of wonderment nearby, then a hiss of desire. Someone shouted, "Greystalker, no!" Then a Siamese, contestant 17, scrimmaged across the marquee. Before Roach knew what was going on, Greystalker flew, trimmed claws out and teeth bared. Roach shrieked. I watched several other cats leave their neat pedestals. The furry mob converged on Roach, who ran into the bleachers. Andi covered her mouth with both hands, in a gesture of horror. You could only tell she was laughing by her eyes.

Oh, Andi. You're all the genders I want to be naked with. I've plugged your name into every search engine on the planet and ego-surfed you until three in the morning. I've read your biscuit recipes and your thoughts on campaign finance reform. I've followed you to work and lurked in the audience when you've delivered position papers. I've written over 300 E-mails about you to my friends. (I just checked. I did a word-search on your name in my sent-mail folder.) I started watching *Buffy the Vampire Slayer* because you said you liked it, and even bought the *Buffy Companion* book. Why can't I be your Buffy companion?

I remember when I met you and Roach at the Total Relationship Awareness retreat in the hills north of Marin. I wore a dress to a workshop on male-female communication and drew scowls. You wore a bomber jacket and wife-beater. You were butch in a way that only a genetic woman could be. Your creamy neck and ankles curved like breasts. You and I sat together and giggled as Gerald, the facilitator, talked about sex and communication and why the two sometimes coexist. The building that housed and us looked like a chateau on the outside and a high school gymnasium on the inside.

When you and I both whispered jokes about "sexcommunication" and Roman Catholic pedophile priests, I knew I was in love. I suspected, anyway. And that night, we sneaked out of the compound and went skinny-dipping in the koi pond. It was barely deep enough to wade in, but we squatted among the angry orange fish. We shivered and embraced and laughed, and then you went back to bed with Roach.

Oh, Andi. When I finally got to spend the night with you, months later, my joy nearly capsized my rib cage. You'd just broken up with

Roach for the third time, after he'd decided he really needed more space to exercise all the nonmonogamy skills he'd learned in a "Yondercourse" workshop. You'd run away from the home you shared with Roach, and I offered you a Platonic place to crash. We cuddled a little, and when you fell asleep, you had a nightmare or a sex dream or both. I stroked your hair until the noises stopped. I never told you what I was feeling.

The Geo Prizm we were chasing turned onto Divisadero just as I spotted Gerald waiting for a bus. I could tell Gerald's mind teemed with aphoristic brilliance. His goatee twitched as he read a book about communication styles. His turtleneck and corduroys screamed "Facilitator." The Geo sped up Diviz, taking our pigeon and my beloved further away from us.

"Hey, pull over," I shouted from the front passenger seat of the Chaosmobile, a Dodge Pacer glue-coated with Smurfs. Barnstable's tape player blared the Doobie Brothers from the left speaker and Philip Glass from the right. "That's Gerald," I yelled. "He's just the guy I need to talk to about my relationship problem."

Barnstable's Doc Marten stomped the brake as hard as it had the gas pedal. We went from 70 miles per hour to 30 in a fart's lifetime. He cranked the wheel so hard we nearly crashed into Bus Stop Pizza. "Hey, why we slowing down?" Keitha asked from the back seat. "We need to catch those guys. They've got my vibrator!" She cocked a lacy arm at the escaping Prizm.

I ignored Keitha. We nearly rammed the van parked in front of the bus stop. "Hey Gerald," I yelled out the window. "Jump in. We'll give you a ride." Gerald appraised my crimson frock and fishnet stockings. Then he looked at my companions, a roughneck and a septuple-pierced crinoline-dyke. Then he looked at his watch.

The watch won. He climbed in next to Keitha, and carefully avoided sitting on her skirts. "Thanks. I'm going to the Women's building to lead a group on creating life abundance in 15 minutes."

Keitha shouted over Gerald's explanation of his talk. "They're getting away, damn it! Get going!"

"Gerald, I'm really glad you're here," I said. Barnstable raced the engine. I turned to face Gerald just as Barnstable revved, so my nose bopped my headrest. "Ow! So Gerald. I really need your relationship-ping skills here. That car we're chasing has the woman of my dreams in it. You remember Andi, don't you?"

"Wait," Gerald yelped. "We're not heading to the Women's build-ing. Where are we going?"

"It's all your fault, Gerald. You introduced me to Andi at your sex and communication retreat, didn't you? You led us through endless workshops designed to fill us with giddiness. You can't stir up the pot and then leave it to boil over."

"Please don't mix cooking metaphors," Keitha rumbled from the back seat. "I missed lunch." Divisadero rushed past us, half fragrant old barbecue joints, half yuppie sports bars. Gentrification hasn't died; it's just gotten sick and ugly. The four of us in this car, even Gerald, rep-resented something the new city wanted to purge. Not by raising our rent, but by making sense of us. The Geo Prizm that held Andi, Roach, and Keitha's beloved vibrator turned onto Geary.

"Let me out! A dozen women will live a scarcity narrative if I don't get to them." Gerald groped for the door handle as Barnstable grudg-ingly slowed down for an upcoming red light. Then the light turned green, and Barnstable revved anew. "Roy, this is not a very aware thing to do, kidnapping me like this."

"I'm not kidnapping you. I just need your help. I'm desperate."

"Hey, wait," Barnstable shouted. "That's a great idea for a prank. We kidnap the head of Total Relationship Awareness and hold him for ransom. What would we demand? Five hundred sacred orgasms? Free communications workshops for deaf mutes? I say we do it."

Gerald screamed, which harmonized with the Glass-Doobie tape. Keitha slapped him with her nonpierced hand. Barnstable nearly hit someone running out of the Honeybaked Ham store at Geary and Diviz. I saw the Geo Prizm two blocks ahead. Roach chafed the road with staccato bursts of speed, the driving of an approval-deprived nympho suffering multiple purebred cat scratches. Andi held our vibrating pigeon up to the light. If only the pigeon could talk, I thought. It would tell you of my longing.

We turned the music down. Gerald led us through a visualization workshop. "Close your eyes, all of you." I heard screams outside the car, and the sound of machinery in conflict with its environment. "Not you, Barnstable!" The car pitched left. Horns sounded. Then Gerald told us to imagine a space far away, where the sun gilded every knife-edge of foliage. There we would meet someone we loved, from whom life's scat-play had separated us. See them standing in front of you, naked and smiling.

"Daddy," Keitha said. "Put something on. You'll freeze."

"It's warm," said Gerald. I heard more horns and a man's voice cursing from a moving vehicle ahead of us. Barnstable floored the gas again. "Imagine that you and this person embrace, and they ask you, Why have you kept me away? For in this realm, you're powerful, and it's your power that has created distance from your love-object. You try to explain, but only chirruping comes from your mouth, like an insect by a balmy pond."

Something struck inches from my face. I heard a jolt in front of me. Then something buzzed at me through glass. The world shrieked. Our car rammed its own momentum. The sudden slowdown shoved me forward. I opened my eyes. A vibrating pigeon cavorted past my line of vision, along our windshield. "Roach," Barnstable said. "The bastard threw it at us."

The pigeon hopped off the car's windshield and onto the street. Barnstable tried to pull over without getting rammed. This took a few moments. I couldn't see the Geo anywhere. As soon as the car stopped, I jumped out and ran back along Geary. Forty yards back, I found a wheel-crushed pile of feathers, catnip, plastic, wires and batteries. Geary traffic had claimed our nameless comrade, the bird with a heart of Hitachi. I scooped the remains and tried to think what I'd tell Keitha about her vibrator.

But when I got back to the car, Keitha had her eyes closed. "How can I communicate? I need to tell my daddy how I feel."

"You don't understand," Gerald said. "The insects are beautiful. The noises they make express desire for each other and the location of choice leaves or dead insects."

I held the remains I'd gathered from the road in front of Barnstable. He shook his head and started the car again. "But my dad's not a bug," Keitha keened. "He can't live on flowers; he won't understand."

We got Gerald to his workshop only about five minutes late. Chaos wrangling may not pad your resume, but it definitely helps you master

San Francisco traffic in an emergency. Keitha went with Gerald, the remains of her vibrator in a fast-food paper bag.

"Admit it," Barnstable said while I sucked his dick that night. "It's not that you love Andi. It's that you hate Roach. You know it's true. Oh, yeah, like that." Barnstable spoke in a faraway throaty way, like after a bong hit. I would never interrupt a blow job to talk, so Barnstable enjoyed holding forth uninterrupted. Sometimes I could make him lose his train of thought with wily tonguework, but not this time. "Face it. Roach gets to screw all these other women, and he gets to have Andi hanging on him whenever he wants her attention. He's irresponsible, self-centered, and unhygenic. He totally gets whatever he wants. You hate him."

Barnstable's apartment had a "Bing Crosby in Hell" theme. Big Hieronymous Bosch prints hung on the walls, with Bing Crosby's face pasted onto random nude bodies on fire. Barnstable had painted Day-Glo orange flames onto Bing's own album covers. That sort of thing. The apartment smelled like cat litter, but I never saw a cat. Barnstable was more weird than interesting—the sort of person who could get his shindigs promoted on the Laughing Squid E-mail list, but not a great conversationalist. Not like Andi.

Finally, Barnstable leaked into my mouth and grunted. I spat out his dick affectionately and went to his bathroom to gargle Listerine. "I don't see why it's an either-or thing," I told Barnstable on my way back in. "I love Andi and I hate Roach. The two things jibe. And if I had Andi, I'd probably never give Roach another thought."

"You just enjoy tormenting yourself."

"Who doesn't?"

I made a lunch date with Andi a few days ahead. The night before our date, I barely slept. When I did, I saw myself in a wilderness, each leaf honed to a knife-edge by the whetstone of the elements. I saw Andi, naked but for a pair of bloomers. I told her everything—my months of pangs, the feelings I hadn't wanted to dump on her while she was in relationship turmoil. "The way a politician craves victory, the way a fundamentalist dreams of the Rapture—that's how I think about you, Andi. I can subsist without you, but not live."

In my dream, Andi just frowned. "That's supposed to be funny? Try a little more wryness. You always overdo absurdism and skimp on the emotional core of humor, Roy. The soul of the joke. It's the difference between a prank and an artistic statement." She was still lecturing me on theories of comedy when I woke, soaked with chilled sweat and drool. I got out of bed, in a predawn frozen cloud, and played video games for two hours.

That morning, I stared at pages of Asian trade statistics without seeing anything. I work with a horde of nice people, the kind who put out a jar for the ASPCA in the break room and ask what I did yesterday evening. I always lie and say I watched television, which turns out to be what they did. Or maybe they're lying too.

The one break in my morning hell was a call from Keitha. She was suddenly closer to her dad than ever in her life, thanks to insights she'd gleaned from Gerald about communication. "It's not the content, but the nonverbal carrier wave that matters. When someone talks to you, pretend they're making insect noises and listen to what they're saying in insect language." I promised to apply that rule to all my conversations for the next week. "Speaking of which, I'm still in mourning for my vibrator. We need to teach that Roach bastard a lesson. Any ideas?"

"Not really." I stared at my sheaf of Taiwanese shrimp export stats, then looked at my coworkers, all married and mostly parents. "I think we should leave the guy alone." Keitha rankled at my sudden equanimity, which I couldn't explain very clearly. I probably wanted to prove I loved Andi more than I hated Roach, but I mostly explained myself in platitudes.

By the time I met Andi for Thai food, I felt as if I'd stayed awake for a *Twilight Zone* marathon. One of those classic TV onslaughts that gives you irony fatigue.

Miraculously wilted plastic flowers perched on every table at the Chiang Mai restaurant. The tables had plastic stands holding crumpled beer flyers and daily specials that never changed.

Andi and I arrived a few minutes before noon, but the hostess still wrote our names on a scrap and told us to wait 15 minutes. We stood out on the sidewalk and watched sputtering buses and ad-plastered cars grind past. Andi wore ball-kicking boots and jeans that were almost Capri pants. Her eyes crinkled like chiffon. Her smile had a sigh's ancestry. I couldn't bear her vividness. My heart sickened like those plastic flowers.

So we had our talk right there on the sidewalk. "You know," I said, "the trickster is a good companion, but a lousy suitor."

"I don't know," Andi said. "I mean, it depends on your cultural frame of reference. Within Native American lore, there are dozens of stories of the trickster taking a lover or lovers. In fact, the trickster's ability to transgress makes him or her a major babe magnet to a lot of people. Or is there a different tradition that I'm missing out on?"

"Oh, fuck." I tried to think of a clever way to swerve the conversation off ethnography. "Andi, I'm not being witty now. I'm maddeningly in love with you, and I can't shut up about it any longer. Come stay with me again. I'll bathe you with scented oils and pour every tear I haven't yet cried over you into your hair to moisturize and give it sheen. I'll kiss every inch of your body. Andi, please listen. I adore you beyond absurdity."

"Roy, what are you saying?"

"I've been in love with you for months."

"You've got to be kidding. I don't believe it. I totally thought you didn't like me at all. You've always acted so weird." Our hostess appeared and told us we had a table.

Andi went very, very quiet. We ate half a plate of pad thai and some green curry that reminded me of the dead caterpillar I might have brought Andi had I been a courting insect instead of a human. We got through most of the meal without saying much. I was giving Andi lots of space to have her reaction on her own. At one point I heard her mutter, "Oh, fuck, I cannot handle this right now." Then more silence. I ended up eavesdropping on the conversation at the next table between a guy who'd just lost his job and his girlfriend who'd just found Eckankar. Apparently if you get really high up in the Eck movement you can travel to other planets in your spirit body.

Andi put one hand on mine and burped gently. "Roy, one of these days you're going to find a life partner who adores being confused. You'll spring your little surprises, like long-buried passions or mechanical pigeons, and they'll just want to drink your spunk for it. You two will be so happy together. I just hope you invite me to the wedding." I promised I would.

When I got back to the office, I had the urge to call Keitha back on my cell phone and give her the go-ahead to organize some major prank on Roach's ass. Maybe nominating him for a spurious Webby award, or sending out press releases listing him as the spokesman of the Gentrification Association. But instead I surrendered to apathy, the next best thing to kindness.

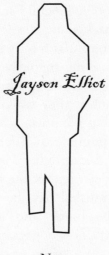

Jayson Elliot

NEW

There's something under my left arm, and it's growing. It started out a little tender, like I had a paper cut in my armpit and I just needed to keep my arm from swinging when I walk.

It didn't really matter at that point, since walking was not something I had time to do anyway. For about three days I had been sitting in the Green Room, a twelve foot square corner with no door, just wooden planks on metal pedestals hugging all four walls, placed there for desks. The Green Room was part of a large concrete space, separated from the high-ceilinged former warehouse by two other hastily constructed rooms, with walls that stopped about a foot before the ceiling. Aspirin-green paint gave the whole thing an institutional, public school feeling. And, of course, supplied the room's name. The decor in the rest of the office was more carefully thought out, but no one had yet gotten around to repainting this first misguided attempt.

Large metal framed windows exposed one wall to Third Street, two floors below through 24-inch square panes of glass that stretched the full length of the building. Two sections of the window—each three panes wide—could be opened by forcing an iron handle upward and swinging the glass out. A notched metal bar could then be used to keep the frame from slamming back shut.

In the daytime, Third Street was a busy shortcut to the Bay Bridge. The sound of frustrated honking mixed with the sound bites of 23-year-old self-styled executives blurting out trade secrets, always half-heard from the Green Room as they walked by too fast to complete their sentences in front of that window.

At night the Banana Republic crowd faded away to be replaced a few hours later by Asian and Latino boys in tight Mossimo tank tops, their conversations just as fleeting, but the topics changed from band-width to boyfriends. The muffled bass beats of the clubs sometimes made their way down the block and in through the windows. Sometimes, later in the night, the wet gagging sound of vomit splashed onto the pavement, its source unaware of the open window above, or that anyone might witness his disgrace, if only with ears.

Once or twice there would be a soft thump, like hamburger falling on a kitchen floor. By three or four in the morning, everything would be quiet, and there would be a few dark hours left before the sky would start to turn light again, and the commuters would return.

For three days I had been sitting in the Green Room, tapping at a keyboard that grew oily from my fingers. People would come and go; in the daytime as many as seven other young designers sat at the home-made desk that occupied the room. For the first two days, someone would bring me food whenever they returned from outside—burritos, croissants, peanut butter cookies. By the third day, the food began to collect on the desk next to me, leaving a greasy film on the papers underneath.

20 people worked in the office, but only one other person was there with me to hear the lovers' quarrels at 2 A.M. and the delivery trucks in the early morning. Noel, my boss, was one of the young executives that had been giving the neighborhood its new reputation.

Noel was Dutch, but he spoke with an accent that always sounded like an art student who had watched *Roman Holiday* too many times. He grew up speaking English—his mother was a fashion model who traveled constantly, so she enrolled him in one of those international schools with the sons and daughters of diplomats and bankers. He had his mother's bone structure and an enviable frame, but his orange-hued skin and stringy black hair gave him something that evoked the word *cartel*.

Noel could have done whatever he liked—he had access to universities all over the continent, and his mother's connections meant open doors were the rule rather than the exception. All children are rebellious, though, and he had come to California to be a journalist, meticulously avoiding any advantages he might be given, and refusing to accept any money (he said) from her.

Somewhere along the line, Noel had noticed that the Silicon Valley types he wrote about were beginning to mention something called the Internet, and he followed this with a keen interest. He spent his nights learning what they were doing, writing his own code, teaching himself to design graphics, and carefully reading trade reports to see where the money was being spent.

Eventually, he convinced one of the older tech types to pay him for a Web site, and since then, he had parlayed charm, bullshit, and late, late nights into a company with 20 employees and a tendency for inconsistent interior design.

I am not Dutch; I was born in Baltimore. My mother wasn't a fashion model, and I've spent enough time in public school to know that aspirin-green is not an attractive color. I *have* watched *Roman Holiday* too many times, though, so I found something of a friend in Noel.

I have never rebelled against my parents. I was always too busy rebelling against my friends instead.

When my junior high friends got into sports, I got into cars and music. When my gearhead friends started blowing off school, I studied and got into college. When other people chose poli sci and business majors, I entered art school. When the art students painted and sculpted, I wandered into the computer labs and used the scanners and illustration software instead.

Through endless temp jobs and stolen hours on the computers at Kinko's and other people's colleges, I learned to design. I spent my time designing club flyers, DJ promos, and zines. I spent a lot of time awake. I learned to bullshit.

I worked very well with Noel.

There were 20 employees in the office, but Noel and I still worked like we had when there were only three or four of us. We overpromised, we underpriced, we exaggerated our skills and crammed all night to learn what we had just claimed to know.

When other people came to work in the office, they brought their college degrees and people skills. They were team players with a can-do attitude. They were in by 10, out by 7, they got a salary, and they did what they were told.

Noel and I would forget to bathe. We would come in at 2 o'clock on a Monday afternoon, still wearing our clothes from the clubs, and leave the office at noon on Wednesday to go shopping at Rolo and Diesel. We'd get cleaned up and dressed up for a night at the Stud, then end up trailing glitter through the corporate offices of a client the next day.

Last week, Noel convinced Miramax that we were experts in streaming video, and that we'd be the perfect people to create an ad campaign for their latest film over the Internet. They agreed to pay us for a demo of the campaign, so we quickly found all the books we could (there were only two written so far) and began scrounging up articles that we could use to teach ourselves.

On Tuesday morning, I started doing sketches for the storyboards, and Noel began to see whether he could figure out how to send video over a phone line. By the time we heard the first club kids outside the window that night, we had a whiteboard filled with ideas, and Noel had written lines and lines of code that looked arcane, impressive, and utterly failed to work.

The Green Room is the corner of our workspace, where it is cornered by two other rooms. One room also looks out over Third Street. That's the smoking room. Smoking indoors in any California business is illegal. The smoking room has a black couch scarred with burns, stacks of boxes, assorted ashtrays that never get emptied, and a refrigerator that hasn't been opened for months by an unspoken mutual agreement.

The other room has no windows; it is an interior room. The other room is our conference room, where we take clients, in a *Boy's Own,* clubhouse version of business meetings. In the conference room are six matching chairs, white walls, and the only table that was actually purchased rather than made. In a moment of corporate largesse, Noel chose to fit the conference room with a large glass-topped table that four people managed to squeeze through the door in a marathon topography experiment that no one bothered to record. The table has become a permanent fixture, sure to remain long after we leave—a Stonehenge for future generations to ponder and never remove.

On Tuesday night, the last employees had gone home, and Noel and I fumbled with cables, trying to feed video clips of Kelly MacDonald into a reluctant computer. I fished a Vantage from the box in my Diesel jeans and stuck it in my mouth, wandering off to the black couch in the smoking room. Noel followed with his Camels, and we sat and smoked, and wondered about how much we had left to do before the demo next Monday.

Noel unsnapped the chest pocket of his green vinyl overalls, and dug out a plastic Ziploc bag, the kind that hold jewelry from ear-piercing stands at the mall. I finished my cigarette and threw the butt out the window; the ashtrays were all too full to go near. Noel headed for the glass table room while I dug in the couch for a discarded drinking straw.

I got a pair of scissors from my desk and made a neat diagonal cut across the center of the straw—one half for each of us. I've known Noel for years now, but his skin always has such citrus colors, and I've heard that hepatitis can be transmitted through the nose.

Tuesday night became Wednesday morning, and our storyboard had become an epic drama. By that second morning the video was working, though we still had no idea how it was supposed to stream. All the employees were team players, and they brought us food as we sat in the Green Room, typing and coding, sketching and designing. We smoked and worked, and had conferences in the conference room from time to time.

By the third morning, I was no longer hungry, and Kelly MacDonald's face was moving jerkily on my screen. Noel left for a while that day—we hadn't planned to be in the Green Room for so long without leaving. I stayed and stared at the screen, getting up to sketch changes on the storyboard or to march to the bathroom.

There is only one bathroom for each floor, and ours is only one of many spaces in the old warehouse that has become an office building. There is no lock on the bathroom, and I always use the stall, never the urinal. I feel too vulnerable at the urinal, my back to the door, a tiny partition the only thing between pisser and sink. I just can't stand there, dick in one hand, jeans in the other, while 10 inches away someone runs their hands under the faucet and stares at their face in the mirror. Even in the stall, though, I never seem to be able to sit down without someone going up to the urinal. I can see their shoes and ankles under the wall as I sit in contempt of the Dockers and Doc Martens next to me. I cover my ears, but it never keeps out the heavy splashing sound as the piss begins. The splashing goes on and on, until it finally turns to a few spurts, usually accompanied by a heavy sigh and a flatulent finale. The ogre zips up, then stands at the sink for an eternity while I hold my head in my hands and wait for the monster to leave so I can clear my bladder in peace.

I hate that bathroom.

Noel returned, equipped for a long stay, and we had more conferences.

By the third night (Thursday night) my armpit felt like it had a paper cut running right through it. I hadn't shaved my underarms since Sunday, so they were itching anyway, but now the sweat seemed to be running into a sharp line at my side, and it would sometimes sting.

By the fourth night, by Friday night, I was typing with one hand.

Weekends are an artificial construct—a marketing scheme and a method of control. Weekends are the reward promised for five days of loyal service, just enough time to rest weary eyes and arms, to pretend to forget that it will all start again, to stay up late one or two nights, sleep in one or two mornings—a tiny taste of freedom. Not too much— one or two more days without the routine of work and the soul gets restless, starts to get creative, wonders if there might be *more…*

Two days is just right. Only one day, and people wonder why there aren't more, start to think about packing it all in. Give them three or four days, and the work ethic slips, life starts to feel like life again, it starts to become clear that you are selling your time, selling your hours, chipping bits of your youth away to make money for someone else. But two days, that's just right. In two days, people will go shopping. In two days, people will visit bars. In two days, people will watch prime-time television and feature films, rent videos, eat at restaurants, take a drive down the coast to a charming countryside attraction, and spend money on tasteful local crafts made with naïf affection.

We don't believe in weekends. We are a new paradigm.

We have created the new economy, and we can create the new work ethic. There are 365 days in an average year because the Earth spins on its axis and travels around the sun. There are 24 hours in a day because the circumference of the Earth requires it to spin at a certain speed, and somewhere in the European thought patterns that defined the hour, base 12 seemed like a pretty good idea at the time. There are 12 months in the year, corresponding more or less to the cycles of the moon. There is no reason whatsoever to have seven days in a week, and certainly nothing in the heavens above that would suggest that two of them be designated the front and the back, meant to be taken as days of rest. In our new work ethic, work gets done on the days that it is there, and when the work is done, the rest is taken.

Friday night means nothing.

The best clubs happen on weekdays anyway.

By Friday night, we knew what we were doing. The video was streaming, Kelly MacDonald was looping, and the storyboards were solid. All that remained was to muddle through, create the screens, compress the streams, design some buttons, and wrap it all up.

Things were taking a bit longer, since typing was coming slowly for me, and conversations were starting to wander a bit too far. Noel and I realized we were starting to plug up a bit: too much time in the Room.

"We need more cigarettes."

Noel patted his pockets. "I've got a couple left in a pack somewhere, if you want one."

"I think we need a carton. I'll split it with you."

"I smoke Camels. You smoke Vantage."

"I only smoke Vantage because they're more Mod. I don't really care what I smoke. We'll get Camels."

"You think they're more Mod?"

"Of course they are. Look at the pack."

"It's a circle. What's Mod about that?"

"Think parkas. Think Vespa. French fighter planes from World War I. It's completely Mod."

"Quad."

"Huh?"

"'Rophenia."

"Right. Yeah. Quadrophenia. Completely Modroquadrophenia.

175

Anyway, whatever. I don't care what I smoke. We'll get Camels, we'll split the carton."

"No, I think we should get Vantage."

"OK, we'll get Vantage then. It's all the same to me. We just need to go out for some cigarettes."

"Right. Great. So we can go down to the liquor store on Harrison. They'll still be open, right? "

"I don't think they sell Vantage. They're not that popular, you know."

"How do you know? Did you ever try to buy them there?"

"No, it's just that I usually get them at the liquor store over on Howard and 11th. They special order them for me. I told Turtle about them, so we make sure to buy them there, to keep them stocked."

"Turtle? Turtle smokes Vantage?"

"Yeah, he's the one who turned me on to them."

"Turtle's about as Mod as a museum curator. The boy hand-paints his own clothes with florescent paints."

"So we'll get Camels. I don't care."

It was more Saturday morning than Friday night, but if you think about it, midnight is another arbitrary construct, and we are the new wave. We saved everything on our computers again—you can never be too safe. I set the alarm on the office while Noel dug his keys from underneath an oatmeal cookie wrapper, and we made our way out of the office, my first foray into the world since Tuesday.

The air outside was warm, still, and dry. As we walked, I made a little breeze for myself. I could not swing my left arm, and I wanted to hold it out at a 90-degree angle, let the tiny breeze blow underneath and cool me. I lifted my arm, but ended up holding it up just slightly, enough for some air, but low enough to keep from stretching it out and making the tender lump in my armpit hurt even worse.

Noel noticed me walking funny. From the right, I could walk perfectly normal, but from the left, I had one arm dangling outward from my side, like a scarecrow getting ready to pop some robot break-dance moves. Of course he asked about it.

"I don't know what it is," I said. "It just hurts to put my arm down or lift it up too high, so this is how I need to hold it."

"Oh, Sweetness…"

Noel calls everyone Sweetness. He's Dutch. His mother was a fash-ion model. He has to talk like that.

It's Sunday evening, and there's something growing under my left arm. I'm not typing anymore, or trying to move the mouse. I'm just sit-ting in a chair in the Green Room, directing Noel through the screens I've made, telling him where to put each one as he matches it all up to the code he's been writing. I'm drinking a Diet Coke and smoking a Camel, resting my left arm on the back of another chair, trying to wait for the swelling to go down.

Tomorrow morning is the demo for Miramax, and I think we are going to be ready. We've gone through the storyboards so many times that I'm afraid they've pushed other more useful knowledge out of my head and replaced it. The video is working, and the interface looks great. I feel like there is a tangerine under my arm, dipped in a stinging acid and pressed up against a paper cut. I am sitting in my chair, going over tomorrow's presentation with Noel.

Everything is perfect. They'll hire us for sure with this. I have been hoping the swelling would go down, but if anything, it feels like it's get-ting larger. I tell Noel to save the file; we are done. There's nothing left to do but relax until the 10 A.M. meeting.

It's 6 A.M. I haven't tried to look at the acidic grapefruit pushing out from under my skin. I try to pull off my T-shirt, but with only my right arm, I am just tugging pointlessly. I enlist Noel's help, and with a little wincing and pain, manage to get the shirt over my head. It feels like I am ripping my skin in two, but I lift my left arm, and try to see what is the matter. The grape-fruit is there, but it looks smaller than it feels. It's a kiwi, or a satsuma, it's under my skin, and my armpit is a bruised, sweaty purple.

"Noel, take a look at this."

"Oh, hell. What did you do? Did you hit yourself?"

"In the armpit? When would I hit myself in the armpit?"

"Well, get it home. Get some rest. It'll go down."

"It hasn't gone down so far. It's been getting worse for days now."

"Since when?"

"Since Thursday or so. I thought it was a little cut or something. It really, really hurts."

"Alright, love, let's get you to the emergency room. Best to have them take a look at that."

We set the alarm; we lock the office. Downstairs, outside, the sky is getting lighter and the newspapers are lying on the sidewalk in clear plastic bags, dew and frost collecting on the plastic, the headlines hazy. We walk south on Third Street, to Townsend, and to the huge parking lot that used to be an RV park, where Noel parked last week. The lot is empty, space after space of asphalt and paint, waiting to be filled in the short coming hours. Noel's Kharmann Ghia sits alone in the center of the lot, dark green and waiting.

I open the passenger door with my right hand and wince into the seat. Noel takes a little too long flipping through his keys, then performing a series of in-car isometrics, but eventually we do leave.

The hospital isn't too far away, and at this hour we are the only car on the road. Up Townsend, through San Francisco's only roundabout, then up Potrero with its gauntlet of untimed spotlights. Now that I'm actually on my way to have this looked at, I think my body has decided to go ahead and provide a full and accurate pain report to my brain. Someone is threading a flat, sharp loop of metal through my skin, pulling it slowly and at just the wrong angle. Every time we hit a bump, the metal turns and hurts a little bit worse.

We pull up to the hospital, a large brick building with hopeful wisps of ivy creeping up the walls. Noel stays in the car, which is really OK because he has to get home to get some sleep before meeting Miramax. If he comes inside they'll ask who drove, and when they find out he drove they'll look at his eyes and they'll smell his skin and he'll be stuck there in the emergency room with me, only he'll have the added feature of an uncomfortably attentive policeman.

The woman at the window takes my name and I describe the pain, and I take some yellow photocopied forms to fill out while I sit and wait. You know how you would think an emergency room in San Francisco's Mission district might look at 6 A.M.? How you'd expect murmuring, crusty shufflers to wander back and forth through the waiting area? How you'd picture at least one aggressive male in his mid 20s to be hassling the staff, and police to be standing around passively disapproving of everything, and lots of truly disturbing bodily sounds and smells to punctuate the atmosphere at odd intervals, all under unflattering florescent lights? At 6 A.M. in this emergency room, you would think all that, and you would be right.

I finally hear my name, and navigate through the police and the patrons to make it into an examining room. A wide-faced nurse comes in first, and starts asking me questions, thinly disguised inquiries like how have I been eating, and have I gotten enough sleep lately? This is a waste of time—I'm in a hospital, not a courtroom—I stop her and explain. I've been up for five days and some hours now. I've been doing lines since Tuesday night. No, I couldn't say the exact amount, let me do some math, I'll estimate. I don't know, maybe seven, eight grams total? No, it wasn't all meth, but mostly. You know, there was some coke, and you take what you've got, huh? Anyhow, that stuff just gives you 30 minutes of clarity and then it's all twitches.

The nurse is gone, and I'm still trying to do the math on my fingers. Now I'm really interested in exactly what I did do. It's kind of like a high school kid counting his beers—as long as I've done it, let's get a good score. My fingers are so oily.

The nurse is back, with a doctor and a needle. They want to get some kind of sample. They're saying something about blocked glands and allergic reactions, and I can hear the guidance counselor tone welling up in the doctor's voice. I lay back on the caramel vinyl table, and listen to the crinkling of the sanitary tissue covering.

I can hear the doctor and nurse talking, not addressing me directly, but lowering their voices just enough to pretend it's not for me to hear, when of course it's exactly the opposite. I hear comments about parties, and "kids," and responsibility. I can feel their eyes on me, even as I close my own.

They don't know about responsibility. And I'm sure they don't know about parties. I certainly don't, not any more. I have sacrificed the world that passes at night beneath the Green Room's window for the new one that we are making, day and night. I am not here, in the small hours of the emergency room, in the pursuit of thrills. I am here as a casualty, a Purple Heart in the new economy.

The doctors and nurses, the team players, the weekend clubbers—they don't understand. With their weekends and their schedules, their A.M. and their P.M.—they are missing the point. New technologies are hatching. New paradigms are emerging. IPOs are on the horizon. This is the New World. This is the Next Wave. We are not subject to your rules, your old ideas. Everything is different for us. We have fuel. We can not run down.

The doctor and the nurse are still talking. I don't bother opening my eyes. I hear words in their conversation like "lance," and "drain." Somebody lifts my arm, and I don't bother to protest. I'm resting.

The needle pierces me with such careless tearing that I become made of metal, and I can feel my metal ripping apart. Something is wet. The thing under my arm is shrinking. I will be repaired. I hear more words. Words like "lesson," and "learn."

I ignore them. I have no lesson to learn. This is the new economy, and I am the new wave.

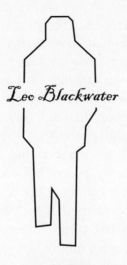

Leo Blackwater

E.I.P. BID
(Early Intervention Program Twice a Day)

I.

Dr. Wakayama, a short Asian woman with a big head and black hair shaped like a Darth Vader helmet, moves her gaze from the thick chart of medical facts to the subjective, imprecise human being. As a medical condition, fatigue is elusive. Tilting her head, she gives me that face she too often gives me. I've never been able to figure out whether 'tis smirk or smile, with that skeptical voice that could either mean "I don't know how to help you" or "You're full of shit, you hypochondriac!"

Instead, she says, "Your labs are fine. Your fatigue couldn't be caused by the HIV."

"Would cancer show up in the labs?" Now I really sound like a hypochondriac.

"Yes, I think it would. Anemia. Liver counts..."

"Just asking," I say, trying to save face.

"I think it could be depression."

I stare at her. Dizziness, blurred vision, joint pain, and fatigue. *Depression*, obviously.

"Have you ever taken antidepressants?"

"I've tried them all."

181

"You've tried them all? Well, which worked best? We'll try that one."

"None. Of course I was high most of the time they weren't working."

Sarcastically, "They don't work when you're high."

"No, I don't want to go through that again. Paxil made me impotent. Amitriptylene knocked me out. Zoloft made me dizzy. I did a 180 over some railroad tracks on Prozac."

"If you won't take antidepressants..." she focused intensely on the ceiling for a second as if she were trying to feel the presence of the Force. She shook her pen and peered back at me. "I could take you off your medications for a week and see if that makes a difference."

Take me off what was delaying AIDS? "What about viral resistance?"

"Well, it's not the greatest combination you're on, anyway. You've never even been on a protease inhibitor."

"Would I be able to go back on the Epivir and Zerit after the week is up?"

"Yes, I don't think it'll make much difference."

"OK," I sighed.

I went home second-guessing the good doctor and second-guessing myself about the wisdom of this risky move. Would I develop viral resistance and not be able to tolerate the 17 other medications available? Would I be switched to meds that would cause me to develop a buffalo hump on the back of my neck? This reasoning didn't sound much like reasoning. What was real? This fight against microbes fought only with good numbers and bad numbers that guessed how close you were to dying. The pills that made you sick, now they were real.

Did depression count as hypochondria?

II.

I woke up the next morning and reached for my bag of plastic bottles and then stopped myself. I did not take my Epivir and Zerit. I also declined my cimitidine (generic for Tagamet), my Tylenol, and even my vitamins. Suddenly I felt ordinary. A regular person. Not someone fighting a terminal disease, but an ordinary person on any ordinary morning annoyed at having to go to work.

For a few days, I live life as if no clock is ticking. I do not feel better physically, but I am in better spirits.

I go to movies and visit with friends. I listen. I water my cactus. I clean up my apartment and open the windows. I feel a connection to the clouds and the sky, the flowers and the grass.

I do not rush places.

I begin to plan what to do with my life.

On the seventh day, in telephone consultation, Dr. Wakayama nonchalantly remarks, "You can resume taking your medications."

"OK." Silently, I add, "In the afternoon."

Afternoon comes and goes sitting on the porch reading: "Later."

Evening comes with the rain lulling me to sleep: "Tomorrow morning."

Sunlight pours in the windows. I hear Max the German shepherd digging outside. We wrestle with him over his rubber ball.

III.

In the Evening:

A last meal. At Maria's Italian Kitchen with its checkered tablecloths and good food, I have a tasty Calzone with pepperoni, light on the ricotta (that cottage cheese lookin' stuff). I cut open the golden shell and pour in the accompanying dish of marinara sauce and sprinkle a blizzard of Parmesan.

Then, I unzip my backpack with the sound of opening teeth. From its gaping mouth I pull the bag of bottles, sounding like a bag of baby rattles, or a rattlesnake. I search for the correct bottles memorized by color, size and childproof cap, and pull out the hard white diamond, the ugly brown capsule, the jungle green cimitidine, the orange daily vitamin. One by one, I wash them down with the cleansing glass of ice water with a thin slice of lemon.

As I resume the BID ritual, the room dims ever so slightly as I return to death row. The deathwatch and fight for survival resumes...against the invisible abstract foe of microbes and numbers and windmills, only made real in the sickness and deaths of my friends, the side effects of medications, and the whispers in my head.

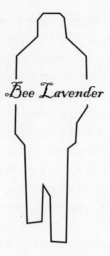

The Theory of Maternal Impression

I grew up on the Kitsap Peninsula across the Puget Sound from Seattle. Every so often we would drive from our house deep in the south end of the wooded county around the inlets and bays. I stretched out in the back of the car and looked up at the hills covered with trees and the occasional quarried ledge with a trickle of a waterfall, or sat up and watched to see if the tide was out, uncovering green slime and barnacles. We drove through Gorst, where my grandparents once had a dairy store, and then into Bremerton, making that sharp left turn next to the massive warships.

We would park the car downtown, next to J.C. Penney's or Woolworth's or in the cement-walled parking garage. We walked out to the old rickety ferry terminal next to the big cranes and cavernous buildings where secret military things happened with ships and chemicals. Twelve-foot chain link fences with rolls of barbed wire marked the entrance to the shipyard, which was patrolled by armed guards. Large signs warned against approaching by land or sea. My mother worked behind that gate, doing secretarial support for a nuclear office. I'd been inside a few times when the yard opened for family visiting days. The waterfront was dirty and unremarkable—just a few bars and a fish restaurant and the YMCA where I used to swim until someone noticed my chlorine allergy. We waited inside the cold wooden terminal with dark painted wainscoting and ancient vending machines and then boarded a ferry to go to the city for the day.

Walking on the ferry at Bremerton is free, but you have to rush to get a brown vinyl booth next to a window. The best seats were in the middle, near the snack area and away from the deck and the evacuation instructions posted on the walls. If we were late we had to sit in the chairs near the door and the endure blasts of cold air that rushed in every time someone walked out on deck. The walls of the ferry were lined with faux wood laminate, and everything was always slightly dirty, with cigarette burns here and there and graffiti scratched on most surfaces. The bathrooms were orange and brown and had scrollwork along the big mirror, and the water in the toilets swished back and forth with the motion of the boat.

I went to the city with my parents or my teenage aunt and her husband to see the laser Pink Floyd show at the Science Center, play games on the midway, or ride the big scary rides I hated. We visited bookstores to pick up novels and magazines we couldn't find at home, or went a movie that might never make it to our county. Often we went to see a specialist at one of the hospitals. I had a series of mysterious symptoms that no doctors in our town could diagnose, and the city doctors poked and prodded for years trying to find an appropriate term to explain my unusual eyes, skin, and skeleton.

The buildings in the city scared me with their enormous height; as we walked up the steep hills I was always halfway convinced that one would fall down and crush us. My eyes couldn't handle the scale of the place—everything doubled and tripled and wobbly, moving around too fast. There were no trees.

Every time we went to Seattle I wanted to eat fish at Ivar's and throw French fries to the seagulls swooping above the water. I begged to be taken to see the displays of odd things at one of two little shops. On Pier 51, a dark and crowded store built to look like a longhouse sold souvenirs. The middle of the store was devoted to all the usual tourist stuff—shot glasses with images of the Space Needle, boxes of seashells, taffy, suede bags filled with sparkly rocks. Machines vended pressed pennies that said THE CURIOSITY SHOP, and a small wooden machine showed a peep show for 10 cents. The sepia-toned flip images showed a lady taking a bath and her maid dressing her afterwards, with no actual naked bodies.

Lined up against the back wall of the store were displays of native artifacts like totem poles and old canoes and beadwork. Glass cases held a stuffed armadillo, flea circuses, pins with poems written on the heads, a tiny mermaid mama and baby, and pictures of odd and wonderful things. There were bottles of deformed farm animals, a pickle jar containing a pig with extra legs, and a two-headed cow. There were also two human mummies: an old withered woman and Sylvester, found shot to death in the desert. The bullet hole in his creased and shriveled brown chest was right at eye level.

Another little store inside the Seattle Center was less crowded and had more detailed examples of freak show artifacts, with pictures and histories of Siamese twins, men who bicycled with no legs, and bearded women. I could stand and look at the pictures without being jostled by tourists, and read the detailed descriptions of the lives of the curious people on display. I was endlessly interested in the displays, and once I could read I started to collect more and more information on weirdness from *The Guinness World Records*, *Ripley's Believe It or Not*, and *The Book of Lists*. The stories of spontaneous human combustion and children who vomited frogs from hell were interesting, but I was mostly interested in the freaks.

Cheng and Eng, the brothers for whom the term "Siamese twins" was created, were shown posing alone, and then with their wives. The caption said they had 24 children between them. They made a fortune showing off their bodies, then retired to become farmers and raise kids. Tom Thumb was shown in his formal, miniaturized splendor, with pictures of his wedding to Lavinia Warren, which had attracted more newspaper coverage than the Civil War that week.

I was entranced by people who had figured out a way to make a living off the curiosity their physical difference piqued in others. I watched after-school specials about people who were inspiring and had pretty, swift diseases like leukemia or brain cancer. But I had never seen people like me, with differences that were remarkable and incurable and terribly interesting.

The freaks posed in pictures to demonstrate their signature trait, and I thought about how I was often examined by groups of doctors instead of one doctor in private. I thought about how I was made to walk naked down orange carpeted hallways while medical staff evaluated the way my spine moved, scrutinized the pattern of my walk, and loudly discussed possible explanations for my strange symptoms.

I thought about the full-body scans in the cold public hospital. I recalled how the radiology technician on duty, twisting his curly brown hair and fidgeting with his glasses, had been so excited by the novel working of my digestive system that he made two sets of images and kept one for his private collection. I was in glassy anguish, entering puberty with cancer in my endocrine system and malnourished from test-related fasting and surgeries and depression. Radioactive isotopes flowed through my body. I wanted to sleep but had to hold still without moving for two, three, four hours at a time strapped to a table as the machine moved slowly back and forth over my body and the gamma-camera collected images. If I fell asleep I might twitch or move—then the test would have to start over again. I looked out the window at naked tree branches and played albums in my head: Blondie, the B-52's, the Clash, the Violent Femmes.

Sometimes a song from the hospital corridors would intrude: Whitney Houston or some other repetitive and maudlin thing corrupting my internal soundtrack. The technician didn't tell us what he saw in the scans, only that it wasn't what he was looking for. Whatever it was, he found it more interesting than the thyroid cancer metastasizing in my lymph system, though he frowned and said the specific type of cancer creeping downward from my neck was unheard of in a child.

I thought about my thyroid, removed when I was 12 and sectioned for review in labs because it was determined to contain a rare and lethal cancer, again unheard of in a child. The tissue samples traveled the country and eventually ended up in a teaching hospital on the East Coast, preserved for study—a permanent violation of my privacy. Over the years, generations of medical students would solicit more information about the cancer, ask politely whether I would participate in their research study or drug study. Could they please have another piece of my body to study?

I thought about how each new doctor demanded a set of photographs of my back and neck, of the white and clear and red bumps trailing across my body, many hundreds of lesions on a person so young the medical textbooks denied that they could be a serious problem. Before they were diagnosed as cancer they tore against the collars of my shirts or caught in the links of necklaces, bleeding and healing and growing bigger every day. It took four years of monthly appointments to cut them all off, a few dozen at a time, a shot for each one and then a digging, cutting motion, an electrical charge to cauterize the tissue. The doctor stood on a stool and wore a magnifying glass on his head, like a coal miner. He scrutinized every inch of my torso. He was twitchy and excited to have a case for the textbooks under his control. He said there were only five other people like me on the West Coast. The first dozen cuts hurt but after a while I learned not to feel it, not to notice, even if they forgot to give me the anesthetic. After the tumors were removed the doctor blinked rapidly, examining my body, and said I was mutilated—not fit to be seen by other children. He gave me a permanent waiver for PE.

The oncologist's office at the teaching hospital was above the primate research lab. The oncologist always had a cigar clenched between his teeth. "At some point the strands of your DNA just missed a connection," he said, and demonstrated by holding two hairy fists together with one knuckle out of order. But he couldn't explain why it happened, and he couldn't tell me how a genetic disorder could show up with no prior history in the family.

"You're a first-generation mutation," he said. "You probably won't be able to have children since we don't know how much radiation to give you and we are estimating on the high side," he said.

"But even if you can, you shouldn't. It would be wrong."

What power created freaks? The old books didn't always say, and though some of the disorders were things I knew about, like cleft palate, others were mysterious to me in much the same way my disease was mysterious to my doctors. I was comforted by the fact that other people had been born with spectacular, unknowable damage, and that they had survived, even prospered. They didn't hide their bodies; instead, they made people pay to look at them.

At one time people believed that misshapen babies were judgments from a deity, but after the Dark Ages, maternal impression became the scientific explanation for people born with odd traits. The theory explains things simply: A mother scared by a wild rabbit would have a child with a harelip. A woman who saw animals shaking as they were slaughtered will have children with epilepsy. Women who craved strawberries would have children with a strawberry birthmark. The imaginationists believed that the specific circumstances of the fright or distress bore no necessary relationship to the shape the child. They thought that the mother's imagination and moral integrity were the real issues.

Tom Thumb and other freaks were not allowed to perform in some European countries because the government believed that a pregnant woman viewing a human oddity might be so traumatized that her unborn child would be marked forever.

Maternal Impression was a commonly accepted scientific theory, agreed upon by everyone from the court anatomists to high-profile surgeons to radical thinkers like Charles Darwin. It was a theme in popular literature produced by Sir Walter Scott, Henry Fielding, Goethe, Zola, Ibsen, Strindberg, and Voltaire.

There is no proof of what happened to my DNA, no easy way to describe it. I lived in a county with six military installations, with toxic waste lying without comment on the ground. In my grandparents' generation the ships used for atom bomb testing at Bikini Atoll were brought to the shipyard and sandblasted, the workers wearing simple overalls and no protective gear. The nuclear waste was dumped directly into the bay, and therefore circulated throughout the Puget Sound, including all the inland waterways of my hometown. My parents and their sisters and brothers and cousins swam in those waters.

The government says officially that there are no cancer clusters in my hometown, though the Department of Defense Centralized Tumor Registry has been in touch recently, asking for the details of my survival. My doctors say there is no specific scientific reason to explain the fact that many of my family members and friends are dying rapidly of rare cancers. Nor can anyone explain why I have an aberrant disorder expressed in a more esoteric fashion than has ever been seen.

Nobody can tell me why I have two different kinds of cancer and an auto-immune disorder and cysts eating the bones of my face from the inside out.

Nobody wants to guess at a proper empirical reason for the wreckage of my genetic code, though they have more than hinted through their treatment of my case that I'm an old-fashioned freak of fine interest.

My mother met my father at a destruction derby. They were married at a wrecking yard. During her pregnancy, she saw war ships on a daily basis, sitting in dry dock downtown. She lived a half mile from the undersea naval warfare station where nuclear warheads are assembled for submarines.

Without a better explanation, barred from making the logical connection between toxic waste and childhood cancer, I've decided that my life can only be explained through the theory of maternal impression. Since I'm told the environmental pollution did not change my DNA, I'll have to believe that it was the sight of the warships in the bay that caused the damage. Or perhaps it was more subtle, a combination of metaphoric factors, both the presence of weapons of mass destruction and the fact that my parents married in a wrecking yard.

You have to pay to take the ferry back from Seattle to Bremerton, half price until age 12 or so. Most of my trips to the city happened after I had to pay full price, when the cancer was diagnosed and I needed lots of expensive tests and doses of radiation. It was important to get to the terminal at least 30 minutes early. I needed a booth so I could lie down.

I'd settle with a coat over my cold body; then, hands covering my face, dream of circuses and carnivals, places where my mutilation was a gift to show an audience. The spotlight came up and I posed with all of the scars on my back exposed, then turned and threw my head back to show the fresh cuts across my neck. The audience included doctors, but they had to sit with the crowd, had to pay to see my flesh. I was the one who decided what and how to show off, and the crowd murmured with excitement. A gamma-camera slide show flashed on a giant screen behind me, showing the distribution of the cancer and all the strange inner workings of my body. The audience whistled and cheered to see my spectacular damage.

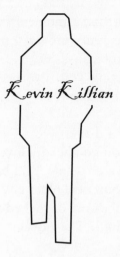

Kevin Killian

MAN AND BOY

On a deserted stage a boy, Kevin Killian, age 20, sits facing the audience wearing a suede fringe jacket à la Joe Buck's in the film of _Midnight Cowboy_, except purple, to match the era of the '70s in which he lives. His long hair climbs halfway down the middle of his back, cut into luxuriant brown curls like the film actress Jacqueline Bisset or the rock star Jimmy Page; and his eyes are clear, though he's full of Scotch whiskey. He keeps pouring Scotch from a pint of Johnny Walker into the little hole in a can of Tab. The blue of his eyes, the shocking pink of the Tab can, the brown of the Johnny Walker, and the deep purple of his ridiculous suede jacket make an unsettling stage picture. Onstage now walks a nondescript middle-aged man, Kevin Killian, 45, dressed in a suit. His hair, how flecked with gray, is cut short. He's 20 pounds heavier and perhaps an inch shorter than the boy he sees before him.

MAN: I woke up one morning with a stitch in my side. Then it wouldn't leave me, it became part of my life, so I walked around tilted, compensating for my loss—a phantom pain, I didn't know what I had lost. Later I realized it was my youth. Since then I've continued to age but never as sharply. For all of us, a moment comes sooner or later when the feeling hits, when the years crowd too closely together. At some point the vertiginous drop begins.

BOY: It's so strange meeting you. I've been thinking about you my whole life. Would you like a drink?

MAN: How flattering.

BOY: Oh, come on, have a drink.

MAN: No, thanks. But you go ahead. Have one on me.

BOY: You know, if you weren't "me," I'd be trying to seduce you. For you're exactly the sort of quizzical older guy I'm always trying to make.

MAN: And you are just the sort of fucked-up 20-year-old I find most attractive. Grist for my mill. The novelist, you know, must take his inspiration from real life.

BOY: Where did you get those bags under your eyes?

MAN: *You* gave them to me, I guess.

BOY: Big bags—deep luggage. I could smuggle drugs in them.

MAN: Enough already about my eyes.

BOY: I like your asperity; I don't have that. I'm naive, kind of a blank. All I want is to be cool. Like a diamond in a big refrigerator. All the same I'm crestfallen, and it's you, Kevin. You've settled down, become a bore.

MAN: Maybe that's what happens once a person turns 30.

BOY: Or 40.

MAN: Exactly! What nobody ever told me about aging is that I'd age both ways—past and future.

BOY: What the hell does that mean? Don't be cryptic.

MAN: I'll try and slow down, though that's not my forte. OK, you grow older and older—if you're lucky, but that's another story—

BOY: Then tell it another time.

MAN: And so you try to preserve what little currency you've got; at the same time, you're losing track of things—no longer can identify the bands in heavy rotation on *120 Minutes*. That's one part of it. But at the same time you find yourself craving the things you used to hate; you wind up liking the things your parents used to like. John Wayne movies, for example.

BOY: Oh, how I hate John Wayne.

MAN: Schoenberg. Ella Fitzgerald. Perry Mason. Ten years ago I couldn't have carried around these wants in my basket. There wasn't room, I suppose. All around me the taste for Henry Mancini and Ferrante & Teicher now blossoms like a sick rose. I feel myself growing older before and after, like the Push-Mi Pull-Yu animal in the Doctor Doolittle stories, or, or, or—

BOY: I think you've had enough caffeine for one evening. Come here and lay your head on my lap and tell me, show me a picture of what you're thinking.

MAN [*lowering himself and lying down with his head in BOY's lap*]: Or picture a kind of Gumby with a flexible rubber waist so squashed in that his head and feet are heavy with rubber, his stomach a thin membrane like a rope of spit.

BOY: Uh-huh. Say, are you seeing anybody?

MAN: That's what aging feels like.

BOY: Nobody? I have an absolute devotion to one man, an older man, maybe your age. He's so smart—smarter than either of us. Sometimes I lie at his feet and he reads to me, from books. Every kind of book, *interesting* books.

MAN: I remember. His name was Carey.

BOY: What do you mean, "was"? Don't we go on and on forever? *I know he's married, but*—

MAN: Oh, Kevin, grow up!

BOY: *But he doesn't love her!*

MAN: No, don't grow up, what am I saying?

BOY: In *Alice in Wonderland*, Alice says that books should have either pictures or conversations. I'd like to put a picture in one of Carey's books—a picture of me—

MAN: And deep down you must know you're not that important to him. I remember asking him once about mutual funds. Have you done that yet?

BOY: No. Am I going to?

MAN: In about two months. His eyebrows will rise a little at that one. It will turn out you had them mixed up with mutual masturbation.

BOY: But I like watching his eyebrows rise, like two sleek humps, for his hair is the soft buttery color they call "camel's hair," when you see it in coats; and I want to get him a coat made of camel's hair.

MAN: You never will. *He's* the one with the money.

BOY: Most of the time however, we don't do much talking. Tell me, Kevin, what's *120 Minutes* anyhow?

MAN: It's a show on MTV.

BOY (*sarcastically*).Oh! That's crystal clear.

MAN: As I get older I dream less often, but what I lack in dreams I make up for in memories. When I wake up in the morning, squelching the alarm again and again, my head is fuzzy with thoughts, and fat, like a down pillow newly plumped. *What were you dreaming about?* All I see is a big black space—the absence of something that once really happened. Across that vast blackness I see two figures turn and cavort, me as a young man, and me as myself. The big person teaching the little person certain practices, and how to avoid stress. The little person saying, shaking his head sadly, "Let's get old together."

BOY: Do I get to be rich?

MAN: No.

BOY: Famous?

MAN: No.

BOY: How much grief am I supposed to swallow? Am I still a writer? Do I publish any books?

MAN: Several—all duds. I do have one piece of advice. Everyone you think is gay is straight, and everyone you think is straight is gay. [*To himself*] That'll save me some time.

BOY: Even Lev Raphael? He's in my creative writing class in school and he is like Keir Dullea and Lou Reed wrapped into one! If he ever turned around and spoke to me, I think I would die.

MAN: Even Lev Raphael.

BOY: But he can't be gay, I always see him with that girl.

MAN: Even Lev.

BOY: That awful girl who I hate, but now, if what you say is true, I'm registering strange feelings of empathy for her, she's not so bad, she's just misguided, perhaps? Let's drink to her.

MAN: Make it a stiff one. But none for me, none for me.

BOY: Did you guess that you'd be married by the time you turned 40?

MAN: To a woman, no less! I always thought I'd live on Cape Cod with the sea breeze splashing my face and four or five faceless kinds of stud men of all nations would be running in and out of the surf in daring bathing suits, building world peace with candles and soda crackers. But instead I live in San Francisco with a woman. When I fell in love with her it was with an abrupt kind of violence—a hook in my heart, like *The Texas Chainsaw Massacre*. Love does funny things, violent things, to all kinds of people, and I should not have expected to be immune.

BOY: I'm nervous about that. Look at me! I'm not the type to have sex with a woman.

MAN: Well, this will all be in the 1990s when you can have sex with *packages of Kraft Swiss cheese* and there will be support groups to share your struggles with.

BOY: I better have a drink first.

MAN: For years I've been writing a biography of Jack Spicer, the San Francisco poet who died in 1965, quite young, of alcoholism. Survived by most whom he cared about, Spicer, like Frank O'Hara on the East Coast, was the center of a cult, or school of younger poets who idolized him, and his own peers, whose feelings were more mixed. I tracked down dozens who had known Jack Spicer, and I kept asking them, in different ways, how it felt to be a gay writer in the middle of the 20th century? And how disgruntled I was when they couldn't remember. I felt furious when they'd refer to events that clearly took place after Stonewall, for example. "But he died in 1965," I would insist, politely as I could, gripping a pencil so hard it snapped. "Contain your memories to one period."

Then a young woman called me on the phone, said she was writing a paper on the life and work of Sam D'Allesandro, a young writer who died several years ago. She knew I knew him and had found me on the Internet. "Of course I'll answer all your questions," I cried, "and I'll be frank, honest and direct," I added, thinking darkly of my age-befuddled respondents. "I won't hold anything back." She must have been thrilled. But then when push came to shove (and it always does) I was such a flop. The big thing was, I couldn't remember. She asked, "When did you meet him?" I said it was in the spring of 1985. Dodie said, it was the summer of 1984. He was wearing a brown leather jacket. I said he never owned a leather jacket in his life. On and on it went until we were both numb. And yet how could I ever forget the animal attraction he shot out from every pore of his body, nor the way my cock felt hardening in his mouth, and his pink lips around its shaft like a rubber ring.

BOY: Like me and Gary Ross. When I woke up I felt a sugary ring around the base of my cock, and a heavy unfamiliar weight bobbing up and down atop my thighs. His chin tucking into my balls. "Get it on, bang a gong."

MAN: I don't remember Gary Ross.

BOY (*furiously*): How can you forget! He is *The Maltese Falcon*, the hottest man on the whole Lower West Side!

MAN: And I guess I was stoned.

BOY: And what's the Internet?

MAN: Um, wait and see.

BOY: You're hard on yourself, and that means hard on me.

MAN: I remember.

BOY: I don't want to know about all the things that are going to happen to me in your life, I don't want to know about AIDS or anything like that. I just have one question—it's about Christopher Isherwood.

MAN [dumfounded]. *Huh?*

BOY: See, it's kind of dumb, but I have this thing for Christopher Isherwood. I've read all his books and I know he lives in California and my question is, Do I ever get to go to Santa Monica and *meet* him? I know he lives with a younger guy, a painter, or something, and I was thinking, maybe I could go and somehow get rid of the other guy and move in with Christopher Isherwood. So does that happen?

MAN: I forgot about this part of my life.

BOY: Do I? I know it's eccentric of me to have this fantasy, where somehow Don Bachardy falls off a cliff into the Pacific. But I'm there to console Isherwood, whisper in his ear it's time to lie down now, life is a cabaret old chum, my young arms and hands will massage you to sleep while my cock wobbles in your face, Mr. Isherwood. Your cute little blue-eyed face while you sleep, forget about Don Bachardy, he was just a nothing. So Kevin, do I ever go there?

MAN: God, how embarrassing!

BOY: I'll be strong, I'll cast off my schoolgirl crush like a second skin, and be me, me, Kevin. Oh, but how can I when I don't even have the right to be myself? Which of us is the "real" Kevin Killian?

MAN: I don't want to spoil your party by telling you about your future, Kevin. I want to keep you just the way you are, a halo of idiocy around your head, your hair reeking of sweet Moroccan hash, your knobby knees, your big hands and your erection that sticks straight out 24 hours a day.

BOY: Feel it! I'm into exaggerated gestures just like my idol Christopher Isherwood—he who told the world, "You did not live in our time. Be sorry!" Ah, Kevin, if I *don't* get to push Don Bachardy off a redwood deck in Santa Monica, and I *don't* get to fuck Helmut Berger, what happens to me and where's the fun in life?

MAN: I must be a sad disappointment to you.

BOY: Oh, no!

MAN: You sure?

BOY: I've grown to like the "me" I became. Your wrinkles and your crinkly, Brillo-like hair are dear to me now, like tiramisu of the damned. But how about you, Kevin? Will you ever care for me? Are you too old to have erotic feelings for the boy you once were?

MAN: I'm speechless as vinyl. Have you grabbed the wrong end of the shtick?

BOY: Will I grow into that sexy body like a hand between your legs? If you had teeth I would bite me.

MAN: I don't remember being so bold. But I must have been.

BOY: One of these days I'll remember this encounter and I'll write about it, and when I do I'll be cruel. Solipsistic and cruel. Grr!

MAN: I must have kissed my ancient body with your young turbulent lips—

BOY: At one time or another.

CHEERS

It's hard to imagine now that someone could be 15 years old and not know anything about sex or alcohol, but I was raised in a succession of church pews—a snug little existence of God and church family. Those things just were not spoken about, unless they were included in a list of evils that the nonchurch people did. I really didn't know "those" people. And it certainly never occurred to me that the very fact that I was there in church, as was my sister, meant that at some point, as terrifying and unholy as it may have seemed, my own parents had to have had "sex" at least twice. *My* parents—the most God-fearing, divine, law abiding people in the entire world? No, no, *no*! Too heathen a notion to contemplate.

One day I came home from school to find a little paperback book from the Christian book store that said some sort of thing about God and babies. I looked at it. It was never spoken about. Not a word. The book was sort of interesting. It was more chapter and verse—in Southern speak, that means "from the Bible"—than anything useful for a little girl who was about to accidentally learn about sex in one of the most brutal ways.

My best friend was a boy. He was from a big ol' Italian family with tons of brothers and sisters. They were a nice family, but they also said curse words here and there, and oh, my God, they were *Catholic*! So racy! We were pretty much inseparable and fooled around in our own childlike way. Childlike, although I was a teenager. But it was nothing, I would *never* have sex until I was married—married and ready to produce for the world perfect offspring to be raised in a perfect environment. I didn't even understand guys flirting with me; I just thought they were being friendly. And I was friendly! I was kind and outgoing. I was spreading God's love. I thought those winking boys must've been in their own church on Sunday and heard a good lesson on fellowship, and they recognized me as a fellow Christian. I knew my best friend was a little wild and kooky. My dad didn't like him all that much, didn't trust him—he was Catholic. But my friend was fun and funny. And I was fun and funny, always had been. And I loved him. He made me laugh.

So when my best friend and I found out that another kid's parents were going out of town, I was all ready for the fun and frolic of that. You know, the "suburban night club," some family-friendly house with the paneling and the couch. He knew some of the older kids from school because he had older brothers and sisters, and he lived in the subdivision where most of the kids lived. I didn't. I lived on a lone street with only two girls my age, but one of them had said "shit" once and my father overheard, and besides, their lawn was unkempt, so I couldn't play with her.

Anyway, I went with my best friend. I don't remember where I said I was going. I know I didn't say "party with someone's parents out of town." I loved my parents and wouldn't want them to worry. There wasn't a church activity that night, so maybe I said, "I'm going to get something to eat," which was always what I said. There is no doubt I had already had a fabulous meal cooked by Mom. I always did. Feeding people good food is Southern love. But they let me go, so there I went.

I remember the house. It was typical—it looked like every other house in that subdivision, which looked like all others in every state in the country. People may paint their shutters a different color, or install a different door, but they are all the same. It was on the corner near a public pool that I often wanted to swim in because those who lived in the neighborhood got to, but I could not.

We went in. Fun! All these people laughing and carrying on. Music playing. Lots of boys. Mostly boys—I was too inexperienced at the time to know that always means trouble, unless the boys are gay. Football players were there, which I was too inexperienced at the time to know that always means trouble, no matter what.

After a wealth of hellos, or "He-e-eys" (three syllables down South), I wandered into the kitchen where there were "college guys." Hmm, interesting. The eternal man-children, and at our high school party, how flattering! They were sitting in a circle, drinking fluid from these tiny little glasses. Tiny! So small and cute. Looked so much like our communion cups, only in church they were plastic, filled with grape juice, and certainly no one cheered when you drank one.

One of the guys offered me a knee to sit on his lap. Wow, they were friendly too. This was great!

So they gave me a little glass, and I drank it. Swiftly and with character, like they did. Everyone cheered. How *fun*! My best friend came in and said something. I couldn't make it out. He sounded strange. Almost mad...no, couldn't be, everyone was having such a good time. What? He's leaving or something. OK. I love him. He always does what he wants. I'm sure he'll tell me what's going on tomorrow. Several people said they'd drive me home. I was saddled up on this nice college boy's knee, drinking out of the little cups, people cheering and laughing. It was truly fellowship.

Stairs. That's the next thing I remember. I don't know how many. One? Three? One hundred and three? But I wasn't really climbing them, sort of being dragged. It's only a flash of a memory, but I remember thinking, *Am I drunk?* I knew these words from testimonies at church. Some man told the congregation how he had been a drunk but he had found God and now he no longer drank. Oh, no. Was this it? Me—drunk? Wow. Weird. But someone was helping me up the stairs. I was safe. Among friends. I'd figure it all out later.

Later. I don't know how long "later" was. But I wasn't on the stairs anymore. I was on my back in someone's bed. And all I could see was the huge sweaty head of a football player who had his hands on my wrists hovering above my...oh, my God...stripped naked body? What had happened to my clothes? He was furiously going up and down, up and down. His head was large, then less large, but still large. And where on earth were his clothes? And what was he...?

Oh...my...God.

Terror. I am not married to this man. I don't know this man. I don't even know if he's a Christian. My entire "narrow path God willed perfect respectable" life flashed before my eyes. In between the pumping of my aggressor, I saw the rest of the football team on the sidelines. Oh, thank you, God—I understand I'm to be rescued from an unimaginable fate by the strong hands of these ample boys, your servants. So I say, with a limp, twisted, unfamiliar, intoxicated tongue, "*No!*"

I couldn't make it loud enough.

"Stop," I say. I'm slurring. Why? I don't slur. I'm an articulate, smart, funny, God-fearing, good Southern girl.

I don't slur.

"No! *Stop!*" I try again. I see the watchful eyes of the team: They are smiling; they love me. No, wait. Cheering? What is this? The homecoming game? What the heck?

Later. I don't know how much later. One minute? Three hours? One hundred and three hours? One of the football players is pulling me out of the house and putting me in his—probably his parent's—car. I become aware enough to at least have an idea of what just happened and how much this running back or whatever is saving my life. In my slur that has become a gurgle, I say thank you...thank you...thank you.

He is silent. Saintly. He is a soldier of light.

I try to fix my clothes. Wow. I had my clothes back. My hero here must've done that for me. The unknown blur—that was him, driving me through that subdivision—was becoming such an important person in my life. During the fading in and fading out, I must have told him where my house was. I saw the familiar homes on my street. My neighbor's unkempt lawn. I told him two more, because we were in front of the empty lot two doors down. He stopped before he got to my house.

I think, *Right, very smart.* If I were this fellow, I wouldn't want to face some girl's father at whatever o'clock with his drunk, deflowered daughter in the car. I attempt to straighten my crooked self, and *wham*—

He must've been pretty strong, whoever he was. With one swift move he had lifted me and thrown me down and was on top of me. He didn't get any at the party. Not fair. What would the guys say?

Somehow, in that moment, I drew upon a latent strength that would only become a fully developed part of my being years later. Confused and dizzy—wow, was I ever dizzy—I kicked and kicked and kicked at that car door. Miraculously, it opened. Maybe the alcohol in him allowed me to slip from his grasp. Stumbling, with objects moving in circles around me, I made a winding path to my front door. I remember when my feet hit the lawn that my father meticulously cared for. I remember how familiar it felt underfoot. And how unfamiliar my feet felt. I remember the scene out of a horror movie of trying to get my keys in the door. I really remember the next three days.

Me. Loud, funny, bright. My mother called me "sunshine." But in the dark days that followed, there was little light. I sat in a little ball in the corner of my room. Rocking back and forth, forth and back. My cat would periodically come to check on me. I would robotically move through family meals. I hoped my mother would think I was reading in my room, like my sister always did. I didn't want her to worry. In the haze of my existence, I had some very clear thoughts. *If my dad finds out, he'll take a shotgun off the rack. If my dad takes a shotgun off the rack he will pursue Alabama retribution. If that happens, my mother won't have my father. And she needs my father. She loves my father. I love my father. I love my mother. And all the people at church will know. And my dad's an elder. And how stupid of me not to recognize the evil of the little glasses. I am ashamed.*

It was right at Christmas time. At some point, during those next few days, I got a little present in the mail. It was a bottle of my favorite drugstore perfume from my best friend. There was a card attached. It read: "Merry Christmas. You're a whore."

EXCERPT FROM *TINY LADIES*

"Every word I say has chains round its ankles; every thought I think is weighted with heavy weights." —Jean Rhys, *Good Morning, Midnight*

In some people, trouble runs so deep no part of them is left unaffected. You spend your time trying to help them fix a thing here or there, but they cut you like a handful of shards. People are fragile; once they're broken you can't piece them back. Not that anyone has the time to try, at least not those of us working for the state. We're wearied by quotas, the endless cycling of people through the system. Concern is invariably measured. And that, they will tell you, is how it has to be. The world generates more need than satisfaction—there's simply not enough to go around. Be sparing with care. Cautious. That's what I've learned, and I'm happy to have learned it.

Frances says, "Carrie, you don't have to tell your story to get your clients to share theirs." I don't answer her. What she says is not unfamiliar—she says it with brusque concern. But her reminder is crushing.

I have been a caseworker for seven years, and it always comes to this point—a vantage point—between who sits behind the desk and who is in the chair. It's give or take, and you can't do both.

That, of course, raises another point: Only the blind are willing to lead the blind. And often they don't want to. Just because someone's had a tough life—endured some struggles of their own—you can't assume they're empathetic. Empathy is hard-won, rare. Frances finds empathy dangerous, disorienting. But if you've survived—even if you don't know how you managed it—you might have something to offer someone who doesn't believe they can survive. You're a kind of example, a museum piece. Suddenly there's something valuable in you, admirable. When I walk into the office, I can't help thinking of my coworkers, at least the good ones, as artifacts; they seem detached from their lives except to exemplify their history, to convey its lessons. Their bad choices make them good counsel.

I started doing casework in San Francisco. They interviewed me before a panel of eight representatives from various field offices. They put a heavy gray reel-to-reel recorder at the center of the table and sat sipping from Styrofoam cups.

"Why do you want to work for the Department of Social Services?" a young woman asked. The left side of her face drooped, as though she'd had a stroke or had been in some kind of accident. She was hard to understand, but I didn't ask her to repeat herself. When I smiled at her, she averted her eyes, so I stopped smiling. Through most of the interview I sat quietly, looking at the face of each panelist. Their inquiries were strangely laconic, their silences more demanding than their questions.

Feeling pressed to respond, I answered, "I feel guilty not helping people who need it. When I needed it, someone was there for me." They suddenly stiffened, as if to dam a flood of potentialities in my answer. Their expressions turned unenthusiastic, like a wary parent, or a distracted police officer. *Just the facts, ma'am.* They had done this for years; they asked their questions, biting them off before they could provide revelations. Not one organization in America can ask the pertinent questions. And if they stumble on one, just by accident, there's an automatic shutdown in the person who has asked it. The parts just settle and turn off.

So when I got the job, and they told me about the pool of two thousand applicants, I said, "You've made a mistake." But I was wrong. They didn't want any more than what they got. They sent the recording to Sacramento where my answers—and my silences—were impartially scored. If they'd made a mistake, it was not irreparable. There were 1,999 people waiting for my position.

Now, in Iowa City, the expectations are considerably different. I hurry into work clutching files. My coworkers—four of them—are at their desks before 8 A.M. I say good morning to them, making sure they hear me. They are sensitive about these things. If I brush past them and don't speak up, they talk about it. Frances says, "Treat it like another part of the job, being nice to them."

I look out at the lobby. Empty. Some days only one or two people make it in. In San Francisco, my case load was never under 50. People took numbers, sat on hard plastic chairs waiting to be called. Selfish of me to think that was better. Frances, when she hired me, told me this wasn't a busy office. "Iowa City is hardly a city," she said. "Still, people have problems here."

Frances is black. She's a heavy woman who wears a base too light for her skin. She smokes incessantly, often with the patch on. She smokes until she's dizzy, sitting outside when it's warm enough, with her head in her hands. "It's not easy to close a case here," she said during our interview. "It's a college town mostly. Students come in when their financial aid doesn't cover them. They want food stamps, that's about it. Your job, really, is to keep your stats." She looked at me with surprising concern after laying out such cynical objectives. "Are you sure this is the right place for you? I know you've worked with much tougher cases."

I didn't say anything about Victor, about what came before, and how an easy case load would inevitably present challenges for me. I made my job in San Francisco practically impossible. I could do that anywhere. She never asked me why I left San Francisco. I don't think she even called my references. She took me at face value, and I'm glad she didn't tell me what she read there. But I've never known her to do anything that rash since. Even after three years of working here, we still seem to be stumbling around that first encounter. I sense her regarding me with a concern that borders on distrust, and I either feel indebted to her or humiliated by her attention.

I start going through the files on my desk. Last name first. Social security number, and on and on. Jones, Gloria. November 9, 1989. A week ago, but I can't imagine her face, so I read on. Mother of two. Court case pending. Substance abuse. I remember her now. She looked anorexic, her eyes enormous in her face. Her education was minimal. She wanted work as a home health attendant, emptying bedpans, cooking oatmeal. She had less than a week clean. She was still shaking.

She never made her follow-up appointment—one of those people who gets clean on New Year's. *Not my failure*, I tell myself, as though I'm new to this and need to justify the incompleteness of case files, of lives they contain. I know what it means to sit on the other side of the desk, to spill your life out to someone you've never met before, thinking they're the last safety net, the last hope. I know what it means to sit shaking in a chair, listing your skills for a skeptical job developer. But that experience doesn't keep me from feeling a sense of personal defeat when I come upon the abandoned cases, the early terminations.

Frances is on the phone behind me, talking to her boyfriend in Washington. They're planning to build a home in Virginia. She whispers, but speaks just loud enough for me to hear her making plans. She's starting a new life. It makes her purposeful and energized. I've felt that way every time I started over. Except the last time, when I left California. Then, I just felt tired.

The door swings open and a chill wind whips through the office. As though we've planned it, none of us makes a move to admit the young woman who takes a seat on one of the orange chairs in the lobby. We push files aside, lift our phones to make calls. We're adept at looking busy; we do it as a defense. We prepare a front of orderliness to address whatever chaos we might encounter on a given day. Eventually, I stand up and call the woman to my desk.

She has hair like a rooster—pomaded so each strand looks thick as a pencil. It's cut short, exposing her face. She doesn't wear much make-up, but I continue to look at her, drawn to a kind of toughness and a sadness that is its own shadow. I ask her name, the first in a litany of questions before we begin.

"My name's Carrie. What's yours?"

"Fisher. Hannah Fisher," she answers indifferently.

I ask who referred her, and she responds with a name I don't recognize. Then she just says, "The hospital."

I know instantly what she means and write the words *South Wing* on a post-it. Sometimes writing informal notes—rather than composing long-hand in their files—keeps them from embellishing too much. When I first met Victor in San Francisco, he used to lean over my desk and tell me when I'd left out something he considered important. I became a kind of biographer in his mind, though no one would read his file, except maybe the police a few years later. I wonder now what I wrote in it and whether they noticed the dangerous attention I gave him. The fond slant of my notes was unmistakable.

I look at her, lean forward in my chair, and give one nervous tap of my pen to the blotter. "How'd you end up in the hospital?" I ask.

She looks at the pen for what feels like minutes. "My best friend died last winter." She meets my eyes and smiles for the first time. "I think I may have had something to do with her death."

I recognize but can't place her, and begin to consider my limited spectrum of activities in town. I don't see her face in the Deadwood— a dark paneled bar I sometimes stop in—or Pierson's drugstore with its fountain in the back, or the Bijou theater. I imagine myself walking in and out of these places alone, and Hannah Fisher doesn't appear in any of my recollections. My time outside of work seems suddenly full of dark and aimless meandering, untouched by any interaction. It's distressing not knowing anyone here. Only part of it's intentional.

"Do you mind if I smoke?" she asks.

"We'll need to go outside," I reply. "I'll join you."

Outside I realize how young she is—maybe 25. Her hand trembles while she lights her cigarette, and when she looks at me I notice one pupil's more dilated than the other—a reaction I've seen before in people on the drugs they give at the hospital.

"Do you mind if I have one?"

"Oh, sure." She's flustered, sorry for not offering. She rummages through her purse, then the pockets of her winter coat before she finds them.

"So, they must have mixed some strong cocktails for you at the hospital?" Her dilated eye almost vibrates.

"I beg your pardon?"

I explain how South Wing patients sometimes call their pills cocktails.

"I wasn't there too long, but I did like the chloral hydrate." She laughs briefly.

"In the old days they called them Mickey Finns." I say it, gloating a little, something my father taught me.

The sky is still dark, and I think it will be another impossibly gray weekend. A fine snow covers the cars in the parking lot and the fields stretching away from us. She turns to look out over the faint snowdrift, and I notice her profile is startlingly beautiful. Her green eyes and orange hair sharply contrast against a sky the color of purple contact paper. She turns to look at me, exhaling smoke from her nose.

"I noticed the pictures at your desk."

"I've been collecting them, cutting them out of books. I've had some of them since I was a child." I remember sitting by the canal near our house as I paged through heavy art books. My father sold them, but he wasn't a bookseller. The books were one of his many occupations. He had a trucking job when he married my mother, but when I was 10 years old he lost it. He went to jail, came back, and went to jail again. We call it recidivism.

"Someone always needs something fixed," he'd say. That's where he came in. Most of the books he'd get from people who had died, or from the Salvation Army drop box. Sometimes, if he saw one for cheap in a used bookstore, he'd buy it and sell it for what he knew it was really worth. That's another thing he told me: "You've got to learn the real value of things." There was no shame in picking around for what others—through either laziness or negligence—discarded.

I'd sit under the bridge, which amplified the sounds of the canal—damp sounds you felt in your bones. If I found a picture I liked, I'd scramble out from under the bridge, wiping away the pebbles and dirt embedded in my knees, and open the page to the sun. My eyes would adjust slowly, and then the picture would assemble itself. The pictures I'd look at the longest depicted women in the midst of battle: *The Rape of the Sabines* or *Liberty Leading the People*.

"I love 19th century painting," I say to her. "Do you like painting?"

There's dead silence, a windless snowfall. At the mention of painting, I notice a flash of curiosity in her eyes.

"That's what I was in school for," she says, dropping her cigarette in the snow. "I finished last year."

"Do you still paint?" I ask.

"A lot of people at the hospital liked my yarn-and-felt work."

It takes me a moment to discern her sarcasm. "I guess that was a stupid question."

"No," she says in a careful, correcting voice. "It's not stupid. I just don't think of myself as a painter right now. Besides, I have a hard time believing it matters to you one way or the other."

"It does matter to me. I'm here to help you if I can." I watch her light another cigarette.

"People shouldn't burden each other." There is something disheartened in her tone, as though trying to convince me of this is too much. She looks at me squarely. "You're awfully young."

"No I'm not. Not really. I'm 29, and sometimes when I look at myself I see someone older. I have these dark rings, for instance." I point to my eyes. "They're genetic, but they say something about my life."

I notice Hannah has them too, but I don't point this out to her. "Where are you from?"

"Sioux City," she answers. "I came to Iowa City to study painting. I got my MFA here last year."

"And you decided to stay?"

"My friends expected I'd be the first to leave. All of them have moved on. They'd be shocked to know I couldn't."

That's how these college towns are. If you're not connected in some way to the university, you immediately become the town idiot, delivering newspapers, chewing your own tongue. Or you've had some misfortune no one's ever asked about but everyone knows. You carry this dark aura with you, and people watch you a little closer. It's not difficult for me, having never attended the university. I drove in from San Francisco and decided to stay. Anything they might say about me is true.

Hannah Fisher, however, does not belong here. I trust my instincts on it.

She stubs out her cigarette, and we go back inside. I continue for a moment to write out her case notes.

"Do you want to tell me about your friend?"

"Not really." She laughs, picking up the taxidermic baby alligator I've carried for years. "You have the strangest things on your desk."

My father first took me down to the canal after a particularly dry summer. The water level was low; the canal was like a long skeleton baring itself. He carried a big branch, turning over old cans and plastic bottles, pieces of clothing.

"Why would someone take their clothes off here?" I asked him when we chanced upon a muddied pair of panties.

"Probably to go swimming." He raised them up before us on the end of the branch.

"Why didn't they take them when they left?"

"This little girl must have lost 'em," he said. I could tell he was thinking about her, so I started thinking about her too. I thought of the girl who wandered the block eating the prettiest flowers. We had angel's trumpets growing at the side of our house. My mother cut them with scissors and threw them into the trash.

"One day that girl is going to die on somebody's lawn but it won't be ours," she said. I called her the "Poison Girl" from then on.

That's who I thought about when I saw those panties on the end of the stick. Perhaps she'd eaten those flowers before she went in, paralyzed by their poisons or succumbing to the delusion she required no air. I imagined her body falling slowly through the murky water and settling on the soft bottom.

We were just about to move on when my father discovered the alligator, a tiny little guy wriggling alone in the mud. My father immediately grabbed him and looked into his half-lidded, perfectly round eyes. His legs paddled as though he were still moving over ground. "Smart little fella," he said. "He ain't supposed to live here. This guy was probably flushed down someone's toilet and has been living on his wits ever since. You want him?"

We took him home. My father went into the shed and brought out an old grill and splashed some water into it from the hose. I went around the backyard pulling out grass, clumps of dirt, rocks. We put him on the patio. My mother had just gotten out of bed though it was well past noon. She gathered her night robe around her and looked in. "That's the saddest thing I've ever seen," she said. And though my father insisted it was a great life there in that rusty black drum, the alligator did look sad. Sad and confused, sitting on a little rock with mud and grass and sooty bars overhead.

We rarely had pets growing up, but I remember the Wallaces' horse. Sometimes they kept him overnight in their backyard. I'd sit and watch him from the window as he gracefully bent forward to eat patches of the grass. He belonged to Karen Wallace, who was a few years older than me and who used to charge me money to pet him. So I just watched him over the fence when Karen was asleep.

I also remember the commotion when that horse got loose at 3 A.M. one morning—my father out in his shorts with a flashlight, my mother standing beneath our yellow porch light. It was my father who brought him back. He rounded the corner cocky as a hero and put the horse behind the Wallaces' gate. My father always said that the best way to calm an animal is to look in its eyes.

I often look in my clients' eyes, angle my chair to sit a little closer to them. Frances says I get too involved. She prefers an impartial interrogation. I don't think looking into a client's eyes is necessarily coddling; many of them are unnerved by it. So I don't look into Hannah's. I just tell her, "That's from Florida—where I grew up." I take the alligator from her hands and run my finger over the little, bared teeth and the hard ridges down its back.

I put it back down near my pen holder and bottles of White-out.

Hannah looks amused, thinking about something.

"Ellen was…mischievous," she says. "She was always surprised by the trouble she'd find herself in. I think that's what I liked about her, at first. She seemed so lawless. Naive, but brash at the same time."

"How'd you meet her?" I ask, sensing immediately that this is about her dead friend.

"She was in painting class with me, and I liked her work. She painted these almost primitive self-portraits engaged in petty crime—shoplifting, pouring coffee on an unsuspecting lady, perched in a tree with a slingshot. Really funny paintings, some of which I still have.

"I talked to her once about them. I think I just said something mildly encouraging, like how funny they were—nothing really critical. Then, a couple of days later, I found this box of homemade cookies she'd baked and placed on my front doorstep. She'd made a box for them with miniature paintings on each side, and all the cookies were glazed and decorated with different color icings and silver candies. It was an amazing effort. And I remember thinking she must have followed me home, which I found kind of childish and flattering. I knew we'd be friends."

"The last time someone followed me home, it was an ex-felon on my case load." I don't tell her that I invited him, that I was an ex-offender specialist in California. No. Why should I tell her about Victor? You don't need to tell your story.... "That sounds a little scary," I reply. She loosens her scarf and draws it from her coat. She carefully drapes it over the back of her chair, but she keeps her coat on.

"Well, fear was something I had to learn. I'm better at it now." I recognize stability—what some might call common sense—as something Iowa affords. I remember San Francisco—my whole life, really—as demanding something else from me: blind courage, perhaps. I have some simple things now that I can depend on: a quiet cottage, a loving dog, this job that many of my coworkers plan on retiring in, a checking account, and a little savings. And my car. God bless my rusty old Valiant.

This is what I'd suggest to Hannah: a safe place, a few simple amenities. Though I'm sometimes afraid of the quietness of my life—how the walls sometimes whisper, conspire—I prefer it to what came before. What came before is always on the tip of my tongue, but I'm no longer in its mouth.

She leans forward over my desk, cupping her face in her hands.

"Did you get some kind of training to do this work?"

"I'm not a therapist," I tell her. "I had some training when I worked for the state in San Francisco. I'm a case manager. I'm primarily here to make referrals, coordinate some kind of plan for you."

"I'm good at planning myself," she says. She leans back and inspects me coolly. "I'm very quick," she says, clutching my stapler and pointing it at me. "I'd probably be pretty good at your job if I wasn't so fucked up."

I put her file aside and move my calendar to the front of the desk.

"I don't doubt that you might be good at this," I say. "But for now we might just want to concentrate on one thing at a time."

We schedule an appointment for the following week, but I notice her drumming her fingers on the chair, shifting in it as though she has something else she wants to tell me. I look up at her once I've written the appointment date on my business card.

"Is there something wrong?" I ask.

"I was just wondering if you might really be able to help me," she says. She looks off for a moment, then stares into my eyes, "I'm not comfortable asking too much of anyone. I have a way of screwing things up, you know?"

She stands up abruptly. "I enjoyed meeting you, though. I'll see you next week." She walks out the door before I notice her scarf piled by the leg of the chair. And then the phone rings with the day's first cancellation.

The road home is desolate and lunar, the flatness of the landscape relieved only by a little wooden fence and a railroad crossing. Nothing else for a few miles. I put a cassette into the tape recorder I keep on the front seat, and the Byrds' *5-D* scratches its way out of the box: "Oh, how is it that I could come out to here and be still floating and never hit bottom and keep falling through..."

I light a cigarette and look over at Hannah's scarf on the seat beside me. I pull up to the little cottage I'm renting with its shrunken path and the insulating, waist-high wall of snow up to the doorway. It seems like the entrance to an igloo. How I arrived here is a question that persists for me, but the place is so remote, I no longer seek an answer.

I have to keep the porch light on all day so when I get home from work I can make my way up the path. I haven't shoveled it in the past few days, and the mottled ice is slippery as the back of a prehistoric fish. I spot King in the window—my beautiful white Samoyed, fogging the glass with his panting. I picked him up on my way to Iowa, riding on the highway at 2 A.M. in a terrible storm. I saw him running along the side of the road, just a strange white flash at first, a dwarfed ghost. Then I saw him turn in someone's headlights, stilled there with his mouth and eyes wide open, a terror and incomprehension that made me brake dangerously fast. I had only to open the back door of the car and he jumped in, wringing wet, overly excited for the next three days.

For a while we lived in the car together. Once I got this place, we slept on the floor—just the dog and me—with a few layers of blankets. I had some cocaine left, and I was shooting it, cramped by paranoia and visions. At least I thought of them as visions. I imagined Victor outside, as patient as any judge. I spent the first nights convincing myself of the impossibility of his having followed me. But when you pull yourself out of a place as low and desperate as the one I'd escaped, it's easy to imagine things and hard to stop.

King would cower in the corner, and I'd spend hours peering from the windows, hiding from shapes the shadows took on, or trying to coax him to me, staring into his eyes as though I could communicate with him—some crazed Dr. Doolittle. At one point he lunged through the screen door and ran out to the pond. I ran after him, calling to him in my underwear, my eyes dilated like black lakes. I saw him out in the water—I was paralyzed with the certainty he'd drown.

He didn't drown. He eventually came out, shaking with cold and afraid of me. I began to get a hold on myself, approached him carefully, and dried him. That was the last time I did drugs. I gathered up the syringes and paraphernalia, dumped them into a milk carton, and threw it all away. Two weeks later, I interviewed for my job with the Department of Social Services. I was wearing a belt with my teeth marks in it. Once I got the job, I threw the belt out too.

I got the job three winters ago. I'm still trying to convince myself that it's possible for life to move at this pace. Maybe it has something to do with my not using drugs, and the tentative return of sanity, but the days have a dream length—entire lives played out in the inching forward of a clock hand. And only recently have I come to appreciate each day's slowness, a languor that makes me wonder whether I didn't drive into some lost or swallowed-up town, where sands move backward through the hourglass, the past reassembling itself, ready to fall again in different configurations.

This two-bedroom cottage has a peculiar warmth. I appreciate its accumulation, a kind of organic decorating that seems to have happened without my intervention. Some of it was here when I arrived, the lamps and a couple of the rugs. I purchased the furniture almost entirely at the Mennonite store: a used '50s sectional and a recliner with a worn plaid cover, forest and pale green. Now there's a nest of King's white hair in the lap of the chair. His toys are here and there, and records everywhere.

I take King out behind the house. He loves the snow and runs over the slick surface of the frozen pond. I worried at first, fearful of a break in the ice. Now I just assume that dogs have some kind of sense about these dangers. Animals know trouble; you can see it in the eyes of the alligator on my desk.

I don't follow King out over the pond, but pack my heels down along the natural embankment, admiring his bursts of energy. He's a beautiful dog—healthy and with a full winter pelt—but there's something sad about him too. The image of him running along the highway remains there for me, and I sometimes hug him too tight, give him too much love, and talk embarrassingly like a child with him.

I look away from King and scan the flat landscape, the one large hill like an Indian grave that casts a shadow up to the door, the few dead trees and the abundant snow pillowing the roof of my house and virtually camouflaging it. I rarely recognize my loneliness anymore, except in this silence. And it isn't silence, really. I hear an owl, the wind, and my breathing. I bring my mittens to my mouth. The heat of my own breath is a comfort. There was a time when this weather would have killed me, when I couldn't find any warmth in my body, bone-thin from drugs. But I like it now; it points to the change in me.

When I turn away from the cottage and the pond, the white seems to go on forever. I often think of Jack London stories when I come out behind the house. My father loved London's stories—he read them while he was incarcerated, dreaming, I guess, of some other wilderness with its different sense of justice.

El Luté

EXCERPT FROM *THE GEOGRAPHICAL CURE*

The trees seem extra crisp today, whizzing by the window of the cab as I ride. Every leaf outlined against the sky in sharp contrast, their pointed edges blocking out the noontime sun blasting from directly above. Blackstone Boulevard has tons of trees on it. The Boulevard, as its inhabitants refer to it, runs through one of Providence's snootier neighborhoods, along the Woonasquatucket River, which runs gray water past sludge banks.

Two lanes on each side, with a grassy island running down the middle, dividing the traffic. The grassy island is also tree-lined, with benches and an asphalt walkway running the length of it. I look out the window of the cab and watch joggers jog up and down the middle of the island. Secretaries and intake nurses from the hospital speed-walk down the middle of the boulevard, wasting away their 50-minute lunch break on the grassy island before speed walking back to work. I'm convinced they're insane.

My cab is maniacally speeding down this path, heading toward the ancient hospital grounds that await my arrival. Every shift of the cab, every bump in the road is an assault on my hypersensitive shell, and I curse the driver every time he applies the brakes. *Slow down, pal.*

The hospital I'm going to consists of several large mansions, each one specializing in a different diagnosis. Some people are placed in the psychiatric mansion, where they are received, evaluated, and promptly stabilized with prescription drugs. Other people are directed to the drug-rehabilitation mansion for detox, to suffer a hellish withdrawal from the tranquilizers and housewife speed that were prescribed to them, just next door, in the psychiatric mansion.

To avoid any confusion, I was placed in the "dual-diagnosis" mansion, which stands dark on a hill like a lone soldier in the war for sanity.

My head is starting to wad like cotton. I haven't been well for about five hours now, and it's all starting to come down as I ride in this death car toward the pointed iron gates surrounding the hospital. I still have a needle in my pocket, and I take it out of my pocket every few minutes to make sure it's there and roll it in my hand. It's been used twice so it's not exactly sharp. But not completely dull either.

When the driver drops me off, I place the needle into the trash can outside of the main building before going in. I try to keep it near the top of the garbage, knowing that I'll likely be attempting to fish it out again in about five hours, while I wait desperately for a cab to take me away from this unforgiving place, over the tracks and across town.

The other new patient sits on the couch across from me, tapping his small feet together. I think he said his name was Bob. I'm trying to sit still.

My eyes are twitching back and forth faster than they can focus on any fixed object. The wallpaper fuzzes into an uncomfortable hallucination every time I try to catch its pattern and decipher its oscillating codes. I can feel the warm white glow of the nurses station coming from somewhere over my left shoulder.

Bob's arms look like two pink sausages ready to explode from their thin casings. His hands clench into balls wound tight with discomfort.

I notice that my hands are doing the same thing: curling into white-knuckled fists, as if every ounce of nervous energy in my body is slamming quickly into the walls of my every cell, trying to force its way out through my extremities. I can just sit and wait for it to finally rip itself through the tips of my fingers, shredding my nerve endings with its barbed tail.

"Did you get checked in yet? The nurse says you're checked in?" Bob's voice sounds like he is speaking through a megaphone held an inch away from the back of my head.

"I don't know," I whisper impatiently, lying. I had been checked in.

When I arrived I spoke with the head intake nurse under the heaving glass dome of the front lobby. I was told to sit in cubicle two and wait and she would be right over—more of an order than a suggestion, really. The naugahyde seat squeaks as my body collapses into it, and Billy Joel attempts to mellow the atmosphere over the transistor radio. My temples have fire running through them.

"OK, Are we ready?" she chirps loudly as she sat down across from me. She likes to help people, likes her job—I can tell. The shine of her healthy face makes me wonder whether she is one of the speed-walkers from the boulevard. Everything is really starting to hurt now: my muscles crying and my dirty veins begging *please please please.*

She ignores two blinking telephone lines as she prints my name on some sheets of paper and shuffles them around. The blinking red lights of the telephone threaten me with every warning flash.

Answer the fucking phone.

"I'm a nurse, not a switchboard operator," she giggles, confusing me with her career talk. I see her as neither.

Her cubicle is decorated for some cryptic holiday, with ribbons and cards placed thoughtfully around pictures of what I assume to be her two nieces. Her sister's kids, maybe. The shiny gold edges of every framed photograph poke sharply against my eyes as the smiling faces of the children pop violently from the wall, like plastic witches at the haunted house.

"How are you doing today?"

I rudely answer her question with a question. "Do you give me any meds for the detox?"

My throat is closing up.

"We'll do our best to make you comfortable," she answers, really meaning it, but I knew it was bullshit.

She probes my sizzling mind for links to my psychosis and addiction. Clues from my past.

"What do you use? How often? Are you violent when you are

using? Suicidal? Have you ever had sex for drugs? Ever been in jail?"

I just kept nodding like a robot, waiting for her to make me comfortable.

"Do you have any drugs or paraphernalia on you now?"

I think of my needle sitting in the trash can outside the door.

"No."

Her words lunge at me from behind her razor teeth, questions ripping through the air and morphing into riddles, before slamming themselves against the invisible tautness of my eardrum.

I crave darkness.

"Whaddya mean, you don't know? I mean either the nurse checked you in or she didn't." Bob's interrogation is beginning to get on my nerves.

"I guess I have then, yes. I've been checked in, Bob. OK?" He is oblivious to the knives in my voice.

He engages me in obligatory rehab chatter.

"Did they give you any meds yet?" Bob's face radiates desperation.

"Nope, not yet."

"Whaddya in for? Crack head?"

I hear my voice reply: "Heroin."

The word slips thinly from my mouth, meaning everything and nothing, leaving a hole in the conversation. Its three syllables separated, written down, and stuck to the wall with thumbtacks.

Bob sits like a waiting synapse until I finally fill the void with the customary reply.

"How about you, Bob? What are you kicking?"

"Oh, just pills. Vicodin, you know. I love them fuckin' beans."

Just pills. His dead gray eyes flip to orbs of icy blue when he thinks of them, when he whispers about the secret stash he had waiting at home. His loyal beans sitting lonely in his junk drawer, awaiting his imminent return with pursed lips and a knowing wink.

Welcome home, big boy.

During conversational pauses, when Bob and I stop talking for more than three seconds, you can hear it, hovering and vibrating like a foghorn. A constant hum draped over the facade of silence. The audible hum of dementia shatters the quiet. Madness spiraling away from my body in waves like radio signals—shrill screaming like a dog whistle.

"Psst. You hear that, kid?"

"Yes, Bob. Constantly."

The nurses are switching shifts, the incoming nurse getting the low-down on the new intakes. She is younger, closer to my age. She doesn't seem as if she likes her job as much as the previous angel of mercy. Something about her timing is off, waiting until I am just visibly able to daydream before cutting in with her lengthy intake process.

She goes by the book, this one. I can tell.

"When do I see a doctor about meds?"

Bob opens his eyes when he hears me mention meds.

"The doctor will only be in later but I can give you some Motrin if you'd like. Helps a little." We know this is not true.

"So when the doctor gets here I can get some methadone so I can at least feel OK?"

The nurse runs the cap of her blue pen down the edge of a manila folder that has my name on the tab.

"Oh, we don't administer methadone for heroin detox. We only give it to people who are already on methadone maintenance."

My face cracks.

"I assure you we will do everything to make you comfortable."

Her words are swallowed by an undertow of panic. I can tell this was not negotiable. My pattern of thinking heads directly toward rationalization.

"There's no way I can kick in here cold turkey are you fucking crazy I could have done that at home. Who is the barbarian responsible for this and who do I speak to about changing hospital policy?"

The nurse's face suddenly becomes very tough-love, glowing with unsympathetic concern.

"Maybe you should experience the detox *without* methadone, so you can remember how painful and tough this is, so that you'll never want to go through it again."

She is serious about this hypothesis. Maybe she is writing a dissertation. She must be fucking insane.

I look at Bob, hoping to find an understanding eye. He just

shrugs. I don't think he understands the gravity of the situation.

"Bob, you know you'll probably want methadone too. You're on the same shit as me, just in pill form. Opiates are opiates, Bob."

I'm hoping he will join my resistance.

"Nah, I'll be OK, kid. She said she'd give me something in a while." He's not getting it.

"Bob, you're going to be awake for the next three weeks. Motrin doesn't help. Trust me. You're going to need more than that."

I look in his eyes and see tumbleweeds blowing through his brain behind them.

I need someone who understands, but they have all left me. All three of my running partners just up and left me. Moved to Texas, leaving me alone and shivering like a crack baby in this Northeastern hellhole. I am nothing but the shadow of a monster habit.

How dare they leave me when they helped me get here? My company is gone and my misery grips me like a wet blanket. My habit is off the charts and now here I am. With Bob.

I have to get the hell out of here.

"C'mon Bob. Whaddya say we take off?"

"Whaddya mean, kid?"

"Like take off, you know? Get the fuck out of here? Leave?"

I always want to take people with me when I flee rehab. I once convinced a small group of fishermen that the rehab we were in was inhuman. Within moments we all signed ourselves out against medical advice and loaded into my car for the short trip from Rhode Island to New Bedford, Massachusetts, a tightly wound fishing community with a lot of bars. The people who live there would always pontificate about how strong the dope was there, so I got a bundle when I dropped off the fishermen. It seemed just like any other dope I had ever done. Maybe there was too much build up. Maybe it's just never enough.

"You sure you want to stay, Bob? I still have room."

"Naw kid. I really can't split. You sure you want to leave?"

"I'm sure, Bob. I've got to bail, but you take care, buddy. Hang in there, Bob."

I can't believe I'm already using words like "buddy" and "hang in there" and I've only been here for three hours. I have to go.

The nurse huffs as she prepares my release papers for my signature.

They really go whole-hog with the guilt tripping when you leave a detox early. Like disappointed parents, they lecture you on how you can't run from your problems, that they fester and grow like sea monkeys.

I tell her I'm moving to Texas.

"You can move to Timbuktu and this will move with you. There is no geographical cure for this." She smirks as she said this, hoping that her words would cement the deal.

I vow to myself to prove her wrong. I *could* move away from this monster. I can run away just fine.

I walk quickly away from the hospital grounds, stopping only to retrieve my needle from its place in the garbage can.

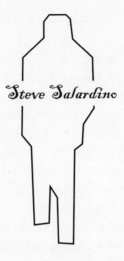

Steve Salardino

ANYWHERE IN PARTICULAR

Rusty is placing pieces of egg and pancake into his mouth all at once. I mean at the same time. And I can see it: dull yellow, shiny white, brown, and tan, going in then down. I can feel the little winces of pain as it hits Rusty's diseased stomach. It is just a slight, instant pain, like being stung by a bee that almost doesn't exist. And it doesn't faze him. But I feel it even if he can't. We go way back.

I look down at the sandwich in my hand—which I ordered blindly— take a bite, and look up at Rusty again. He seems oblivious but not empty. Somewhere inside him he is even overflowing. Still able to put the fork to his mouth but not able to engage the fullness, the whole-ness, due to the meds.

I wonder about chronology and causality and cancer. Was it pain then brain or brain then pain? This place, a 24-hour coffee shop, a place from our past, a refuge at 2 o'clock and 10 o'clock and any o'clock, now seemed an intrusion—eaters and servers clanging and chomping. But all I notice is the space around Rusty, almost glowing— a cloud or nebula—and his mouth is the center where things (like food) go in and where things (like words) come out and I hear him say some-thing slow:

"Steve...fucking roller-coaster...knife...running...off...tied...
wave...you..."

He might actually be making sense here. It could be me—my inability to concentrate on his words. In fact, he could be talking about his eggs: "Steve, these eggs are really good," or maybe, "Steve, how's your wife doing," and what I am hearing could be a collage of other conversations from the past five years. A chronicle of deterioration. The more I watch him the more I feel myself becoming unstuck and pulled in. He's still talking and I can't stop watching his mouth move but now his voice seems to be coming from even farther away.

We're standing on a lake. Standing on water, frozen—ice. But it's bright out. Real early. We're 10 years old. Our parkas are dirty with oil stains and grease. Fluff bulges from a tear on my sleeve that was not there before. We're panting. It hurts to swallow. Rusty has built an engine. Not really built one but removed one from the lawn mower of our neighbor Mr. Wagner who has a gardener now that his wife is gone, now that it doesn't matter. We're panting because together we've shoved and towed all morning. This is what I hear as Rusty pours gas into the engine that has been reassigned to a purple and gold plushy comfy chair with ice skates tied to its feet. This is what I hear as I inspect the late lawn mower attached by many gears and belts to a drum, a crazy wheel thing with spikes and teeth and metal points resting on the ice, a Seussian nightmare. This is what I hear as Rusty stops and pours a little on a rag and hands it to me and as I huff I think something then forget it. (*Am I cold?*) And he takes the rag and the bag from my hands and inhales and exhales a bunch of times and I see little clouds come out of his mouth and disappear and this is what I hear:

"Are you ready? Are you ready to fly? Cause we are going to go, my brother! We are going to ride this purple rocket ship until we burn up or run out of gas or crash or something—I don't know what. It came to me when I was eating. Mom had just made me breakfast. My mind works like that. I'll be doing something not complicated, something completely regimented, and I'll get an idea. And this one is really going to work. This one I'm actually pulling off. I'll steer with my foot and take it once around the lake and fly by you so fast you won't even have a chance to wave. Just kidding, I'll pick you up. You helped me, didn't you? Helped me drag this awesome machine out here. Brother, we are gonna move. Are you ready for the ride? Ready to ride with me?"

But now, in the coffee shop, I take a bite of my sandwich, a sandwich that is new to me, one I don't remember ordering now, one that I don't even know the name of, don't even know if I like, and I say: Do you want something else, Rusty? Are you ready to go back? But am I ready? Back to what? I mean, to where? Is there somewhere you want to go, Rusty?

Rusty gets home from school—I mean college, because he did go away to college. For a while. And his dad can't get off the couch and there is a package on the little low table there in front of the couch and Rusty offers a "Hey, Dad" and his dad, the dad, just nods. Isn't that strange? I think there is a photograph on the table too. But the package, is it a gift? Is it a giant Baby Ruth? Some drugs? A carburetor? A calculator? I think it's a knife. A buck knife, six inches long, locking blade, with case. I watch Rusty unwrap it. Green shiny paper. Who wrapped it anyway? Am I there? I am there. Wait, maybe the knife was on the table and the gift was the photograph. And the photograph, the photograph is (of course) of his mom, and where'd she go?

The eggs are gone and my sandwich is gone and I might not really be there but Rusty doesn't seem to notice and now I hear him say bright and clear: "I want to go now."

We are in my car because he doesn't have one, he doesn't have a license, and in any case he shouldn't be driving with all those meds in him. I'd let him if he asked but he doesn't ask. I pull out of the parking lot of the coffee shop and I put on my sunglasses because the sun just bounces off everything and it is just so bright that everything looks white like the whole world is bleached like a snowstorm, like whiteout. And Rusty squints. I can tell he doesn't think about wearing sunglasses even though I can feel how sensitive his eyes are. It's a side-effect. He just squints. It's like squinting is a way of life. Like eating. Like drugs. Like white. And I say anywhere in particular with a little lift in my voice at the end because it's a question and because I'm hoping he says no because I have to get home to Susie soon and she's already going to be mad that I won't be hungry for dinner. And he says this (and I'm pretty sure he really says this and it's not in my head and not a memory), he says: "Where do you go if you die and you don't believe in anything?"

Did you get the invite? I ask into a phone. (This is before marriage, before sickness, before hearing was a problem, before meds.) Are you coming to the wedding? I say. But he is not coming. And not ever going back to school and…

"Besides, I'm writing all the time nonstop on this typewriter I found like it was meant to be and it takes all my concentration and time and this typewriter doesn't have a lowercase d or capital D either so you can see how hard it must be for me but don't you think the present tense is more interesting anyway? And why did you call again?"

But Rusty, you called me.

We're still driving. I look over out of the corner of my right eye, hidden behind my sunglasses, and see Rusty. The blankness makes him look cool, withdrawn, except he really is withdrawn. But I can also feel that thing almost stirring inside, whirring inside but not greased, stuck—the effort small. Minor torque.

The hospital is made of glass, reflecting the sun, and the brightness gets brighter and streams right through the car window, right through my sunglasses, and I am blind for a second but somehow I still manage to pull out of traffic and turn into the long smooth driveway. In the loading zone I turn off the engine. I must remember that I am dropping him off and not the other way around. Visiting hours are over. Rusty opens the car door and gets out right away—swiftly—aware that he is home, at ease here as he is everywhere now. He turns around and squats down to be even with me. It's hard to see him because of the sunspots in my eye. He says "Thanks" and "Goodbye" and then he turns back, and I watch as he walks up the steps and through the glass doors. The world seems so bright now that I'm squinting to see him, even behind my sunglasses, behind everything; he's still there but fading.

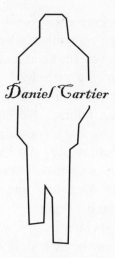

Daniel Cartier

Every Time I See Me Falling

"Have a nice *fucking* time *fucking* each other you *fucking* assholes!"

Need attention? Screaming this at the top of your lungs in the middle of a crowded public space is always a sure way to get some. Dramatic arm movements and door-slamming also help, but be sure to break something on your way out just to drive the point home and make that lasting impression.

The sad truth is, I've already had *two* ex-boyfriends scream this at me in public, complete with all the gestures and ensuing hilarity. So what I want to know is, How the hell does someone get to the point where they feel so melodramatic they actually yell that? It sounds like something a toothless, overweight guest on the Jerry Springer show would scream at her brother, whom she's dating, after she discovers he's been fooling around on her with their mom.

But it wasn't a crazy Jerry Springer guest. It was two people I was actually dating. So my next question is, What the hell was I doing with them?

"Have a nice *fucking* time *fucking* each other you *fucking* assholes!"

The first time was in 1988 at a nightclub in Dover, New Hampshire, of all places. My boyfriend, Paul, saw me talking to some guy, whom I guess was cute, or at least cute enough for Paul to be jealous of. The stupid thing is, I don't even remember what the guy *looked* like. The next thing I knew Paul was screaming at me. "Have a nice *fucking* time *fucking* each other you *fucking* assholes!" And then I was flying...as New Order blared all around us, and the singer sang, "every time I see you falling." I was falling...falling...Nothing seemed real. The wind knocked out of me. I felt my back crashing through the table behind me, and out of the corner of my eye, saw half-empty two-for-one margaritas splashing everyone. And then I was on my knees, a bouncer screaming in my face about the drinks and the mess. I looked around. Paul was gone. He'd proven his point.

The second time was years later in a New York City video store. And even though it was a different boyfriend, it was the same fucking thing: totally out of nowhere. Each time, I was so taken aback that they might as well have yelled "You raped me!" or "Burn in hell, cocksucker!"

And there was always an audience to deal with after (of course). What do I tell them? Do they think I'm pathetic? Do they *at least* feel kind of sorry for me? I mean, we might as well have put up a stage and lights and just screamed, "Hi there! Welcome to the *Two Crazy Gay Guys Show*! We're two totally insecure, *miserable* gay guys who shouldn't even *be* in a relationship, let alone be with each other! Join us tonight as we scream accusations and throw things at each other, all the while involving you, our beautiful audience."

Of course we never know going into the woods that there may be traps set, or land mines that can blow us to bits. All love starts sweet, of course. Otherwise, why would we bother?

I was 16 when I first laid eyes on Paul. I watched him walking toward my friends and me, his silhouette framed by crisp October stars. And the daunting task I'm left with years later remains how to describe him to you and do him justice. How can somebody possibly describe the *feeling* of instant love? What words can I muster? They all seem so stupid and lifeless when I think of the pounding ache in my teenage heart—and how it changed forever with his sudden appearance.

Paul possessed worldliness I couldn't even come close to knowing.

And he was older. *At least 23,* I thought. *Maybe even 24. He's been places, I can tell.*

And the one word pounding through my head as he walked toward my little ragtag posse, huddling outside a Seven-Eleven trying to score beer, was *sex.* And with each step he took toward us, the word became louder in my head: "sex, *sex,* SEX!"

Alongside him was a beautiful girl. I could tell she possessed world-liness too. The way she walked alongside him with such ease informed me of it. They were laughing: laughing and walking, walking and laughing. And they were in slow motion, still managing to descend on us in very quick time. Before I knew it he was mere feet away, staring down and grinning at us. He was instant and dazzling, and very, very blond. His white teeth flashed, and he said, "Hey there! What are you kids up to?"

My poor little brain pounded away: "sex...sex with him...sex with him..."

"Uh—we're just waiting for someone to help us out." This was my friend Stacy talking. Witchy Stacy. Stacy of the clove cigarettes and creeper boots and black smudgy eye makeup. Stacy had a room full of posters for the Cure, and ended up becoming bipolar and flipping out. But that was later on, when we were juniors. Bela Lugosi would always be dead at Stacy's house.

"You guys need me to get something for you inside the Seven Eleven?" he asked. There was laughter in his eyes as he loomed over us, staring us down. I instantly saw what he saw, and I cringed.

He saw kids. He saw some little high school, death-rock wanna-bes sitting Indian-style outside a convenience store, in a stupid jackass town way out in the middle of nowhere. He saw acne and combat boots and Manic Panic hair dye. And I felt far removed from the ele-gance I knew he was accustomed to. The year before, in ninth grade, I'd read *The Great Gatsby.* Thinking about it now, only F. Scott Fitzgerald could've done Paul justice. Paul was elegant. He harked back to a different time. I pictured him in the countryside—wind whipped and smiling behind the wheel of a Model T, all his schoolboy chums crowded in the back, just having pulled ivy off the walls at Yale. Or maybe it would just be him and this elegant girl, only in my head she became a flapper, and they were laughing and drinking gin while tinny

1920s radio music crooned love songs as the whole world listened. I always daydream with a soundtrack. I should probably be a music supervisor for television, but I guess it's a pretty hard field to break into. Seriously though, if you ever hear of anything…

Suffice it to say I felt idiotic sitting there with all my overdressed baby-fat-faced friends, while he and his ravishing companion peered down upon us. He was all sleek lines and cheekbones, and when he turned and caught my eye I shuddered with embarrassed lust.

He bought us some beer, which we giggled over and carted like mice into an alleyway. My friends thanked him with a pseudo casual, "Thanks man, you're all right." I stood there and gawked.

He smiled. His companion smiled. "Nice mohawk," He said to me.

My whole insides were instantly spinning. *Oh, my God, he talked to me! He talked to me! Oh, my God, he just talked to me!*

Stupefied, I said "thank you" like I was underwater. A hyperactive loop went round and round my cranium: "Did I really just talk to him? Did I really just talk to him?"

Then, as in any good celebrity sighting or UFO encounter, they were gone as quickly as they'd arrived: down the street and into the night's darkness. As they got smaller, he leaned into her saying something, a little private joke between two winners, and she arched her head back, laughing heartily and loud. It was glamorous laughter I would try to mimic later on, when I was alone in my bedroom, and nobody could see me pretending that I was her, and he was telling the joke to me, a secret joke only his ghost and my reflection in the mirror fully understood. And from that night on, his ghost was my untouchable companion. His face was the pillow I found myself hugging every night. Kissing every night…smiling…laughing…pretending…

New Hampshire is a *very* conservative state. It's all woods and war memorials and old people who think Reagan was a misunderstood genius. However, Portsmouth, which boasted an art gallery and two sidewalk cafés, seemed wild and bohemian. It had a *scene*. By scene, I mean a bunch of leather-jacketed, spiky-haired older kids who hung out in the middle of the town square looking distant as they nursed hangovers each day with coffee and hits of acid. Alongside them were the other groups not fit for the rest of the state: the gays, hippies, performance artists, and skinheads.

And then there were my two friends and me: the goths. Portsmouth was the only place we could go unless we trekked down to Boston, and since none of us drove, this rarely ever happened. So Portsmouth became our world. We'd have to force our parents to drive us in after school so we could hang out in the town square's outskirts, watching the older punks, who all seemed like rock stars. They never really acknowledged us. Being 16 and still living with our parents, we were considered poseurs. These guys were real.

We'd brag to one another if one of them even looked at us. In the interim, we got to know all the other people—the poets and shop owners. It seemed everybody knew Paul. He was referred to in the community with a hushed reverence. We heard rumors about the wild parties he gave, and his dramatic habit of leaving these parties at their zenith, just letting his guests have free reign over his apartment. "Why would he leave?" my friends and I would wonder. "Does he just want to be alone? Doesn't he like his friends?" And then of course, "I wish we could go. I wish he'd invite us."

Time passed. I'm not sure how much. Two years? Two and a half?

There's so much I could say about these years, but I just don't have the energy to right now. Plus, I've rehashed these years too many times in the last decade at parties and eventually in the AA meetings where I ended up. To be brief, there was the acceptance by the older punks of my friends and me. There were parties of endless drinking and drugging that followed. There was me dropping out of high school, giving my horrified parents the lame excuse that I had to warn the world about the oncoming threat of nuclear war.

I also started bands, had my first gay kiss, and my first series of overly dramatic relationships. I went from boyfriend to boyfriend never really taking the time to come up for air (pardon the intentional double entendre). So much to remember and blab on about. And believe me, if there wasn't a point to this story, I would.

At the heart of it all was Paul. He existed in my head 24 hours a day, perfect and untouchable. Every action I took was somehow willing him to notice me one day. It certainly was no secret to anyone else how I felt. Even my series of punky, funky teenage boyfriends knew it. We'd all go to the restaurant Paul worked at and everyone would watch me drool over him. This was the late '80s, mind you. America was learning how to complicate even the simplest foods, so we'd chow down on tuna salad sandwiches with pineapple basil mayonnaise. Pesto was just starting to happen and it was popping up everywhere, in pasta and on salads. You just couldn't get away from it. Paul would stop and talk to us, sometimes even sit down to have a cigarette at our table.

Occasionally I'd force myself to go into the restaurant alone with a book, and watch him as he worked. I'd purposely bring "deep books." Paul seemed "deep" to me. I wanted him to know I was "deep" too.

On one of these occasions, Paul sat down at my table and it was *just us.* I tried to appear fascinated with some book I had by a Greek philosopher. Don't ask me which one it was. I don't think I even knew then.

"Wow," noted Paul, "Some book! Doing homework?"

"What? Oh, um, this? No I uh—"my voice was cracking, "I—I just like this writer."

I can't recall much of the rest of the conversation, just that it was the first time he and I had spoken alone. It lasted five minutes, but to me it seemed every second went by slower than the last. I stumbled over words and tried to pretend I had some bottled knowledge of Greek philosophy, which of course Paul knew everything about.

"Boy those Greeks" he said knowingly. "They were wild."

"Oh—uh—yeah?"

"Yeah!" He purred, "Orgies, drugs—you name it. All those old guys had harems of young boys just lying around. They'd just flip them over and start pumping whenever they felt like it."

"Oh—um—wow!" I replied dumbly.

"Isn't that hot?" he said, looking right at me. I blushed and frantically tried to come up with a response.

"Y-yeah but um, weren't they afraid of, uh—catching anything?"

"Catching anything?"

"Uh, y-yeah, like, um, AIDS?"

"Like, um, AIDS?" he snorted. "Oh, *God!*"

I can't remember anything else. Only that when I left the restaurant he was out front with another waiter. They glanced at me as I walked by and began to laugh. I think I muttered a weak "goodbye" under my breath. I was so sick to my stomach, I don't recall.

A few years passed. So did various hair colors, menial jobs, and boys who meant nothing to me except not being alone...and then suddenly...

Paul was mine. I can't explain how it happened. It seems weird to me even now. I had my humdrum existence and he had this untouchable one, like he'd just fallen from what I like to think of as heaven: Hollywood's golden era circa 1935. And I could never quite believe he was here walking among us in New Hampshire circa 1989.

It happened at a party. I was 19 and had loved him for over three years. I was high on mushrooms and he was suddenly there, tugging me into a bathroom. He was aggressively drunk, something I would become accustomed to later on. I should've known then that it wasn't normal to have someone yank you out of a party all boozy and shove their cock down your throat. But I was so painfully naive and stupid. Oh, yeah, and in love.

He pushed me to the linoleum and whipped it out slurring, "You're really into me, aren't you? Well, dig in, baby." Moments later he stumbled backward and pissed all over the floor and all over my little black bondage skirt.

We became boyfriends, and at an alarming speed, moved in together. I felt I'd arrived. He was 26 and I was 19. He'd never been in any relationship longer than two weeks. As time passed, I prided myself on the fact that I was finally the one who got him, pinned him down, and of course was going to fix everything about him. It never occurred to me there might be some severe reason he had never gotten serious with anyone before.

Feebly attempting to make a long story short, I'll sum up Paul and me this way: I was an alcoholic. I drank every day, nearly killing myself, driving in a series of uninsured foggy blackouts. But compared to Paul's monster addiction, my drinking was like a shy school marm letting loose at a church social.

Paul's drinking was angry and—I learned very quickly—insatiable. There was *nothing* he'd hesitate to break or destroy when he was loaded, which was basically every night. And he *always* had a point he just had to prove. If we were at a party and he vaguely felt like someone didn't like him, he'd immediately be up in their face, screaming and accusing them, wanting to *know, demanding* to *know*, what the *fuck* their *fucking* problem was. He'd act chummy with you at first, like "Oh, aren't we all having a blast? Isn't this fun?" But at some point when you weren't looking, he'd turn. He'd start digging in at you, subtly trying to pry out your deepest fears. Still smiling, he'd pretend he was bonding with you, becoming your confidant, winning you over. He made you believe you'd found someone who understood whatever it was you were going through. He made you feel protected and safe. And of course that's when it happened

"So your mother just died of cancer, huh?"

"Yeah...[*whimper, whimper*] I miss her so much."

"I see...so when did it happen?"

"God, thank you for talking to me about this. [*whimper*] She died about a month ago [*more whimpering*] Yes, it's been about a month.... I miss her so much." [*totally uncontrollable whimpering*]

Paul waits a few seconds, lets them calm down, and then says: "Are you sure about that?"

The stunned victim looks up at him confused, "Am I sure? What do you mean?"

"Are you sure she's dead?"

"Sure I'm sure...wha—"

And then Paul's off. "Well, I just think it's weird, you being at a party going on and on about your mom dying of cancer, and dragging us all into it. I mean, why are you at a party in the first place if you're so bummed out? Huh? What the fuck? Do you really need attention that bad? Because if you do, I'd be glad to get it for you." Then Paul's up and pacing about the room and bringing the party to a standstill. "Oh, gee! Look, everybody! So and so's crying 'cause his mother just died of cancer, or at least that's what he says!"

"Paul, come off it..." someone whispers.

But Paul's on a roll now, "Come off it? Come off it? No! I will not fucking come off it. I will not fucking come off it at all! Listen, I'm fucking sick and tired of all these fucking self-centered assholes needing attention, so they come here and start laying all their shit out for us to smell!" Paul turns now to face the crying cancer-mother offspring. "Do you think we give a shit? Huh? Do you think you're the only one feeling anything right now? Huh? Do you? *Do you?*"

Stunned silence, and then Paul is grabbing cancer-mom boy's arm and dragging him to the window. "You want to see pain? Huh? Do you want to see what a real suffering person looks like? I'll show you pain, you asshole! I'll show you pain, you fucking fucking fucking—" Paul's hand is crashing through glass. Sharp shards rain down everywhere, on our laps and in our drinks. Blood is spouting now from his arms and he's lost in a world where the only word left is *fucking*, which he screams over and over and over and over. And over fucking fucking fucking and over and over and over fucking and over...

I lived with this. Every day I felt this rage directed at me—like he was blaming me for loving him. Paul's mother didn't die of cancer. Paul's mother had given him up for adoption. Paul's adoptive parents were Southern socialites. They didn't want kids, but felt compelled to adopt some anyway. They wound up with Paul and his sister, and let both children know in subtle, lifelong ways what a burden they were. "If I'd a had my way, I would have gone and seen the world," his mother would sigh. "But we were expected to have kids...that's what married people did where we came from. And since we couldn't have any ourselves, we ended up with you two. But I really miss being free..." (Insert disappointed sigh here).

Paul was convinced that the rest of the world felt this way about him too. We'd all desert him eventually. When I finally began to *dare* to dream about *maybe* leaving him someday, I would suddenly flash on the image of a little boy looking at me, eyes pleading. "So now you're leaving me too?" he would say. I'd feel so horrible, like I'd caused him all this pain, and it was my entire fault for ever even entertaining the idea of not staying.

So stay I did. I simply stayed and stayed and stayed for years longer than I wanted to. I was the first person in Paul's adult life that he'd ever let in. And so I became the hardest person for him to let go. Usually when somebody got too close, and saw the *real* Paul, not the one he played for acquaintances, they were dropped so fast they didn't know what hit them. But I was kept around. I can't say why. Was it because I came to the table with such an insane case of idol worship? Or was it my naïveté, my gullible little prayer that I could make it all better? Or maybe it was just my complete and utter inability to speak up for myself and to fight back? Whatever the reason, Paul was not mine—I was his.

My most vivid memory of him is the day he checked all of our dirty towels for semen stains. He arrived home convinced that while he was away I had masturbated, and the thought of me doing this had driven him into a jealous frenzy. He *wanted some answers,* he said. He *wanted to know who the fuck* I thought about when I shot my *load all over the place*!

I had no answer. I just stood there, mute, not knowing what to say.

He said to me one morning, as I swept broken plates from the floor, "Daniel…I'm sorry about last night…when I did what I did…I wasn't doing it to you, I swear—I—I feel like I was doing it to my mother."

Again, I just stood there wondering, *What do I say?*

Part of me wanted to tell him I wasn't his fucking goddamn mother. I was his fucking goddamn boyfriend, for Christ's sake. But that part of me was buried so far beneath the surface, I couldn't get through all the other shit to retrieve it. I couldn't say that. There's no way; I'd hurt him. He'd leave me. He'd hate me. He'd hurt me again.

If I came home 10 minutes late, he'd be there waiting—a list of questions scrolling past his eyes. "Where were you? Oh, really? Who was there? Uh-huh, I see…Well, you said you'd be gone till 5. It's 5:25. What the fuck is this bullshit? Where the fuck were you? Where? No really, don't give that answer again. I want the truth. Who were you with? Who the fuck were you *with* you *fucking asshole? Tell me*! You know I'll fucking find out. Who was it? Was it Sean? He's cute. I bet you think about him and his big *fucking cock* banging into your mouth all day, don't you?"

Again, me silent.

Again, me not knowing how to respond.

And again, me not a psychoanalyst, but a stupid kid who was too scared to speak; his words moving too fast to catch up with anyway. So far as I could see, there really was only one thing for me to do. And so that's what I did.

I just kept silent. It's a defense that stayed with me for a long time afterward. And as others came into my life—boyfriends, managers, and record labels—I'd sit and watch them trample over my dreams and pulverize my opinions. I'd watch it all in slow motion and remain silent, so scared to say the wrong thing. Barely managing a threadbare smile, I'd finally mutter, "Don't worry, it's OK. I understand. Uh-huh, no, I'll be fine. I'm sorry. No, I understand.... uh huh...I know.... I understand."

I'm not with Paul anymore. I left him, and New Hampshire, 10 years ago. I'd like to say I've changed completely, but I'd be lying. I speak up for myself a little more, and actually have days when I find myself daring to like the man I've become. It's a weird feeling, and it seems wrong, but I try to just let myself feel it. There's still a part of me somewhere that's not sure whether my ideas are stupid and my opinions are dumb.

I'd like to say Paul was the last of my crazy, possessive lovers, but he wasn't. I met more along the way. A boyfriend in New York was so overbearing that if I even looked in the general direction of another man, the rest of the day would be shot. The whole year of my life with him became an alleyway littered with name-calling, insults, plate-throwing, and of course the constant questioning that I had no answers for.

We were in a crowded video store on a Friday night. I was paying for our videos and in the process of handing the clerk my $6. I heard: "Have a nice *fucking* time *fucking* each other, you *fucking* assholes!"

And then I was flying again. I collided against a video display, knocking over all the "employee favorites." People gasped and my lover stormed out, leaving me to help put everything back together. In front of shocked onlookers, I apologized for everything. I didn't know what the hell I was apologizing for. Apparently the fact that I'd looked at the clerk when I was attempting to pay him. Maybe I should've tried paying with my eyes closed. Perhaps that would've been OK.

But time goes on, and as we learn things we slowly change. It's not like in the movies where somebody realizes something about themselves and they have that "lightbulb moment." You know, where all of a sudden they're like, "Oh, my God! It's because my father never

hugged me that I'm a heroin addict." And then of course they're totally 100% better and everything's different. And then the sun comes out
and there's this big music playing and everybody starts to dance in the
streets to a Phil Collins song. I mean, it would be great, you know? If
life could just be that simple. But it just doesn't seem to work that way
most of the time. The most important changes we go through usually
happen without us even knowing it. One day, after having worked on
myself for years and years, going to AA meetings, writing in my fucking journal, and saying my fucking serenity prayer for about the fifty
billionth time, I realized, "Huh, I guess I don't want to be with people
like Paul anymore." And then I realized I'd felt this way for quite a
while, but I simply hadn't recognized it until then.

Epilogue

I was in a rush a week ago. I was doing errands that needed to be
done, but I felt this strong urge to get home. I felt like something terrible would happen if I didn't drop everything at once, get in my car, and
go. I tried to ignore it but as the day wore on the feeling became more
insistent, like I was toting around a 5-year-old who had to pee really
badly, but I just kept shushing him, saying, "No, not now. Just hold it
a little longer and we'll be home soon."

I couldn't tell where this feeling was coming from. These were
errands I wanted to do all week but just hadn't had the time: buy groceries, send out bills, and get Banjo her flea medicine. By the time I got
around to going to the bank, I couldn't follow through with it. The
feeling I had deep down in my gut was so overwhelming I couldn't see
through all the guilt. And the "tick-tock, tick-tock" of the minutes I'd
been gone from my apartment started to unravel me.

So I found myself rushing home, cursing every red light that slowed
my way. When I arrived, the parking was hurried and the elevator was
stupid. "Stupid fucking elevator!" I clattered. "What the fuck's the
deal? I'm in a *hurry*!" And then banging on the button a few more
times, as if the machine could respond to my desperation.

Finally I'm inside the elevator, but the goddamn box moves too
fucking slowly for my liking and I want to swear at it some more. But

I can't now because some old lady who lives a few floors above me has stepped in, and is asking me all these *stupid* questions about my dog, like, "What kind is he?" and "How long have you had him?" I want to tell her: "Look lady, not now! I'm not in the mood. Really! My dog hates you too. OK? And I've had *her* for a year."

Floor four and I'm out the door. Banjo's at my side panting and try-ing to keep up with her crazy gay owner. And then I'm at my door and there's the fumbling with the groceries and the dog leash to get my keys. I struggle to find them, but after some digging I do. They're inserted and the deadbolt is turned.

I am home.

And all is fine. Craig sits at the computer in his office. "Honey, is that you?"

His voice trails down the hall, a lilting, unassuming happiness.

"Yes. Sorry I was gone so long."

He doesn't hear this last part and asks, "Did you have a nice time shopping?"

"Uh—yeah, I did. I just—"

I stop in the middle of my psychosis, and I'm frozen. The sound of keys clicking on his keyboard a few rooms down begins to comfort me, his calm clicking against my pronounced breathing. And I realize that he's just gone about his business as if nothing's the matter. And then it dawns on me: Nothing *is* the matter. Everything's just fine.

Craig isn't going to grill me on where I'd gone and why I hadn't come home sooner. He's not going to start listing all of our friends' names, demanding to know which ones I've been sleeping with.

But for the last two hours I was acting like he would. And the scari-est thing is I didn't even realize I was doing it.

So part of me—the psychotic part, the post-traumatic stress part—sighs a heavy sigh and retreats into its cavern. It seems to be hibernat-ing more and more these days, which is nice. Maybe someday it will go to sleep for good and just never wake up.

I walk into Craig's office. The screen door is open to the deck, and I see the tomato plants he grew from seeds getting amazingly tall.

"Wow. Look at those tomatoes," I exclaim as I kneel down by his chair.

He stops typing and turns to me with a big smile on his face. "Honey! I didn't think you'd be home so soon."

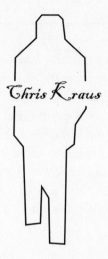

The Blessed

Dear Chris,

I left a message on your answering machine about why I couldn't come last week. Maybe you never heard it. It was about the accident. God's latest evil trick. The car you helped me buy is wrecked, and it is just the last example of how every time my life seems to be OK God sticks out his foot and trips me. No, it's worse. God is a malevolent asshole. Sometimes I think he puts on his cowboy boots and kicks me. You have been very kind, but even though I owe you five more cleanings I have to let you know I can't come back.

Because every time I go to work I break something or something new goes wrong. My T-cells are down below 200 now and I feel like a ghost has wrapped its hands around my neck. I can't breathe or catch my breath and I don't want to infect any other people with God's curse. It was no coincidence the washing machine and dryer broke the last time I was working at your house. God did that, and God only knows what else God will make go wrong to hurt me.

I am four months behind on rent and now the social worker at LA County Hospital says she can get me Section 8 and disability. I have decided to wind my business down and take everything they give me.

Ten years ago I promised God I'd never go on welfare, but why should I keep my promises?

God is an evil fucker and the accident was just his last revenge. Two months ago he started to reveal his true intentions when he let those kittens die. What kind of cruel and heartless person would leave seven innocent kittens out to die in a cardboard box next to a Dumpster? I spent the last money that you gave me taking them to the vet and still I couldn't save them. Do you know what it's like to have a four-week-old kitten dying in your hands? When I got sober and started up my cleaning business I thought God would help, but I was wrong. God wants everything to die. Myself included.

Your friend,

Bo

Bo left this for me when I was away at Yaddo during the month of June. Actually, the letter is a reconstruction. When I got back to LA my boyfriend or ex-boyfriend and his 14-year-old son and my husband or ex-husband and his girlfriend's shaggy taffy-colored dog were all living at my house. The house was my great hope. It is a large three-level stucco thing ambling down a slope at interesting angles, with a courtyard and a guesthouse, built by an architect for a female client in the early 1930s. It is the kind of house—"suitable for entertaining"—that a young, ambitious acolyte of the art world might dream of someday occupying. Not grandiose, but "comfortable" enough to give you that irreplaceable, invisibly supported, timelessly upper-middle-class WASP ambiance. I bought it at a bankruptcy sale two days before I turned 45, thinking it would save my marriage, but neither of us lived there. Now it's rented.

When I got back in June, all the furniture was moved around. My boyfriend or ex-boyfriend's teenage son had boxed my books and clothes and papers, and the bedroom, which I'd done up to match the cherry tree outside, was covered with sports and military memorabilia. The three men were living off one giant shopping trip to Smart & Final and Bo hadn't been there for three weeks, so everything was dirty. I read his letter standing in the living room beside the fireplace and I remember being very worried that the son, whose friend was visiting from Christian church camp, would not have to think that there was anything unusual about this situation. Everyone was talking and I was confused about where or who they wanted me to sleep with, and I felt Bo's letter pulsing in my hand like it was an amputated finger. I remember holding it at arm's length, blinking, my whole body tensing up to shut it out 'cause it was too painful to absorb, and then I put it down or threw it out. All I was thinking was, *I don't even have a place to stand.* I was a stationary object, teetering without a station. Bo's letter hit me with centrifugal force, and like I say, I probably lost it.

Bo lives in an apartment in the slummy part of Silver Lake. His landlord, J.J. Sherman, keeps forgiving him back rent, and he is much beloved by all his neighbors. I went to Yaddo wanting to write a book about my husband, who was lost to me. Every day I sat at Sylvia Plath's old desk, sobbing, filling a spiral notebook and producing the four pages every day everyone expected. It had been five years since I left the East Village for LA, and Yaddo was like a refresher course in hierarchy. There were the ingenues, the stars, the doomed reformers and experimentalists. Everyone behaved exactly as expected except there was this undertow of beauty—the goofy vulnerability of grown-up children trying to make something of our own in the wake of all this legendary greatness—that bound us all, the envied and the envious, together.

I met Bo about three years ago when I was living in a tree house in Mt. Washington. I was looking for someone to clean because I worked at home a lot and things got messy. The house—which I eventually traded for the three-level thing—was an asbestos-shingled cabin built in the armpit of a rubber tree. It was romantic. At that time, I was Pippi Longstocking and my husband was Pippi's father, the Absent Sea Captain. Pippi's father left her well provided for. Twice each month two checks arrived: a small one in Pippi's name, and a large one for the Sea Captain. Both checks were issued by the same Institution. No matter how many hours Pippi worked, or how infrequently the Sea Captain visited the Institution, their checks would always be the same. The Sea Captain lived 3,000 miles away and anyway he had other means, so with his consent she kept them both. Pippi had always been quite poor. Now she had an income of about $60,000.

To reach the house you climbed 72 concrete steps that zigzagged from the bottom of the canyon. It had been built in the 1920s as a hunting shack, and the elevation gave the house a *Deliverance* kind of feeling, protecting you with clear sight lines and cover from all your enemies.

When Pippi and the Sea Captain bought the house it had already been abandoned for 10 years. The night before they made the offer, they sat on the stoop and smoked a joint, leaning back against the splintered door that looked straight out across the canyon. There were still trains on San Fernando Road. Outside, you could hear the distant whistle. Pippi and the Sea Captain leaned against each other, feeling twinges of romance that had long since been replaced by kinship. Together they formed a single perceiver—some kind of tropical plant imbued with listening devices, wide open to the rustling night. It was the end of summer.

They knew the Sea Captain would leave again, this time maybe forever, and Pippi would be on her own. They mumbled words about mortgages and tax incentives but really they were summoning the house's past to see whether there was any substance that could help them in the future. And it—the house—felt good. Strange and familiar at the same time. It was the kind of New Zealand bungalow Pippi remembered from her childhood. There were old cupboards, a lemon tree, and cottage windows. Pippi adored the past, and the Sea Captain knew that she'd be happy in this setting. In this way she could wait for him forever. The house was feminine and tough, but mostly it was very solitary.

In June all that was gone and as I recall Bo's letter now, I'm amazed that someone with an IQ of maybe 95 had such a keen sense of form. A letter is an act. I will gather up my thoughts for you and put them in a letter.

When I met Bo my husband had been gone about two years.

At the Institution, Pippi had a job teaching a group of mostly troubled girls how to write their diaries. For the first time in a long time she was free. In Los Angeles there was very little competition. People seemed to take her seriously. Her students published a magazine called *Obscene Thoughts* and, strangely, this was very controversial. Back in New York, heartsick at being known only as the Sea Captain's quirky daughter, Pippi had asked the Sea Captain's famous artist friends, "How can I become famous?" And naturally, they'd laughed.

But in Los Angeles everything was quantifiable. Success, therefore, was both attainable and boring. Conceptual art was now what West Coast real estate had been to the immigrants of the 1920s: a blue sky opportunity. Any graduate of an East Coast university willing to work a 60-hour week in New York could come out here and within three years become a leader in their field. You didn't have to be that smart, that rich, or especially lucky. While Pippi's old friends languished in New York, dozens of recent Institution graduates were becoming name-brand artists.

There wasn't much in the environment that interested me, and I was lonely. Attached irrevocably to the Sea Captain, Pippi had sex with people from the most unlikely places.

Eventually I called an escort service in the South Bay catering to men and "ladies." The first escort, James, pressed his hands onto my throat until I nearly choked, and this was surprisingly erotic. James was maybe 32. He had a short, compact body and bad skin, gold jewelry, a Mercedes, and a cell phone. Obviously this was safe, 'cause James was a professional.

Josh, the second escort, was 22. He'd never done this, but since every girl he'd ever slept with in Hermosa Beach said his penis was the best they'd ever seen, he thought he'd be a natural. When he couldn't get it up, I didn't really mind or take it personally. Adventure was the chance to find some commonality with anyone at any time. Who was this person? Josh, stoned and embarrassed, thought I might have some connection to the music business, so he started pitching. He had this band, and their influence was mostly techno, except they added this kind of gangsta thing. The studio engineer was so impressed he comped them on their demo, but really it was hard to talk about because their sound was so unique it was inexpressible.

When Gary, the third escort, threatened to decapitate me, I switched to answering personal ads. At least it would be cheaper.

When all value has become exchangeable, stupidity becomes a topic of investigation. California is a chance to rethink everything.

I met a New Age dom who made me promise to comply with all his orders. He was a leader in the men's movement, an EST graduate, and a member of Agape. He taught me all about transcendent mind—how each person is the master of their fate, and poverty and sickness are created by the negative thought-patterns of the individual.

In Los Angeles, Pippi had decided to become a writer. The night her book came out, when her students were all gathered in the tree house for a party, she escaped downstairs to be beaten by the dom. She didn't want to be a role model.

When Pippi was a little girl, the Sea Captain used to tell her stories. The purpose of a story is postponement. When physical contact—sex—is too immediate or violent, the only possibility is to circle round the space that separates you with words.

Before Bo, there'd been a Guatemalan cleaning woman. She brought her child to work and had no transportation, so of course I baby-sat and drove. There was some awful story about a murdered uncle, he'd been hiding in a tree, and the child had seen him shot. Maybe she'd even pointed him out. The girl, Diana, at 11 seemed so protective of her mother, and she liked to read. Thinking she could be a friend, I asked Maria if I could take Diana on an outing. We went to the beautiful playground with the Witch's Hat at Elyria Canyon, but Diana, who was fat, cried and hid from all the effortlessly hip blond children of location managers and environmental lawyers, and when I took her out to lunch, she vomited.

Bo arrived with an arsenal of earth-friendly cleaning products and a feather duster. He seemed like a big improvement. He was a large square-jawed man with skinny legs, about 42, who looked like the Jolly Green Giant. Bo was clean-shaven, had hazel eyes, and described himself as a Virgo fairy. He said: "I live to clean." So, yes, he was a bit slow-witted.

He didn't seem to have a boyfriend, and since he idolized young sullen ethnic types with exquisitely developed bodies, I wondered whether he ever had. It was like he'd learned queerness from the wrong book. Bo hummed show tunes while he alphabetized my groceries. His shining moment had been the time he placed the winning bid on a pair of scuffed-up mules—tenth cousins to the ruby slippers that Judy Garland once wore in a movie. He retold this story to me later, sniffling, eyes misty, when things got really bad. By then he'd lost them in a fire. But his greatest pleasure came from rescuing abandoned cats and kittens.

Bo is standing in the living room, chest pumped out, brandishing his feather duster: "If I ever catch the bastard who abandoned little Calico in the trash, he'll have to mess with this faggot!" His two-room apartment shelters more than a dozen pets and strays. He feeds them, tags them, takes them to the vet, medicates them, names them. On Friday nights Bo likes to take a walk to Circus Books around the corner. He buys a root beer, browses the rack of porno mags. Vaguely aroused, he goes out to a row of Dumpsters in the parking lot and listens for the mewling sound of desperate kittens. Bo moves according to God's plan. God has placed these kittens in his path. Therefore, it is God's will that he save them.

Bo, an orphan, is terrified that any cat might die unloved, uncared-for.

Bo charges $40 for a weekly cleaning. On weeks when no one cancels, driving between Mt. Washington and Silver Lake and the Valley, he earns $400 and then he has to pay for litter, cat food, and the vet.

Pippi and the Sea Captain fly around the northern hemisphere on tickets purchased by the Institution. When it occurs to her, she picks up the phone and makes a thousand bucks selling their frequent flyer miles to a Florida developer. The absurdity of this does not escape her.

I love myself the way I am
There's nothing I need to change
I'll always be the perfect me
There's nothing to rearrange

were the lyrics of a Self Empowerment anthem that the New Age dom would play while he was beating her.

I used to like to read a lot of books about Buddhism. (My husband's girlfriend is a Buddhist.) I liked the parts about chrysanthemums and autumn moons, and the way the koans gave a structure to emotive logic. (My husband's girlfriend is a literary critic. She says my writing is "pathetic.") Mostly, though, I gravitated to the parts about morality. The Buddhist teachers say, "Strive to do good," but then they qualify this by adding, "If you can't do good, at least don't do any harm," and this seemed very realistic. Because at that time when I was living in the tree house I was seeing myself as something like a fulcrum. My husband was 3,000 miles away and we no longer had sex or slept together or told each other dreams or even talked. The ocean of our symbiosis had been diverted to a narrow stream of enterprises that we shared: investments, checks, and money. Therefore we saw each other as the Greater Good. Things came our way. I believe that marriages are sacred. Each time Pippi made easy money due to luck or cleverness, she vowed to give part of it away, and the Sea Captain supported this. Because there was no longer so much actual love between us, we thought we could create an atmosphere of love by giving things away.

Bo, the rescuer of orphan cats, was also seeing himself as a fulcrum.

Bo's whole life is a catastrophe, and he often gets confused. Once I hired him to pick up some flooring 80 miles away but then he couldn't remember why he'd come or what to do two hours later when he got there. Bo dates these lapses back to childhood. He never knew his father. His infant memories include an imprint of his mom's high heels—the way she threw him to the floor and kicked him in the head. He was a fat, effeminate child. Other times, she used belts and straps and one of those old heavy plastic telephone receivers. Bo thinks his slowness might be due to a concussion. But then again it might be sensory deprivation because Bo's mother swooped him up and locked him in a closet every time he opened the refrigerator. Refrigerator, closet—two dark boxes in Canoga Park, where the temperature stays up around a hundred half the year. One time the punishment went on so long that he was missed at school. Social Welfare sent him to some distant relative in Nevada. Bo found a starving, short-haired black-and-white stray cat that had been abused, and finally he had someone to talk to. When he was old enough to leave, he bought a Greyhound ticket to LA, but the driver wouldn't let him bring the cat without a regulation crate, and this was the first bad thing that happened in Bo's adult life.

The New Age dom said I could no longer use the word "depressing," so I stopped. Later "luck" was added to the list, and all its synonyms like "chance" and "fortune." He saw me as a victim of a "negative evil culture" that included Andy Warhol, the early records of Lou Reed, tailored suits, the use of alcohol and tobacco, the entire island of Manhattan, cropped hair, films without a plot, all forms of gay and lesbian culture, and hyperbolic antonyms.

On the anniversary of our first cleaning, Bo gave me a heart-shaped cut-glass ashtray with the words I LOVE YOU on the bottom. And then I didn't see him for awhile because he had pneumonia, and when I did he came up the 72 steps winded and hysterical and announced he'd tested positive for full-blown AIDS. He quickly phoned his 13 other clients, seven of whom canceled. And then an uninsured drunk driver hit his '89 Chevette at Sunset Junction. Where does luck begin and self-determination end? Bo had no liability and the car was wrecked. His chest and face were covered with exotic sores and he couldn't climb the steps to Pippi's without wheezing. Bo lived in Silver Lake, and the Free Clinic where he got his medicine was 15 miles away, and then he had to catch a string of busses to be able to make $40 or $50 cleaning. It was unbearable.

Pippi and the Sea Captain gave Bo $1,500 for a car. He called up his 28-year-old butch cousin, who was just finishing his second round of chemo, to help him buy a car, and Kevin called his married sister, who'd just bought a Ford Windstar. The dealer wouldn't take her '91 subcompact as a trade, so it was still sitting in the yard. She'd let it go to Bo for $1,800.

What kind of family is this, that would sell a junk yard vehicle to a relative with a terminal disease? Pippi wondered. Bo and Kevin towed the wrecked Chevette to Kevin's yard because Kevin had just made friends with a homeless single mother. She and the kid could move into Bo's old car—and everyone lived happily ever after. Pippi wondered, *What kind of country is this, where moving into a wrecked Chevette could be construed as a step up?* She started to feel panicky and sick, but Bo was happy to be someone else's benefactor.

When Pippi was 15, she resigned in protest from the school debating team. She was quick, and she would have been the first girl captain, but she passionately believed that it was wrong for schools to single out the quick because the quick would always be rewarded.

There is a certain preemptive emptiness that pervades the artwork produced within the Institution. The art is well made and conceptually coherent. The greatest triumph of this artwork is elusion. The way it references so much, content dancing on the surface like a million heated molecules till it's impossible to ascribe any particular meaning to the object. All around it there is a patina of topicality, of edge, but then you can't say what it is. The artwork is an embodiment of corporate practice: It is better to be everywhere than somewhere. Never put in writing what can be mumbled on the phone. The object has cosmetic meaning. Pippi guesses this is Beauty.

In Los Angeles it is possible to achieve a measure of success.

Freeways make everything accessible. The airport's close. She gets up at 7 to spend three hours doing business in New York. She talks and writes. She buys and sells. No one questions her invented pedigree. The only meaning she holds onto is what she remembers when she was living in the country with the Sea Captain four hours north of New York City. Time did not have any use at all and the dark-red apples clinging to the crooked branches in November on the road to Harrisburg reminded her of a Flemish painting. It's like she's skipped five centuries.

My husband writes to me about the happiness he's found with his new girlfriend: "She is so frail and helpless. She's like a little bird."

Pippi replaces time with projects. She spends two nights a week sleeping on the New Age dom's storeroom floor. He teaches her how to receive and process pain with absolute detachment. He shows her how actions can determine being, and that a mask of femininity can replace her "true" androgynous self. Connecting this to the gestural tradition of non-Western drama, Pippi finds this pretty interesting. When she tells him this, he makes her promise to stop reading. The New Age dom loathes analytic thought, especially in women. "Look at you!" he screams. "You live in self-created misery. The books you read, the clothes you wear, your AIDS-ridden housekeeper infecting everything he touches in that slum you live in." Pippi gives Bo $300 to pay for surgery on his cat Lucy's malignant tumor. Her house, in fact, is chic and she is richer than the dom. She knows the New Age dom is crazy, but her life has become a bunch of menu options. When there is nothing to believe in, you compose a landscape, you make Choices.

Gypsies believe in a cosmogony of fate. Each person is part Judas and part Christ. Luck decides which one will win. Chance is larger than both gods and devils, but poverty has its own momentum.

The New Age dom explains that Santa Monica is "more spiritual" than the northeast suburbs of LA because money signifies God's love. The beach, the mall, and Laura Ashley. I was trying then to follow an emotive logic chain as far as it would go. I thought that emptiness could be offset by acts of kindness...

Bo took personal responsibility for his wellness. He changed his diet, took the drugs, but still, infections and their cures just made him sicker. He had flu, pneumonia, lesions, and shingles. The night his wisdom tooth became impacted he was too sick to get himself to LA

County Hospital, so Bo asked his new friend Aston if he'd drive. They took Bo's car and left it in the street because they didn't have 10 bucks for parking. While his tooth was being pulled, someone popped the hatch and stole Bo's vacuum cleaner, which he'd been too weak that evening to unload. In the morning Bo went home, but he'd lost $250 in canceled cleaning jobs and then he had to borrow 50 bucks to buy another vacuum cleaner.

Pippi watches a video installation at the Institution. A camera has been placed in front of a makeshift set, featuring a rope and pulley exercise machine suspended from the ceiling. The artist, Student X, has also installed a disco ball, some Astroturf, and mylar. For 30 minutes, various art students walk in and out. Some of them try hanging from the pulley. A boy and three cute girls are all dressed as cheerleaders. The boy wears a skirt too. They shake some pompoms, shrug and leave. No one can get the exercise machine to work. Student X is 36 or so, and Pippi wonders why he isn't making Volvo ads or infomercials. "Um, what's it about?" she asks, bewildered.

"It's about video," says Student X, thinking Pippi must be really dense. And she considers this. "The color," Student X helpfully explains. "It's pure video. The Astroturf is the same shade of green as on the color bars." And yeah, he's right, the green is kind of smeary.

Then she recalls there is a discourse about how color saturation can dissolve the boundaries of the pixels, hemorrhaging across the surface of the screen, although video paradoxically defines a surface without depth: a geo-ontological fourth dimension. Additionally, the video posits the reductive nature of performance because the Astroturf and the exercise machine comprise a play space. Given no direction, the art students behaved in a self-conscious way. Pippi guesses that this underlines the difference between being 5 years old and 30. It occurs to her that watching hours of surveillance tapes would be equally enlightening.

Bo has an old vinyl 33 LP record that he's carried around with him forever. The man's face on the cover is caught in ¾ profile. He is clean-shaven, and his chin points up. The face (like the faces of its intended viewers) is worn out just enough for us to trust it. Bathed in the glaring klieg lamps used for early color print film, the face becomes exemplary. It is frozen in a mask of aspiration, bitterness, and hope. The man who posed for it—Bo's dad—is dead now. Bo's dad came west in the 1950s, when Route 66 dead-ended in Pasadena, which was then the Nashville of the West. The record was his father's first and only because the studio went bankrupt just before it got released. Bo doesn't know the songs or what they sound like. The record's sealed in cellophane and he's promised himself never, ever to open it. It's like the seal contains the spirit of his dad and he doesn't want to lose it.

When Heidi's parents die, a kindly uncle presents her with a snow-globe. Their chalet in the Alps has just been sold and she's about to be deported. The snow-globe is the only thing she has to remind her of her home when she is living with her guardian in the city. Each time she shakes it, she remembers phlox and cow bells, her mother's face, feather beds, and cocoa. She sniffles. Her wicked guardian, sick of this, wrests the globe from the orphan's tiny hands and throws it down the staircase. Glass breaks. Water spills. The object is destroyed. Why is it some people are born to become magnets for other people's cruelty?

The New Age dom provides me with a safe word but he says that if I use it he will leave and maybe not come back. And so I never did, until one morning in November. It was a new game he'd invented, where I was handcuffed and blindfolded on the storeroom floor, and I had to dodge the lashes of his whip, except I couldn't. My neck stuck out, I howled and stumbled while he laughed at me for being such a stupid clumsy girl. It was Enough—Enough was the word. Enough sleeping on the floor, enough having to be with him before I drank a coffee, enough being taunted as a child, enough having to watch other kids throw garbage and scream "Retard" at my younger sister.

The word "blessed" is used a lot in Southern California. An official memo from the Institution reads: "And we were blessed to have the services of the renowned Ms. XYZ as a consultant." If we are blessed, then who are the unblessed? And do we celebrate our blessedness at their expense? I help Bo and Bo helps dying kittens.

I am living by myself in a cabin in the mountains. My husband's girl-friend is now teaching him about Buddhism. I don't know where Bo is. I imagine he'll die soon. I am no longer taking comfort from the small ecology of kindnesses.

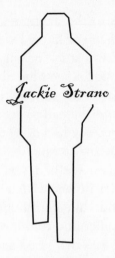

Jackie Strano

KARAOKE KING

Last night was a good night. At the Ramada Inn in Sacramento I won $500 at the Northern California Karaoke Competition Semifinals. I brought the house down with "The Rose" by Bette Midler. I was up against "I Will Always Love You," the Whitney Houston version, which was sung by a fancy queen from Chico. But I walked away with the cash and an invite to the finals down in Fresno in about a month. I did a line of coke to sober up and headed out on 80 East for Reno to get a suite at the Silver Legacy and call Donna. I used to work with her at this phone-sex place. I was the night manager and credit operator and she was one of the fantasy girls. I would dispatch the calls, and she was a big busty blond college girl with an oral fixation. Little did the guys know they were talking to a petite 30-year-old with red and pink dyed hair, piercings, and tattoos who dropped out of high school to have her first kid. There were plenty of guys that called for that scene too, but she only took the college bunny calls. *Keeping a safe distance,* she called it. Her voice is so sexy—we had this phone flirtation that went on forever. We would banter back and forth until one day I just came out and said that I had to meet her soon and I didn't give a shit how inappropriate it sounded. Well, the next day she walks into the office to pick up her check. She usually did this in the daytime so I never saw her, but this time she came in after 8 when she knew I would be there. She was *fine*! She walked right up to me and stuck out her hand and introduced herself. I kissed her hand and said something about getting some dinner or something. We made it as far as my car. We fucked furiously for an hour. I had to get back upstairs and she had to get back home to her old man, some biker dude who supposedly had done time in Soledad Prison. The thought of him busting in on us and blowing my head off played through my mind every time we had sex. The mental image of my bloody demise added to the urgency I felt every time I put my hand inside her. This went on for awhile until I quit the job and she moved to Reno. She gave me her number and told me to look her up whenever I was passing through. That was two years ago.

Last night as I walked out to my car in the warm central California night with that full moon putting a fever pitch in my brain I had a vivid memory of her smell and I knew I had to see her. I got to Reno in record time, settled into the room, took a hot shower, lit a joint, and called her. I rehearsed out loud how I would fake a wrong number if he picked up. She answered after the first ring like she was sitting on the phone just waiting for my call. An hour later she was in my bed and we were relentlessly making up for lost time. I didn't need to ask her how life was treating her. I could see it in her eyes that she was happy to be distracted for a night and that if I had asked her to right then and there to run away with me, she would have. I knew we would probably get as far as Texas and then she would leave me in some little shit town in the middle of the night and get a ride back to the biker from hell with the first willing truck driver she could find. She needed a man to hide behind, but I didn't care. I wasn't looking to marry her. I knew what we were doing with each other wasn't something that was ever going to see the light of day. So when the midday light and heat started creeping in and I slowly and somewhat painfully started to wake up, I was too hazy to notice right away that she was gone. I could still smell her on the pillow next to me. I held it to me and inhaled deeply, sighed out loud, and rewound the images of the night before in my head to make sure it hadn't been some drug-induced dream. There was a note on the TV next to my wallet that said: "Good morning baby, no time to linger—didn't want to wake you. I'm sorry. Love you always, D." In the two years since I had last seen her, she had had another baby. Now she had three. I had dated here and there, some more serious than others but nobody like her. She was never going to leave him. She was never going to let me see her with no makeup on. She was never going to say out loud why she cried last night after we had sex. She was never going to wake up in my arms. I started to picture her with him, pictured her turning to stare at the wall while he snored, while the kids slept, while the world was quiet and still but her heart was beating hard making a deafening and demanding sound pounding against her chest. I got angry. I got to feeling dramatic, like a righteous avenger, and I knew what I had to do. I had to see for myself what kind of true day-to-day life she lived. Without washing her off me I slicked back my hair, put on my shades, and jumped into my car to go to her. On the way over I pumped myself up by blaring the radio and singing at the top of my lungs while barreling down the freeway. Singing along to that Pat Benatar song, "We Belong...We belong together" and Head East's "30 Days in the Hole." I pictured myself in prison. There had been a fight and a gun had gone off and cracker biker dude was dead from one bullet straight through the heart. I would be the envy of everyone, including the guards, every time conjugal visits happened. Donna would show up all glammed out and we would disappear for days into the dilapidated love shack they provided. Donna would bring silk scarves to drape over the garish lights and burn incense so we could pretend we were in a motel room. I would be teaching music as therapy to the other inmates and writing my memoirs and pumping iron out on the yard, joining the sisterhood of *vatas* and *cholas* and home girls, making connections for when we all got out. I would read every book in the library and start college correspondence classes. I would get out early for good behavior and Donna, me, and the kids would move to Pomona and we would open a bar and grill and put in a karaoke machine.

As I turned onto her street my heart was stuck in my throat making me choke and making my chest feel empty and sucked dry. I gripped the wheel to steady myself. I was full of lust and rage and fear and such a sense of overwhelming dread that my breath just came out in little puffs of sound. There he was...outside, washing his motorcycle. He was standing there holding a hose spraying it down standing back on his heels with flip flops on and his beer belly sticking straight up and out. His posture said "fuck you" and "don't fuck with me." He looked like someone who either felt that the world owed him big time or that he felt like he owned everything he pissed on. I slowed down and stayed back, pretending to be parking at the house across the street and down a ways. Just as I was ready to burn rubber past the house and drive away, the front door opened and out came Donna. She handed him a beer and kissed him as he pulled her up onto him and across his chest as he grabbed her ass.

Son of a bitch!

I dialed her number furiously on my cell phone. I watched her go back into the house while cracker asshole kept hosing down his Harley. "Hello?"

"What the fuck is going on, Donna?"

"What the hell is the matter with you?"

"What's a matter with me? You fucking leave in the middle of the night to go back to that motherfucker—that's what the hell is a matter with me!"

"Where are you?"

"I'm across the fucking street."

"Oh, God!"

"Yeah, fuck me, right?"

"You have got to get out of here.... Please, I promise I'll call you. Just go."

"Do you love me?"

"What?"

"Do you love me?"

"... Yes."

"Then let's go. Walk out the door and let's go. Let's get the fuck out of here, together."

"Baby, I can't."

"Bring the kids. Let's go. Please come away with me."

"This can't happen—"

"It's happening. This is the way it's going to be—now, let's go!"

"I'm...pregnant."

It took me a minute to digest the information and add another little face to the picture.

"I got room. Come on, babe, life is too short."

"It's not his."

"Whose is it?"

"Someone I can't leave right now."

"Oh, shit, Donna, what the hell? Goddamn, girl. Goddamn... Goddamn!"

I threw the phone down, slammed my boot to the pedal, and peeled out down the street. As I passed suburban biker dude, he looked up with a scowl. We locked glares for a moment as I zoomed by. I actually felt for a fleeting second that he and I could have been friends in a different lifetime, commiserating over a cold beer about women while someone in the background tried to do George Jones justice on the microphone.

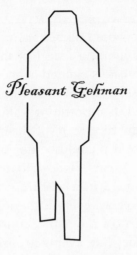

Pleasant Gehman

LADY, DON'T BE PANIC

The fat businessman flashing his brassiere in the middle of the street should've been a red flag, but being a Hollywood native, stuff like that happens to me on an everyday basis, so it took a moment to register that I wasn't at home but in Cairo. I'm a freak magnet. Weird circumstances and insane people actively seek me out. Once in a while, the way 5-year-old girls dream about being Britney Spears, I have fantasies about living like everybody else. But no matter how hard I try to behave, to act *normal*, it never seems to work.

I was travelling with my friend Tracy. We both belly-dance professionally and had been to Egypt before, but this time we were in Cairo for a huge dance festival, classes and workshops by legendary choreographers of *la danse orientale*, many of whom had been famous for decades. Performers from all over the world were attending. We'd been giddily planning this trip for months, leaving messages blasting Arabic music on each other's answering machines, saving every penny for dance classes and costumes. We were not only excited about going to Cairo but more than happy to leave our everyday lives behind. Tracy was going through a divorce and I'd been dealing with veterinary and automotive problems on a constant nightmarish level. Counting the minutes till our departure, we breezily waved away everyone's concerns over terrorism. Anything would be better than what we'd both recently been through! Tracy's mom, a nice Jewish housewife from the San Fernando Valley, was almost as excited as we were. She stuffed Tracy's suitcase with munchies, trial-sized shampoos, and travel accoutrements; she even scored us a bottle of Valium for the plane. But the pièce de résistance was the tiny, state-of-the-art video camera she gave her daughter so the entire trip could be documented.

"This is going to be so great," Tracy gloated, standing in the middle of LAX, stroking the camera in a gesture not unlike a lover's caress. "We're going to be able record every little thing that happens to us!"

The second we stepped off the plane, conservatively dressed, trying desperately to look and act like average tourists, the Fellini shit started. It began with the hotel, which was a dump even by Third World standards. We'd both agreed to stay in a budget place, being tough chicks who'd back-packed through Europe and camped out on beaches and stranger's floors. We didn't need cushy surroundings, we both reasoned. We'd hardly ever be there.

The Amon Toushka's lobby said it all. There were a couple of dead palm trees sitting in decomposing clay pots filled with cigar butts and crumpled up tissues. Old men loitered smoking *sheesha* pipes, their ratty turbans and food-stained galabias barely visible through the haze of stale smoke. The desk clerk was a nastier-looking vampirical version of Sirhan Sirhan. We considered offering him a pen (for some reason, Western style pens are in huge demand in Egypt and are considered a status symbol that can be given as tips or tokens of esteem) but it didn't seem as though it would change his sneering attitude. He demanded our passports immediately, as though he'd sell them on the black market the second we stepped into the elevator.

Fortunately, the elevator took almost 15 minutes to come. The creaking ride up to our seventh floor room was terrifying; we expected to plunge to the lobby with every lurching second. We wended our way down a narrow corridor barely lit by naked lightbulbs. The dirty salmon walls were pocked with holes every few feet, threadbare oriental carpets were littered with piles of chipped plaster, and discarded food wrappers were spread haphazardly over bare concrete.

Our room, of course, wasn't made up. Damp, ragged towels covered the floor and sagging beds revealed dirty sheets with black pubic hairs interwoven. The sun-bleached curtains, now torn and rotten, had once been a gay Flower Power '70s print, and were falling off their hooks. The indoor/outdoor carpeting was stained with grease, and a dead radio hung by its own wires from a trashed cabinet within the bedside table. Amazed to see a television set, Tracy touched it and the front control panel fell off.

There are only two phrases one needs to know to survive in Cairo. One is *in sh'allah*, which means "if God is willing." The other is "no problem." They are used ubiquitously as well as interchangeably by natives, and cover everything from the answer to a simple question, to the rationalization or solution for a major emergency. If something is going to happen, it will—*in sh'allah*—so you wait—*no problem*—as long as you need to, until God wills the outcome.

Delirious from lack of sleep and urgently needing to flee the fleabag, after hearing 45 minutes of *in sh'allah* and "No problem" (without tangible results) from the front desk, regarding everything from getting clean linens to making an overseas call, Tracy and I locked our valuables in our suitcases and made for the street. We waited the requisite half-hour for the elevator. While I was looking for the stairs, I made the rather unsettling discovery that the hotel simply *did not exist* between our floor and the lobby. There were six stories of twisted metal and raw cement (courtesy of the last earthquake) with no stairs or even floors between us and the ground floor. Comforting!

Walking on Giza Street between the Ministry of Culture and the upscale Cairo Sheraton we were approached by a tubby, balding man in Western clothes. Seemingly reaching for his cell-phone, the guy lighting-quick unbuttoned his shirt, revealing a gray J.C. Penney's–style no-nonsense grandma-type bra. It was so threadbare and dirty it couldn't even qualify as lingerie—even a bag lady on crack would've been ashamed of it! Looking directly into our eyes as he passed, he tongued his lips lasciviously and squeezed his left nipple. Stunned and speechless, I asked Tracy: "Did that just really happen?"

"*I can't believe that just happened!*" she replied in amazement.

Our first impulse was to reach for our cameras, but by the time we had them in hand, he was gone. The soldiers guarding the Ministry of Culture hadn't even noticed him. But we sure noticed them. And it wasn't just their snowy white Tourist Police uniforms, a beret tilted jauntily to one side. How hard is it to miss lithe, café au lait–skinned 19-year-olds with Pharonic features and puppy-dog eyes—especially when they're smoking casually, wearing gun-belts, and packing gigantic automatic weapons? Since our cameras were already out, we tried for a photo-op. Instead, we succeeded in attracting the attention of their first-in-command: a pot-bellied, toothless guy who screamed that we were violating an Egyptian law we didn't know existed. It is illegal, we learned, to take pictures of *anything* having to do with the military. As we left, Tracy whispered, "No problem," launching us both into fits of punchy giggles.

That night, we were determined to paint the town, even though I'd developed a nasty bladder infection. We'd been guest-listed to see the Dina, the most famous belly dancer in the Arabic world. Dina is a household word, like Cher or Barbra Streisand. We couldn't believe our good fortune. At 9:30 we began our toilette. By 10 we discovered the shower wouldn't turn off. By 10 we'd begun a frantic series of calls to the front desk. When 10:30 arrived, the bathtub had began to fill up, and the whole room was inundated with steam.

" No problem," said Sirhan Sirhan, in a lackadaisical, offhand tone.

The bathroom floor was completely flooded, so I called again at 11:45 and tried to describe in detail, slowly and clearly, what was happening.

"*Lady, don't be panic!*" he hollered in disgust, banging the phone onto the receiver.

I calculated that we'd need at least 20 minutes for the elevator to come, so if we weren't going to miss Dina, we'd have to leave now.

"Fuck it," I said to Tracy. "We're out of here."

We piled our suitcases on top of the dressers, left the windows open to allow the water vapors to escape, and bailed, drenched as though we'd come out of a steam room.

Dina was awesome, and for a climax she danced to a song by Om Kulthoum, and the entire crowd lost it. Om Kulthoum is to the Arabic world what Elvis is to Westerners…and then some. Like the King, after she died she became even more famous, as though canonized. Every cabby in Cairo has a picture of her in his wallet. The first time I heard Om Kulthoum, I was an immediate convert. Then I saw her picture...and let's just say that she makes Fat Elvis look dignified.

The passion in her voice is stunning, but toward the end of her career she was old and bloated and didn't really manage to cover it up in voluminous caftans. Nearly blind, she wore oversized Jackie O sunglasses; she had a number of double chins, which were only accented by her massive beehive bouffant hairdo. She always sang with a white handkerchief in one hand—some said because her songs were so full of sadness and longing. Others insisted it was because she was an addict who concealed cocaine in her hankie, sniffing it onstage during her lengthy concerts.

Whatever; the handkerchief, like the glasses and scary hair, were her trademarks. I've got to say that Om Kulthoum, more than any living human being, resembles those scary old ladies in the comic strip "The Far Side." But even mention her name and Egyptians get misty-eyed...and seeing Dina dance to a 30-piece orchestra playing Om Kulthoum made me and Tracy so crazy we *had* to go out and party with George, a jovial Lebanese guy we'd just met. We went to the casino he managed, got shitfaced on his tab, and listened to stories about the multitudinous times he'd been arrested in various countries. Then he took us to a disco. Somewhere along the line, we changed his name to "G-Dog." We went with G-Dog to his place, right around the corner from our hotel, to have a nightcap of juice and *sheesha* pipe before turning in.

We arrived back at our room after the sun had already come up. Unbelievably, the shower wasn't running. Utterly stinko and jubilant that our entire room wasn't soaked, we documented our hotel room's "splendor" with Tracy's video camera. We showed off every carpet stain, duct-taped piece of furniture, and mildewed towel. Reaching new heights of delirium and laughing so hard we ached, we then discovered that the shower hadn't been fixed—they'd merely covered up the problem by turning our water off! A series of phone calls to the front desk ensued, all answered with the standard "No problem." By the time the plumber arrived with a shifty-looking security guard, it was so bright in the room we were wearing our shades.

"Look, it's the water doctor!" Tracy cried, sticking the camcorder in the men's faces the moment they came in through the door.

She filmed everything, from the Arabic curses streaming out of the plumber's mouth as he wallowed on the bathroom floor getting soaked, to my slap-happy commentary and Roto-Rooter jokes. Finally, the water pressure restored, the guys left. Brushing my teeth with my sunglasses on, my hair wadded up into a sloppy bun on top of my head, I was struck with my resemblance to Om Kulthoum. Grabbing a bedsheet and draping it around my body to resemble a caftan, waving a piece of Kleenex in my hand, I stepped onto the balcony, and started prancing around, bellowing the lyrics to "Ya Msharni," a famous Om Kulthoum song, at the top of my lungs. Tracy filmed my psychotic histrionics with the Nile as a background, until I stepped inside, laughing so hard the sheet fell off.

"Keep singing," Tracy cried, maneuvering camera angles like a guerrilla filmmaker, "Do X-rated nude Om Kulthoum."

Of course, I obliged her.

We spent most of the day running around town wired on mud-like Turkish coffee. So it wasn't until late that night, as we were about to go clubbing again, that Tracy noticed her camcorder was missing.

"Are you sure?" I asked, thinking it was just buried in her suitcase jumble of blow-dryers, panty hose, and lunch-box-sized snack foods.

"It's gone," she said mournfully. "I looked everywhere."

Our luck was such that Sirhan Sirhan was on duty again. I went to the lobby to call the woman running the dance festival, who spoke fluent English. Meanwhile, Tracy came down and started shrieking, causing a major scene. Sirhan Sirhan, the hotel's manager, and all the old men sitting around smoking *sheesha* stormed up to the room, throwing everything around, arguing with each other in Arabic, trying to find the camera, which they figured we'd just misplaced. All they succeeded in doing was (as we call it in the States) "tampering with a crime scene." In other words, they destroyed evidence and got fingerprints all over our belongings. The festival's representative, Mohammed, arrived looking like a near-Eastern version of Don Johnson in "Miami Vice," dressed head to toe in silver sharkskin.

Pissed off and keyed up as she was, Tracy took one look at Mohammed, and began covertly pointing and frantically mouthing to me: "*He's cute!*"

Trying to be serious, even in the face of Tracy's cartoon-like libidinal display (in spite of his garish taste in clothing, Mohammed *was* pretty damn easy on the eyes) I kept a straight face and attempted to answer questions posed in pidgin English. Tracy alternately ranted, giggled, eyed Mohammed lasciviously, and wept.

"There, there, Trashy," Mohammed said, mispronouncing her name as he patted her back while she gave me a covert sidelong glance. "Trashy, please, don't be hysteric! Is OK...no problem."

Mohammed had me write up a statement for "Trashy" to sign, flashing his silver Bic pen for us to use. At this point we'd been in Egypt long enough to be duly impressed—a man is only as good as his pen, after all. So this was Mohammed's way of saying he was on top of the situation. He assured us that Egyptian police were "very clever." Out of sheer nerves, Tracy and I were compulsively munching our way through her stash of junk food as Mohammed stared in disbelief.

Tracy remembered then that the camera also had footage of my nude Om Kulthoum act, something I'd thought of the moment she discovered the camera was missing. In fact, I was sure it was probably all over the Internet by now. Tracy told Mohammed it was an absolute necessity she get her camera back, and whispered that there was footage of me naked. At this, Mohammed's eyes nearly popped out of his head in shock over the sinful antics of "loose Westerners."

"We must get the camera and tape back," he said, gravely. Then, leering at me pointedly, he said, "So I can see this!"

After more Arabic arguments with the contingent from the lobby, who were chain-smoking cigars at a rate equal to our junk food consumption, Mohammed made it clear that we had to go to the police station to give a report. As Tracy and I grabbed our sweaters, Mohammed looked us over dubiously.

"Ah...I mean no offense," he said as politely as he could muster. "But you cannot go to station looking like..." He threw his hands up heavenward, "Like...*nightclub womens*!"

Washing off our glitter makeup, we changed into baggy, "decent" clothes. Even though it was fucked up that the camera had been stolen, and that we weren't going to go out, we both were a little excited and adrenaline-charged by the prospect of going to the police station in Cairo. It would, after all, be an adventure.

The moment we entered the station, our illusions were shattered and we started to get scared. It was as though we'd stepped out of a James Bond movie and into *Midnight Express*. As our eyes adjusted to the dim, flickering fluorescent lights, we took in the cracked, filthy linoleum floors; rat-traps in the corners; the battered file cabinets, their drawers open and bulging with folders; not to mention the the surly-looking, middle-aged cops lounging on dilapidated naugahyde chairs, cleaning their rifles. Tracy gripped my hand so hard her bubble-gum pink acrylic nails dug into my palm. Mohammed and the head cop started yelling at each other immediately.

"Not Without My Camcorder!" I whispered, trying to put Tracy at ease with a joke.

Mohammed frantically motioned us to be quiet as the head guy, who had a huge scar down one cheek, stood up abruptly, adjusted his gun belt in a macho pose, and said to Tracy in deadly calm, perfect English, "Whom do you wish to accuse?"

"Accuse?" Tracy asked, her voice barely audible and quivering with panic.

"Yes, you must accuse someone," the cop said, his gaze steely.

Tracy stood silently, eyes darting around, finally meeting mine. It seemed as though maybe we should just forget the whole matter, go back to the hotel, get some rest, maybe do some light sightseeing the next day...anything just to get out of this situation. What's a camcorder, anyway? *Just a material possession that can be easily replaced.* And really, what would happen if they *did* get it back, and saw Naked Om Kulthoum, then what?

Suddenly, I felt panicky about what I'd done—if it had at home, in Hollywood, it would've been a joke, even with the cops, but what about here? Surely there were laws about nudity, not to mention lewd conduct. Was I completely insane? What the hell was I thinking? Egypt may not be as hardcore as Saudi Arabia or Iran, where women are mandated to wear a veil and not even allowed to drive. But still, it's an unbelievably conservative, 98% Muslim country. I had the distinct feeling that what I did would *never* fall under the umbrella of Allah's having willed it, and there'd be *no way* I could ever explain away my flagrant display by saying "No problem." Suddenly, I felt the need to pee. Badly.

"Mohammed," I whined, like a kindergartner about to have an accident, "I have to go to the bathroom."

Tracy was biting her cuticles, saying nothing as he regarded me and said emphatically, "But you cannot go to the bathroom here. You must wait."

I resigned myself, rationalizing that it was just nerves and not my bladder infection. I was trying to breathe deeply and think calming thoughts when the hotel's plumber was brought in, looking absolutely terrified. The cops threw him onto a bench facing us and began harshly interrogating him. I stared at his cheap rubber sandals and worn-out pants and his haggard face and felt horrible. After 45 minutes of everyone in the room screaming at each other, my teeth were floating.

"I have to go to the bathroom," I said urgently, pummeling Mohammed.

"*You cannot go to the bathroom!*" he hollered, "*This is bathroom only for criminal!*"

"*I have a bladder infection!*" I yelled right back, as all the policemen's heads snapped around like Linda Blair's in *The Exorcist*.

"But Pleasant," Mohammed said carefully, as though he was talking to someone with a severe mental disability, "This bathroom is...*inhuman!*"

"I'm going to wet my pants," I said truthfully, through gritted teeth.

Another agonizing 10 minutes went by as Mohammed explained my situation to the cops, who regarded me dubiously. Mohammed took my hand tightly, and with an escort of two cops, I limped down a corridor to the toilet. There were a bunch of men loitering around in pimpy-looking '80s sweatsuits with pagers prominently displayed. I noticed that they were linked together chain-gang-style with iron leg-shackles. Standing near them was the most over-the top, freakish hooker I'd ever seen. She momentarily made me forget my bloated bladder. Tall and corpulent, she wore a luridly patterned, mismatched skirt and low-cut blouse, looking even more psychedelic than it really was under the strobing fluorescent lights. Shiny taupe Spandex tights led to white pumps almost completely black with scuff marks. Her massive, badly permed 'do was bleached a sickly shade of orange and filled with plastic flowers. Her clown-like makeup resembled Joel Grey's "Emcee" character in *Cabaret*: Two symmetrical circular splotches of red on her cheeks complimented harsh, silvery blue shadow that almost—but not quite—hid a huge shiner. She was handcuffed, and on one arm wore bracelets up to the elbow. From the noise they made—a tinkle, rather than a clank—it was obvious they were real gold.

The guards went into the bathroom first, roughly dragging out a man in traditional *saidi* dress as he protested violently. Actually, the toilet was no worse than any other Egyptian bathroom I'd been in, except for the feces smeared on the walls. There were two metal foot-forms on the floor flanking an open hole in which to relieve yourself. No toilet paper, no light. As I urinated, Mohammed guarded me, providing a human barricade so no one could open the door, which didn't have a lock. I could see his feet planted firmly, inches from my own, outside the stall door.

Tracy was still sitting morosely, looking small and scared at being left alone in this hellhole. More arguing ensued—perhaps "Trashy" had brought the camera to Cairo only to lose it intentionally, so as to collect insurance? How did we know it wasn't one of the maids?

Tracy had never even insured the thing, and if she had, it would've been much easier just to "lose" it in Los Angeles. Why go through all the red tape of doing it in a foreign country, for Christ's sake? We both thought that the culprit was the hotel security guard who had accompanied the plumber. First of all, the door hadn't been forced, so it was probably an inside job. Second—and more importantly—the security guard was the only person besides the plumber who'd even seen the camera. And the plumber was here, shitting bricks, probably thinking he was about to get his hand cut off or something. Plus, we both thought it odd that if indeed the thief had been one of the naive-looking teenage chamber maids, why hadn't she stolen any of the beauty products or feminine clothing we'd left out? With the severe language barrier, all this was almost impossible to translate to the police.

Finally, Tracy was made to sign a statement that she couldn't even read—it had been typed up in Arabic, of course—and we were allowed to leave, just as dawn was breaking.

"I feel as though you are my sisters," Mohammed said as he dropped us off in front of the Ammon Toushka. He handed us his business card and said he would get the matter sorted out, which we severely doubted. We'd both written off the possibility of ever seeing the camcorder again.

We immediately started packing our belongings, planning a hasty exit.

There was no way we were going to spend another minute in the hotel. Tracy called G-Dog, who was just arriving home from his casino job.

"*Guess where I've been*?" Tracy shouted almost gleefully into the phone, "*I've been in jail*!"

After hearing an abbreviated version of our ordeal, he commanded us to get a cab to his house immediately. We could stay with him, or he would help check us into a five-star hotel. As Tracy struggled with her bags, waiting impatiently for the elevator, she suggested taking the stairs, too delirious to realize that her bags would've been totally unmanageable.

"Let's just wait," I sighed, too exhausted to explain to her that there was literally *nothing* between our floor and the lobby.

As we tried to leave without going through the proper check-out procedure with Sirhan Sirhan (whom we never, ever wanted to see again) the scene at the front desk could've been any random newsreel footage of people trying to escape a Third World country as a coup took place. Everyone sitting around the lobby—the old men, even a bunch of newly arrived, jet-lagged, hippie-looking Norwegian tourists—got involved. Sirhan Sirhan was going apoplectic, pounding on his ledger, shrieking, and gesturing wildly. Our cab driver, bribed with a 10-pound note, was simultaneously stuffing our luggage into the trunk of his car while bellowing loudly and playing suitcase tug-of-war with three gun-toting, uniformed members of the Tourist Police. We finally got out of there, and at the entrance to G-Dog's building, I started laughing hysterically while Tracy broke down in the tears that had been threatening all night. At this point, we hadn't slept more than four or five hours in, like, six days.

Later that day we checked into the Ramses Hilton, where the Oriental Dance Festival was being held. The employees at reception were charming and fawned all over us, sending our bags up to our room and offering us a gratis cocktail while we waited for the paperwork to go through. We were amazed at the cleanliness and luxe modern amenities of our room. Feeling like we'd won the lottery, we noted the sparkling clean bathroom—with a tub, shower, and bidet, plus fluffy, pristine bath towels and tiny sized soaps and lotions all sealed in wrappers. There was a big-screen color TV (that actually worked) with a remote control, double beds, and a phone whose receiver wouldn't give you hepatitis or some leprous skin condition. We put on our bikinis, went down to the pool, crashed onto chaise lounges, and ordered drinks immediately, charging them to our room.

After the festival started, Mohammed came by, wearing an unfortunately Mafioso-like combo of a black polyester shirt and skin-tight, white brushed-denim jeans, which showcased his beefy thighs. He was sweaty and seemed harried, in need of a shave yet reeking of cheap aftershave.

"Still no news on your camera, Trashy," he said, trying to look all official with his clipboard.

We knew through the grapevine that he'd been bungling things all week, including taking care of some other festival attendees who'd been staying at the Ammon Toushka and had had property stolen out of their rooms. As he flipped through some paperwork, looking for a police document Tracy needed to show at customs upon departure, Tracy eyed him and leaning in close to me whispered, "You know, Mohammed's not that cute. He's kind of a dork, and he's sort of fat."

I nodded in agreement.

"All he really has going for himself," Tracy yawned, "is a good pen."

We stifled giggles as Mohammed continued earnestly: "But the police, I am sure they are working on it."

"I know, the police, they are very clever," Tracy sighed, her sarcasm sailing with an almost audible swoosh right over his head, "*No problem!*"

The Hell House Affair

In the spring of 1984 I rashly agreed to move in with a strange and nefarious boyfriend named Hank. His flat—universally referred to as Hell House—occupied the bottom floor of a ramshackle Victorian in the Lower Haight, then a seedy, decaying neighborhood. The house's gingerbread exterior had faded to a color best described as "weather-beaten" and its tiny front yard was a botanical necropolis, but the real disaster area was inside. Leprous walls shed paint and plaster, leaky plumbing irrigated micro-jungles of mold and mildew, and the place tilted alarmingly to one side—a vivid reminder that in San Francisco the ground beneath one's feet is apt to shift whimsically.

Hank had grown up poor in some Central Valley hick town, but possessed the fine manners, dry wit, and jovial disposition of a musical comedy playboy. He loved to play host, something he did with graciousness and elegance, always keeping the witty conversation rolling and the drink glasses filled. His urbanity, however, never interfered with his rock-and-roll feistiness. He wore his dishwater-blond hair a little too long, dressed like the Velvet Underground circa 1967, and waged a cold war against piss-elegant queens, spray-painting "Queers Against Gays" on walls years before all the punky activists decided to be queer instead of gay.

Hank romanced me as no one ever had. He was always holding my hand in public, meeting me at the door with a kiss, sticking flowers in my hair, tracing "I love you" on my arm with his finger, or giving me tiny presents. He made me feel pretty. And did I mention that he looked like the young Steve McQueen? His only drawback was that he shot speed. Sure, all us trendy young gay boys dabbled in drugs, but Hank would reach for a needle with no more thought than you or I would reach for a salad fork. I chose to ignore this little failing because I was deafened, dumbed, and blinded by love.

Hank and I shared Hell House with an enormous, ever-changing cast of trendy young flat mates. Our common bond was believing we could change the world for the better—or at least keep it from changing us for the worse—by honing our cynicism to a weaponlike sharpness, dressing like the wackier New Wave musical groups, and hanging out at nightclubs. Deluded? Perhaps, but what were we supposed to do—wear alligator shirts, eat croissants, and watch *Dynasty*?

Though we all worked or went to school (in my case both), we devoted the bulk of our energies—which, given Hank's endless supply of amphetamines and generous nature, were prodigious—to a never-ending debauch. In the louche chaos of Hell House people blasted their stereos at all hours, swilled beer, turned tricks, cut and bleached their hair, dabbled in bondage and drag, watched *The Jetsons* on mushrooms, sculpted with telephones, wrote poetry, dyed fabric, had snit fits, orgied, feuded, debated politics, and danced on the furniture.

We each paid a $120 a month for our rooms—supercheap, even back then. The landlord was a portly old queen who insisted we pay the rent in person, then answered the door without any pants on. He'd originally lent the space to Critter, the prettiest boy alive. Straight men cruised Critter right in front of their wives, traffic on busy streets ground to a halt when he skateboarded by, and legions of admirers showered him with food, drugs, money, and lodging, getting nothing in return but a half-smile. By the time I moved in some rich girl had spirited Critter away to her penthouse, but once he came back to visit. Seeing the way Hank looked at him, the way everybody looked at him, made me crazy jealous. I started fantasizing about plastic surgery so men would look at me that way. Fortunately, Critter didn't stay long.

Hank was mad for '50s design and continually scavenged Dumpsters and thrift stores for boomerang-shaped coffee tables, Eames chairs, and other high-modernist treasures. Alas, drug mania made him somewhat indiscriminate, and he also dragged home mediocre table lamps, appliances that didn't quite work, broken toys, scratchy records, amateur oil paintings, and, oh, anything that wasn't nailed down. Tsunamis of junk flooded from his room into the hallway and kitchen, eliciting complaints that were invariably met with sincere apologies and frantic clean ups. The neatness never lasted long, though, as Hank had a way of absentmindedly disorganizing things with abandoned searches and aborted projects. The boy could really make a mess.

Hank also scavenged people. His best find was this achingly sincere blond girl with high cheekbones and expensive clothes whose claim to fame was having written a song for Pat Benatar. She'd drop by for a little visit and end up staying for weeks. Invariably she'd buy drugs, do them, spend a few days going from room to room socializing, and then when she started to crash say, "Oh, I think I'm coming down with the flu." We'd all laugh and say, "No, Genevieve, you're crashing." But she'd just shake her pretty head and insist it was the flu, then curl up on someone's bed for three days till she felt well enough to buy more drugs.

The phone number at Hell House was UNDEAD-7—too perfect because there were (usually) seven of us living there and we all just assumed we'd be dying of AIDS. Back then there was no treatment. People would just disappear—*poof*—and the government did nothing because America preferred homosexuals dead. So, feeling sassy as well as scared, we determined to make the most of our last few years, leaving no drinks undrunk, lines unsnorted, or boys untricked with. If you must judge us for the lives we led (and really, nobody's saying you have to), please remember we thought we were goners.

Once, Hank got arrested for possession. Having no personal experience with prisons but having seen a lot of movies, I was terrified for him. I ran down to the jail and found him standing behind the thick plate glass window of the visiting room, looking sheepish. I think getting caught embarrassed him. He told me I shouldn't worry since he was in the queen tank and wasn't getting raped or beaten. He really seemed more concerned about my anxiety than his own predicament. Two days later they released him and dropped the charges, but the image of Hank in his prison uniform stuck in my mind. He was so handsome!

Eventually I got mad because Hank kept leaving me to sleep alone while he did speed. I would have joined him in his narcotic frenzy, but I lacked the stamina. Drugs are hard work. Waiting for the dealer, finding someone to do the drugs with, finding a place to do the drugs, doing the drugs, crashing—it's like a full time job. Being lazy, I figured it'd be easier to get Hank to quit than to keep up with him. We had a big fight about it that I won and for a few weeks he stayed clean, just drank beer all the time and cuddled up with me at night. The apartment got a thorough tidying and I could really see myself growing old with Hank. Then, without warning, he went back to his old ways. I asked why, and he said because when he shot up he could "see God." I'm not the least bit religious, so that meant nothing to me. I sort of wanted to leave him and sort of didn't, so I compromised by staying with him but sleazing around a lot on the side.

When he relapsed, Hank really went berserk. He lost his pizzeria job (stealing?) and started working at an erotic bakery. Our refrigerator was always filled with cakes shaped like penises and breasts. He also began leaving his works in the sink, making me hysterical as I have a nervous dread of syringes. Worse, he increasingly ignored me to hang out with scary weirdos, including a fellow whose picture had recently appeared in the paper for biting a policeman. He even invited a skinny skinhead named Stove and his chubby, witch girlfriend to stay in our basement, where it was rumored they performed Satanic bondage rituals.

During the '80s homelessness was becoming a national shame, but instead of housing, the government poured billions of deficit dollars into a nuclear weapons buildup and Central American death squads. Wildly popular President Reagan gutted environmental protection and civil rights laws, slashed taxes for the rich, and insisted ketchup should count as a vegetable in school lunches. Smarmy televangelists ranted against homosexuality and claimed AIDS was an instrument of God's wrath, while the mainstream media promoted the boring, white-bread traditionalism of preppie chic and gross, yuppie-style conspicuous consumption. I only mention all this so you'll see that the depravity and dissipation of Hell House took place in a society that excluded us and which we didn't much want to join anyway. OK, back to the story.

Once after a long day I came home cranky and tired to find Hank busily disassembling the toaster for no reason. Surrounding him was a motley horde of drug fiends who—I realized with horror—were finishing off the last of a lasagna I'd baked from scratch and hadn't even tasted yet. The kitchen (which I'd recently cleaned) was a sea of rubbish: macrame plant holders, deflated inflatable wading pools, dented car parts, dirty stuffed animals, I don't remember what all. Use your imagination and go wild. I screamed that it was over between us and stomped off. Hank told his buddies to clear out and ran after me, apologizing profusely. Before I could go into my room and slam the door, he grabbed me by the hand. I tried to pull away but he kissed me ever so sweetly and coaxed me back to the kitchen with a line. I snorted away my anger and gave him one last chance.

Since I was the most responsible person in Hell House (Virgo, Virgo rising), the utility bills ended up in my name. Did I say responsible? I meant gullible. Every month I'd have to hound these crazy drugged-out people for money, and every month it got harder and harder. Finally I complained to Hank: "We owe $400 and everybody's broke and the house is a mess and you don't make me feel pretty any more." He mumbled that he was too busy to talk just right then, so I did what any sensible TV sitcom wife would do. I stomped my foot and said, "I'm going home to mother!" He didn't even try to stop me. My mom's basement had a cold cement floor and I couldn't make any noise at night because the lodger upstairs drove an ambulance at 5 A.M., but it seemed like heaven. What a relief to come home from Statistics or European Intellectual History without finding any lunatics in the kitchen or garbage in the halls. I didn't miss the anarchy one bit.

Hank, however, I missed terribly. I just couldn't stay mad. Nobody's perfect, I reasoned, and if somebody was, they'd probably be really annoying. Before I could call Hank though, he called me. I was thrilled until I discovered he was upset because I'd taken my name off the utilities and they'd shut off the electricity. Nobody living in Hell House had good credit so they couldn't get it turned on. Would I reopen the account, please? I was still paying off the four hundred I already owed, so I told him absolutely not, but he wouldn't give up. Didn't I still love him? Didn't I care that it was winter and they couldn't use their space heaters? He still cared about me! He still wanted to be my boyfriend! He loved me! In the middle of his impassioned plea,

Hank started laughing at himself—he knew he was lying and being terrible and knew it wasn't working. Lesser junkies would have gotten angry, but he just wished me well, hung up, and disappeared from my life. 16 years later we met again and he apologized.

Michelle Tea

PARIS: A LIE

I would guess that any relationship begun in the throes of a black-out would leave you doomed to it. Aren't blackouts similar to sleep, which halves your consciousness like a fat melon and bares all your dark engines—your sleepy, psychic wiring—to the streets? It's like rip-ping the face off a TV (you see them dead in my neighborhood all the time). Heavy, cracked hulks leaking their gleaming, coppery insides, the fragile tubing, the mechanics behind the projection. That's a blackout.

I was in one when I roared into the bathroom where this one girl had her hand up inside this other girl who was bent way over the toilet, her face squished up against the chrome plumbing, heaving over the bowl. Or so I imagine—I really have no fucking recollection. Which is unusu-al, because I handle my liquor superbly. Often I have watched dear friends plunge into extreme boozy sloppiness, losing all sense of space, lurching with slack faces and wet mouths, puking, falling, falling into their puke. Often I have watched this and sent a tiny prayer of thanks to Bacchus or Dionysus—whatever big holy goat-guy ruled the world of the drunken. I would pray, *Thank You Stinky Hairy Holy Horned Wino, for making me simply sleepy, too sleepy to heave the sloshing cup of suds to my mouth one more time,* I'm turning narcoleptic, where's the

285

cab? I just conk out. Or sometimes I get all sugared up and hyper, maybe a little loud, sure, but I always know what I'm doing. Which is handy, because I love to drink and it had appeared that this would not be a problem, until the shifty girl showed up at my house.

First my bedroom door just swung open, because the house that I live in is like one big free-love commune, with no locks on the doors and roommates barging in on you all day. And if we catch one another doing something shameful like licking butt or impaled upon an electronic pleasure device, everyone just giggles and trots back into the kitchen. And when the phone rings you gush to the caller, Oh, My God, I Just Walked Into My Roommate's Room And She Was Totally Licking That New Girl's Butt! Yes, That New Girl! The One With The Short Hair? A Performer, Kind Of Butch? Works At The Health Food Store, Rides A Bike, Has That Tattoo? That One! And the caller gasps, and you gasp, and at the end of the hall the new girl gasps as her butt hole gets tongued. And everyone is happy and truly alive, living the wild life, sex and talking, coffee for the talking and booze for the sex and snacky bites of cigarettes in between.

I was not doing anything as exciting as receiving a tongue in my ass when Camille hip-checked my door open and craned her neck around the bend. I was in bed, and we were both surprised. *I thought you were gone...?* My room is curtainless—so bright with the sun—and outside all the noise that comes with living on a stretch of chop shops and garages that clank with mechanics was streaming through my open windows. It was like three o'clock. My crappy little travel alarm clock on the floor said this.

I sat up quickly, quickly like in a dream where it feels like you should be quick, you're running and running and there's a serial killer with a big knife right behind you, but you're so woozy, you move like molasses. That was me in my bed that afternoon, I sort of oozed up my wall like an ambitious slug.

Camille grinned. She looked like the Cheshire Cat: All you could see was a floating set of choppers; everything else was wooly hat pulled low, greasy hair spanning over cheeks that were chubby as a chipmunk's. But you would only know this if you lived with Camille, like I did, and occasionally caught her dashing out of the shower, steam billowing behind her as if she were escaping a burning building.

Like a little white rabbit she hops into her room and slams the rickety door, a rickety door with a big hole patched with electrical tape, broken from when the last roommate punched her hand through the wood. But that's another story. Right now I'm explaining Camille's fugitive fashion, very incognito; maybe she's on her way to rob something. Baggy dark work clothes. Underneath she's all sweet cheeks, pink and young, soft. The whole town is filled with people whose insides don't match their outsides. It's a long process of hiding and disguising, of coaxing your inner tough guy or princess or tormented philosopher-poet-rock-star out from the skin shell by buying it toys. I looked like shit when I hit San Francisco, but I knew that a witty and confident person lurked beneath my twitching, nervous frame—I just had to draw her out. Like poison from a wound, or alchemy. That was a while ago. I'd learned to wear my poison so well I'd forgotten there was a wound beneath, leaching it.

I banged my head against the wall, just a little, to jostle some brain fluid back into place because everything felt pooled in my forehead, like I'd slept all night with my head hung off the bed. Which could have been possible if my bed wasn't a frameless futon, so flat it was flush with the floor. *What's up, have you been in here all day?* Yeah. *You've been getting phone calls: I've been telling everyone you're not home.* I'm Not, I assured Camille. I'm Totally Not Home. My face felt rubbery—no, plastic. Not exactly pliable. You know how after a night of drinking, memories rise slowly to the surface, like bits of shipwreck knocked free by a fish? Something—a door slam, shouting on the street, a slight earthquake—sets a new brain wave shimmering and you reluctantly open your eyes and experience a moment of pure peace before scenes from the night before come trickling in.

Drip. You were really loud. *Drip.* You stole that girl's drink, and she totally caught you. *Drip.* Oh, fuck, you *swore* you weren't going to ask that girl to make out with you again. I was back against the wall that afternoon, waiting for the big bucket of shame to dump on me, but there was nothing, a dark expanse. I tried to push at it with my mind, like Uri Geller bending keys.

How did I get home from the bar? I pushed at the mystery. *Eew, what are you doing? Stop, you're grossing me out, you're going to pop your eyes out of your head!* Camille, I started, Do You Know How I—

Listen, she said, and ducked into my room in a shady way that really worked with her thuggish attire. She shoved my door shut with a clunk, and came down onto my futon with me. *There is a really cute girl in the living room, and she's here to see you.* Who Is It? *I don't know!* she howled gleefully. *I've never seen her. She looks young.* Camille herself was young—she was 20, so I didn't know what young meant to her. Twenty-five was young to me; I was 30.

What Does She Want? *I don't know, she said she gave you a ride home from the bar last night and you told her to come see you this afternoon.* I Have An *Appointment?* I rubbed my hair; a spike from my bracelet punctured a snarl and stuck there. Ow. *I don't know!* Camille was very intrigued by the whole scene. *Should I send her in?* What The Fuck, Send Her In! I hollered grandly. Waved my hand in the air, the one that wasn't trapped in my messed-up mess of hair. I extracted myself from myself, pulled the covers around me, and languished there like a sickly starlet. There's a real glamour to hangovers if you work it properly, if you ride it out and aren't consumed by guilt or barfing. My hair felt dry and springy as I pushed it back from my face. My throat caught on itself when I swallowed, like velcro.

Tell Her To Come In, But Make Her Bring Me Water. Camille nodded and smiled, slunk up from my bed. Mine was such a happy house, everyone ready and willing to facilitate and even participate in each other's dramatics. It was really beautiful.

I sat there trying to remember things I couldn't, and got distracted by the carousel of flies rising and falling in great arcs around my room. You open the window and they rush in like air, like the hot and sour stink of the meat factory on the corner. A dark cloud of them, unreal. Eventually I shut my windows, eventually they're gone. It's a great mystery—where do they go? Occasionally I find a plump little carcass like a raisin on my floor, but that's only occasionally. They darted and frolicked with each other in the air above my futon, like tiny, flying puppies.

My door opened and a very young girl walked in with a pint of water. One of the pint glasses smuggled out of the bar at last call. I accepted it gratefully. *Hey*, she said, sort of sheepishly. She had really big eyes. Camille was right: She was cute. Not as ecstatically cute as my roommate seemed to think, but I had 10 years on Camille and was sorry to report that everything—girls, puppies, flies—got less and less cute as time wore on. The girl glanced around my room as I guzzled the water. It went right down, the whole pint. I rarely drank water, but when I did it was magnificent. *You remember me, right?* She meant it to be a kind of icebreaker, I could tell, but I'd never seen this girl before in my life. I Have Never Seen You Before In My Life, I declared. I hoped that I didn't sound bitchy. I'm usually so friendly, but this was such a weird morning. Afternoon. *You don't remember last night?* she laughed. Did We, Like, Have Sex? I joked bawdily. *No, no*, she said. *Not really.* Oh, wonderful. Whatever that meant.

It meant, of course, that I'd walked into the bar bathroom to find her fucking some girl over the toilet. I had proceeded to stand there shouting encouragement, and when the toilet girl started freaking out the way any normal person would upon having their most vulnerable moment violated by a belligerent stranger, I apparently just started cracking up. Which made my new young friend crack up, which made the poor vulnerable girl with her pussy in the air wiggle off her lover's hand and flee the bathroom with her skirt sliding down over an ass I'll never remember but like to imagine was sassy.

And...We Hung Out In The Bathroom? I asked. This was incredible. A practical joke perhaps, one of my roommates being a little prankster asshole? I remembered everything; I never forgot anything; it was a curse how much my mind retained. *Yeah*, my new pal was laughing. *You were, like, talking about how cool it was that we were fucking in the bathroom, because nobody does that anymore and everyone's so boring and stuff....* Girly seemed to become a bit uncomfortable as she realized that I truly did not remember any of this. She eyed me warily. Well, That Sounds Like Something I'd Say, I assured her. I Mean, I'm Sure I Was Sincere. I didn't want her to think it was just the liquor talking, even if it was. It's true—girls *don't* fuck in the bathroom like they used to. It's a real shame. Being a dyke used to mean something. We have a criminal lineage; we used to be outlaws.

I gazed at this girl I had absolutely no recollection of. It sounded like we'd really shared a moment. I wondered whether people stayed themselves while in a blackout. Were personalities inherent, or a series of poses shaped into habit through repetition? If no one was minding the store, did personality slip away? Who was I? Was I Obnoxious? I asked the girl. *No, you were funny*, she said. Is Your Girlfriend Mad? The girl shrugged. *She's not my girlfriend—I just met her at the bar.* You Guys Just Met And You Were Fucking In The Bathroom? I snorted. She's Brave Enough To Do That, But Gets All Freaked Out Just 'Cause Some Other Girl Caught A Glimpse Of Her Ass? *That's what you said last night*, smiled the girl, whose name was Paris. She wasn't Parisian, she was Greek, though really she was just Californian; she lived with her parents somewhere outside the city. One of those towns I'll never go to, though I know all about their pressing ecological issues thanks to my employment by Conserve California. I'd probably called her house at dinner time and tried to get her mom to fork over $50 on a credit card so I could make my nightly quota and not get canned.

Paris wanted drugs. That's why she was there in my bedroom as I sat on my futon, huddled in blankets and horrified at my life. Paris wanted Xanax. *You said you'd sell me some…?* Her voice trailed off into what we in telemarketing—no, tele*fund-raising*, tele-fucking-*activism*—call "up tones." Enunciating a sentence in a questioning tone. It conveys nervousness, insecurity, lack of confidence. Youth. My boss had explained to me countless times that people did not feel good about giving money to those who spoke in up tones, and I did not feel good about selling drugs to my new young friend. Not for moral reasons—I just didn't have very much. Nothing but a tiny palmful I'd begged off Wiggy. Wiggy who'd been a junky till he couldn't be one anymore, till his eyes were shot with yellow and he was forced to give up everything. Everything but the shit the doctors gave him, stuff that was just as brutal on your body as heroin but with none of the high. $3,000-a-month pharmaceuticals, and a prescription for Xanax to ease the pain of spending $3,000 a month on pharmaceuticals.

Wiggy was lying low with his family across the bridge in Marin. But every now and then he would rail against the injustice of his disease and hitchhike over the Golden Gate, show up at the bar with a good story and the amber vial of Xanax he'd trade for drinks. Wiggy had been a hairdresser before illness had collapsed his life into childhood and shunted him back to his boyhood bedroom and the care of his parents. Once he'd done the hair of every punk-rock legend to pass through Los Angeles. He carried in his wallet a photo of himself sweetly holding back the hair of a certain puking icon. Wiggy held the hero's ruined, colored tresses in one hand; in the other, a silver pair of shears glinted triumphantly. *He would not let me cut that fucking hair*, Wiggy recounted every time he flashed the picture, shaking his head like a queenie mama. *I'd say Ig, baby, you look like a muthafuckin' hippie. So I waited till he was wasted, and gave him a little trim.* I'd Like To Give Him A Little Trim, I sleazed, gazing at the legendary picture. Wiggy giggled a sad little giggle and sipped at his highball, sour and strong. Wiggy called cocktails highballs, a blinking neon word from the '50s, or Los Angeles. His glance lingered at the barroom door like someone important, someone glamorous, was going to walk in, but no one ever did. *This place is a goddamn overpriced fishing village*, he bitched, angry at being condemned to the northern half of the state. He'd slam the blue pills on the table like a palmful of coins. *I'd like a pink squirrel.* He'd lean back in his chair until someone dutifully pocketed the Xanax and trotted to the bar.

Last night I'd done it. I usually don't like downers, but drugs were drugs, and I'd been a bit edgy lately and supposedly those tiny darlings filed the edge right down to the cuticle. Wiggy Wants A Pink Squirrel, I told the bartender, and got another trough of beer for myself.

This is not a pink squirrel! shouted Wiggy belligerently, half-way down his cocktail. It had only just dawned on him. *What is this shit? It's The Same Shit You've Been Drinking All Night*, replied the bartender calmly. *This is NOT a pink fucking squirrel!* Bartender's mouth was open, bartender was gauging the situation before bartender spoke. I sprang into action like the codependent adult child of alcoholics that I was. Well, What Is It? I chirped cheerfully. I puckered my mouth around the glass and sipped. Wiggy, It's So Yummy! I chucked his shoulder in the place where his T-shirt was torn and his tattoos leaked through. *Ronnie, you don't even know.* Wiggy began to cry. Fat pebbles of cry-juice dropped from his face, a flash flood, muddy makeup ravines coursed across his face. *Honey, I'm Sorry*, he said to the bartender, whose name was Honey. Honey scratched her dreadlocks stoically, and slapped some bar napkins down before Wiggy. Wiggy mopped himself up. *It fucking sucks being sick like this*, he said, tilting his head to keep more tears from rolling out his eyeballs. *Can you imagine, if you just had to HALT your entire fucking LIFE and move back in with your parents?* No, Wiggy, I said. I realized I was patting him like a dog, and stopped, embarrassed. No, I'd Go Fucking Nuts. *I am going fucking nuts*, he said.

Wiggy cracked open his pill bottle and popped a pill onto his tongue, then mine. They were so teeny—a little crumb of a pill. The last thing I remembered was Wiggy daintily swabbing the dark paste of makeup beneath his eyes, and the foamy roll of beer as I brought it to my mouth. And now this—teenager?—shuffling on my scuffed floor, begging pills off me. Or, at least, prepared to purchase.

Apparently, Paris had driven me home. So she was old enough to do that. She wore those baggy hip-hop pants the kids in my neighborhood wore to high school. I felt old. Again. It had been happening a lot lately. I did not live the life of an old lady, but I could hear it beckoning to me, like a mermaid on a rock. I rubbed my head again, trying to massage and stimulate some intelligence. How Much Did I Say I'd Sell Them For? *Um, two dollars.* Paris had big, fleshy lips, the kind you usually see wrapped around a microphone. She had the impossible eyes of a Japanese cartoon character—enormous brown things that sloped faintly upward, as if her temples were being tugged back by a tight ponytail. But Paris's hair was short, a battleground of cowlicks. Because she had slept in her car, all night, in front of my house. She just woke up when the meter maid, placing a screaming orange ticket beneath the wipers, noticed the body in the back and knocked on the window. That was a couple hours ago. Since then she'd been watching bad TV in the living room with my roommates.

Your roommates are cool, she commented. Then, *Your house is cool.* I felt like the mother of her little girlfriend, someone she was on her best behavior for. A little gentleman. I was confused by her sleeping in her car. Why Didn't You Sleep Up Here? I asked. *You wouldn't let me.* God, Really? I was shocked. I practically invited the homeless into my very bed, people were always crashing all over the place; it was a big house. A big, drafty flophouse. I'm So Sorry, I said. How could I have made this poor child sleep out on the street? Was I truly an asshole? I liked to look upon the enigmatic subconscious mind as the real can of the soul, and I regarded subconscious activities such as sleeping, writing, fucking, and blackouts as demonstrative of the most deeply real part of a person. Was I a monster?

I'm Sorry, Paris, I repeated. Let Me Get You The Pills. I wanted the girl out of my room so I could think, or attempt to summon thought. I kicked off my blankets and climbed from my regal hangover throne. Stood to stumble over to where my jeans lay in an exhausted heap on my floor. Realized I had no underwear on and sunk back into the futon. Paris had jerked her head back like I'd whapped her, became suddenly very interested in a flowery birthday card from my mom that was tacked to my wall. *Darling Daughter*, the ephemeral script swooned. I tried to make a joke about a merkin, but it was dumb, so I coughed. Which felt unattractive. All phlegmy and hacking as I wiggled back into my bed, watching Paris's smooth cheeks burn from a dusky olive to a more glowing crimson. The crumbs in my bed dug into my bare ass as I reassembled myself. Like sleeping on the beach, I liked to think. The oceanic waves of traffic below, the sea gull squeak of rusty shopping carts, my sandy bed. Occasionally I would hear a swimmer being attacked by sharks, but that was the way of the natural world. A brutal place.

I asked my new friend to bring me my pants. She sort of flung them at me. Thanks. I didn't understand the strange obligations I'd woken up to. Entertaining and providing drugs for an apparently surly teen. I shoved my fist into the pockets until I felt the pills, nestled in lint at the bottom. I pulled them out. There really wasn't a lot of them. Less than I had expected, even. I thought...I puzzled at the cute baby blue drugs. *We ate some last night, remember?*

Paris stared at me. She sucked a meaty bit of her lower lip into her mouth and nibbled it nervously. Those lips sat on her face like a gorgeous cut of steak. Almost bloody, they were so red. *You don't remember, huh?* she asked sort of regretfully. I ignored her, busily brushing each tablet clean of pocket lint and placing them onto my comforter. Would You Happen To Know, I began, What Happened To My Underwear? Because I Do Wear Underwear, But It Seems I Am Not Wearing Any Underwear Right Now. Paris's very plush lips seemed to be trying to smile, there was a little war going on in her face. She pulled them straight, but one unruly muscle broke free and her upper lip rose and crested in a Billy Idol snarl. Paris shook her head. I wrenched my eyes away from that fascinating mouth and divided up my pathetic stash. Three for the teenager and three for me. Paris dropped $6 onto my bed, snatched the pills, and stepped back. She seemed afraid to get too close lest I flash her my pussy again. A curious desire to become a lecherous housewife, late in payment to the paperboy, flared inside my sickened body. Come Sit By Me, I flipped back the blankets and patted the flattened futon beside me. Tiny bits of crumb trampolined into the air with each provocative pat.

Are you kidding, of course I did not do that. I was a fucking hungover mess and I wanted this kid out of my room, even if her lips did look like an expensive delicacy served by a restaurant that would never seat me. *OK, thanks.* She was so twitchy; it wore me out to look at her. OK Then, Bye. She stood there in her fancy sneakers. Those enormous pants the kids were wearing these days. What were they trying to hide? They looked like good shoplifting pants. You could drop a canned ham down one of those pockets and sashay right out of the store. Ok Nice Meeting You Paris, Bye. *Bye...*The child slid, finally, from my room. The swish-swish of those giant pants. Why not just wear a skirt?

The slam of the door made me jump even though I knew it was coming. I scrunched back into my futon, plunged my face into my pillow and breathed the funky stink of my sweaty, unwashed scalp. A comforting smell, like farts. I felt gross, sleeping all night in that bed with no panties on. I wasn't a very clean person, but I did have my own set of standards, a thief's code of honor, and knew that my skanky futon was no place for an unclothed snatch. I clamped my legs tight against whatever vermin I imagined might be lurking beneath the covers with me. I sighed deeply, and breathed the hot fog of my own breath. It was not a comforting smell. It was the smell of someone slowly rotting from the inside. Camille! I croaked. I figured I didn't have to dredge up the energy to really holler since Camille was certainly lurking at my door like a cat, waiting to be invited in for gossip. I was right.

She crashed into my room with a gorgeous mug of water. She raised it like a trophy or a torch. The light streaming in the windows seized it, made it glow like ambrosia, like liquid crystal. It would make me well. Oh, Camille, I moaned. I guzzled the stuff until I couldn't stand the feel of my belly pushing against its skin. The word *distended* floated through my mind like a pretty scarf in the wind. The problem with being seriously dehydrated—as I was—with being committed as I am to a dehydration lifestyle, the problem is when you finally do drink water you get all slushy and bloated with it and wind up feeling worse than you when started, only in a different way. My poor body understandably thinks these are the only drops of water it will ever know, so it holds onto them for dear life, a cactus, my belly a camel's hump. It's called retaining water. I know that if I drink the stuff with some regularity, instead of springing it on my system a few times a year, my panicked body would adjust and I would not have the icky feeling of being *distended*. My skin would glow the glow of health, radiant as a pregnant lady. But I hate water. It's got no taste. And I've grown to love the idea of myself as a craggy old woman, a wrinkled and wind-worn dehydrated husk, like Georgia O'Keeffe. I've got no problem with that. But on certain mornings—afternoons—water is medicine.

Camille, I started, once I caught my breath. All that water had winded me. I was sure I smoked a pack of blackout cigarettes last night. Camille, You Hadn't Told Me She'd Been In There Watching TV. Camille shrugged. *She was so quiet, I kept forgetting she was there.* Camille wanted the whole story. I fed it to her in jerks and starts, recounting the mystery of my behavior as it had been told to me by the strange Paris. Oh, *my God*! Camille rolled around my futon like a big puppy in a union suit. *So, you took Xanax, blacked out, didn't have sex but you both hung out and she drove you home?* Yes! I shouted triumphantly. But I Don't Know What Happened To My Underwear. *Could they have fallen off?* Um, No. I wasn't too worried. I'd been known to find it extremely humorous and endearing, while tanked, to remove my panties and make a gift of them to people I don't know very well. I'm sure some stranger was lucky enough to receive the gift of my Hanes Her Way last night in my stupor. *Are you going to see her again?* I Hope Not, I said. Camille seemed let down. But, I added mysteriously, Who Knows? Camille smiled.

Alone in my room at last, I was exhausted. I wanted only to return to sleep, but that would have been pathetic. I decided I would stay in bed, drink water, and smoke—something I usually look upon as a disgusting practice. Smoking in bed. It is loathsome and not glamorous. A bed is no place for nicotine. But this day was such a difficult one. I would drink and smoke and talk on the phone. I hollered out to a roommate to bring me the phone. I had to see if Wiggy knew anything about my teenage Paris.

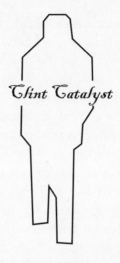

Clint Catalyst

FRIEND OR FAUX: AN EXCERPT FROM
TURNSKIN

But speed just wasn't working like it did back in the good old days—the times of hardcore delirious glamour. Most of the club kids bugged with their campaigns for fame, their paparazzi gossip for conversation, and trumped-up chatter. And nobody got on my nerves more than me. My patience had been worn to an angry frazzle. Meth only heightened the anxiety, the overwhelming sense of despair. Clubland's frantic house beats kept time with the hollow pounding of my speeding heart. And my fellow poets, my associates—performers at the Paradise—weren't at all pleased to witness my shadowy return. Rather than ask me what projects I'd been working on, they looked at me with knowing scowls. "Take care of yourself," they told me. "We wondered if we'd see you again."

New work, my turn on the stage became less and less necessary, done with less and less care. I couldn't even control my shifting makeup, my erratic mannerisms. Somewhere along the ride, I'd picked up a nasty facial tic, an annoying Billy Idol thing jarring the right side of my visage. It couldn't have looked anything but painful, pained. Plus my sentences came out screwed up and gasping, fragments raspy and dry, like I was out of breath. "No, everything's going great," I'd say, though they didn't ask. "I've just been busy. Grad school."

"Grad school, hmm," voices would mock, if they bothered to reply at all. Could they possibly know that my classes were over? I felt like I made everyone who saw me suspicious.

Then I met Filip, which shifted my focus. The desire for an environment where I'd be inspired was rapidly extinguished by my hormones. In short, I rediscovered sex. I say rediscovered since it'd been so long I'd nearly forgotten I could have sex with someone other than me and my sticky collection of porn. But time is such an elusive thing in speed terms, always steaming, streaming, dragging—never linear. Let's talk about getting horizontal. A war was storming in around me, and I moved my forces to the bedroom.

Actually, that sounds like I was the one In Control, you know, Mr. Predatory, I Made the Move. Not the case at all. Filip introduced himself to me or I introduced myself to him; that's the fuzzy part. Point is, we met among the dancing cadavers at the goth club where I worked. Roderick's Chamber, the spin-off of House of Usher, one of my favorite haunts. Both of them. Guess it's a pretty good thing—that I liked Roderick's, that is—since I was scheduled to be there every Tuesday, cohosting with Shawna, owner and progenitor. That sounds stilted: She started the club.

So there I was at Roderick's, lips pursed, tossing my locks like some death-rock Nellie Olsen, offering hors d'oeuvres and chatting up patrons. Typical host type stuff. Dipping into a population that included teenage suburbanites—baby bats from Napa Valley or Carmel, old school scenesters who were there because they really love the music, Victorianas and Ren Faire geeks, and the token degenerates, club freaks. My people. Not very many fags—ironic for a movement heralded by prancy boys in eyeliner. I always preferred my goth served chilled, extra dark, and romantic—the stuff of 19th century lit, of antique furniture. Not the brawny men in flowing skirts overflowing with testosterone. They threw me off at first, but by this time I was so jaded, I thought myself acquainted with all the bona fide butt boys. Assumed I either knew them, had had them, or hated them. Filip proved me wrong.

I'm such a terrible judge of who's available, who isn't. What I'm saying is that I have a tough time telling who likes me That Way. No, no, I was only being friendly / Just kidding around, man / We're much better as friends: These were words I never wanted to hear another human say. But Filip wasn't reciting them; he was hitting on me, shifty eyes and a nervous chuckle I mistook for shade. I countered with something insanely rude, some Black Magic protective B.S., nothing formal like a spell though. I didn't have the attention span, couldn't be bothered, so I made up my own curses. Stormed off in a cloud of huffiness.

"What's up with you and Filip?" Shawna asked me later that night, 3:30 in the morning, front seat of their Toyota RAV-4 as they drove me home.

"Story? There isn't one."

"Story is: He's nice," she corrected. Pause. "You really should talk to him." I couldn't see her face, examine her expression, but I knew what she meant. Me? He liked Me? I'd been down this road before: All signs read No Way.

But next Tuesday, something shifted and Filip liked me, liked me That Way. I was sure of it.

Filip was from San Jose, but his painfully good looks excused that. He was tall, six-foot-something-or-other, intensely blue eyes, chiseled features, massive package. Didn't have Prince Albert in a Can, but he *did* have a thick-gauged one through his cock head. His name really wasn't Filip, it was Brent, an All-American moniker about as dark and mysterious as pastel-colored bobby socks. Initially I joked about his choice of sobriquet, changing his name to go off to the big city, transform into Mr. Big Stuff, until it dawned on me I'd done the same damn thing with my "Catalyst" surname. So I shut up.

He comported himself with rigid shoulders and stiff gestures, as if he had a secret. Turns out he did. Filip was married, had a wife for more than a year now, but they had some kind of crazy arrangement. Days they were a couple, evenings they were free to do as they pleased. Where'd they come up with that idea, Jerry Springer?

"If you wanted to go back to your place, we could," Filip suggested. "But only until dawn." Yeah, right. An affair is an affair the way I see it: What difference is there between 5 and 7 A.M.? Was their marriage some sort of religious fasting thing, starve until the sun sets then binge and party down? I'd never sunk my teeth into married meat, but figured it was a logical progression from my I'm Not Gay But It's Different With You saga. And if I was going to sin, I was gonna sin *good*. That means no peeking to see whether it's still dark outside.

We went to my apartment, but not till after a few whispered conferences and ridiculous arrangements had been made. He'd go with me, but since he'd caught a ride to S.F. with his friend Robert, we had to find a willing female to entertain Rob while Filip and I did the deed. Oh, brother. A lay is not a lay unless it's complicated. Scan the club for single girls. "Madison, you know Robert, right?" I found myself asking. "Well, don't you think he's a hottie?" Blah yakety blah. Luckily first try was a score. Robert really was a hottie, really he was: long raven locks and vintage dinner jackets, a dapper guy. Plus he played guitar for some band—Mister Kill or something—which certainly didn't hurt.

Partners in crime: Robert dumped Filip and me at mine, went with Madison to hers. Filip telephoned once we were finished, and lo and behold, the honey light of dawn dripped through my uncovered window. Business had been delayed while I slammed Vanilla Stoli, force-fed a dirty batch of crank some chump had sold me, took a shower to cleanse my nether parts, then waited on Filip to slide into my silver latex pants. That's how things started. I was heavy into rubber back then, loved the obscene way it clung to the angles of my body. Wearing my own latex gear was such an erotic experience, all sucking noises and slippery and tight in the right places. Mmm. But somebody else in my stuff, him in them in my bedroom, carefully lacing up the crotch, his first time in rubber? Divine.

A smacking of lips, sweaty flesh. Filip's rump in the air. Yes, he was good. Not a molar-splitting, life-changing experience or anything, but also nothing to sneeze at. I was fascinated by the relative sincerity of his delivery. *Do it to me here, here, let me turn like this, this is such a good dick, I love sucking it, it feels great when you ram it deep inside me.* In medias res, I started to think of this swingin' suburban heterosexual thing as something less admirable but clearly more successful than most flaming city fags I knew. I mean, it's not like we want to be farmed out to anybody's wives or anything, but get a straight guy rap and it'll fill your ass with dick for sure. I'm tellin' ya. The more butch they are, the more they want to be poked, and they never have problems getting it. Me, I'm a sissy with mediocre goods and I ended up on top again.

And again and again turned this one-night stand into a Relationship, something new for me to trot around.

I had a boyfriend and a new pair of Luichiny's, and I was very proud of them. Obscenely square toes, white fur tongues—pony, I think, which is even more confusing 'cause it comes from a cow—a black block heel and this brilliant chunky sole protruding half an inch or so around. In, out, in, out, like some brick pattern on those '70s tract homes. Or teeth, fucked-up teeth. Total monster shoes. I loved them, had bought them in the Upper Haight in another master-plan attempt to get clean—blow all my money, every last cent of my living expenses and then some; that way I couldn't buy drugs. Could always manage to get Filip, clubgoers to float me spirited treats when I attended to them: "Put you on the list next week? No problem, but would you be a dear and fetch me a Lemon Drop? I've misplaced my comp tickets. Silly me." My silly shoes would click clack home early those alcoholic weeks—keep pouring the drinks and I'll pour my guts out—my history—till I'm too sloshed to speak. I was walking only because Filip propped me on his shoulder, dumped me in his car.

Funny, I've never liked the taste of liquor but am such a lush. Gulping not sipping myself into oblivion as if that's normal behavior, as if people normally consume substances they don't like the taste of, let alone imbibe them to blackouts. But here I go Telling not Showing.

I have to tell you, though, that Filip fell for me, his wife fell for another guy, and we kept fucking. Then I had something else in common with Airick: marathon sodomy sessions. And I had something new to knock on his door to ask him to borrow: lube.

"More? You need *more*?"

I did need more.

The Walgreens bag beneath my box springs that once held the reserve of Astroglide packets from Haight Ashbury Free Medical clinic, a tube of K-Y—plastic now, no longer in a tin—chocolate cream flavored lube—really raunchy stuff that seemed like a good idea in Salon: Video for the Discriminating Adult when I was shopping on Ecstacy—ditto the bottle of Probe—How could I have resisted the name?—even the two Tupperware containers filled with Wet Nonoxynol 9 that

Hannah had given me partly as a joke but mainly because I hinted that I needed some. Empty, gone. All of it gone.

I always needed more.

"You are one sick puppy," Airick gushed approvingly.

One sex-craved bow-wow having a helluva time avoiding crystalline treats, that is. My meth addiction had reached new, sundry, and secretive lows. The collective disgust of my associates only fueled my despair, hence my intake. Filip hated me on it because I was acerbic, impatient. Shawna and Z hated me on it because I was irrational, egotistical. Irresponsible—no longer to be depended upon at the club, regardless how small the task. One Tuesday I even went so far as to throw the hors d'oeuvres tray at an unsuspecting patron. I cast it away like a bad omen—a game of hot potato (Here, Catch) without so much as a Head's Up. Grapes and cubes of cheddar the only language exchanged between us.

Desiree hated me on it 'cause, well, we've already covered that. Even Airick hated me on it 'cause I was such a voracious fiend, needed more, more, more, more. So I resorted to clandestine arrangements, transactions with dealers that were harder to check up on, unlike James or Jonathan and the Roderick's regulars. Natch I was convinced people were Meddling in My Biz.

Insert Chynna here. Desperation breeds the lowest common denominators, and dealing with Chynna was more than a mere dip in the shallow end of the gene pool. I'm trying not to be judgmental—seriously—but since this is my point of view, I might as well tell you she was a rancid ex-stripper skank. Chynna. I hate when people name themselves after countries or continents. Hi, I'm Antarctika, I'm Africka. As if altering the spelling changes the meaning so much. That's the way it worked with Chynna, though—hate to admit it, but I have to. This one was her own planet.

She was white and something mixed, maybe Latin. Doesn't really matter. Point is she was anything but Asian and had taken on the moniker because she was so little, she said; like a china doll. Massive groan over that one. Her? A figurine? Crack baby was more like it. Ghetto braids, 100% synthetic, blue-black and lilac poly that screamed Bargain Bin. Juicy nails—press-ons, of course—and jet-black lip liner, frosty pink lips.

But appearances are thin and watery. What counts is the person who's beneath. Or in her case, who isn't. Here's a prime example of what I'd have to endure to score: Ensconce the cordless in my room. Dial her pager, wait. Page, page, anxious. Wait for an interminable period of time. "'Sup?" She'd bark. "Sure, I'm holdin'. Be there in a flash / Comin' right atcha." Then, hours later, she'd show, come trudging over to claim, "All I got's a quarter but we can share." Sharing meaning I cough up 30 bucks—an obscene amount even if the entire baggie were my own. But I had to cover cab fare, you know, her expenses. Her. Cracking gum and her braids like a licorice whip, tossed over the shoulder.

Chynna spoke a brand of slang I didn't understand, talked in Hella Bum Rushin' Phat Scrub Stix Clownin' Flix, and lots of it. Talked and chopped the drugs, talked and chewed my ears to a bloody pulp. Did I Hear About the Guard Who Fiddled Her Pussy Last Time She Was Inna Pen? Somewhere when I was verging on furious, she'd push a rail at me—a speed bump, as it were. Chynna'd string me out all night with a series of splinters, miniscule rails laid on the enormous jagged piece of mirror I'd procured from the basement of my last apartment, back before I became too paranoid to take out the trash. It was haunted downstairs. Now the trash came to me: little lines and some of the biggest lies I've ever heard. The Little Lady had ripped off two friends of mine, these fags I knew, a couple. Mopped their rent cash they'd yet to convert to a money order, then constructed an elaborate tale of how she hadn't taken anything. In fact, they owed her. Oh, of course.

Boring cover-ups she volunteered—at least her Tall Tweak Tales, what I called speakin' Tweakineze, were perversely fascinating. Too bad she had to stop payment on the house she bought her family in Marin with full scholarship funds from a private donor at the Art Institute because she dropped out to dance on tour with the 2 Live Crew who totally fucked her over, Dude, when she found out she was carrying the lead singer's baby and his woman was the tour manager so to cover it up the band left her locked in a dressing room in Minnesota where the auditorium's security found her later and thought she was some obsessive groupie they turned over to the police who believed she was a juvie because of course she didn't have an ID on her, only a G-string, she was a dancer for 2 Live Crew not New Edition so she hitchhiked back to S.F. with this really nice trucker who gave her a ride all the way but now she was sort of hiding out from him because at the end he went kinda psycho and told her he loved her and got so touchy-feely she freaked out and stabbed him in the neck with a fork from his can of Beenie Weenies which of course really pissed him off so she jumped from the window of the rig and has heard he's been looking for her ever since. No way, really, Chynna? That's so terrible to hear.

What was great was when she'd get all heart-to-heart and shit. What's that term again? For when a person mixes up the meanings of words? Inversion, I suppose. She'd lean in close and whisper, "Me and Herbie's gonna have us a little déjà vu this weekend in Vegas," her eyes sincere as a doe's; she really meant it. Or she'd slap her forehead, exclaim *Rendezvous!* trying to be all psychic that way long-term amp addicts tend to do. I never corrected her, bit my tongue as she went on about how what she really needed was a monotonous relationship and it had been such a monogamous day. Besides, I doubt she would have even heard me. It was kind of endearing—just like when she informed me she was Doing Me a Favor while ripping me off, pocketing my belongings in her nappy nylon backpack.

I never really got high with Chynna. At best I got an extensive Almost ending with me passed out on the black velveteen fold-out couch that weighed a ton and felt like a casket. I'd saved up the 250 bucks to buy it back in Arkansas. I made the money nude modeling at UCA, clutching props and holding ludicrous poses buck naked 20 minutes at a stretch for an icily air conditioned classroom of students who sketched my privates. The couch was one of the few remnants of my past life, back when I had things like schedules and a savings account. Its cushions were dusty and sinking, like me.

When I woke the next day my throat was a cesspool of postnasal drip. It felt like I'd swilled battery acid. Eyelids drooping like broken window shades in that atmosphere pumped out on missing CDs, broken promises and tattered To Do lists—I'd resorted to changing the date, since the items remained the same. My morning recitation of events still started with No New Work—was such a harsh reminder that I had to kick drugs. But that was a desperate chasm to leap over.

My life was a movie I didn't want to watch anymore, wanted to fast-forward through. The plot development—the Easy Move for me, it seemed—was to play doctor. Feeding my needs and craving more of my insanity, I practiced shooting up in the bathroom. It was such a drag being at the mercy of others.

The enhancing frame of this violently lit WC—approximately 2 feet by 4 feet—was the only private place when I had company. I kept the tools tucked away in my shaving kit—the outside pocket of a faded black pleather medicine bag that I'd extract from beneath the sink. Balance the tools around the basin.

I was bound to the fineness of my tablespoon with its arched arm, Q-Tip cottons, worn cc-marker syringe with a dull point, clear splash of water from the faucet, healthy pinch from the emergency reserve of Tina. Bound to those inked-in colors: my face growling into the mirror, red cheeks swollen like a newborn. An angry reflection. Teeth buried in the black leather of my belt, eyes narrowed into slits, determined, until the drugs hit and punched out that tiny white world. Went off like a firecracker in my head, took the back of it right off. It was so delicate and dramatic, like Neve Campbell in *The Craft*: "Take my scars, take my scars."

Clearly this was a stalling action. It fractured whatever I was trying to do—including my need to declare myself a junky, not an occasional user. I wasn't even able to have an orgasm unless I'd stuck a needle in my arm.

Which leads us back to Filip. He became another fixture in our household, the Married Guy. My roommates never referred to him by name. "Is the married guy here? / Phone for the Married Guy / Hey, pass me the pan Clint's Married Guy brought us," Then *shazam* he's overcooking pasta and grotesque over-the-counter tomato sauce. He announces his marriage is over, which transforms him from Hitched to Ditched and Divorced in one fell swoop—*kersplat*—like a cartoon character.

"She's moving out at the end of the month," he said. She being The Wife—or rather The Ex—and he explained, "She's not so crazy about, um, us."

So much for arrangements.

"And you know, I have a really big place and everything so—"

Actually I didn't know, had never been inside. A scooped-out hollow in my gut signaled what was coming next. It was an incredibly tense moment—the air between us loaded with the brisk buzzing sound of flies stalking the living room. The kitchen was lemony-smelling. Had someone actually cleaned in here? A citrusy, garlicky spaghetti stew Filip stared into, silent as he stirred our steaming dinner. He gulped, his Adam's apple bobbing like that thing when people go fishing and I thought, *I don't know this guy at all. Are we supposed to Care About Each Other?* Then there it was, hanging thick and awkward as a semi-erect penis, dangling between us:

"You could move in if you wanted to."

Shit. So I could've gotten married, become a kept boy, if that's what I'd wanted to do. I didn't know what I wanted to do. I wanted to write, just because I couldn't think of anything else. It's kind of scary, looking back, because my wonder years and all my life had been comprised of Big Plans. What I was going to do next, what I needed to do to get there, blah blah blah. When had everything become such a big deal, or had nothing been a big deal after all? I'd been reduced from High Expectations to just high. Abbreviated. Left to Think About It and huff on my cigs, smoke curling in my 12-pack carton of a room, firing up PM Int'ls, the attractively maroon-boxed brand he turned me on to. A brand I've since been able to find only in San Francisco—ironic since PM stands for Phillip Morris, a corporation I assumed was pretty much omnipotent, i.e. International. Apropos though, since S.F. thinks of itself as its own cultural hub, its own Mecca. Personification / Hasty Generalization. Yes, I digress.

But this is one detail I can't omit. Late one afternoon, 4 or 5 or something, Filip was off at work and Desiree was coming in from work, stepping off the 24 Divisadero as I was struggling with the locks downstairs. I hated those fucking locks: two keys for the protective gate, two for the general door, two more for our place upstairs. Then add another for my bedroom, but that hadn't happened yet; I'm getting ahead of myself.

"Eww, what stinks?" queried D-Rock as she clomped up our apartment's staircase in platform Mary Jane's, wide and pigeon-toed, her nose crinkled in disgust.

"I dunno," I said and quickly scanned the soles of my shoes.

On the heels of this inspection, Desiree noticed something in the hallway. "What the—" Dark brown splatters on the oak floor: a winding, chunky trail, a tarlike path leading from the bathroom. Stopping at Airick's door.

Quickly we surmised this was something wrong, something sick. We knew that.

"Oh. My fucking God." It couldn't be. No way, it couldn't be. But the ardent way she spoke assured It Was.

"Oh, my fucking God!" D-Rock attacked his door, really pounded on it, wailing with both her fists. Then—"Oh! My! Fucking! God!"— she launched into a Grand Mal, full-on thrashing and stomping and spitting out obscenities with Airick's name. "This! Is! So! Disgusting!"

"*What?*" The door flew inward, half-open, blocked by Airick's nude torso. A dense musky smell rushed at us, a pungent mix of gamey pubes and poop.

"What do you mean, *What?*" Desiree's arm shot out to an index finger, a point. "This!"

Airick laughed a tiny, nervous laugh and shrugged his shoulders. I just stood there, taking it all in. Such a performance.

Airick had upped the ante in the illicit substances department. That's to say, he'd graduated to booty-popping—slamming speed up the butt. Pull the needle out, slide the apparatus in, and voila! Warm waves, ripples of euphoria à la Billie Holiday without going all the way. The Other Way.

But the way it went for him was right back out. Yes, he took a shit. Or rather it took him, this exhaust trail to his bedroom.

"Clean. This. Up!" Desiree gave the churlish proclamation and stomped off. *Slam!* goes her door, then there around Airick's comes a second one. Head, that is. Bug-eyed and shriveled, painfully skinny, blistered with sweat. Surveying the situation, it/he looked eerily familiar. Not in that "I think I've seen you somewhere before" kind of way, but the OK, now *Who is this* point of reference.

"Omigod," I Valleyed. "Tim?"

"Y-Yes? Clint?"

It was. Upon arrival in San Francisco, my first job had been at Kinko's Copies. I lasted a week and a half, including training. These two cool girls who worked at Act One had yanked me up and placed me in a better paying temp position since I had a college degree. Why would you want to work at Kinko's, they waxed rhetorically. Before the great escape, Tim had been my manager: the guy who'd interviewed me, hired me, and shipped me off to Burlingame for a barrage of lengthy introductory videos and Q&A sessions. But now a drugged look was so deep in his eyes, all personality was drowned in it.

What I learned in a few minutes—what he'd been reduced to in that four-year span—sent freon up my spine. Fifty pounds lighter and aged at least a decade, living in a residential hotel on Market, living off out-calls he made through a "Models/Escorts" ad in the *Bay Area Reporter*. Glamorous. Oh, yeah, and I shouldn't forget his shoulder—the right one—still propped up by a makeshift brace from a couple months prior, when he'd broken his collar bone. A wrong move—he fell out of a tree. A 35-year-old man had the urge to climb trees and Be One With Nature. Just for grins, in San Francisco. I need not say more.

Quasi-civilization had now officially slipped away. I was living with a guy who not only defecated on the floor, but also didn't bother to wipe it up. Moreover, when he conceded to do so his Act of Retribution consisted of his casually strolling out with a towel wrapped around his midsection like a sarong, thin and flowing, and dabbing at the mess with a handful of napkins. More rubbing it into the cracks of that scuff-marked floor than cleaning it up, his lips curled into a sneer.

Was this a passive-aggressive act? His demented version of sincerity? What the common folk would call a joke?

Whatever the case, Mark sure didn't find it funny. Not that Desiree and I were exactly doubled over in laughter, but Mark was livid to our two counts sicked-out.

Oh, I almost forgot to mention him to you. Mark was an Art History major at SFAI, one of those militant vegan neohippie types with a polite Connecticut upbringing. So fortunately he took showers. And he just happened to live with us—D-Rock had lured him in with a sublet flyer that she posted on the campus corkboard. Mark was filling Steffi's slot, space. Actually more like quarter of the rent.

That is, until this incident. Then Mark became remarkably involved in our apartment's goings-on.

"Wait a minute. He put speed...up his butt?"

Shh, Desiree nodded, as if Airick overhearing our late-night kitchen conference would have made any difference.

"Is that a gay thing?" Then, editing himself so as not to offend me: "I mean, does it work that way?"

Mark had to make sure he was getting this right. Total sociobehavioral study. I was doing the same with his Fimo clay bracelets and dreadlocks tipped with neon-colored beads.

"Yeah, sure," I explained. Actually, I'd read about the workings of the butt in *The Joy of Gay Sex*, so maybe it *was* a gay thing. "The tissue up there's the consistency of toilet pap—"

Desiree tossed me the penciled brows, a violent pitch of *Shut the fuck up / Don't let him know how intimately you're informed about this type of thing / Stop incriminating yourself* that I happened to catch. She was right: I shouldn't shock Mark any further if I was going to be on his team, which undoubtedly this was turning into, completely Us versus Them, only fortunately this time I was on the side of the Us. Thank God. I couldn't imagine another housing search. And my relations with Mark were already borderline delicate. Recently I'd startled him—the Straight Boy—when he saw me naked with cock head raised at attention—pumped full of lusty thoughts—as I tossed the cordless phone from my room. I mean, he kept paging and paging it, that excruciating high-pitched beep going off when Filip and I were in the middle of things. What did he expect?

"Worked enough for him to crap all over the place," Desiree countered.

"'Nuff said," Mark nodded, his meat- and processed chemical–free skin visibly crawling from the thought.

"And he's got a *hooker* over here?"

The way he said "hooker" made it sound like *Radar-Range* or *persnickety* or *commode*, one of those archaic words.

"When I've got a camera, supplies—when we've *all* got stuff?"

Group nod of agreement at that one.

"Well, then it's settled." He clapped his hands a single time in that decidedly male way, more of a deep cuff. "That guy's gotta go."

Wow. *This* guy had balls! Not even on the lease, a measly sublet of something like a month, and already there he was, throwing people out on the sidewalk. Quite a change from the meek health food store boy I'd seen. Then again, I guess we all have our breaking points. Shit on the floor just happened to be his.

Which is what nudged Mark into handyman mode. I couldn't tell you much about his artistic merit, but he could install locks like a mother-fucker. The fact that Desiree, he, and I all had individual locks on our doors before dusk the next day amazed me. We were Good to Go.

That is, until Mark went into the rest room to clean up and wash his hands.

Aagh! He sprinted back into Desiree's room, where we were comfortably sprawled across the bed, listening to Depeche Mode ("It's No Good") on her unpredictable boom box. Mark's face, usually a robust melon-pink, was pale and ashen.

"There's more."

"More what?" I asked apathetically, dull from Klonopin.

"All over the bathtub." His words were clipped.

"No!" D-Rock's face registered sheer horror, her bouncy ringlets trembling, as if the blood had suddenly drained from her head.

We ran to the back room and examined the evidence.

This time it was no measly trail. It was an enormous brown sludge eclipsing the tub, a grisly mud puddle we knew wasn't mud. And it was ripe. Fresh. There are few things in this world I cannot easily give nomenclature to. The way this smelled is one of them. Overwhelming and profound, the stench rose and seemed to mat the mucous membranes of my nose. I fled down the hallway and fought my gag reflex.

When had this happened? I hadn't seen Airick since the incident yesterday, though I assumed he was still home—Thrill Kill Kult seeped faintly through his door. From where had this materialized? Was it some karmic fecal matter of the cosmos? I hadn't heard Airick lumber across the hallway and into the shower, and that clumsy Dung Hag was about as quiet as I was straight. This had turned into a series, *Sex and the Shitty*. When did he have the chance to spew more poo?

In my bedroom, I lit nag champa and listened to D pow wow with the poop meister. Sometimes incense is nice and everything, but it made my closet-size sanctum smell like a Grateful Dead parking lot. Anyway, Desiree was noticeably calmer than the last time they chatted; he was—at best—monosyllabic. In what could be best described as an extensive experiment in sleep deprivation, Airick had reached the primal grunts and syllabic-fragments-of-the-serotonin-depleted stage, a brain-melt zone I'd been reduced to countless times myself. Methamphetamine is so *Flowers for Algernon*: All that superhuman cerebral ability fades to

limited physical activities like stapling carpet scraps to the wall or masturbation antics worthy of *The Guinness Book of World Records*.

Yes Airick was responsible for the rest room defecation project; yes
Tim was still shacked up with him; yes they were both defiant in their
body language and yes, all of this was a problem.

A cursory *knock-knock* and D-Rock entered my lair.

"He's cleaning it up," she said, sitting down on my infinity print rug.

"I should *hope* so. Desiree, he *shat*"—she nodded, extracted a
Kamel—"in our shower."

"Mm-hmm," she agreed, acerbic grin curled around her cigarette. "He did."

"Now we have to get flip-flops," she said in a breath of smoke.

Flip-flops? I was going to have to shower in *flip-flops*? What a fashion nightmare. Plus one of Desiree's eyebrows was smudged.

Lisa Archer

The Shitty Schoolgirl

My brief and scattered history of shit play began in 1993, when my best friend Emily started pissing on the owner of an obscenely prosperous New Age book company. In my experience, the clients who talk endlessly about peace and love are always the ones who eventually ask, often quite tentatively, "Do you think you could maybe—shit on me, please?" Emily and I had started turning tricks together back in '91, when we'd both worked for the same agency. In the spring of '93, I was taking a sabbatical from sex work to study for my Ph.D. exams. Since I was consequently broke, Emily persuaded me to take a study break one day to drive out to Half Moon Bay with her to shit on her illustrious New Age john. "He keeps asking me to shit on him," she explained. "It's not that I don't want to—I just can't do it. Do you think you could?"

"I'll do my best," I promised, and indeed I was rather enamored with the idea. In a very abstract sense, it pleased me to defecate on a man who made his billions selling spiritual paperbacks to the purchasing enlightened. I ate beets that day and swallowed a couple Ex-Lax tablets, hoping to produce a lovely liquid fuchsia.

It was a rainy spring day in Half Moon Bay. Emily's client lived in one of those contemporary houses that jutted out of the wet green hillside like a sailboat made of wood and glass. Hrut greeted us coolly at the door. His scant flaxen hair lay flat on his head, and he spoke in some kind of Scandinavian accent. Emily and I followed him through his empty house with folded ladders leaning against the walls and sheets of clear plastic, splattered with white paint, covering the floors. Out back on the wooden deck we soaked in his barrel hot tub in the rain. The deck looked out over a forest of shadowy gray trees, barely visible through the fog. We hardly spoke. Part of Hrut's trip was that he didn't like to talk in sexual situations, so he told Emily what he wanted in advance. Then, whenever he changed his mind and wanted something different, he whispered to Emily, and she in turn whispered it to me. It was like the telephone game, and I was starting to feel slightly feverish, as I sometimes feel when I have to shit really bad but can't.

Finally we got out of the hot tub and dried ourselves in the only finished room in the house—a small, pine-paneled cubicle with a white shag carpet and a vase of tiger lilies in the corner. Hrut whispered something to Emily. She motioned me over to her and quietly explained: "He wants us to stick these flowers up our butts and chase each other through the house like wood nymphs, while he sneaks around watching us. Then he wants us to come back in this room and piss and shit on him." I looked at Hrut, who was solemnly covering the white wool carpet with a large plastic sheet and multiple layers of paper towels.

"OK." I prodded my butt hole with the stem of the tiger lily. It slid in smoothly like a long, slimy icicle. I clenched my anus around it and cautiously let go. It stayed in for a minute or so, then slowly slipped out and dropped to the floor. (Since I'd been holding my shit all day, this really fucked with my control issues.) Emily couldn't get her tiger lily to stay in either, so finally we just said to hell with it and started scurrying through the house, dodging ladders and paint buckets, while holding flower stems in our butt holes so they wouldn't fall out. I didn't think we looked much like wood nymphs, but the show wasn't for my benefit.

About five minutes later, we rushed back into the pine-paneled cubicle. Hrut was holding a video camera. As we entered the room, panting from exertion, he grabbed Emily by the arm and whispered something in her ear. He wanted us to film each other as we pissed and shat on him respectively. "He's the only one who's going to see it," said Emily. "And it won't have your face in it anyway." Hrut was already lying on his back in the middle of the room—upon that bed of plastic and paper towels he'd made earlier.

"Can I go first? I'm dying to take a shit!" My bowels were ready to explode.

"No, you're the finale!"

"OK fine—just give me the camera and hurry up and piss on him." I held my poop and focused the lens on the upside-down V of Emily's legs, as she straddled Hrut and spouted a sparkly yellow stream. It missed Hrut at first, so she repositioned herself until it landed on his neck and chin, then petered off in an occasional dribble.

"Here." She took the camera from me. "Now it's your turn."

"Where does he want me to shit?" I whispered.

"I dunno. Just do it on his stomach."

I straddled Hrut, squatted and relieved myself of a single purple turd—so hard it practically bounced off his belly—which was strange, considering all the Ex-Lax I'd taken. I don't know what I was expecting, but it seemed so utterly banal. Here I was, shitting on another human being, and it felt no different from shitting in the john. I looked down at Hrut, who didn't even make eye contact. He simply scooped up the turd in a towel and vanished into the bathroom with a resounding flush. Was it possible he saw something transgressive in this? A few seconds later, he came out of the bathroom, walked out onto the deck and climbed back into his hot tub. My asshole felt strangely empty and ached from constant tensing.

Emily handed me a stack of crisp twenties. "For you," she smiled. We dressed and left.

I've shat on four people in eight years—each time for pay. The folks I've shat on fall into two categories: the experimenters, who court it once or twice as the last taboo—the final frontier of their desire—and the hardcore, dyed-in-the-wool fetishists. Hrut falls into the first category. So does football-player Bob.

"Once when I was a teenager," explains Bob, "I was fucking my girlfriend up the ass after football practice. She took a shit and was so embarrassed, but I just thought, 'Oh, that's so hot.' Then, after I came, it just looked like a big mess to clean up."

A friend who'd heard me talk about Hrut recommended me to Bob. I've been seeing him every couple of weekends for the last few months. He called me yesterday afternoon.

"It's OK if I talk, right?"

"Yeah, go ahead." We'd agreed he could talk over the phone as long as he didn't say anything about the money.

"What I'm interested in this time is anal," he says under his breath. "And could you, maybe, not clean yourself out, so there's like some, uh—you know—on the condom when I pull out? D'you think you could you do that for me?"

"Sure."

"And could you, maybe, hold it all day, so if I put a few towels down on the floor you could maybe go, like, after I pull out?"

"Yeah, I could do that."

"I want it to be real realistic, you know. You wouldn't mind that or nothin'?"

"No, I'd say so if I did."

"And how about farting? Can you fart?"

"Yeah, I can fart."

"So how much time do you need? You know, to prepare?"

"Give me as much notice as you can. At least five hours."

"So, if I want this tomorrow afternoon, how early can I call you?"

"10 or 11 is fine."

The phone rings again a few minutes later.

"What are you going to eat?"

"Broccoli."

"And that'll make you fart?"

"Yeah."

"I can be there at 5:30. And I can give you a little extra, 'cause I know you have to eat all that stuff you probably don't want to eat."

"Thanks Bob. I really appreciate it."

"I was also wondering if you have, um, like…teenager clothes?"

"I have a schoolgirl outfit. It's a red plaid jumper."

"That's great. What I'm looking for is something young and innocent, you know—like 16 years old and real embarrassed. Like 'Oops.' You know what I mean—like you're doing this thing and then—'Oops!'"

"I can do that. No problem. See you at 5:30, OK?"

"And—and I have like one of those glycerin enemas, but I'd rather do it without the enema. I want it real realistic, you know."

"OK, Bob. I'll be there at 5:30. I'm looking forward to it."

"Good, that makes me happy."

I usually have complete and total confidence in my ability to fart, but the day I'm scheduled to fart on Bob, I start having doubts. So I call Michael, a male pro dom who specializes in farting.

"Does he want sweet farts or rank stinky farts?"

"I pretty sure he wants stinky ones."

"Then black beans, sauerkraut, and hard-boiled eggs. It's the deadliest combination. What time are you doing this?"

"5:30."

"It's almost one now. That's pushing it. You should be able to produce some gas by then, but you better hurry up."

"I've already had some broccoli and milk products."

"Broccoli should work, but black beans, sauerkraut, and hard-boiled eggs—that's much ranker."

"I'll go to the corner store right now."

"Oh, I forgot—you have to eat really fast too. Just don't ever pull this one on me, OK?"

In the next half-hour, I gulp down a can of black beans, a can of sauerkraut, and five hard-boiled eggs. By 1:30 I have to shit really bad, but I hold it for four hours, including the hour-long drive to Fremont, where Bob lives. When I finally alight on Bob's doorstep in my plaid jumper and white oxford shirt, I feel like a superhero, having escaped incontinence by a narrow margin.

Bob, a retired football player from Texas, ducks under his front door. Wearing nothing but boxers, he scoops me up in a big, bristly bear hug. Bob is 6 feet 5 with squinty eyes, a bald head shaped like the Frankenstein monster's, and a face that's weathered in vertical stripes. He hands me a wad of bills to count while he throws some towels down on the living room rug.

We start pawing each other on the sofa. The scene belongs on the front seat of a Chevy pickup, not on a couch in front of a warm fire and a bookcase full of football trophies from 20 years ago.

The black beans, sauerkraut and hard-boiled eggs aren't working. At most they yield a few mild puffs, but no rank, sputtering farts—at least not until after he comes. Ultimately that doesn't matter. Bob throws my plaid jumper over my shoulders and fucks me doggy-style. He's relatively good at this, and I think the shit in my rectum provides a cushioning effect. When he pulls out, I deliver a long, mushy brown turd—the one I've been holding since 10 this morning.

"Whoops! Oh, no!" I squeal on cue.

"That's OK, hon," Bob reassures me. Squeezing his cock back in my butt hole, he goes right on fucking me doggy-style over the log-shaped turd, which just lies there like an innocent bystander, not even smelling particularly bad.

"Oh, baby! That's so hot!" Bob comes with a spasm.

When he pulls out, I turn and look at his still-erect cock. The condom is covered with so much shit that it looks as if he dipped the head of his cock in chocolate icing.

The scene with Bob was the first shit scene I'd done since 1998. I thought my scatological career was over after I met Garvey. Garvey was the one hardcore, dyed-in-the-wool fetishist I had the pleasure of pooping on. In Garvey I encountered my limit in shit play.

Garvey was a petite, tidy-looking man with slicked-back gray hair and a thin mustache. Garvey liked enemas—I mean he *really* liked enemas. He wanted to lie down in his tub while I gave myself an enema and spewed shit all over his body. He didn't actually say this on the phone. I try to keep the details to a minimum, just in case the guy's a vice cop. Nonetheless, he told me enough so that I came prepared. I brought a shower shot (a long metal hose—one end of which screws into the shower nozzle and the other end into my butt), hydrogen peroxide, and a bottle of antibacterial soap. I was definitely ready for some unhygenic acts.

Shortly after I arrived, we climbed into Garvey's bathtub. He sat behind me, as I poked the cold nozzle of the shower shot into my butt, let the water run into me and fill me up until the pressure got to be too much. When I let it out Garvey immediately stuck his head into the downpour between my legs. Most of it was water at first, then the shit began steaming down my thighs. It smelled like a port-a-potty—warm and putrid.

"May I eat some of it—please!" Garvey pleaded.

"I really don't want you to."

He lapped at the insides of my thighs, apparently not paying any attention.

"Stop that! You'll get sick. It's full of *E. coli*!"

"I've never gotten sick before. Do you mind if I put some in a jar to save for later?"

Oh, God, I didn't even want to think about it. Garvey scraped some of the poop off the insides of my thighs with a spoon and shook it into the jar.

I showered right afterwards, scrubbing down my whole body with anti-bacterial soap and rinsing my legs with a mild hydrogen peroxide solution too. The stink was really getting to me. I asked Garvey to rinse off.

"I'd really rather not," he said.

"If you don't, I'll have to leave right away. I'm gonna throw up."

"I understand," he said in a voice of compassion. "It bothers a lot of people." With a sigh of regret, he climbed into the tub.

"I'm sorry—I have to get out of here!" I fled into the next room—Garvey's bedroom—and collapsed on his perfectly made bed. I looked at the clock. Only 20 minutes had passed since I'd arrived. *Shit*, I thought, *we have another 40 minutes to go.* Garvey's bedroom was impeccably neat, but I was afraid to touch anything. I imagined that Garvey walked around his house all the time with shit on his hands, covering everything he touched in minute particles of feces like an uncouth Midas. When Garvey entered, wrapped in a blue towel, I didn't want him to touch me either. I suspected he'd just wiped himself off for my sake—or maybe even licked himself off—since he'd been so reluctant to shower. I felt both disgusted and sorry for him.

"I'm wiped," I breathed.

"I'm wiped too," he chuckled at the pun.

"Do you mind if we take a break?"

"Not at all."

He flopped on the bed next to me.

"So you like this more than anything else, huh?"

"Yeah," he said.

"It must be hard sometimes finding people to do it with." I bit my tongue.

Why was I being so presumptuous all of a sudden?

"No, not really," he said. "I've been married and divorced four times."

"Were they into it too?"

"Not in the way I am, but they were willing to do it for my sake 'cause I liked it so much."

We were silent for a moment, as I took this in. I wondered what this guy had going for him that four women—who weren't into shit themselves—would do this with him. Some of them for years maybe.

"And they knew this was your main turn-on when they married you?"

"Oh, yes, I told them right up front, and we did it all the while we were together. But I think the reason they left me," he began slowly, "was because they found out I was more into their shit than I was into them."

We were quiet for a moment, as we both took this in. I could tell it was hard for him to say.

"So how long have you been into this?"

"Oh, as long as I can remember. When I was about 7 years old I got hit by a truck. I was in a coma for nine days, and, when I came out of the coma, the nurse in the hospital was giving me enemas. When I was a kid, I didn't know what fucking was for the longest time—until I was real old, like 12 or 13. One day I asked another kid on the playground what fucking was, and he told me, and I thought, Oh, *that's what that nurse in the hospital did to me.*"

We both laughed.

"What did the kid say that fucking was?" I asked curiously.

"Oh, I don't remember. It was so long ago."

"But you thought it had something to do with enemas?"

"Yeah," he chuckled. Little had I known I was awakening his oldest sexual memories by sliding that cold nozzle up my butt.

"You don't have any more left—like a hard one—do you?"

"No, I don't think so."

"Well, before you go, I'd like you to watch me. You don't mind that, do you?"

"No, go ahead." At the end of the bed, there was a platform that I'd hardly noticed before. Garvey mounted it on all fours and let a long turd drop onto a light blue towel. Then, turning to face his stool, he bent down to kiss it, cooing and patting it on the head as if it were a small animal.

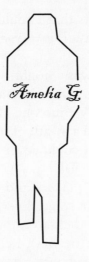

Amelia G.

RESTRAINT

Looking at him standing in the back of the courtroom, I was miserably aware that he could have been made presentable to meet my parents. He was wearing khaki pants and a blue button-down and his hair was dark blond and cropped short. I felt horribly guilty about his hair.

John's hair was the first thing I noticed that first time we went to see Joy's Demise play. The club was packed, given that this was the band's first DC show in years. Apparently they'd been living in San Francisco or LA or someplace like that for the last three years. A bunch of my housemates knew members of the band, so I tagged along.

The six members of Joy's Demise all dressed kind of alike. They had high-speed fans on the front of the stage which blew around these huge sheets of gray gauze they wore. It seemed like the band was made up of just this great wall of gray gauze and bleeding wrists. I knew the wrist thing had to be a special effect, but I couldn't figure out how it was done.

John was the lead singer. He was differentiated from the other five by this fact. By that and his hair. His hair fell to the middle of his back. It looked heavy and it was striped in perfectly alternating black and orange tiger stripes. No roots that I could see. It looked like the stuff grew out of his head that way. *Tyger Tyger burning bright / In the forest of the night.*

My own hair at the time was a bright, sloppy pageant of most of the red, pink, and purple shades in the Manic Panic pantheon. I couldn't make up my mind, so every time one shade faded some, I slapped another one on with it. I had a swath of my natural brown hair which I kept virgin on the top, so I could cover up the funny colors if I had to. Like to go to court for a DUI.

They had two keyboard players and the other four members of the group whirled about the stage. Everyone had black hair except John. Even though I know dick-all about music (except that some kinds of performance make me wet), I could tell John and the other three nonkeyboard band members were making part of the music with motion-sensitive instruments that clanged and boomed as they danced. They were all very androgynous, and just watching John move around the stage got me more worked up than I'd been since I was a 15-year-old dry-humping in the front seat of my (then) boyfriend's silver Porsche.

John was lean and moved with a sort of feminine grace. My housemate Lars teases me by saying that what I really like is chicks with dicks. I really just like pretty boys.

Joy's Demise played music that reminded me a lot of early Sisters of Mercy. I later offended John by telling him so. I was always surprised that Joy's Demise hadn't gotten a major record deal the whole time they were in California.

They closed with a number called "Church," which they claimed to be singing in Latin. I didn't take Latin at Georgetown, so I couldn't say for sure whether they were singing in the dead language.

John and the three dancers were like dervishes during the final crescendo. The curtains of fabric billowed wildly and pseudo-blood spattered everywhere amid the thick fog the fog machine was pumping out. A good show has what it takes to transport me—this definitely was it.

Afterward, I pointed out to Lars that I had gotten red liquid all over my clothes. I demanded that he take me backstage and introduce me to the band so I could tell them to replace my duds. "I'm certain that's the reason," Lars replied.

Over the protests of one of the bouncers, he dragged me and three of our housemates into the dressing room. The bouncer backed off partly because Lars really was a friend of the band, but more because of how Lars looks. Lars got his name (not from his parents, who are perfectly decent people) because he looks like a Viking. He's 6 feet 4 and wall-to-wall muscle with shoulder-length locks and a big blond beard. He is employed as a construction worker, and he actually does pushups for fun. Even if there's no bimbo lying under him. No lie.

"So does this stuff stain?" I asked John as I put my red-slicked hand in his. Handshake. Not over-eager or limp, just neutral and firm.

"Would you be able to tell in that outfit?" he asked. His voice was husky and sensual. Some singers have boring speaking voices, but his sounded like everything he said was a sweet, low-pitched obscenity. I immediately felt like the two of us were alone.

I ignored Lars as he tried to introduce me to other members of Joy's Demise, and I was only vaguely aware of his leaving the room some-what huffily. John was only wearing blue jeans and sneakers and my attention was focused on drinking him in. He was thin—almost emaci-ated—and he had this horrible scar parallel to the ground on the left side of his rib cage. But he had these wiry muscles. I wanted to touch his abdomen to see whether it felt soft or hard, like it looked.

"Are you criticizing my attire?" I bantered back to John as we both worked to convert our handshake to holding hands. I was wearing shredded jeans and a half-shirt I'd painted myself and been told never to wear to work again. Not that I gave a fuck what they thought of me at my dumb telemarketing job. Like that was really my future.

"I'M A SLUT. I KILL WHAT I EAT," John read from my shirt.

"Uh, it's a Big Black thing. You wouldn't understand," I told him. I was really into noise bands and industrial music at the time.

But he did understand. He did get the joke. He was horrified that I also liked jangly guitar college rock and what he called hippie music. At school I had always had a hipper-than-thou attitude, but John made me wish I were cooler. I wanted so bad to say the right thing to make him like me, to make him ask me to go home with him. As it turned out, the right thing to say was: "That fucker Lars left without me, and it's after midnight so the Metro is closed. I'm going to leave cold Ramen noodles in his bed." Like I could afford to waste a perfectly good meal.

"Make sure you overcook them with a little extra water first," John advised. He had one of his bandmates drive us to the group house where John lived. John didn't have a car. His bandmate had a big old rusted-out green Pontiac Ventura that looked like it had survived at least two horrible wrecks. I had a little convertible red BMW that I couldn't sell because my mom was also on the title. I wanted to drive it around and stop short at stoplights until someone hit me and I could collect the insurance. Unfortunately, I couldn't legally drive the stupid thing until next March. That DUI sure was a fucking inconvenience.

John's place was at the edge of a construction site. He held my hand on the lawn and told me the house had been condemned, but that he and his 13 housemates could live in the three-story hovel for four more months supercheap until the bulldozers came. We stood on the lawn, holding hands and talking about his home's impending doom. It was a little too warm for comfort—our palms were sweating against one another.

When I look back on that moment, I wonder whether right then I could have done something to make it different. But I didn't think John and I were really going to be anything at all at the time. That first night I just wanted to get inside and get him the rest of the way naked.

But moments pass. I kept seeing John, and two months after that first night I found myself holding hands with him on his lawn again, picking our way around the treacherous cinder blocks and nails left by the construction workers. I asked him, "What are you going to do when your time is up?"

"Find some nice girl who wants me to move in with her."

I took my hand away from him. "Not this nice girl," I told him. "This nice girl has been burned one time too many." Maybe I said it because the construction site made me think of Lars and how he would tease me for being mushy. I don't know.

It was around 7:30 at night and, being November, it was not quite dark but dark enough that I couldn't quite make out his expression. I reached out a fingertip to stroke his hair, but he jerked away. I wanted to tell him that was the wrong response to my comment. I wanted to tell him the right answer was to avoid hurting me. I wanted to tell him that was my way of communicating that I liked him and it scared me. What would I tell my parents? Like we were speaking anyway.

Maybe I would have expressed myself to John the less hostile way if we'd talked that night. But he walked in the door of his rotting house and slammed it shut and locked it before I could follow him in.

I didn't see John for two weeks after that. I didn't miss him much. Lars and I spent a lot of time catching up. Obviously we'd seen each other during the preceding month, but I had spent an awful lot of it with John. Not that Lars and I had anything particularly new to talk about as we wandered around Georgetown (the neighborhood, not my school). We wrote in soap on the car windows of parked teens and picked out new boots for Lars and cut holes in my leather so I could add more studs. About the only new thing we had to discuss was my breakup with John. Lars pretty much had the attitude that it was good riddance to bad rubbish.

"It's just been so long since I liked a guy enough to go out with him on another date after we'd bumped uglies already."

"He's a sick little freak who does too many drugs. Stay away from him."

"Fuck you, Lars."

"You never get hung up like this. It must just be the way he fucks."

Technically, John actually had a lot of trouble fucking. Something to do with all the smack and hallucinogens and who knows what else his mom did while she was pregnant with him. He can't remember a time in his life when he didn't see trails all the time. So we never really successfully completed fucking. The oral sex, on the other hand…John loved to go down on me. I don't even like getting head that much normally, but he had this rough, almost catlike tongue, and he could lap patiently for hours. When I think about the relationship, my main memories are the constant sense of things left unsaid and of his hand in mine while his slow-moving tongue drove me to a place without pain.

"I'm serious. Emotions are for the weak," Lars told me.

So Lars and I went out to slash the tires on the car of this guy who stood up one of our housemates for a date. Technically, I guess I slashed the tires and Lars drove the getaway car, but it made me feel more cheerful. After, we went to Denny's to see whether there were any people we hated that we could loogie on. I would get this dissociated feeling at times like this—this feeling that I was not really participating in my life, that I was not the sort of person who would be doing these things. I know that a lot of what Lars and I did for fun was horribly juvenile. It's just that when I was at an age when it would have been more normal, I was busy being serious—I was bucking for the grade so I could go to a good school and have a good life. Sometimes I thought maybe I was stupid to abandon Georgetown (my college, not the neighborhood) with only one year to go, but I'm not sure what choice I really had. Spitting on jerks with Lars just gave me such a feeling of freedom. Freedom from expectation, freedom from social constraint, freedom from fucking maturity.

Unfortunately, although there were a few people at Denny's that night whom Lars and I disliked, there was no one we hated that much.

Lars and I were about to leave when John showed up. He'd just gotten off work at the used CD store across the street. I'd conveniently forgotten that he worked there.

John walked straight over to where Lars and I were waiting for a table. For some reason, Denny's never seats us.

"Hi," said John with his heartstring-plucking voice.

Lars spit a humongous glob of snot on the front of John's shirt. But Lars couldn't save me. I not only made him apologize—I made him drive the two of us to John's place.

John made no mention of my harsh words or of the way he shut me out, so I didn't bring them up either. He showed me some song lyrics he was working on, along with a comic strip about employee theft at a record store. The comic strip in particular was amazingly good. I knew he drew, but I had no idea how well. Plus it had me laughing out loud.

"You'll get arrested if this is ever published," I told him. I was sitting on his bed reading his stuff while he paced around the room like some angry, caged tiger.

He stopped pacing when I said that. "I'm planning on having a friend of mine who works at Kinko's make poster-size copies of it and then I'm going to use some adhesive I snagged from the construction site to put the comics up around town."

"Cool," I said, wishing he'd sit down on the bed next to me.

"You really like it?"

I replied, "I normally make it a policy not to say anything nice to anyone I date. Otherwise I would tell you that you are incredibly talented and witty." And he kissed me. I thought that if I was ever going to tell him I loved him, I should do it then. He kissed me like "I love you." But he didn't say it. Maybe because it wasn't the case, but more likely because he knew I ultimately wouldn't stay. He knew we only had the moment, so he just kissed me. And I kissed him back. Hot and wet and searching. Tongues entwined deeply, probing in a way that would have been invasive if we hadn't wanted one another so badly. I kissed him back and his kiss was like "I love you." And the moment passed, but I stayed kissed.

"Why do you make it a policy not to say anything nice to anyone you date?" John inquired, his breath in my ear making me shiver, his long tiger-striped hair cloaking me, toasty warm across my shoulders.

I told him about that prick I'd been going out with when I was at Georgetown. "We were coming back from a club in Adams Morgan and I was so smashed I was practically passed out in the passenger seat. So he stops driving and tells me his car needs a tow and I should get in the drivers seat 'cause I've got Triple A and he doesn't. Next thing I know I'm in the police station and they're jabbing a needle in my arm and they're doing a bad job. On purpose to make it hurt extra I think." After I jabbed my inner elbow with my index finger for emphasis John leaned in to kiss the sensitive skin in the crook of my arm.

"Did you like him before that?" For a moment, I just thought about what a beautiful voice John had. And I thought maybe I could take him away with me when this part of my life was over. He was talented. He could get signed to a real record label or be a commercial illustrator or something. I was sure of it.

Then I thought about his question. "Yeah, I liked the guy before that. But I've got bad taste." And John and I kissed some more. I recalled another time we were kissing in his room when he told me how his mom resented having to buy him food when he was little and how she never told him who his dad was. And I suddenly decided not to tell him the rest of the story. I left out how angry my parents had been about the arrest. I left out the part about how they had left me locked up in a DC holding cell for two days and none of my supposed friends had come to bail me out either. And I left out the part about how my parents had railed at me about how I have no discipline and no restraint and how they threatened not to pay my tuition for my senior year at Georgetown and how I said, "Fuck you very much for your unwavering belief in me! I don't want your fucking money." It had seemed like a dignified yet amusing line at the time and I hadn't wanted to apologize for something I genuinely hadn't done.

But I sure had hated being poor these last seven months, and knowing John didn't have those options to throw away made me feel guilty for my fury. And then John went down on me and, for just a little while, I forgot to be angry at the world.

For the next few weeks I was really happy, even if Lars did give me endless grief. Mostly about what a great lay he knew John had to be if he commanded so much of my attention. The teasing did irritate me though. Partly because it was supposed to irritate me. And partly because John actually couldn't fuck. In the time we'd been together, we had successfully completed intercourse once—and then without a condom. Mostly John just couldn't stay hard, but he definitely couldn't stay hard inside a condom. I'd used a contraceptive sponge that time, but I didn't want to do it again because the sponge is not the world's most reliable method of birth control. But mostly because I knew John had shot up and his mother shot up before him and it wasn't like he'd been to the doctor to make sure he was safe even if I was the first person he'd had sex with in 4½ years.

John's mom shot up so much when she was pregnant with him that he had to have open-heart surgery when he was five. It's like his earliest memory—the doctor telling him it's his mommy's fault and then giving him drugs that he was probably jonesing for since his exit from the womb. I told John that I'd never heard of prenatal drug use causing health problems like that. I held my breath for a second, unsure whether he knew the word prenatal.

After a beat he replied, "The whole time I was a kid, the doctors told me it was my mom's fault for using so bad when she was pregnant with me and me being a preemie and all. Could have been lies. I don't give a fuck. Either way my mom's a stupid junky cunt. A cold-blooded cunt."

I thought about whether I would describe either of my parents as a cold-blooded cunt and thought that I might want to but could not fairly do so. I didn't know my father that well. He's a neurologist on Long Island and he makes incessant brain surgery jokes which I find funny.

But he works long hours and my mother and I never saw him much. I assumed my mother still didn't. She keeps busy working at the library. Not that her job pays much—and she is always at pains to point out that she has a Master's in library science. My mother read to me a lot when I was a child, but she was uncomfortable advising on matters of the real world, so we grew apart when I hit puberty. I felt guilty that I sort of enjoyed the freedom from trying to impress my hyper-successful folks. Their only offspring had gone astray.

Anyway, John and I were having an awful lot of fun together. And Lars did warm to him a little. One day the three of us went to Springfield mall and a little kid saw me and John necking on a bench, got a load of John's orange and black hair and my pink, red, and purple tresses and screamed, "Mommy, mommy, it's zebras mating!"

"No more *National Geographic* for that kid," Lars observed.

Lars teased us about the zebra thing afterward, but by then it was more an in-joke for the three of us, rather than Lars giving me a hard time.

One time when John was over at our town house hanging out with me and Lars and a couple of my other housemates, we were laughing about the zebra incident at the mall. We got into a free-for-all where everyone was telling stories about awful scenes they'd made. I told the one about how when I was 14, I went to this event at my grandparents' country club and my cousin dared me to throw one of the icing flowers off this big cake at him, and I did it, and my cousin respected me more after that. But I never got invited back to that club.

After I finished telling my story, John said it was time he got going and got up to leave. I pulled him back down to where we'd been sitting together on the living room floor and whispered, "Why do you have to go now? Do you have a ride?"

"I'll take the Metro."

"It's after midnight; it's closed."

"It doesn't matter."

"Why do you have to go?" We were both whispering, but I was embarrassed that my housemates might overhear and think I was a wimp. Emotions are for the weak and all.

"We're getting too serious," John hissed, his feline features curling up into a snarl.

"I'm as serious as you. What's the problem if we're the same amount serious?" I stroked his hair and then held a lock of it in my fist so he couldn't leave without making a scene. Around us, my friends chattered on about making scenes. They were having a loud, raucous good time and probably heard almost none of the whispered conversation between me and John.

"I didn't say *I*'m getting too serious; I said *we*'re getting too serious." If only his voice weren't so beautiful, so desperately sexy. John tugged his head to try to get out of my grasp, but I held firm.

"Why are we too serious if we're both serious?" I implored. My brain screamed at me to tell him I loved him, but I just couldn't. He made me laugh, but I laughed more with Lars. He made me come, but he certainly wasn't the first. He was witty and cool, but surely there were other witty and cool men who wanted me. He didn't care that I'd dropped out of college, but I might go back some day. He kissed me like he loved me, but maybe that was just a technique thing. So I remained silent.

"It's stupid," John told me, using his hand to jerk his hair out of my grasp. "I mean, what do we have in common?"

I sat there for a moment, unable to speak. I thought about music and sense of humor and what we liked to do for fun and sex and the way we sometimes clicked. I thought about how we could tell each other things neither of us had ever told anyone else. I was speechless.

"Well?" he said louder. "What do we have in common? Nothing, right?"

Maybe it was because I realized my friends were paying attention now. I'll never know for sure why I said anything. But I said, "I don't know. We've both got cool hair."

Even though it was the third week of December and fucking cold in the DC burbs, John walked home. Maybe I could have avoided the rest of the story if it hadn't been December, but before I'd had even a week to get over being sad about John my housemates were all heading off to Christmas dinners with their families.

It might have been the drugs I took for my unusually hideous (could it be stress?) menstrual cramps. Or it might have been the spirit of Christmas. But I decided to go over to John's place to apologize. All of my housemates were with their various families, but I was nowhere, since my family and I were not on speaking terms. I was sitting there wearing a little green elf dress and red stockings and drinking egg-nog by myself on Christmas and having the worst cramps, so I decided to take the Darvocet that Lars had left for me in case the cramps got too bad.

His mom was a nurse and she never let her boy suffer. I've met her a few times and she is so sweet. I can't imagine how she had Lars.

So me and my opiate-clouded brain got in my car even though it would be three months before I could legally drive it and I'd been pretty good about that up until then. I figured it was Christmas so I could not possibly get pulled over for DUI. In my lonely, drugged-out state, I found some poetry in the idea of getting away with another DUI.

"I'm not leaving until you accept my apology," I told John.

Or rather I told his back. One of his housemates had let me in and told me to go on up to John's room. He'd come back early from his mom's. I was surprised he'd gone there in the first place, but people do funny things for Christmas. "He's in a mood," his housemate warned me.

John's room reeked of pot smoke, and John refused to speak to me. I was sitting on his bed and he wasn't pacing for once. He was, however, loudly playing this weird cassette tape on his boom box. Something with serious disharmony and lyrics about serial killers—the sort of thing I normally really like. But John refused to answer my question when I asked who the artist was. In frustration, I jerked open the door of the cassette deck and pulled out the tape. A streamer of tape fluttered behind the cassette as I hurled it.

He turned around and half-smiled. He came over to where I was on his little twin bed—where we had spent so many nights curled up together—and he climbed on top of me, straddling my lap. I felt the warm glow of the Darvocet and the eggnog and John's closeness and I started to put my arms around him. Then his hands were clutching my throat. I grabbed two fistfuls of his hair and tried to pull him back off me. *What immortal hand or eye / Could frame thy fearful symmetry?*

He shook me by the neck and pushed me back on the bed, pinning my hands under his knees. He smelled like pot and his long big cat hair obscured my vision, making everything into an orange and black haze of marijuana-scented demise.

Because of the Darvocet, his grasp had not hurt that much at first, but then it started to hurt a lot. I couldn't breathe. I couldn't tell him that he should stop because I loved him. I couldn't tell him anything at all. And it bothered me that I was sure I looked ugly lying there on the bed with my mouth reflexively open, trying to gasp. And I thought that I'd never be able to thank my parents for getting me the lawyer who got me off with no jail on the DUI, for getting me an attorney even though they didn't believe me. And I thought that maybe, after eight months of uncommunicative penance, my parents would want to talk to me, to work things out. But everything was orange and black and my eyes felt huge even though it was hard to see with them and there was pain everywhere in my stomach. The pain had come back and I had the horribly mundane epiphany that perhaps I had been trying to destroy myself to avoid having to put my life back together. Only I wanted to live.

Then John's tongue was in my mouth and he loosened his grip as he kissed me hard. He held my head, framing my face with his hands so I couldn't move. I was desperate for air, but partially blocked by his greedy mouth. Abruptly he pulled away and stood up. He gave me that creepy half-smile again and said in a measured tone with his heartbreak voice, "I'm going to kill you." Then he went to the bathroom.

I lay there for a minute on the bed, sucking air and gingerly touching my throat. I realized there was something wet soaking through the front of my elf dress. One of my little red stockings was also damp. Then I fled.

Lars was the only one of my housemates home when I stumbled in. He gasped.

I laughed and then cried out triumphantly, "I am even with the State! I didn't get pulled over tonight and I sure deserved to!" Then I tripped over my own feet and pitched forward onto the cheap carpet. It looked to me at the time more like the room rearranged itself than like I fell.

Lars had his mom come over to our town house and look at me. She said very matter-of-factly that the wet spot on my stocking was semen and the wet spot on my dress was blood. "But he didn't cut me," I told her.

"You're having a miscarriage," she told me.

"Well, that explains the weird, lumpy, purple period I've been having," I laughed. If not for the Darvocet, I would never have been that crude with Lars's mom, but well…if, if, if. It wasn't like I'd wanted a baby or anything, but I'd thought my period was late and painful 'cause I couldn't afford to eat right. At the time, it just seemed humorous.

Because she's a mom, Lars's mother made me go file a report with the police. And because Lars kept punching the wall and offering to go kneecap John.

"You should file a report no matter what," she said. "You can decide later whether you want to press charges."

"I'm not going to mess him up if the cops are involved," Lars told us angrily. This news did not seem to perturb his mother. She helped me out to her big brown station wagon and took me to make the report.

During the whole ordeal the only time she seemed distraught was when the cop asked me whether I was going to get back together with John. "Did you just hear anything I told you?" I was incredulous.

"I've seen worse," the cop told me, "much worse. And they always go back for more. I bet you don't press charges." Looking back on it, I guess he dared me because domestic violence pissed him off and he wanted to prod me into pressing charges. At the time, because of my DUI ordeal and all, I did not feel like the police were exactly looking out for my best interests.

I did not see John again until the court date. Or maybe I just didn't pick him out when he didn't have cool hair. He looked so respectable, so normal standing there in the back of the courtroom. With his close-cropped, dark blond hair and his chinos, he could have been any of a score of boys I went to college with—boys who never piqued my interest in the slightest. But there were deep shadows under his eyes and I wanted John to cross the distance between us and tell me something that would make it so Christmas hadn't happened yet. Something that would turn back the clock just enough that Christmas was next week and I could take him to Christmas dinner with my parents.

It had been a while since Christmas, but I still needed a neck brace the day I told the prosecutor I was afraid John was going to come after me to finish the job. I couldn't bring myself to send him to jail, but I wanted a restraining order. I didn't want to die. "How bad did he beat you?" the prosecutor asked me. I told him in unflinching detail. Saying it aloud to someone who had heard it all made the whole thing somehow seem simultaneously more serious and more like no big deal.

The only part I didn't tell him was my second reason for wanting the restraining order. I really was afraid John would come after me to kill me, to choke the breath from me, to make sure I would never have the oxygen to declare my love for anyone else. But I was even more afraid that we would get back together first. I was afraid that that cop was right and I would go back to John and he would kill me later and then it would be my fault as much as his. But the restraining order would make it harder for him to come courting and it would make it harder for me to admit I still wanted him. But, to the prosecutor, I just described the attack and told him I needed restraint.

Finally, even though I said I wasn't looking for John to go to jail, I had to talk to the public defender guy. The attorney for the defense asked me why I had gone out with John if he was such a terrible person. I thought about telling him how John had held me at night until the nightmares and the rage went away. How he'd kissed me like "I love you." How he had moved like a ballerina. How he had made me laugh by scaling streetlights. How he had gone down on me for hours and made me come more times than I thought possible. How he had introduced me to new things and new music and new perspectives on life. How he'd helped me come to terms with the need to go back to school. How he'd made me realize I wanted to live. I thought about telling the public defender about how John always made me think of that line: *Tyger Tyger burning bright / In the forest of the night*. How he had the coolest, most beautiful hair I had ever seen.

Or at least he used to. Before I ruined it.

But finally, I just made a strangled sort of choking noise that was probably ironically appropriate. My first thought was, *I don't know why I went out with him...well, he* was *in a band*.

But all I actually said was, "I just need restraint. I just need restraint."

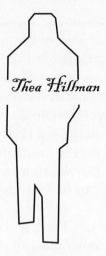

Thea Hillman

DEAR KATH AFTER

I take feeling bad personally.

There are so many things I want to tell you. I have a list. The same lists I had when we were together. Stairway walks, recipes, movies, and poems. Little lists, same as the one I have now except those lists got done and this one won't.

I want to tell you about Marty. I want to tell you how she almost saved my life. That just hours after you had called and broken up with me, there I was at that club, drinking double shots of tequila. And how typical and tragic that more than one dyke actually found my double fisting attractive. And that then there she was—Marty—telling me she knew me from somewhere, telling me she'd been hearing about me for years, telling me I was beautiful. She followed me around like a puppy that night. She came on so strong I told her if she wanted to go with me, she should back off. And she did. Back off, I mean. And she did come home with me. I barely told her anything about you, but she could feel it, emanating from me like a toxic sunburn.

And I want to tell you about last night. I felt like such a woman last night, Kath. Why is it that misery has me feeling more female than ever? Maybe it's the mascara shadows, the lack of sleep, the tequila. Maybe it's being so far outside myself, getting fucked by strange girls and seeing myself the way some new girl does. I look at myself and feel desirable. Funny what a breakup can do for you. Funny what being so deep in love with you can do for me. I put on my red slip last night and the slutty white mules you love so much and danced in front of the mirror. I was so satisfied with myself last night. Everything looked so good and so right and it was OK to be beautiful and sad.

And last night was so crazy. There was me, Victoria, my brother, his girlfriend, and a stripper from Texas, all going together to the queerest event in town—the drag king show at the King Street Garage.

And last night, I could almost have fun. There were all the girls with mustaches and all the femmes dressed so high they could've been drag queens. Last night gave me hope. I could almost enjoy it, except for all those girls kissing each other. I could handle everything except the girls making out. Why do they have to do it in public like that?

And Nic was there. Nic who's been way more broken-hearted than me. All my exes: Nic and Kim and Zed, each of them has now broken up with a new girl and each has shown me how ordinary extreme pain and self-pity are. Sorrow is humbling. I want my pain to be fabulous. I don't need my pain to be worse than anyone else's; I just want it to be strangely, uniquely mine. Art to someone else's breakdown.

And so I almost felt good last night. And then there was Marty, in her mustard—or would that be ochre?—shirt and skinny tie. She grabbed me and kissed me and squeezed hard, her arms around me from behind. And I was careful not to touch her too sweetly or kiss her at all because there were two other girls at the show that she was dating and she wanted to be single this weekend she said. Which would have been fine if she hadn't kissed me and run her hands down my hips and told me about the party after the show. Which would have been fine if then, when the dancing started, she didn't get hot and heavy with this girl I'd seen around town, whose shoes I had loved and then hunted down and who had gray eyes that glinted, dangerous and enchanting. Marty danced with the girl, right next to me. She twirled her and then brought her close against her body the way I already after only two weeks knew she did. And I started feeling sick and like a voyeur and moved away on the dance floor.

And so we went to leave—me and Victoria. And I felt so stupid for giving a shit about Marty when I really didn't and for letting myself hurt any more than I already did, and then there she was, Marty. She asked, where are you going? She asked are you mad at me, she says I'm not dating her. She kissed me, she said come to the party with me, she said you look so pretty, which didn't help, but I want everything to feel good so I said yes. And Victoria said make sure you have fun.

And it all would have been fine except all the girls Marty had ever dated and happened to be dating were at the party. And Kath, your best friend Paul—well, his housemate Carolyn was at the party. Which made me panic thinking Paul would be there and that then he'd tell you I was there, with Marty, holding hands, looking like a couple at 2 A.M. or actually maybe I was wishing he would tell you because he never would do that to you. Just like he didn't tell me he knew you were going to break up with me.

And the party would have been fun except on our way to get away from the girl in the basement that Marty was dating we went through the kitchen and ran right into the girl with the gray eyes from the dance floor. And the girl strikes up a conversation with me and we compliment each other's hair, dresses, shoes, and Marty is dying next to me, obviously hot for this girl or awkwardly having dated her, but I didn't start the conversation and I'll be damned if I can't play along. So Marty says, can we talk?

And she takes me outside. And she says she wanted to be single this weekend and here it is two nights in a row that we've seen each other. She says, I didn't want to leave your house this morning. She says, I want to slow down, she says you could get back together with your girlfriend. Knowing you, I tell her, trying not to cry, that just isn't going to happen. I tell her, it's over with you, trying not to sound too heart-broken because this discussion is about her and me, not me and you. I tell her it's a little too late to decide she wanted to come to the party alone. I tell her I'm leaving. We're at 24th and Bryant at 3 A.M. and I start to walk home because Marty doesn't have a car. She makes dildos for living—social service work, to quote her—and there's not a cab for miles and as I start to walk, a car slows down, a man leans out and honks at me. Clearly, I can't walk home. And fuck Marty for putting me in this situation. I recognize two of her friends leaving the party, getting into a truck nearby, and so I march back over to Marty and tell her to ask her friends to drive me home. Knowing they can't say no, I'm already on my way over to the truck and I hop into the back and fold myself up behind the two front seats of the cab. The women are nice and don't ask any questions and take me home.

Breaking up is so ordinary. There is nothing dramatic about break-ing up. I am not special.

The best thing about breaking up with you is that it has nothing to do with me.

I love you.

Thea

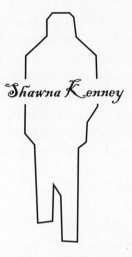

Shawna Kenney

SHINY BAUBLES

We hit the piercing parlor about two weeks before the breakup. It was his last-ditch attempt at salvaging our relationship and my last sorry-ass grasp at threads of my self-esteem. He bought me a nose ring. It cost $50, and I was flattered that he'd splurge such an amount on me. Never mind that the money came from our collective cash, and that we had no phone or groceries because he'd blown his last paycheck on alcohol for his "friends" down at the club. The fact that he'd just given me a $900 bike while I drove a $200 deathtrap of a car seemed perfectly normal at the time too. He held my hand while tears squirted from the corners of my eyes as the piercer punched a hole into the side of my right nostril with a needle. I left feeling pretty damn cute, wearing a teeny sapphire chip that lay so flat against my nose you couldn't see it unless you were really close.

I was throwing up a lot by then—in the bathroom, with the door locked, retching into the toilet with the water running, careful to use different fingers so as not to get those tell-tale scars I'd heard about. Sometimes even "fantasizing" about something especially gross aided the process along—thoughts of eating cigarette-and-baloney sandwiches or rotten mayonnaise worked well. Usually just the smell of the toilet was enough. He'd poured my cans of powdered Slim Fast down the drain, but I figured out a way to hurt myself without him knowing anyway. My little secret. When my ribs started to show I was quite proud of what I'd "accomplished." He didn't notice.

Two weeks later I woke up puffy-eyed and headachy, not knowing exactly where I was. One look in the mirror at the necklace of blue and purple fingerprints just above my collarbones reminded me. I still can't remember what started it. I remember police, who came because the neighbors had called them again. *How embarrassing* was all I could think while they questioned me. Like I still had some dignity left or something.

This time, instead of hiding in the bedroom and refusing to press charges, I nervously called a friend for help. She drove an hour from Baltimore to Washington, braving rush-hour traffic and the hellish city layout that always terrified her. She offered me a place to stay, but was a newlywed dealing with being a punching bag herself at the time, so we drove on to a hospital and later to a battered women's shelter. I posed for mug-shot-like photos, turning to each side, lifting my thin Steve Steadham skate T-shirt's short sleeves, finally facing front as instructed, while they took Polaroids "for possible future evidence." Blinding flash, over and over. At least I didn't have to smile. I told and retold my story to the counselors. They gave me the rules for living there and I went to work on getting back on my feet. I didn't want to throw up anymore—I didn't feel fat or skinny. I just felt nothing for a while. I don't know what happened, but for some reason once I started therapy and chores and planning a new life, I was hungrier than ever.

A few months later I found myself living with friends in New York—a new city for me, one I'd heard was a place of new starts. The ex-boyfriend showed up on my doorstep one month into my "new life," crying, holding a ring, and begging forgiveness. Maybe he was getting help. Maybe people *could* change. The ring was an emerald flanked by two diamond chips, set in white gold. I slipped it on and it transformed my hand into someone else's hand. The hand of someone prettier. Someone fancier. Infatuation still had its choke hold on me, and I visualized our new future together. We looked at little houses in Queens. He went back to DC and called me incessantly. I guess I knew in the depths of my heart that things could not—should not—work out, but optimism has always been my downfall. Maybe we were different. Maybe we weren't an Oprah cliché. I was wrong. We were. His anger flared again and I finally knew enough to run—and to Fed-Ex the ring back.

Legal procedures were already rolling. Six months later I'd have to face him in court. My first gift to me on the way back to self-love was a tattoo. And not some little flower or butterfly-type thing—an Isis-style armband, like I'd always wanted. We'd always planned to get matching tattoos together but somehow never had the money or the time. This one was all mine. I wanted something Iroquois—to honor the Native Americans way back in my family—but couldn't find a design I liked, so settled for an Aztec pattern. It took six hours in one sitting for her to do the outline and top shading. I talked and laughed and read books while the new artist scratched away on me in her basement. By midnight I felt like someone had been trying to saw my arm off a few inches below the shoulder. I returned a week later for the finale—shading underneath my arm. No laughing this time—I lay down with my arm up and over my head and let the tears flow while she finished.

I applied the ointment religiously afterward. Avoided the sun and even passed on the chlorinated jacuzzi at a party a week later. The design went from raised to flat with the rest of my arm, and the soreness faded daily. I walked into the courtroom two weeks later, confident (and sleeveless, of course.) He was standing right at the back and I smiled and almost said "hi"—just a natural reaction to seeing a familiar face. Remembering why we were there made my knees soften and shake. They shook while the lawyer read the allegations: assault and battery. They shook while the shelter-appointed court-companion led me to a front-row seat. They shook as I brushed by his staring, emotionless face on the way out. A face I once kissed and loved and held and pulled the in-grown hairs out of. A face I thought destined to be the face of my future children's father. A face now chiseled by hate and revenge—the face that visits me in nightmares still. The face I sometimes see when I flinch from a falling object or when any man makes a too-quick arm movement toward me.

We met there at court four more times, until the ruling was decided, and my knees shook every time. He got community service, had to pay for my medical expenses, and was ordered "no further contact." I got another tattoo, marking the end of a bad time-period and the beginning of a good one (college), but mostly to commemorate my newfound ability to make my own choices. I ran into him a year later. He wanted to formally apologize, and I let him. I wasn't really ready to listen. I definitely couldn't yet forgive him. But I smiled smugly when he said, "I'm jealous of your tattoo."

Twelve years of experience, love, laughter, tears, marriage proposals, and hindsight have passed. My current boyfriend knows better than to buy me jewelry. Karma took good care of my ex. I only throw up now when I have the flu. And I'll forever be grateful to the girl who drove me to the shelter that day.

The idiot who said diamonds are a girl's best friend definitely never had one—a best friend, that is. Best friends are a girl's diamonds.

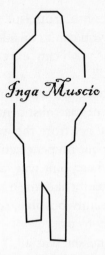

Inga Muscio

Days With Inga and Bridget:
An Excerpt From *La Journal de Inga la Gringa*

july 3rd

last night, me 'n' bridget hung out.

we went out for a drink at a total dive bar where we were the only women present and every man in the joint gaped at us when we walked in. i tensed up, but bridget sensed it and was all, "i promise this is ok. i've been here before." so anyway, we're sittin there talkin, and we mosey onto the subject of sex and love.

bridget's all, "you know i've been thinking about which relationships in my life have been really lasting and fulfilling, and i end up at my relationship with you. you, lisa darms, and rachel jones are my total soulmates. you know everything about me, never pass judgement on the things i do, and are always there for me when i get into trouble." and i (the neanderthal) am all, "but bridget, we don't fuck."

true, bridget and i enjoy a highly erotic relationship.

and true, i put my hands up her skirt and down her blouse every chance i get. and true, bridget has been known to accommodate me by not wearing panties when she knows i'm gonna be around. but our relationship, though tinged with eroticism, is not based on sex. so i'm all, "bridge, we don't fuck. you can't consider me in the way you'd consider a lover." and she's all, "*yes*, i can. except for the fact that we don't fuck, you are my soulmate."

and that got me talkin about my little tumble with homer. homer's all into being something she defines as "abstinent." what i learned this means is as long as i don't penetrate her from the waist down, then she is abstinent. so we did lots of stuff, but no penetration was involved, so according to her, we did not fuck. her point was, after people fuck, everything gets all weird, and since she really likes me a ton, she wants to keep things as seemingly platonic as humanly possible, so none of the freakouts that apply to fucking would apply to us.

so i told bridget all this and she was all, "*yes*. i want to *meet* this girl. i totally understand where she's coming from."

and so do i.

i totally respect and understand this way of thinking. it raises a lot of questions for me about being sexual with someone. i mean, once i start fucking someone, they somehow think they know me better than anyone else. they think they should take precedence over all my other friends, even though i haven't known them as long as i've known all my friends, and even though our shared history might tally up to a month or so.

it's ridiculous.

i am wondering if ol' homer isn't sincerely onto something with her shaky definition of "abstinence."

me and bridget talked about all this over our drink.

then we went where she had invited me to go in the first place: a jerk-off porn theater in the tenderloin that showed 16 millimeter films from the '70s. the porn theater ended up providing me with an historic and present day heterocentric overview of sex in my society. nights like this really make me wonder if bridget doesn't carefully plot these things out. conspiracies aside, we were, alas, destined to spend the majority of our evening in environments where we were the only women present.

we walk pass this turnstile that buzz-z-zes, but only after bridget ascertained beyond a shadow of a doubt that we would be watching 16 millimeter films, not videos. she made attendant guy show her the film reels, for gods sake, i love that woman.

we walk into the theater, and all i smell is sperm. i am grossing out enough to fucken faint. bridget had felt my body tense up in the dive bar, so she is already prepared to physically restrain me from running away. as my vision adjusts to the light, i see the uniform rhythm of hands stroking cocks. it looks kinda like that "wave" thing people do at céline dion concerts. one man is sucking another one off. on the screen, pussy is being eaten. ok, this is familiar to me.

i kinda relax when i see the comforting vision of pussy being eaten. bridget seizes the moment and leads me to a "seat," which is much, much more like an upholstery-covered stale sperm sponge. i stand in front of it for a long time, bridget slightly yanking my hand to pull me down into it. i reason, "ok, well, i've got my leather coat on. none of the surface will touch the immediate layer of clothing between my skin and the seat." as i desperately try to convince myself to sit down, bridget cops a mantra: "it's ok, sit down, it's ok, sit down. it's ok, sit down." i guess she kinda hypnotizes me, because i manage to place my ass on the very edge of the seat.

so let's see.

the fucking is pretty entertaining. total '70s white hetero sex with highly unprofessional actors who have problems with things like keeping their cocks hard and coaxing wetness from their pussies. fucken driest crop of pussies i've ever seen. so then comes up dude who insists on sitting in our row. we find this unacceptable and i move to the edge of another seat. our bridget, she reclines.

so then dude moves to talk to us. bridget puts her hand in his face and goes, "we're together."

and i go, "get the fuck away from us."

we say these two things over and over until he finally goes back to his corner in our ex-row. then, across the aisle, but at the row in front of us, i notice a dude pull his pants down to his ankles. i am so astounded that someone would let their bare ass touch any surface in the entire room, it takes me awhile to realize he's maybe 5 feet tall and has a gargantuan cock that requires two hands to stroke it properly. i look at bridget, who is also pondering this same phenomena and we both start braying like jackasses.

after we calm down, we watched dry pussy-fucking some more.

two drops of come dribble out of porn-star dick.

somehow, my pussy is wet.

go figure.

so then bridget deems it time to completely destroy the meager safe-ty level i've worked so hard to achieve.

"i hafta go pee," she says, "wait here."

i'm all, "*no.*"

one of the other things i'd been watching, besides the film and shorty two hands across the aisle, was a lit doorway to the side of the screen. men kept going in there, but none came back out. or if some-one did come out, it wasn't one of the ones i saw go in. i knew that beyond that doorway, they were doing things i had absolutely no inter-est in seeing. and *that* is the doorway fucken bridget is talking about when she says, "i hafta go pee, wait here."

it is also why i say, "*no*" so vigorously.

again, she's all, "wait here."

i grab her arm, and say, " *no.* i will not let you go in there alone and i will not sit here alone. *no.* hold your pee. pee your pants. piss on the floor, it would probably make this place smell better. *no,* bridget, *no.*"

oh, my god, she squirms out of my grasp and stands up. i am hav-ing full on cardiac arrest. i realize she is going to go pee in this place, come hell or high water, for this glowing reason: the doorway inter-ests her.

herein lies one of the big differences between bridget and me.

she is brave and curious.

i am terrified and uninterested.

there is nothing i can do to stop her. so i go with her, mumbling, "that fucken dude who was trying to talk to us is gonna follow us you fucken doorknob. oh, god, i'm gonna die of a heart attack in a porn theater in the tenderloin. please explain this to my mother." and on and on.

bridget ignores me, which is what i would do if i was her.

up stairs of a narrow hallway painted fluorescent bile green. men waiting on the stairs. we walk this gauntlet, and turn the corner and this is when i see *i am all wrong*. me and bridget *aren't* the only women in the establishment. there is a woman sitting on the toilet, sucking the dicks of the men waiting in the line. her pimp, who turns out to be rather a decent fellow, says, "someone's gotta use the john." (i got the feeling he likes this pun, and uses it whenever the situation arose.) so the woman and the dick suckee come out and wait in the hall with me and the rest of the gang while bridget pees.

dude who wanted to chat earlier walks in.

duh.

he asks mister pimp for a hit. money and a crack pipe are exchanged. dude walks up to me and offers me a hit of crack. my heart warms to him a little. i see he is trying to offer me some kind of happiness. mister pimp—my friend—goes, "fucken she don't want no smoke, you dumbfuck."

i smile at mister pimp with all the love in my heart.

dude tries to offer me crack again—how long is bridget gonna pee-e-e—and i shake my head, "no."

mister pimp goes, "fuck, leave her 'lone."

then he asks me what the fuck i am doing here. that's exactly what he says, "what the fuck are you doing here?"

and i'm all, "she, uh, she, uh, she wanted to see these films." he nods. i get clearance because i'm trying to be good to my woman. he respects this kind of love ethic, and just as i'm about to actually relax and maybe socialize a little, bridget niagara falls comes out.

when we sit back down again, we notice shorty two hands has relocated to our row, but still across the aisle. we watch a well-to-do-looking elderly gentleman smoke crack with a scratchy crackhead. limp dick/dry pussy fest continues. then it's over and a new feature starts. this one with reprehensible sound quality, but starring an incredibly wet pussy. dude attempts engagement with us YET again and i say, "i can't follow the plot with you interrupting me." bridget laughs.

shorty two hands across the aisle really starts going for it in a big way. me and bridget stare, which is why he moved in the first place, but he smiles sheepishly anyway. he strokes and strokes his big ol' mammoth. i can't believe how big this guy's dick is. we want to see him come, but just then this really massive dude sits down in front of us. he's got to be like 6 foot 5 or something. he immediately pulls his pants down. me and bridget look at each other, then stand up together to peek over his shoulder at his dick and it is tiny. miniscule.

between shorty two hands and green bay packer pencil dick, me an bridget just fall into hysterical laughter and cannot regain composure. me and my soulmate, we barged out laughing and didn't get to see shorty come.

mother's day

it was very early monday morning or very late sunday night, depending on how you look at things. i was at bridget's since i went home with her on saturday night. we stayed in bed all day and i completely neglected to call my mom for mother's day.

i suck.

i kept waking up in the morning—it was a stunning day here in san francisco—but i felt icky and slipped into my subconscious relaxation mode. i kept surfacing while bridget was watching an intense gymnastics competition. women's college, if I remember correctly. finally, i got up and took a shower. i put on bridget's white slip—or at least one of them—and promptly crawled back into bed.

bridget started "cleaning" her room—an event one must see to believe. she picks up an object or a piece of clothing, mumbles something about it, such as, "oh, here it is," or, "how did I get a grass stain on the sleeve? damn," or, "oh, heh, heh. I remember the last time I used this, heh, heh, heh." i watched her for around an hour or so, the wind blowing in through the window. it is funny, with bridget. she fascinates me so deeply. i feel as if i completely understand her, even though she will always remain a total mystery.

a few days ago when i woke up at bridget's and she was still sleeping, i spent around an hour sitting this old bunny on her chest and then thinking for a while until the bunny toppled over from her breathing and then i'd stand it up again and think some more. bridget inspires a very strange meditation in me. and i find her room cleaning schtick perfectly riveting. bridget's room looks like it sprouted up due to the results of a land mine and then someone came and put nice pictures on the wall and carefully inserted lovely lamps, for effect. and the truly, truly amazing thing about bridget and her room is she knows where almost every single item is. piles and piles of papers, letters, photos found on the street, journals, folders full of film stuff, toys, and books all crammed onto her desktop, and she can tell you exactly where to find the receipt from safeway dated april 22, 1999.

so, yes.

i watched her for quite some time, in silence, before growing bored. then I snooped through her stuff and read an "art" magazine. (which

featured a "review" of abercrombie and fitch's new magazine-as-cata-
logue-product featuring photos of white young men, by bruce weber.)
(gag.) then bridget got bored too and asked me if i wanted to watch tv.
we watched absolutely fabulous (three episodes). then we watched the
last half of st. elmo's fire. i couldn't take it. but bridget tends to view
movies more than just watch them, like me. she gets more stuff out of
the raw medium than i do, and can therefore sit through the tritest shit
imaginable. st. elmo's fire was on tv though, not video.

after the movie, bridget ate toast with orange marmalade (yuck) and
i ate top ramen. then she popped in the auntie mame video and we
watched rosalind russell be stunning and wear lots of fabulous clothes.

bridget is such a drag queen.

after that, it was normal tv and we ordered pizza.

simpson's	*waiting for pizza*
the family guy	*waiting for pizza*
x files	*eating roasted potato pizza (bridget had chicken on her half)*

me and bridget watched more dumb tv, and finally went to bed.
well, we had been in bed all day, more or less, but we turned off the
lights. and I could NOT sleep. duh. and thought about how i didn't
want to get up in the morning and have to GO to peri's house. i'd
rather BE there when i woke up. so i finally got dressed, wrote bridget
a note and kissed her pretty forehead. skateboarded to safeway. there
were a couple of scary blocks and my heart beat fast and i kept thinking, *why did you leave the warmth and safety of bridget's house?* it was
like 3 A.M. but I got to the safeway and made a few breakfast purchas-
es and the cashier called a taxi for me. the driver had a nice, deep,
rolling voice and i liked him immediately. he asked me if i called my
mom for mother's day and that is when i realized i suck.

that bridget.

i have the best fun with her.

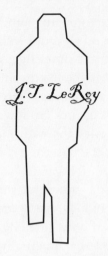

J.J. LeRoy

WHEN TO BE A GIRL

Last week I made out with a movie star. A film director introduced us. He sweetly keeps inviting me down to the set of the Hollywood film he is making. And I think about going all the time. But he likes girls. And he knows I am not one, but that is easy to push away, because when I met him I looked really pretty.

I saw him watching me throughout dinner. He chewed his big fleshy lips as if he were tasting me. And I felt the boy part of me shoved away. I went into the woman's bathroom and put on glossy maroon lipstick. When we went out to smoke, I got it all over movie star's mouth. We were so into each other he changed his flight so he could stay the rest of the next day.

The next day I wore a black satin skirt with a lacy slip. I fish to eat. I got to see a tattoo not many folks get to see. We kissed at the beach while it rained on the porch of a cement park bathroom. And later he filmed me, filmed us kissing. He tells me how beautiful I am. He is beautiful too. I am in awe of how he moves: confidently fluid, with the rights of a boy on a playing field he has mastered. With the right of a handsome boy to claim a cute girl.

I never move like that even when I am a boy. And when I am with

353

him all I want to be is a pretty girl, for him. But then I talk to someone that knows me, wants me as a boy and I feel "her" start to slide off like a silk shawl. And then there are times I get a lot of attention for being a boy. A pretty young boy. Maybe from someone that wouldn't like me if I became a girl. They want me as a pretty young boy. And I feel potent in my boyness. I call up my Hollywood Star and I swagger on the phone with him, and he laughs with me, but I can tell, I can feel him shifting away. I am not the passive girl he digs. But I feel defiantly male, and cannot stop.

Sometimes I really miss the power of standing out on the street, a boy for sale, a cute young blond blue-eyed boy. Men would pass me hungry for meat like a pack of lions smelling their first deer in a month. And as long as I could forget that I actually meant nothing to them, I could feel important, like I had a place in the world. But sometimes the emptiness I would feel after could be ignored. Just to be valuable, even for a little while.

Like one time I was with this New York big-time art dealer guy and his sycophantic friends at a fancy restaurant. They were all amused at me, at how I ate, what I ordered. How I put jelly on everything. That's how we do it in Appalachia. I escaped to the bathroom and when I got back, the New York big-time art dealer guy told me to go again. I said I didn't have to, he said, "*Go again*!" I slid out from the booth as the table giggled like teenage brides. I returned to the bathroom and tried to go again. When I came back they were all blatantly laughing at me, the New York big-time art dealer guy asks me what the fuck did I do? I tell him I tried to go again like he told me to. And he says, "I just wanted you to walk to the bathroom, you blond airhead idiot!" They all choked on their Riesling in hilarity.

He ordered me: *Go, do that again, walk.* I envisioned grabbing a bottle off the table spraying it in their faces, smashing it spectacularly and screaming *Fuck you*! But I didn't do that. I got up and walked to the bathroom again and felt my face hot under their comments about my ass, about my body. I didn't yo-yo right back to their table though. I walked into the empty women's room and stared at myself. Knowing if I was a girl it would be different.

I dug out a pink lipstick in my back jeans pocket and put it on before returning. When I am a girl, they can make comments about my body, they can be interested in me only because of my appearance, in sex, me, as a pretty young girl, but it doesn't hurt like it does when it is me—a boy. It feels wonderful.

My mother, Sarah, said it always makes everything easier, being a girl. When we went to a new town, and she was looking for a new Daddy for me, well, telling a horny man, *this is my son*, well, that man might take it as a challenge. Might not make him want to marry a girl with a son around. But if you are two pretty girls, sisters, that alters the situation for the best. Men like that more. It's easier to get free food in a restaurant or store, get a landlord to slide you a month more as two pretty sisters that just ran a little short. As a girl, I feel powerful, like Sarah, luring men in, live bait in a cage. I can move with her command of the feminine. I can match a similar authority my Hollywood movie star holds over his body, with my subtle downturned eyes, graceful caresses, and sinuous motions. Because it is not me.

I am hiding somewhere deep inside the lustrous decoy, waiting till it is safe to resurface.

Contributors

Charles Anders (www.charlie-girl.com) eats more duck feet than you do. She's the publisher of *other magazine*, the magazine for people who defy categories, and the author of *The Lazy Crossdresser*, a how-to manual for slack t-girls. Her writing has appeared in ZYZZYVA, *Comet, Mad Scientist, Strange Horizons, Peep Show, Best Transgender Erotica, Best Bisexual Erotica 1* and *2*, and many other magazines and anthologies.

Lisa Archer and her two cats are diehard San Francisco sex radicals, struggling to make a living in the post–dot-com economy. Lisa's fiction appears in *Best Bisexual Women's Erotica, Best Fetish Erotica, Best Woman's Erotica 2002* (all from Cleis), *5-Minute Erotica* (forthcoming from Running Press), *Mammoth Book of Best New Erotica Volume 2* (Carroll & Graf), and *Best of the Best Meat Erotica* (Suspect Thoughts), among other publications. She has also starred as Lisa Lixx in *Bend Over Boyfriend 2, Slide Bi Me*, and on *Playboy Sexcetera*.

Cheryl B. is a writer who has performed her work throughout the United States and internationally. Her writing has appeared in numerous publications, most notably *The Milk of Almonds: Italian-American Women Writers on Food and Culture* (2002, Feminist Press), *The World in Us: Gay and Lesbian Poetry of the Next Wave* (2000, St. Martin's Press), and *His Hands, His Tools, His Dress, His Sex: Lesbian Writers on their Fathers* (2001, Harrington Park Press), among many others. Cheryl received a Master's degree from the New School in 2002. A native New Yorker, she lives in Brooklyn with two cats and online at www.motoroilqueen.com.

Don Baird resides in San Francisco, where he has penned a regular column called "Beat This" in the *Bay Times* for over 15 years, bringing rock music criticism to a predominantly gay readership, reassuring queers who live for the devil's music that they are not alone. He furthers this crusade as a DJ, spinning rock music at two popular San

Francisco bars. His writing often veers into other areas besides music, including sociopolitical commentary, sex, high school shootings, amusement park fatalities, personal stories about his family, and serial killers. He proudly embraces a rock-and-roll lifestyle, punctuated by sex and drugs.

Dodie Bellamy has written a novel, *The Letters of Mina Harker* (1998), a collection of memoirs, *Feminine Hijinx* (1990), and *Real* (1994), an epistolary collaboration on AIDS with the late Sam D'Allesandro. Her latest book, *Cunt-ups,* a radical feminist revision of the "cut-up" pioneered by William Burroughs and Bryon Gysin, won the 2002 Firecracker Alternative Book Award for Poetry. "Phonezone" is a chapter from her novel-in-progress, *The Fourth Form.*

Leo Blackwater is a writer, composer, and musician based in Los Angeles. He has a BFA in music and a BA in mathematics. A major in English has continued to elude him, however, because he doesn't speak Spanish well enough.

Cara Bruce is editor in chief of Eros Guide (www.eros-guide.com) and Eros Noir (www.eros-noir.com). She is also the editor of *Best Fetish Erotica, Best Bisexual Women's Erotica,* and *Viscera.* She owns and runs Venus or Vixen Press (publisher of *Viscera* and *Embraces: Dark Erotica*) and VenusOrVixen.com. She is the coauthor of *The First Year—Hepatitis C* with Lisa Montanarelli. Her short stories have appeared in numerous anthologies, including *Best American Erotica 2001, Best Women's Erotica 2000–2004, Best Lesbian Erotica 2000, Mammoth Book Best of the Year Erotica 1* and *2, Uniform Sex, Starf*ckers, The Unmade Bed, The Oy of Sex, Best S/M Erotica,* and *Best Bondage Erotica,* to name a few. Her writing has been published on many Web sites, magazines, and newspapers, including Salon.com, *Playgirl, San Francisco Bay Guardian, While You Were Sleeping, On Our Backs,* GettingIt.com, and many more. She lives in San Francisco. Check her Web sites for more information: www.venusorvixen.com and www.carabruce.com.

Daniel Cartier is new to creative writing, having spent most of his life focusing on his dogs, various boyfriends, and a crazy music career. His three CDs have received unanimous critical praise, and his music is regularly featured on television and in film. He dedicates his story to anyone who's willing to keep on playing the game of love, even when the game continually seems to be a losing one.

After an extended career in degeneracy, **Clint Catalyst** has settled in the city of smog and stardust, where he has picked up the occasional writing gig from *Instinct,* the *LA Weekly, LA Alternative Press, The San Francisco Bay Guardian,* and even *Hustler,* and witnessed the swift sucking noise that accompanied each paycheck as it was absorbed by his insurmountable student loan debt. With a BA with honors distinction in English from Hendrix College and an MA in Writing from the University of San Francisco, Catalyst has learned that authoring books such as his premier, *Cottonmouth Kisses,* is not just a labor of love, it's a pain in the posterior—but at least it's one he invited there. Mr. Double C accepts suitors online at www.clintcatalyst.com and www.purpleglitter.com/clintcatalyst, and is especially fond of punk-rock *papi chulos* and Krispy Kreme doughnuts, especially when combined.

Dennis Cooper is the author of *The George Miles Cycle,* a sequence of five interconnected novels that includes *Closer* (1989), *Frisk* (1991), *Try* (1994), *Guide* (1997), and *Period* (2000). The cycle is published by Grove Press and has been translated into 13 languages. His most recent novel is *My Loose Thread* (Canongate, 2002). He is editor in chief of Little House on the Bowery/Akashic Press, a new line of books by adventurous young fiction writers. He lives in Los Angeles.

Jayson Elliot, an Iowa native, is the editor and publisher of *Permission* magazine. He fell into the dot-com world in 1994 after a rock tour dropped him off in San Francisco, where he funded his writing and publishing habit as a graphic designer. He is now recovering nicely in New York.

Mark Ewert really did do the things he said he did in his piece. In fact, he's writing a whole book about his time spent with Allen Ginsberg, William Burroughs, etcetera, which probably will be called *Beatboy.* Mark is a Capricorn who lives in a turret in a beautiful old Victorian castle in San Francisco. He's cocreator of the cartoon *Piki & Poko,* and he's a total nerd when it comes to Dungeons and Dragons.

Amelia G is a writer and photographer who has lived all over the world. Her writing has been translated into German, French, and Italian. Her fiction has been selected for *Best American Erotica, Best Women's Erotica, Best S/M Erotica,* and numerous other anthologies. Amelia has written for everyone from *Tattoo Savage* to *Playboy,* but she is best-known for founding Blue Blood, the seminal magazine of counterculture erotica. Amelia currently edits GothicSluts.com online and the *SWAG* rock lifestyle mag in print at 8033 Sunset Blvd., Suite 4500, West Hollywood, Calif., 90046. Her photography has appeared in venues from *Marquis* and *Gothic Beauty* to *Penthouse* and MTV. She likes pretty boys, pretty girls, sushi, chilled lattés, work, and rock and roll.

Pleasant Gehman is the author of the books *Senorita Sin, Princess of Hollywood,* and *Escape From Houdini Mountain* and editor of two editions of *The Underground Guide to Los Angeles.* Her writing appears regularly in the *LA Weekly* and *Los Angeles* magazine as well as many national and international magazines and literary publications. She is also a painter, belly dancer, singer, and actress. Pleasant is helplessly attracted to bright sparkly objects and people. Visit Her Royal Highness's Web site at www.dikenga.com/plez.

Trebor Healey's fiction can be found online at the *Blithe House Quarterly* and *Lodestar Quarterly.* Anthologies where his work appears include *Best Gay Erotica 2003, The Badboy Book of Erotic Poetry, A Day for a Lay, Sex Spoken Here, Between the Cracks, Wilma Loves Bette and Other Hilarious Gay and Lesbian Parodies, M2M* and *Beyond Definition: New Writing from Gay and Lesbian San Francisco,* of which he was coeditor. Trebor also wrote a hit single, "Denny," for Pansy Division. His first novel, *Through It Came Bright Colors* (Haworth Press), was published in August 2003. Visit www.treborhealey.com.

Thea Hillman is the author of the critically acclaimed *Depending on the Light* (Manic D Press). A poetry slam champion with an MFA in English and Creative Writing, Thea has performed her work at festivals, bookstores, and reading series across the country. She has produced many performance events, including "Rated XXY: An Evening of Erotica and Education Benefitting ISNA;" "ForWord Girls," the first inclusive all-girl spoken word festival; and the sold-out "Intercourse: A Sex and Gender Spoken Word Recipe for Revolution" for the National Queer Arts Festival. She is on the Mills College Board of Trustees and Board Chair of the Intersex Society of North America. Visit her Web site at www.theahillman.com.

Poet, youth advocate, and conceptual artist **Kathe Izzo** (katheizzo@hotmail.com) works with love: childhood, motherhood, sex, and community. The ongoing True Love Project, in which she pledges to freely fall in love with her audience for one day, one at a time, unconditionally and with unmitigated passion, has created a stir throughout the United States and Europe. Izzo's poetry, memoirs, and short fiction have been published in numerous journals and anthologies, including *Aroused*, edited by Karen Finley, and *The American Bible of Outlaw Poetry* (Thundersmouth Press).

Tara Jepsen is a writer and actor from San Francisco. Her short film *Fumbling Toward Rock: The Miriam and Helen Story* (Steakhaus Productions), cowritten-directed-acted with Beth Lisick, premiered in June 2002 at the Frameline Film Festival. She cohosts San Francisco's longest-running queer open mic, K'vetsh, with Lynn Breedlove. She has traveled extensively with all-girl spoken word circus Sister Spit (1997, 1998, 1999) and appears frequently in the world of festivals: Yoyo-a-Gogo, Ladyfest, Homo-a-Gogo, and Boston's Out on the Edge Theatre Festival. She is currently writing a feature script with Lisick called *Rusty Citation*.

Shawna Kenney authored the award-winning memoir, *I Was a Teenage Dominatrix*. Her freelance writing and photography have appeared in *Juxtapoz, Transworld Skateboarding, While You Were Sleeping, Slap, AP, The Underground Guide to Los Angeles,* and *Herbivore Magazine,* among others.

Kevin Killian, born in 1952, is a poet, novelist, critic, and playwright. He has written a book of poetry, *Argento Series* (2001), two novels, *Shy* (1989) and *Arctic Summer* (1997), a book of memoirs, *Bedrooms*

Have Windows (1989), and three chapbooks, *Desiree* (1986), *Santa* (1995), and *The Kink of Chris Komater* (1999). His latest collection of stories and memoirs, from Painted Leaf Books, is called *I Cry Like a Baby* (2001). His previous book of stories, *Little Men* (1996), won the PEN Oakland award for fiction. For the San Francisco Poets Theater Killian has written 30 plays, including *Stone Marmalade* (1996, with Leslie Scalapino) and *Often* (2001, with Barbara Guest). His next book will be all about Kylie Minogue.

Adam Klein is the author of *Tiny Ladies*, published in March 2003 by Serpent's Tail Books. He is also the author of *The Medicine Burns,* a Lambda Book Award nominee. He recently contributed to the artist book *SMTWTFS* by Marco Breuer, and was a coauthor of the artist monograph on Jerome Caja, *Jerome: After the Pageant.* His work has appeared in *BOMB* magazine and several other anthologies. He is the singer and cowriter for the band Roman Evening.

Chris Kraus is the author of *Aliens & Anorexia, I Love Dick,* and the forthcoming novel, *Torpor.* A book of her art essays, *Video Green: Los Angeles Art and the Triumph of Nothingness,* will be published by Semiotexte/MIT Press in 2004. She teaches writing at the San Francisco Art Institute.

Bee Lavender is a much-married working-class cancer survivor and the coeditor of *Breeder: Real Life Stories from a New Generation of Mothers.* She publishes and edits the online version of Hip Mama and is the author of the zine series "A Beautiful Final Tribute." Visit www.hipmama.com.

Ricky Lee is a Midwest native who has lived in San Francisco for the past seven years. She is a writer, video maker, and visual artist. She is also MC Strict Chem in the hip-hop group the End of the World. She wrote and directed the award-winning short feature *Reservoir Dykes.* Her writing is self-described as pathetic realism. It deals with issues of queerness and gender as well as the wonders of manual labor, drinkin', fuckin', and survival.

J.T. LeRoy is the author of the international bestsellers *Sarah* and *The Heart Is Deceitful Above All Things* (which is being made into a film by Asia Argento). His third book will be published soon by Viking. He is part of the rock band Thistle (www.thistlehq.com). He is a massive rock fan and can be heard on the Third Eye Blind album *Out of the Vein*. He wrote the bio for the new Zwan record and has in general sold his soul (what is left of it) for rock and roll. Learn more at www.jtleRoy.com.

Ali Liebegott currently lives and teaches adults GED and ESL in Providence, R.I. Her poetry and fiction have appeared in numerous journals and anthologies, including *The Haight-Ashbury Literary Journal, The Brooklyn Review, Virgin Territory II, Long Shot, Beyond Definition,* and others. In 1999 she was a recipient of a Poetry Fellowship from the New York Foundation for the Arts. She toured with the infamous Sister Spit Ramblin' Road Show in 1997 and 1999. She has completed three books: *The IHOP Papers, The Beautifully Worthless,* and *The Crumb People*. But more important than all of this: She loves feeding the ducks very much.

El Luté has been traveling the country for the past 10 years as a writer, performer, and petty thief. He currently resides in Providence, R.I., with his partner in crime and their two doggies. To send money, contact ElLute69@aol.com.

Inga Muscio is the author of *Cunt: A Declaration of Independence*. She is presently working on her new book, *Autobiography of a Blue-Eyed Devil: My Life and Times in a Racist, Imperialist Society,* which will be published in 2004. Her Web site is ingalagringa.com.

Eileen Myles is a poet who lives in New York and a novelist who teaches fiction at the University of California, San Diego. She's working on a novel called *The Inferno* and is just finishing a libretto called *Hell*.

Alvin Orloff began his writing career as a lyricist for the Blowdryers, a San Francisco punk rock band of the late 1970s. After producing several zines, he cowrote *The Unsinkable Bambi Lake* (Manic D Press,

1996), a theatrical memoir with a transsexual twist. His first novel, *I Married an Earthling* (Manic D Press, 2000), a social satire in the guise of a sci-fi send-up, was called "unique" and "a delight" by *Publishers Weekly*. He is currently promoting spectacularism, a new literary movement, and working on his second, third, and fourth novels.

Pauley P. is a homo...sapien who writes things and talks too much. Find out more at www.pauleyp.com.

Loren Rhoads is editor of the annual nonfiction journal *Morbid Curiosity*. Her travel writing has appeared on Gothic.Net and Triplit, in magazines like *Tail Spins* and *Trips,* and in two of the *Travelers' Tales* books. Her first book of essays, *Jet Lag and Other Blessings,* is available from Agua Bonita Press in San Francisco.

In her youth, **Jan Richman** attended charm school in the basement of Montgomery Ward's, survived a scorpion bite between her third and fourth toes, and performed the hula for Jimmy Durante. Currently, she lives in a fabulous rent-controlled apartment in San Francisco, where she's desperately trying to finish a novel about Tourette's Syndrome and roller-coasters.

Steve Salardino's writings have appeared in zines, journals, and exhibition catalogs such as *Skinny Chest, The Mississippi Review,* and *Blind Date,* and his artwork has recently been exhibited at Todd Hughes Fine Arts and the Rosamund Felson Gallery. Currently he plays ukulele in the Los Angeles band Ukefink with fellow artists Jason Holley, Eddy French, and his brother David Salardino.

After surviving the late '90s road trips with all-girl spoken word road riot Sister Spit, **Sara Seinberg** packed up Gus the Wonderdog and moved to New England. She lives in Boston, where she takes some photos, writes some stories, and gets some education.

Anna Joy Springer is a doddering lesbian schoolteacher who wears comfortable shoes and has a yippy little dog.

horehound stillpoint has been called a poet, a pervert, a savior to excess, and a scribe of tricks. His work can be found in *Poetry Slam,*

Poetry Nation, Out in the Castro, Tough Guys, Of the Flesh, Rough Stuff, Sex Spoken Here, and *Quickies*. His own minibook of poetry, *Reincarnation Woes,* is published by Kapow! Books press. Online, his poems can be found at LodestarQuarterly.com, SuspectThoughts.com, and NarcolepsyArms.com, plus an old essay or two might still be floating somewhere within Salon.com under the name Greg Nott.

Laurie Stone is author of the novel *Starting with Serge* (Doubleday, 1990), the memoir collection *Close to the Bone* (Grove, 1997), and *Laughing in the Dark* (Ecco, 1997), a collection of her writing on comic performance. A longtime writer for *The Village Voice* (24 years), she has been theater critic for *The Nation,* critic-at-large on National Public Radio's *Fresh Air,* a member of the Bat Theater Company, and a regular writer for *Ms., New York Woman,* and *Viva.* She has received grants from the New York Foundation for the Arts, the Kittredge Foundation, and the MacDowell Colony Poets & Writers, and in 1996 she won the Nona Balakian prize in excellence in criticism from the National Book Critics Circle. She has published numerous memoir essays in such publications as *Ms., TriQuarterly, Threepenny Review,* and *Creative Nonfiction.* Her current short fiction appears in the anthologies *Full Frontal Fiction* (Crown, 2000) and *Money, Honey* (Deutscher Tashenbuch Verlag, 2000), and her reviews can be seen in the *Los Angeles Times, The Washington Post,* the *Chicago Tribune,* and *Newsday.* She has given readings in dozens of venues, including the 92nd Street Y, Dixon Place, the Poetry Project, Barnes & Noble, KGB, the National Arts Club, and the New School. She has served as writer in residence at the Pratt Institute and at Old Dominion University and as journalist in residence at Thurber House. She has been a member of the faculty of Antioch University's Masters in Creative Writing Program, taught in the Graduate Theater Department of Sarah Lawrence, been a member of the faculty at Ohio State University, and taught at the Paris Writers Workshop. She has had short residencies and given workshops at many other universities, including Cal Arts, Trinity College, the University of North Texas, Art Center in Pasadena, Calif., Mills College, Indiana University, the University of Connecticut, and the School of the Arts at the Art Institute of Chicago. In 1993 and 2001 she received grants from the New York Foundation for the Arts in the category of nonfiction literature. She serves on the board of the

National Book Critics Circle, and this year she serves on the faculty of Fordham University as well as on the faculties of the graduate creative writing programs at the University of Southern Maine's Stonecoast Writers Conference and Fairleigh Dickinson University.

Jackie Strano grew up in taverns, bowling alleys, and roadhouses. She won her first microphone singing "Stop Draggin' My Heart Around." She finally stopped chasing straight girls in Sacramento. Now you can find her in front of and behind the camera showing the world what real dyke sex looks like. Her company, S.I.R. Video, stands for "sex, indulgence, and rock and roll." Strano sings with the bands the Hail Marys and the Servants and is still madly in love after a decade with the finest piece of American femme tail, Shar Rednour.

Michelle Tea wrote *The Passionate Mistakes and Intricate Corruption of One Girl in America*, *Valencia*, and *The Chelsea Whistle*. She lives in San Francisco, where she hides in her pink bedroom and hustles writing gigs out of places like the *Guardian*, *Girlfriends* and *On Our Backs*. She loves—like, really loves—beauty products.